ABOUT THE AUTHOR

USA Today bestselling and multi-award winning author Nicola Marsh writes feel-good fiction ... with a twist.

She has published seventy books and sold over eight million copies worldwide. She currently writes rural romance for HarperCollins Australia's Mira imprint, emotional domestic suspense for Hachette UK's Bookouture and contemporary romance for Penguin Random House USA's Berkley imprint.

She's a Romantic Book of the Year and National Readers' Choice Award winner.

A physiotherapist for thirteen years, she now adores writing full time, raising her two dashing young heroes, sharing fine food with family and friends, barracking loudly for her beloved North Melbourne Kangaroos footy team, and curling up with a good book!

Also by Nicola Marsh

Summer of Serenity

Nicola Marsh

Second Chance Lane

mira

First Published 2020
Second Australian Paperback Edition 2021
ISBN 9781867234647

SECOND CHANCE LANE
© 2020 by Nicola Marsh
Australian Copyright 2020
New Zealand Copyright 2020

This is a work of fiction. Names, characters, places, and incidents are either the product of the author's imagination or are used fictitiously, and any resemblance to actual persons, living or dead, business establishments, events, or locales is entirely coincidental.

Published by
Mira
An imprint of Harlequin Enterprises (Australia) Pty Limited (ABN 47 001 180 918), a subsidiary of HarperCollins Publishers Australia Pty Limited (ABN 36 009 913 517)
Level 13, 201 Elizabeth St
SYDNEY NSW 2000
AUSTRALIA

® and TM (apart from those relating to FSC®) are trademarks of Harlequin Enterprises (Australia) Pty Limited or its corporate affiliates. Trademarks indicated with ® are registered in Australia, New Zealand and in other countries.

A catalogue record for this book is available from the National Library of Australia
www.librariesaustralia.nla.gov.au

Printed and bound in Australia by McPherson's Printing Group

MIX
Paper from
responsible sources
FSC® C001695

*For my parents, Marina and Ollie, who instilled a love
of small country towns in me from childhood*

PROLOGUE

Melbourne
Thirteen years ago

'Natasha Trigg.' The bouncer—sporting five piercings in his right brow, a nose ring and bulging muscles stretching his black T-shirt to ripping point—consulted his list before nodding. 'Head on through.' He lowered the crimson rope to let Tash pass.

She hesitated, fear of what she had to do rendering her immobile, and earning her a glower from the bouncer.

'In or out?'

She willed her feet to move towards the main entrance of the Princeton Hotel in cosmopolitan St Kilda. The pub showcased local talent, but tonight, she didn't care about the music. She'd come here for one reason only.

To break up with Kody Lansdowne, front man for Rock Hard Place.

Ironic, as that's exactly where she'd found herself: between the proverbial rock and a very hard place. But she'd made her decision. She had to follow through. No way would she be responsible for ruining his dream. Even if hers had come crashing down the moment she'd peed on that white stick and glimpsed two vertical blue lines.

Leaving Brockenridge to study nursing in Melbourne, escaping the watchful eyes of her zealous parents, whose religion ruled every aspect of their lives and hers, had been a dream come true. Maybe her do-gooder parents had passed on their benevolent genes, because she loved helping people. She'd kept her head down for the first two years, hiding out in the nursing quarters attached to the university, determined to focus on her studies and not be distracted by the glitter of the city. Until she'd been dragged to the Princeton one balmy summer's night by a bunch of nursing students determined to consume their body weight in vodka and had met Kody.

Her first love. Her first everything. Tonight, she'd come here to tell him the truth. Her version of it, because no way in hell would she be responsible for ruining his dream when her own lay in tatters courtesy of dodgy contraception.

Hiding this secret burned a hole in her gut, making it impossible to keep anything down. Though that could be the morning sickness.

She'd rehearsed her spiel many times over the last twenty-four hours, knowing Kody would use every weapon in his charismatic arsenal to sway her. But she'd made her decision. She had to stick to it, no matter how badly her chest tightened with sorrow every time she thought about having to push him away.

She'd timed her arrival for the last song of the band's set, knowing she couldn't stand around for hours pretending to enjoy herself. A jarring guitar riff assaulted her ears as she edged her way into the crowded room where the love of her life and his band took centre stage. Her heart flipped as it always did when she caught sight of him and she blinked back the sting of tears. Damn hormones.

Kody dominated the stage and it had nothing to do with his six-two height, dark curly hair, mesmerising brown eyes and smile that made women fall at his feet: he had a presence that captivated everyone in the room and when he opened his mouth to sing—she'd never heard anything like it. Deep, gravelly, sexy, his voice transcended time and she wasn't surprised he'd captured the attention of an LA recording studio. Ironic that the night he'd told her all his dreams of being a rock star were about to come true was the night she'd planned to tell him about the baby.

She'd had it all figured out: they'd rent a small two-bedroom bungalow by the bay. Maybe Elwood, Elsternwick or South Melbourne, somewhere close enough for him to continue inner-city gigs while she completed her nursing degree. Kody had a massive network of friends and she'd envisaged arranging babysitting through one of them while juggling her studies. They would make it work, creating a close, loving family, the kind she'd never had.

But Kody had been hyper that night, pouncing on her the minute she stepped into his tiny studio apartment, picking her up and swinging her around until she'd become dizzy. He'd kissed her, deeply, passionately, in the way she'd never been kissed before him, then told her his good news in a rush, the words tumbling over themselves in his excitement.

A leading LA producer had been in Melbourne for a music awards show, seen Rock Hard Place at a gig and waited to speak to Kody afterwards. While he couldn't promise anything, the producer had the power to catapult Rock Hard Place towards the kind of fame most musicians only dream about.

Tash had been genuinely happy for him, swept up in his excitement even as a small part of her died. There'd be no moving in together, no shared parenting, no family. Instead, she'd be forced to move back to Brockenridge to live with her disapproving parents who would alternate between berating her for being so stupid and lecturing her about falling prey to the devil. But it would be a small price to pay if one of them got to live their dream. She loved Kody that much.

As if sensing her presence now, Kody's eyes locked on hers across the crowded room. He smiled, lighting up the part of her soul that would never forget him. He hauled the microphone stand close, caressing it, and she tingled with the memory of how he did the same to her body.

'I'd like to dedicate this song to the most beautiful girl in the world,' he said as raucous cheers and foot stomping filled the room. The lights went out, save for a lone spotlight on Kody, who was sitting on a bar stool, an acoustic guitar resting on his knee. And when he began to sing about love and adoration and soul-deep connection, Tash couldn't stem the tears. She could've sworn the entire room disappeared and it was just the two of them as he crooned lyrics meant for her.

When he plucked the final chord, the room erupted into applause and Tash knew the time had come. Dragging in a shaky breath, she shouldered her way to the side of the stage. One of the roadies saw her and waved her over, allowing her to slip backstage, where Kody swept her into his arms and buried his face in her neck.

She loved the smell of him after a performance: sweat mingled with deodorant—uniquely Kody—and she wished she could imprint this on her memory for the long, lonely nights ahead.

When he released her, he tipped her chin up so he could stare into her eyes. 'You're usually as pumped as me after a gig. What's up?'

'Not here,' she said, snagging his hand and tugging him towards a door that led out into a laneway. When the door slammed shut behind them, she led him to a quiet corner behind some stacked beer kegs.

'You're worrying me—'

'I'm pregnant, Kody, but you don't have to worry because I'm getting rid of it.' She had to say the words in a rush, otherwise she'd never get them out. She needed him to believe she was the worst person in the world or she wouldn't get through this without burying herself in his arms for comfort.

He paled, then blinked several times, before releasing her hand and staggering back like she'd slapped him. 'Don't I get a say in this?' He shook his head, his lips flattening. 'This is my kid too.'

'Yeah, but it's my body, and I don't want a baby now. It would ruin everything.'

His upper lip curled in derision. 'Right. Your precious nursing degree.'

He made it sound like she wanted to pole dance for a living. He'd never stared at her with loathing before and his narrow-eyed glare made her second-guess her decision for a moment.

But she had to do this. Had to make him hate her. There was no other choice.

'Good luck in LA,' she said, managing to stop her voice from quivering as she turned and walked away.

She willed him to come after her, to say that he wanted a baby with her, that he wanted a family, that he wanted her to come with him.

Instead, she heard a string of muttered curses before a door slammed.

Kody had believed her. She should be relieved. Yet all she felt was soul-deep sorrow.

CHAPTER

1

Brockenridge
Present day

Tash slid the last bolt home on the front door of The Watering Hole and joined her co-workers at a table near the kitchen. Usually she loved their evening planning meetings when they brainstormed ideas for the month ahead, but tonight her heart wasn't in it. All she could think about was the argument she'd had with Isla this morning, arguments that were becoming more frequent with her twelve-year-old daughter. Most of them centred around the identity of Isla's father.

It had been easier when Isla was younger. Back then, she'd been satisfied with a vague answer or an 'I don't know' before being distracted with a banana muffin or a blueberry smoothie. But with Isla's growing online expertise, Tash knew it would only be a matter of time before her daughter wanted to do a little research of her own.

Tash couldn't tell her the truth. Not when Isla's father was plastered across the internet. She'd ditched the habit of following his career online years ago, around the time he'd won his umpteenth award. Tash had achieved what she'd set out to do—set Kody free to find success—and while following Kody's every step as Rock Hard Place took the world by storm had been the only bright spot in her lonely existence as a struggling single mother, she'd eventually stopped torturing herself with what might have been.

She'd anticipated help from her parents upon her return to Brockenridge. She'd been wrong. They'd heard her out, glowered at her still-flat belly and announced they were moving hours away. So much for religion fostering acceptance and forgiveness.

'Hey, what's taking you so long?' Ruby pushed out the wooden chair opposite with her foot. 'Take a seat so we can get started.'

'You're much bossier than Clara ever was,' Tash said, glad they'd all reached a place where they could mention Ruby's mum, the original owner of the roadhouse, without awkwardness. It was a year since Clara had died and Ruby had returned to Brockenridge to discover she'd inherited the roadhouse. In that time, Ruby had convinced her high school boyfriend not to tear the roadhouse down in favour of a fancy-schmancy country club and Alisha, the road-house hostess, had hooked up with Harry, the roadhouse's chef. It was a regular love-fest around the place and, while Tash was happy for them all, she couldn't help but feel like a spare wheel at times.

'My bossiness is what's making this place thrive, so you should be grateful,' Ruby said, with a smile. 'Okay, first up—Harry, why don't you give us a rundown of the new menu?'

Tash tuned out when Harry started listing his latest culinary creations, most of them a unique blend of Indian and Aussie tucker. With Alisha being Indian, he'd adopted some of the recipes she'd taught him, and while Tash loved his curry beef pie and chilli scrambled eggs, she drew the line at his *baingan bharta* nachos: corn chips covered in a spicy eggplant stew.

'Thanks, Harry.' Ruby ticked off a few points on her list. 'Alisha, why don't you give us a rundown of the bands for the upcoming theme nights?'

Tash stiffened at the mention of bands as she inevitably did and forced herself to relax. Nobody but Alisha knew the identity of Isla's father and she'd like to keep it that way. Thankfully, her friend never brought up the subject, not since Tash had burst into embarrassing tears several years ago when Alisha had suggested she tell Kody the truth. The thought had crossed her mind, several times, but with every album release, every hit song, every award, Tash's resolve waned. Kody had endless funds to fight a lengthy custody battle and losing her precious daughter was one thing Tash wouldn't gamble on.

'We've got three local bands lined up for the regular blues nights, but no rock band for the gig in eight weeks,' Alisha said, with a grimace. 'I've tried reaching out to a few managers and event coordinators, but nada.'

'Thanks, keep trying.' Ruby ticked off another task and circled 'rock band' on her list. 'Tash, have you found extra staff for the theme nights?'

Feeling like the failure of the group as always, she shook her head. 'I've advertised in town and moved further afield to Echuca, but no luck. Plenty of teens want to apply but they can't work here because of the liquor licensing rules. I'll keep looking.'

'Okay,' Ruby said, running an orange highlighter through the 'find wait staff' task on her list. 'Anyone have anything else to raise?'

Alisha stuck her hand in the air like a kid in primary school.

'What is it, Lish?' Ruby asked.

'Uh … well … the thing is …' Alisha trailed off, a faint blush staining her cheeks.

'For goodness' sake. We're engaged,' Harry muttered. 'And we're not mucking about with any big wedding hoopla, so we'd like to hold the reception here, if that's okay with you.'

The initial shocked silence gave way to an excited whoop as Ruby leapt from her chair to hug the happy couple. 'Congratulations, you two. Of course you can have your reception here.'

Ruby hugged Alisha, then Harry, and Tash followed suit, murmuring, 'About bloody time,' in Harry's ear, and, 'I'm so happy for you, sweetie,' in Alisha's.

Alisha and Harry had been her best friends for years. They'd supported her through her pregnancy when she'd started waitressing at the roadhouse after returning home from Melbourne as a terrified, pregnant twenty-year-old. They'd helped her convince Clara to offer a pay rise when she'd used the last of her savings and had a six-month-old to support. They'd wiped away her tears on Isla's first day at preschool, school and, recently, high school. They'd been more of a support system than her parents had ever been and she loved them dearly. So why the tiny niggle of regret that everything in her well-ordered life was changing?

'When's the big day?'

'In six weeks,' Alisha said, beaming at her prospective groom. 'We're too old to wait.' It made sense, as Tash knew Alisha wanted to have a baby ASAP—she'd just turned forty-three.

'I'm the only old fart around here,' Harry muttered, his bashful grin endearing. 'I'm fifty-two, you know.'

Ruby laughed. 'Yeah, you're old.'

Tash added a guffaw. 'Practically ancient.'

'Hey, you two, settle down. I'll have you know I'm extremely fit for my age.' Harry flexed his biceps in a double cobra that had them all laughing again.

'I can vouch for that,' Alisha said, with a wink, and Tash groaned.

'Too much information.'

Ruby's smile widened as she said, 'Gross.'

'I've already typed the date into the computer to secure the booking,' Alisha said, back to business. 'Because there's nowhere else we want to have our reception.'

Ruby's grin faded. 'Who's going to cater? Harry can't cook for his own wedding.'

Harry shot Tash a look she had no hope of interpreting. 'Well, I was hoping Tash could use her influence with the bakery in town for our cake, and I'll approach our favourite wine bar in Echuca to cater, if that's okay?'

'Perfect,' Ruby said.

Tash nodded. 'Sure, I'll organise the cake. Just email me a few pics of what you want and your budget, and I'll get it sorted.'

Harry visibly relaxed, and Alisha said, 'Thanks, Tash, we knew we could count on you.'

Ruby rubbed her hands together. 'Who's up for a celebratory champagne?'

Tash had pulled a double shift and couldn't wait to get out of here, pick Isla up from netball practice, and head home. But these people were family and she owed them.

'Sure, but only half a glass for me,' she said, holding her thumb and forefinger two inches apart. However, before Ruby could pop the cork, Tash's mobile rang and her heart stuttered when she glimpsed Isla's ID on the screen. Isla rarely called and especially not in front of her friends if she could help it. Which meant this call could be important.

She stabbed at the answer button with her thumb. 'Hey, Isla, everything okay?'

The long pause made Tash's fingers clench around the phone and press it closer to her ear. 'Isla?'

A stifled sob had Tash on her feet in a second. 'Mum, can you come and get me now?'

'Absolutely. What's happened?'

'I pushed Dennie and she's hurt and I'm in trouble and everything's a mess.'

Tash's gut churned with trepidation. Isla was a good kid, she never fought, which meant something had precipitated this out-of-character action. 'Sit tight, honey, I'll be there ASAP.' She paused, adding, 'Everything will be okay,' before hanging up.

Alisha touched her arm and Tash jumped. 'You all right?'

Tash shook her head, blinking back the sting of tears. 'Isla's in trouble, I have to go,' she said, grabbing her bag and heading for the door. 'Sorry I can't stay for a champers.'

'Go,' Alisha said, waving her away.

'Let us know if you need anything,' Ruby added.

'Thanks,' Tash said, before pushing through the back door of the roadhouse and sprinting for her car.

CHAPTER

2

Kody had always lived on the edge. As a foster kid, he'd been the first one to pick a fight, to taunt a bully, to stand up to 'parents' who were supposed to care for him. He'd taken risks: with his body, his music. But nothing came close to the rush of arriving back in Melbourne for the first time in thirteen years. Crazy, because he'd been offered exorbitant sums of money to play concerts here the last few years; huge, seven-figure sums the other band members had urged him to accept. He never did, because Melbourne held nothing but bad memories for him. He'd lived rough in this city, had his heart broken, lost a child he never knew he wanted until the decision was taken away from him.

Melbourne was the pits, which is why he couldn't stay to recuperate. Instead, he'd hired a car and made the four-hour drive north to the Murray River. Yanni, his drummer and best mate, had a holiday shack in some backwater town on the border and had insisted he use it for however long he wanted. Right now, Kody had no idea how long that would be. One month? Two? He didn't care. Time was irrelevant, considering he could barely function these days.

Causing the deaths of seven innocent people did that to a guy.

The silence of the car interior made his fingers itch to turn on the radio but he hadn't been able to listen to music since the accident. It had been a long four hours alone with his self-flagellating thoughts skipping like a stuck LP. He'd never been to this part of Victoria before, with its rolling hills and barren paddocks interspersed with sparsely populated towns. Not that he cared about the scenery. Everything he needed was packed in the car boot: two crates of bourbon, a suitcase of clothes and a box of groceries so he could lay low for at least a week without heading into town. Last thing he needed was locals recognising him and leaking to the press where he was. That's why he really hoped the supermarket did home delivery, but when he'd asked Yanni, his drummer had laughed. Apparently Yanni holidayed in Brockenridge whenever he came home and no one had ever recognised him. Exactly why Kody had jumped at the chance to hide out there.

A sign indicated he had another twenty kilometres to go as he cruised past a roadhouse, labelled THE WATERING HOLE in bright neon light. He'd seen similar places in the USA in the early days when the band's coach would cruise from Alabama to Utah, California to Nevada, Texas to Georgia, keen to play as many gigs as humanly possible to lift their profile.

It had worked too, the slow burn of Rock Hard Place exploding into a furore of fame when they'd landed the prized gig of opening act for America's number one rock band. His dream had come true. Fame. Fortune. Adoration.

Yet here he was, turning his back on it all because he couldn't sing a note anymore. His vocal cords had seized the moment he'd heard about those poor people dying because of him. He'd had to walk away from the love of his life, music.

That had been a month ago and his manager, along with his band, had insisted he find somewhere to get his head straightened out after he'd spent the last four weeks holed up in a Wellington hotel, drinking himself into a stupor or dosed up on tranquilisers. Roger, Yanni, Blue and Daz were the closest thing he had to family and when they'd ambushed him with an intervention-style dressing down, he'd finally admitted the truth: he was a mess. He needed to get away, somewhere off the grid, somewhere he could work through his issues.

They expected him to come back to Melbourne some time in the not too distant future to work out the band's next tour, with the hope Rock Hard Place would be bigger and better than ever. He hadn't had the heart to tell them his music career was over. They'd find out soon enough.

He hit the outskirts of town, not surprised to see the main street flanked by pubs in typical Aussie fashion. There was the requisite bakery, a small supermarket, op shop, cafés and Chinese restaurant, a surprisingly upmarket medical centre and a town square. Yanni was right, the place had an understated charm. Not that it mattered. Kody wouldn't be spending any time here. He'd be holed away drinking himself into oblivion.

Yanni's house sat on a small hillside at the highest point of a dead-end road, Wattle Lane. He should've known his mate's version of 'shack' resembled a sprawling homestead that looked straight out of an architectural digest. The entire place gleamed, with its sandstone façade, gunmetal steel roof and wrap-around veranda in contrasting sienna.

He parked the car around the back and stepped out, wincing as his knee buckled slightly. That'd teach him for doing one too many leaps into mosh pits in his early days. Those heady, crazy days when he'd known he'd had the talent to make it big but needed a break. Those exciting days filled with dreams and promise—and Tash.

Crap, where had that come from? He hadn't thought of her in a long while. That's all he needed when he was already feeling lower than low. The way she'd callously dumped him and announced he had no say in whether he wanted a child or not ... he'd been so mad he'd channelled his fury and frustration into making those first few months in LA count. And he hadn't looked back. Neither had he succumbed to the temptation to look her up online. Not that he would've found much. She'd stayed off social media even when they'd been dating, citing nosy parents.

Back then, he'd been so damn angry with her, though he had to acknowledge a small part of him had been relieved. He'd been on the cusp of breaking out with that LA producer and a baby would've seriously crimped his plans. But rather than supporting her through an abortion that must've been rough, he'd turned his back on her.

Shame burned deep and he muttered a curse as he stomped towards the homestead. He couldn't change the past but for however long it took to shake the funk plaguing him, hiding out here was his future.

CHAPTER
3

As Tash pulled up outside the school sports ground and saw a group of girls huddled near the gate, her heart sank. Usually they'd be running drills on the netball court or having match simulation. Instead, the coaches stood to one side, a hunched Isla between them, while the rest of the girls gossiped and cast sideways glances at her daughter.

Many of the other school mums dreaded the impending teen years but Tash had been quietly confident that Isla was a good kid and wouldn't give her too much grief. Isla had never been grounded or called into the principal's office, but that was primary school. Maybe her daughter was struggling in her first year of high school and had hidden it?

She loved Isla and embraced life as a single parent wholeheartedly but it was moments like this that she missed having the support of a spouse. However, this wasn't the time to take a futile trip down memory lane, wondering if she'd done the right thing in lying to Kody. His countless platinum releases, awards and worldwide fame, told her she had. But at what cost?

She stepped from the car and approached the group. Isla caught sight of her and took a step like she wanted to run into her mother's arms, before resuming a recalcitrant slump. The head coach wore a grim expression while her assistant leaned closer and said something before joining the girls at the gate. They returned to the court and resumed training.

'Coach,' Tash said, giving a brief nod. She'd always thought it ridiculous that a grown woman wanted to be addressed by this moniker at all times. 'Hi, Isla.'

The coach frowned and glared at Isla, before her disapproving stare fixed on Tash. 'There was an incident during our practice match earlier. Isla pushed Dennie hard, causing her to fall and injure her knee. She has since gone home but I wanted you here when I tell Isla the consequences for her actions.'

Fear flickered in Isla's gaze before she averted her eyes.

'We don't tolerate any physical displays of anger in my team, whether against opposition or teammates,' the coach continued. 'So with that in mind, I think it's best Isla is suspended for a month.'

Isla gasped and Tash struggled to hide her dismay. Isla loved netball and was good at it, the best goalkeeper this town had seen in a while, according to many. There'd even been talk of regional tryouts, followed by a national comp in Melbourne. This punishment would gut her.

Making an effort to keep her tone steady, Tash said, 'I understand your no-tolerance policy but a month is—'

'It's a shame you feel the need to question my decision, Ms Trigg, but it's final.' The coach turned to Isla. 'I expected better from my star player and I hope that while you're on the sidelines for the next four weeks you'll think about your actions and how you've not only let yourself down, but your entire team too.'

With that, the coach marched to the courts.

Tash wanted to stomp after her, spin her around and give her a verbal spray for being so damn dramatic. But she understood. Physical violence wasn't okay in any situation and the fact Isla had hurt Dennie badly enough that she got sent home … Tash had to handle this, and fast.

'Let's go,' she muttered. 'We'll discuss this when we get home.'

Isla wisely remained mute for the first few minutes in the car, but she'd never been any good at staying silent so Tash knew it would only be a matter of time before she blurted the truth. She'd never been a nagging mum, preferring to let Isla own her mistakes. But something major had gone down on that netball court and Tash needed to know what had turned her meek daughter into a girl who would resort to violence.

'Mum, I hate when you give me the silent treatment.' Isla poked her in the arm but Tash kept her eyes on the road.

'I told you. We'll discuss it at home.'

'It wasn't my fault, you know.'

Tash bit her tongue, desperate to respond, and Isla huffed, turning away to stare out her window. They drove the remaining minutes in silence, with Tash mentally rehearsing all the correct disciplinary chastisements while wanting to bundle Isla into her arms and make it all go away.

She parked under the carport, killed the engine and turned to face Isla. 'Whatever happened back there isn't right—pushing someone around—but I'm always on your side and I hope you trust me enough to tell me the truth.'

After several moments Isla finally looked at her, tear tracks smearing her cheeks. 'Can we talk inside? I used the water from my bottle to clean Dennie's knee and I've been dying of thirst ever since.'

Tash's heart twanged. At least Isla had felt remorse if she cleaned her friend's knee after their altercation. It gave her hope that this was a simple misunderstanding and the coach had overreacted.

'Let's go.'

When they entered the house, Isla ran to the sink, filled a glass with water and downed it in a few gulps. 'I needed that,' she said, flopping onto one of the wooden dining chairs and eyeing Tash with trepidation. 'Now what?'

'Now you tell me the truth.' Tash sat next to Isla and made an effort not to cross her arms. 'All of it.'

Something furtive shifted in Isla's eyes before she blinked and Tash wondered if she'd imagined it. 'Dennie was being a cow, then she got in my face so I pushed her away. Not very hard … but she must've tripped. I didn't mean to hurt her, it was an accident, I swear.'

'Pushing her isn't an accident, Isla. You've never done anything like this before, so what was different this time?'

Anger furrowed Isla's brow as her lips compressed in a thin line.

'Isla, if you don't tell me the entire story, I'll be enforcing a punishment as severe as Coach's.' An empty threat, because a month off the team seemed excessive. Then again, what did she know? She'd never had to discipline Isla to this extent before and maybe her actions warranted a four-week ban.

Tears filled Isla's eyes but Tash didn't weaken, despite the urge to hug her daughter tight.

'Tell me.'

After a long pause and a loud sniffle, Isla wiped a hand across her eyes. 'Some of the other girls were talking about Swap Day coming up at school next month, then Dennie said no mums were coming, only dads … then she smirked at me and said why don't I ask mine?'

Tash gritted her teeth. Whichever genius came up with the concept of parents swapping with their kids for one day of classes during their first year of high school needed to be slapped. She hadn't been looking forward to it. In fact, she'd hoped she could weasel out of it by citing work. Now this.

'What did you say?'

'Dennie knows I don't ever discuss my dad, but she wouldn't let up this time. She kept going on and on, saying I must know where he is, accusing me of keeping secrets and being an attention seeker, that kind of thing, so when she got in my face I pushed her away ...' She trailed off and the tears were back, and this time Tash gave in to instinct and bundled Isla into her arms.

Her brave tween rarely cried so when Isla hugged back, sobbing into her shoulder, Tash knew exactly how upset she was. She held her daughter until the tears subsided, dreading the conversation to come.

Whenever Isla asked about her dad, Tash gave a carefully rehearsed answer designed to placate and discourage further questioning. But Isla was twelve going on twenty and Tash knew that fobbing her off wouldn't work much longer.

She eased away, bracing for the inevitable question—'Where's my dad?'—the one she couldn't answer even if she wanted to. In the early days, Tash could respond with a truthful 'New York ... LA ... Tokyo ... Singapore ... London ...' because she'd kept track of Kody via the occasional online search. But she wasn't about to do that now. Besides, how would she tell Isla her father was an international rock star who didn't know she existed?

The secret sat like a rock in the pit of her stomach: immoveable, painful, unforgiving. She'd wondered many times whether she should tell Isla the truth, but the older her daughter got, the more chance of her rebelling and acting out against her.

She had to come up with a smart response, one that wouldn't alert Isla to the fact her mother was a lying fraud.

Tash reached for her daughter's hand, clasping it between both of hers, and was thankful when Isla didn't pull away. 'We've discussed your dad many times. I told you he played in a band in Melbourne, we went out for a short time, but then he left for overseas and I never heard from him again.'

'Which basically tells me nothing, Mum.' Isla pouted. 'What's his name so I can look him up? Everyone has a social media profile these days. Except you. Maybe he wants to meet me, now that I'm older? Why can't you reach out to him?'

The questions left Tash winded. What could she say if she did reach out to Kody? *'Hey, remember when I lied to you about aborting our baby? Well, here she is—surprise!'*

So Tash reached for the worst lie of all.

'He had another life overseas, sweetie, and he didn't have time for a child.'

Tash's gut churned as it did every time she uttered the monstrosity, or some version of it. No surprises why she didn't sleep well at night. At first she'd blamed her insomnia on motherhood but as Isla grew older and slept through, Tash knew her wakefulness had more to do with the lie she perpetuated than any mucked-up body clock.

'I hate him.' Isla pushed away from the table so fast her chair hit the wall. 'Anyway, now you know what happened, are you going to punish me too?'

'I think being away from netball for a month is punishment enough, but you can't get physical like that again, okay?'

Her daughter nodded and slumped back into her chair. 'I feel bad for hurting Dennie, even if she was being super mean to me.'

'Why don't you ring her and apologise?'

'I already said sorry in person when I cleaned up her knee, and she was okay.' Isla's nose crinkled. 'Though Coach went ape and gave me a massive embarrassing lecture in front of everyone.'

'In that case, maybe apologising to Coach couldn't hurt?'

Isla visibly brightened, as if the thought hadn't entered her head. 'Yeah, that's a good idea. She really likes those chocolate éclairs from the bakery. Maybe I could buy her one and go to training really early tomorrow before everyone gets there, and give it to her and say sorry?'

'Great idea.' Tash stood and dropped a kiss on Isla's head. 'Now, it's been a long day. Why don't we have leftover spag bol for dinner then crash in front of the TV?'

'Sounds good to me.' Isla stood and, to Tash's surprise, flung her arms around her. 'Thanks, Mum. You're fair and a good listener and better than any stinky old dad who doesn't want to be around.'

Tash hugged Isla tight and willed the tears away. If only her guilt would follow suit.

CHAPTER

4

Kody had done a lot of dumb things in his life but this had to be the dumbest.

How had he thought that hiding away in some holiday home at the arse end of the earth would help him heal? If anything, rattling around Yanni's plush pad by himself left him with too much time to think ... remember ... rehash. He did enough of that in his nightmares every frigging night. Waking to the screams were the worst. Desperate cries for help that went unanswered as the crowd tried to escape the flames and the stampede that followed. Heart-rending, gut-wrenching screams that would haunt him forever.

He'd been responsible for the deaths of seven people. No amount of soul-searching or relaxation or whatever the hell he was supposed to be doing here would change that.

'Fuck,' he muttered, pushing through the back door and letting it slam behind him. Fresh air wouldn't help what ailed him but it wouldn't hurt either and he'd spent too much time over the last month hiding away: from the media, from his manager, even from his best mates in his beloved band. He couldn't face anyone, not when he could break down at any moment.

He trudged along a makeshift path, kicking up tiny clouds of dirt every now and then. The land here was prone to drought but the rolling green hills on the horizon belied that. He could spy cattle in a far paddock, sheep in another and his nearest neighbour's house, about five hundred metres away. He followed the path as it meandered along the border with the adjacent property, the divide delineated by towering pines, and inhaled, his arms reaching overhead, the pungent freshness filling his lungs. The movement calmed him a little so he did it repeatedly, until he felt lightheaded.

'Wow, we don't see many guys doing yoga out here. Weird.'

He jumped, lowered his arms and spun around to see a young girl watching him. She had dark blonde hair snagged in a messy ponytail, hazel eyes and a frown that deepened the longer he took to respond. As she stared at him with curiosity, the damnedest thing happened.

He felt like he knew her.

He'd met many fans over the years so maybe she'd travelled with her parents to one of his concerts or to one of the intimate performances he did for radio stations. Yeah, that had to be it.

'I'm not doing yoga, I'm chilling,' he said.

'Out here?' Her eyebrows shot up. 'Mister, you need to get a life.'

A bark of laughter escaped him, the first time he'd laughed in a month.

'Where did you come from anyway?' he asked, liking this kid and her wit.

'I live next door with my mum.' She jerked a thumb over her shoulder to the house he'd seen earlier. 'I did a dumb thing earlier and I needed to get out of there.'

'So you thought you'd trespass too?'

She rolled her eyes. 'I duck through the pines to walk here all the time because your house is always empty.'

'It's not my house.'

'Then you're trespassing too.'

Her sass got to him again and he chuckled. 'How old are you? Eleven going on fifty?'

'I'll be thirteen in two months,' she said, annoyance that he'd underestimated her age lacing her words. 'How old are you?'

'Too old for you to be asking that question. Didn't your mum ever tell you it's rude to ask old people their age?'

'You're not *that* old,' she said, staring at him with renewed interest. 'You look familiar.'

'I have one of those faces,' Kody muttered, eager to beat a hasty retreat before she recognised him. 'Anyway, I better get back to my *yoga*—'

'I'm Isla,' she said quickly, as if desperate to keep him talking a little longer and it hit him that a kid living with her mum this far out of town wouldn't have a lot of people to talk to.

'Kody,' he said, before mentally slapping himself upside the head. He'd planned on using an alias but this girl had somehow disarmed him and he'd slipped up.

'How long are you here for?'

'Don't know.'

When suspicion glinted in her eyes again, he added, 'Maybe a month or two.'

'Well then, I might see you round.' She paused and pointed at the gap between the pines. 'You don't mind if I walk around here while you're staying, do you?'

He did, because kids these days were whip-smart and if she saw him again she might recognise him. But banning her would draw more suspicion, so he nodded. 'That's fine.'

'Cool.'

She walked away, and he exhaled in relief. Short-lived, because she paused and glanced over her shoulder.

'My mum's a great cook and she hasn't had a boyfriend in forever so if you get tired of being on your own, you should come over.'

She sounded serious so he stifled the grin tugging at his lips. 'I'll keep that in mind.'

As she ducked back through the gap in the trees, Kody realised that Isla had made him feel lighter than he had in weeks. That's the thing he liked about kids. They didn't bullshit, they called it how it is.

But Kody had no intention of going anywhere near the mouthy kid or her spinster mum.

CHAPTER

5

Jane's head pounded as her eyelids cranked open. She didn't know what was worse, the rock band jamming in her brain, the grittiness of her eyes or the dryness of her mouth. She hated hangovers. Not enough to stop drinking though. She knuckled her eyes and used her pinkies to clean the crumbly bits from the corners before pushing into a sitting position. Disoriented, she blinked several times and moved her head slowly to stave off dizziness. Pale blue blinds, ecru walls and a desk ... where the hell was she?

She glanced at the rumpled sheets on her left and had a flashback of hairy legs and a mermaid tattoo. That's when it came flooding back and she groaned, flopping back onto the pillow. She'd popped in to The Watering Hole last night, met a trucker on his way through town and ended up in this motel room.

Shame crawled under her skin and she absentmindedly scratched her arm. Last night had been a mistake. She'd made many of those in her thirty years.

She'd let people wrongly believe the worst of her for too long. Allowing people to judge her for being too spoilt, too lazy, had started off as a game to annoy her mother, Gladys Jefferson, a doyen of the community. Jane didn't have to work courtesy of the inheritance her dad had left her and in a town where most people were doing it tough and her mother practically ran everything, that had been a major black mark against her name.

So she sought validation elsewhere, flirting with guys to feel good about herself. She craved attention more than chocolate—and that was saying something.

A knock sounded at the door, way too loud, like a jackhammer to her head. She grimaced, tucked the top sheet around her and opened it a crack, wishing she hadn't.

Her nemesis stood on the other side, staring at her with ill-concealed concern.

'What do you want?' Jane muttered, hating that Ruby Aston appeared radiant in a peacock blue sundress, her dark hair shiny, her make-up flawless and her eyes clear. Having Ruby discover her hung over and naked beneath a sheet in the motel attached to the roadhouse didn't look good. Jane had been the gorgeous one once, the most popular girl in high school. She'd been a bitch to Ruby back then, doing many things she wasn't proud of. But they'd called an uneasy truce when Ruby returned to Brockenridge.

'I saw your car out the front and I wanted to make sure you're all right. Fancy a cuppa?'

Jane's stomach roiled at the thought of caffeine. 'Got any peppermint?'

'Sure. I'll meet you in the roadhouse. Pop over when you're ready.'

Jane's chest tightened. Ruby didn't owe her anything, especially considering Jane had virtually driven her out of town after

implicating her in a theft on the day of their high school graduation, so her kindness in checking up on her made her want to cry.

'Ruby?'

She glanced over her shoulder, one eyebrow raised. 'Yeah?'

'Thanks.'

Ruby's compassionate smile left Jane feeling more inadequate
than ever.

Thirty minutes later, after a hot shower and three glasses of water,
Jane made her way to the roadhouse, wearing the same clothes as
last night: a tight black dress that skimmed her knees and hooker
heels, as her mum called anything above a sedate two inches. She
hadn't done a public walk of shame before. It wouldn't have worried her in the past, strutting into a place wearing obvious night-out
attire the next morning. She would've done anything over the years
to get a reaction from her mum, to make up for the emptiness that
plagued her ever since her beloved dad died and she'd discovered
the unthinkable: her mum had been responsible for his death.

She'd wanted to punish her mum so she'd hit Gladys where she'd
hurt the most: her precious polished façade. Gladys ran every charity
event, presided over the popular book club, and organised endless fundraisers for everything from the high school to the library,
so Jane deliberately did the opposite. She cultivated her spoilt brat
image by not volunteering, though she did donate anonymously to
a lot of local charities. Flirting with men led to rumours but Jane
didn't correct those. Anything to get a rise out of Gladys. And it
seemed to work—Gladys hated Jane's layabout image. Her mum
had a hang-up when it came to presenting the perfect front. She'd
gone to extremes to maintain the illusion of a privileged life, when

nothing could be further from the truth. Not in monetary terms, because her dad had left them well off, but in every other way that counted, Gladys's life was a sham. Only Jane knew her mum was far from the generous, caring woman everyone in town saw.

But what had Jane's juvenile behaviour accomplished? Her mother would never change and all she'd achieved was loneliness, because nobody in this town knew the real her. This stupid, impulsive one-night stand was the final straw. She needed to revamp her life.

Giving her head a little shake to dislodge thoughts of her mother, Jane entered the roadhouse. Thankfully, the place was empty, apart from a family who must've hit the road early and had stopped for breakfast. She pegged the parents as mid-thirties, wearing the harried expressions of those who'd already weathered too many 'are we there yet?' choruses. The kids, a motley crew of three ranging in age from a toddler to a teen, were making enough noise that her head started pounding again. They should've annoyed her yet somehow the sight of the tight-knit family travelling together brought a lump to her throat. She wanted that: a guy she could depend on; a guy interested in a relationship; a guy who could make her feel secure in a way her wealth couldn't. And if she were lucky enough to have kids, she'd make sure she treated them a damn sight better than her mother had treated her.

'Ready for that cuppa?' Ruby touched her shoulder and Jane gathered her wits. Bad enough she'd been caught out by Ruby, she didn't need to add a weird crying jag on top of her one-night-stand shame.

'That sounds good.' She followed Ruby to a small table set up near the office. Along with a teapot, Ruby had laid out a plate of scones and tiny bacon quiches and, to Jane's surprise, a pang of hunger made her stomach gripe.

'I'm hungry,' Ruby said, taking a seat. 'I thought you might be too.'

'Thanks for all this.' Jane sat opposite and helped herself to a scone, dolloping locally made raspberry jam and cream on top, before pouring a steaming cup of peppermint tea. She inhaled deeply, the familiar minty fragrance soothing her head and settling her tummy.

'You okay?' Ruby pinned her with a steady gaze surprisingly devoid of judgement, and for the second time in as many minutes, Jane's throat tightened with emotion.

'I screwed up last night and I'm not proud of it,' she said, taking a sip of tea, wishing it would cool faster so she could down the entire cup. Though she knew her rumbling tummy had more to do with nerves at having this kind of conversation with Ruby than the remnants of a hangover.

'We all make mistakes.' Ruby shrugged and if she weren't being so nice, Jane would hate her.

Jane snorted. 'What mistakes have you made lately?'

Ruby's mouth eased into a wry grin. 'We're talking about you, not me.' She hesitated, before continuing, 'Look, I know we're not close and your private life has got nothing to do with me, but that guy you hooked up with didn't seem your type.'

'I had a bad day and came in here to chill. Then that truckie started paying me attention and—' Jane shrugged. 'You're so smitten with Connor you wouldn't get this, but that guy gave me the validation of being wanted ...' She trailed off and took another sip of tea so she wouldn't sob. Crazy, to be sitting here offloading to a woman so perfect everybody in town adored her. Like Ruby would ever understand what she'd been through.

'I get it,' Ruby said, so softly Jane wondered if she'd imagined it. 'You forget, I ran away from this town. I knew no one in Melbourne and I often dated guys who were wrong for me, just for attention.'

Surprised by Ruby's admission, Jane leaned forwards. 'The stupid thing is, I don't sleep around, I just like flirting because it makes me feel noticed, you know?'

Ruby nodded. 'Yeah, I know exactly what you mean.'

'But what you don't know is how the small-town mentality of many around here assume that flirting leads to more.' Jane grimaced. 'I haven't helped myself over the years because I didn't correct the misconceptions. Some of Mum's cronies, the old biddies who think she walks on water, got me so mad I flaunted myself on purpose just to get a rise out of them.' She tapped her temple and made circles. 'Crazy, huh?'

Confusion creased Ruby's brow. 'Why didn't you leave?'

How could Jane answer that honestly without reinforcing how crazy she was? Ruby had always had a great relationship with her mum. She'd never understand that Jane stuck around to make Gladys's life a misery.

'I ask myself that question every day.' Jane forced a flippant laugh but could tell Ruby didn't buy it. Thankfully, they weren't close enough for her to push the issue.

'For what it's worth, there's something to belonging in a town like this.'

Jane's throat tightened so she aimed for levity again. 'Are we actually having a bonding moment here?'

'Don't push it,' Ruby said, with a smile. 'I hated your guts for so long—but life's too short to hold a grudge.'

'I was a bitch to you. I know I've already apologised, but I was shitty to you all through high school.' She shook her head, ashamed of how narrow-minded she'd been. 'And for what? Because you lived here?' She glanced around the roadhouse, at the gleaming polished wood of the tables, at the vintage posters on the walls, at the jukebox and stage in the far corner, and wondered what it would've been like to come home to this welcoming warmth every day. Her family may have had money but Ruby had a real home and, given a choice, Jane knew which she'd choose.

'What do you want me to say? That you looked down your snooty nose at me? That you taunted me for no reason? That you were a stuck-up cow?' Ruby held out her hands like she had nothing to hide. 'Fine, you were. But that's all in the past. How did that confident girl end up ...' Ruby hesitated, as if trying to find the right words, so Jane supplied them for her.

'Judged? Shunned? Broken?'

'Is that how you feel?'

'Some days.' Jane shrugged like it meant little when deep down that's exactly how she felt most of the time, like a part of her had shattered the day she'd discovered the truth about her perfect family and nothing she said or did could put her back together.

'Is there anything I can do to help?'

Jane forced a weak smile and gestured at the table. 'What you've done here? Perfect.'

'I mean is there anything I can do beyond a cuppa and brekkie?'

Jane didn't know how to ask for help. She knew what she had to do—reinvent herself—but her intentions were nice in theory but hard in practice.

'Thanks for the offer, but this is something I have to do for myself.'

'You know, several of us have been judged and found lacking by the people in this town at one time or another.'

'Who else, besides you and me?'

'Tash.' Ruby shook her head. 'I can't believe her parents disowned her and moved away when she came back to town pregnant. And I know some of the townsfolk disapproved too. But she proved to everyone how resilient she is and I think you can too.'

Jane wanted to hug Ruby for her encouragement but she settled for a muted, 'Thanks.'

'I'm here if you need a hand, okay?'

'You're way too nice for your own good, Ruby Aston,' Jane muttered, raising her teacup in a toast. 'I might even be starting to like you a little.'

'Wow, lucky me.' Ruby laughed and raised her cup too. 'To new starts.'

'I'll drink to that,' Jane said, clinking her teacup gently against Ruby's, wishing it were that easy.

Buoyed by her impromptu breakfast and the chat she'd had with Ruby, Jane had almost reached her car when she realised she'd left her earrings in the motel room. Ducking behind the roadhouse, she spied a woman pulling a housekeeping cart towards it and made a beeline for her.

'Hey, do you mind letting me in? I left my earrings behind—' As the woman turned to face Jane, shock rendered her speechless.

Louise Poole, one of her best friends back in high school, scowled and turned away.

'Uh … Lou, I didn't know you worked here,' Jane said, wishing she had, because no way in hell would she have approached her for anything. Louise hated her guts. Her old friend had confronted her many years ago for supposedly breaking up her marriage, and their resultant showdown in the Main Street hadn't been pretty. Jane had avoided her ever since and felt sick about what her friend thought of her. Unfortunately, Louise had been collateral damage in the plan Jane had back then to get the attention she wanted. Never in her wildest dreams had she anticipated her crazy stunt would hurt one of the people she liked the most.

'Lou, please—'

'Wait here,' Louise snarled. 'I'll get your precious bloody earrings.' As she unlocked the door, Jane heard her mutter, 'You tramp.'

Tears burned the back of her eyes. She'd been a shitty friend and shouldn't have let the lie be perpetuated for so long. If she intended to reinvent herself, perhaps now was the time to set the record straight?

She followed Louise into the room and closed the door.

Louise came out of the bathroom and blanched. 'What the hell are you doing? Open that door right now.'

'We need to talk—'

'I'm not interested in anything you have to say.' Louise crossed her arms and backed up until she hit the wall. She couldn't get further away if she tried. 'Here are your earrings.' She flung them at Jane's feet. 'Take them and go.'

The old Jane would've done exactly that. But if she wanted to make changes, she needed to start now, by regaining control after last night's aberration.

'I didn't do it, Lou.' She spoke so softly Louise inadvertently leaned forwards. 'I didn't sleep with Ed.'

'You're a bloody liar. He said so and you ruined my marriage—'

'He's the liar. I let you think it was me because I was so bloody jealous of your perfect marriage. Plus I still held a stupid grudge that you turned your back on our friendship after you got married and you didn't ask me to be a bridesmaid—'

'I had three kids under five and a useless cheating husband who was never around!' Louise yelled. 'What did you expect, for us to share spa days and long lunches?' She shook her head. 'Get over yourself.'

'I was selfish and disillusioned, but I did not sleep with Ed.'

'You're lying,' Louise said, her icy tone a match for her glare. 'People said you screwed half the town back then and when you ran out of single guys, you came after my husband.'

Pain sliced through Jane's resolve. Was this worth it? What would really change if Louise knew the truth? Then again, this was about her as much as her old friend and getting people to see the real Jane had to start somewhere.

'There are a lot of assumptions about me that aren't true. I swear I never touched your husband.'

'Why wait until now to tell me? It doesn't make sense.' Doubt clouded Louise's eyes, giving Jane a flicker of hope.

'I've been in a bad place for a long time, but I'm done with self-sabotaging and regrets.' She shrugged, like her plans for a new life meant little when in fact they terrified her—the enormity of what she faced in trying to regain respect from everyone, including herself, was difficult to contemplate. 'Consider this my very own twelve-step redemption program.'

Her self-deprecating smile made some of the animosity in Louise's wary gaze fade. Her shoulders slumped as she leaned against the wall. 'Maybe I should embark on my own self-awareness program? Ed is a cheater and a liar and I keep him around because I'm petrified of being on my own. I don't love him—I despise him—but if it's tough financially now I can't imagine what it'd be like with him gone.'

Jane's heart ached for her friend. 'I can't tell you what to do, Lou, but if you're considering giving him the boot, get some legal advice first and start consolidating your finances, stuff like that. Divorce is tough but for what it's worth, you deserve so much better than Ed.'

Louise bit her bottom lip and nodded. 'If you didn't sleep with him, why did he tell me you did?'

'Because he's an arsehole.'

Her dry response earned a bark of laughter from Louise.

Jane hadn't intended on telling Louise the whole truth but if it helped motivate her to kick Ed out, she'd do it. 'He made a move on me. And I may have been in a bad place back then thanks to some stuff I was going through with my mum, but even I wouldn't stoop so low as to get it on with your husband.' She blew out a breath to ease the sudden tightness in her chest. 'You meant a lot to me, Lou. We were best friends in high school and I would never hurt you that way.'

Louise sighed. 'I think Ed might've always had the hots for you. He drove a wedge between us deliberately. He saw how close we were during the engagement and started implying you were into him, so I ... backed away from you. That's why I didn't ask you to be a bridesmaid.'

'Arsehole,' she muttered again, adding, 'Jealous dickhead,' for good measure.

They laughed and, in that moment, Jane felt lighter than she had in years. Yeah, this confronting and confessing thing had a lot going for it.

When their laughter petered out, Jane said, 'Do you think that maybe we could get together for a coffee some time?'

Louise hesitated. 'Can I think about it? I've got a lot to do.'

Jane tried to mask her disappointment. Then again, what had she expected? She'd let Louise believe a lie for so long. 'No worries.'

Louise slid a hand into her pocket and pulled out a mobile. 'I do appreciate you telling me the truth. It's given me a shove in the right direction.' She brandished her phone. 'I'm making an appointment with a lawyer right now.'

'Good for you.'

Louise still eyed her warily but for besties who hadn't spoken in a decade, Jane felt like they'd definitely made progress. 'Is your number still the same?'

Jane nodded.

'Once I get my shit together, I might call you.'

'Great, I really hope you do.'

Giving in to impulse, Jane crossed the room and enveloped her old friend in a hug. After an awkward moment, Louise hugged her back briefly before stepping back.

It gave Jane hope that the friendship she'd valued and stupidly sabotaged might be salvageable after all.

CHAPTER

6

Tash didn't mind her daughter taking long walks; she preferred Isla exercise than being glued to a screen. She tried to maintain a screen-time limit on Isla's laptop and mobile but considering Tash worked long shifts, she wasn't around to monitor Isla all the time and, like any kid, Isla pushed boundaries. She'd considered reducing screen time as further punishment for what Isla had done to Dennie, but it irked that her daughter suffered the brunt of a penalty because of something that was technically not her fault. If she'd told Isla the truth about her father, maybe it wouldn't be such a big deal when other kids asked her about it. Then again, Isla learning her father was a rock star could potentially bring a whole other set of problems: kids only being interested in her because of her dad and subsequently never knowing if a friendship was real or fake.

No, she'd done the right thing in deflecting the truth again yesterday but it annoyed her that Isla had to miss a month of netball because she'd overreacted to a touchy subject.

She spied her daughter stomping up to the back door so slipped her hands into oven mitts. She'd baked Isla's favourite, white choc and blueberry muffins. She understood the coach had to discipline Isla as physical violence wasn't tolerated, but she wished the penalty hadn't been so harsh.

Isla barrelled through the back door and kicked off her shoes. 'We have a new neighbour.'

'Oh?' Tash opened the oven and reached for the muffin tray.

'Yeah. He seems cool. A little grumpy though.' Isla inhaled. 'That smells so good.'

'Don't eat them all at once,' Tash said, lifting up the tray as Isla said, 'His name's Kody.'

The tray slipped from Tash's grip and clattered against the oven rack. Her hands shook as she steadied the tray, managing not to scorch herself. A second later and the muffins would've been all over the floor.

'Hey, are you okay, Mum? Did you burn yourself?'

'I'm fine,' Tash said, her voice sounding weak and reedy. 'The tray slipped.'

Ridiculous, to have such an over-the-top reaction to a name. There had to be countless men called Kody. What were the odds of her Kody moving in next door? Not that he was hers. He never had been. Not really. Her Kody, the man she'd loved unreservedly, would've never accepted her lie. He would've known she'd never terminate a baby of theirs. He would've come after her, sat her down and figured out a way to make their relationship work.

Instead, she'd been forced to leave her nursing degree behind and come home to Brockenridge, knowing how difficult it would be telling her conservative parents the truth. But never in her wildest dreams had she anticipated they'd shun her, moving away to 'escape the shame', leaving her with little savings and having to raise a baby with minimal help.

So he could never be her Kody. Because her Kody only existed in her imagination, a perfect version of an imperfect man.

'Mum, what's going on with you?' Isla touched her arm and Tash jumped, almost upending the muffins again.

'Just tired,' she said, backing away from the oven and placing the tray on the sink to cool.

'I think you're stuck in a rut,' Isla said, reaching for a muffin. 'You need a boyfriend.'

'Where did that come from?'

'You don't date. Which is kind of weird, because you're young and cool and pretty.' Isla studied her, head tilted to one side in a gesture so reminiscent of her father that emotion clogged Tash's throat. 'I told Kody if he wanted to have dinner any time, he should come over.'

Tash didn't know whether to hug her daughter for being so welcoming and friendly to a stranger or chastise her for the same. She settled for tweaking Isla's ponytail. 'Are you trying to matchmake, young lady?'

'Maybe.' Isla's impish grin lightened her heart. 'Anyway, he probably won't bother, because he looked grumpy and sad about something, so don't worry about it.'

'I won't,' Tash said, hoping she sounded blasé, because saying she wouldn't worry and actually not worrying were poles apart. She'd dwell, conjuring up all sorts of crazy scenarios where her neighbour turned out to be the only guy she'd ever loved.

There was only one way to stave off endless hours of angst.

She'd have to pay her new neighbour a visit.

CHAPTER

7

Kody had never been big on cooking but being on the road for three hundred days a year meant he had a few go-to meals rather than surviving on fast food. Pasta and veg, chicken salad and pumpkin risotto were staples he whipped up when he got some time to himself. The boys used to tease him about his hunger for healthy, 'girly' food but he'd acquired a taste for those particular dishes when Tash introduced him to the joys of fresh food over takeaway and he'd equated them with comfort ever since.

Silly, to associate comfort food with Tash, considering their relationship ended so badly. But being on his own in this place, without his other comfort—music—left him with too much time to think. And he hated that. Thinking left him morose and guilt-ridden, dwelling on what could have been with Tash, and what should have been at his last concert. He should've abandoned the elaborate fireworks when the band's lead stagehand called in sick and the show had to be managed by a less-experienced guy. He should've made the decision based on safety and not on ego, determined to conquer every city in the world including Wellington. He should've done more to calm the panicked crowd before they stampeded and ended up killing seven of the band's fans.

That's what he found the hardest to live with: that those people had been there to see Rock Hard Place, to listen to the band's hits, and had been guilty of nothing but seeking pleasure and escape through music. And because of his insistence on using the complicated fireworks instead of going ahead without them, they'd ended up dead.

No amount of alcohol or prescribed meds could stop the nightmares. He'd eschewed the recommended therapy sessions. He'd had his fair share of counsellors growing up, being forced to sit in faux-cheerful rooms with rainbows and suns stencilled on the walls and unburden himself about what went wrong in the latest foster home. It never worked because he didn't trust easily, let alone grown-ups intent on 'fixing' him. They'd cajole and pretend to be his buddy, and when that didn't work, they'd get him to fill out meaningless questionnaires and draw pictures. He'd toy with them, either acting out his anger at the world or toeing the line by giving the spiel he knew they wanted to hear: 'Yes, I understand I'm lucky to be given a home by people who want to care for me. Yes, I'll do my best to behave in an appropriate manner. No, I won't release my frustrations on those around me.' Blah, blah, blah. On and on until he hit his teens and learned cleverer ways to outsmart the shrinks.

Taking time out had to work, because he couldn't go on like this. Scowling, he turned off the stove and drained the pasta into a colander. He focussed on chopping spring onions, capsicum and snow peas, then dicing the poached chicken, a mindless activity that usually soothed but today, he couldn't shake the feeling of impending doom. Bumping into that kid, Isla, had him in a funk. What if she'd recognised him? What if she told her friends? The news of his whereabouts would spread like wildfire and he'd be screwed.

He needed this time-out. When the boys had railroaded him into it, he'd been angry and resentful, but being here had already had a beneficial effect: he'd managed a laugh at that kid's smart mouth, something he hadn't done in weeks.

Maybe he was worrying about nothing. Rock Hard Place's demographic weren't young teens, so the odds of the kid having even heard of him were slim. But she had said he looked familiar ...

The knife slipped, narrowly missing the tip of his index finger, and he cursed, loudly.

An impatient knock on his door had him cursing again. If that kid thought she could waltz in here and bug the crap out of him, he'd set her straight. Yanni had warned him that country folk thought it perfectly acceptable to bang on someone's back door, even strangers.

He crossed the cool slate floor and flung open the door.

To find Tash on the other side.

Tash blinked. Once. Twice. As though the innocuous reaction could erase the man before her. But he wasn't a mirage. He was all too real, sporting the same shell-shocked expression she must be. A chill swept over her body, a ripple of ice that spread from her head downwards, invading every cell and rendering her mute.

This couldn't be happening. In what warped, twisted world did the man she'd deceived more than thirteen years ago, the man who travelled the world, the man who was recognisable anywhere, the man who'd fathered her child, show up out of the blue as her neighbour?

She had no idea how long they stood there, gaping at each other like a couple of morons, but when her brain eventually kicked into gear and worked in sync with her mouth, she managed a lame, 'Kody?'

Stupid, asking a question she knew the answer to. Of course this was Kody. She'd know him anywhere. The same shaggy dark hair the colour of hot chocolate, the same dark eyes bordering on ebony, the same mouth that could coax the most wonderful responses out of her. Other than fine lines fanning from the corners of his eyes and deeper grooves bracketing his mouth, he looked the same. Sexier, if that were possible.

'What the hell are you doing here?'

His frigid tone exacerbated her chills. No inflection. No warmth. Like he couldn't stand the sight of her. She supposed she deserved it considering how she'd treated him during their last conversation, the night she'd driven him away deliberately. His tone may be frigid but his eyes—they roved over her, hungry, greedy, remembering ...

'Can we talk?'

His lips compressed into a thin line but he flung the door open wider and walked away, leaving her with an impressive view of faded denim moulding a taut butt and navy cotton highlighting the shift of muscles in his back. Tash stood rooted to the spot, enjoying the view. It had been way too long since she'd had sex. She couldn't remember the last time. Three years ago? Four? A pharmaceutical salesman had been passing through town and stayed at the roadhouse for a night. He'd been one of those slick suit types, full of charm and smooth lines. The antithesis of Kody. Isla had been at a sleepover, the guy had said all the right things and Tash had allowed herself to be swept away for a night.

'I haven't got all day.'

Kody's rebuke startled Tash into moving inside, a blush burning her cheeks as she realised he must've caught her ogling. She closed the door and followed him into a large, modern kitchen, where the ingredients for his dinner lay on the island bench. Chicken salad, the way she'd shown him to prepare it.

A wave of disabling nostalgia consumed her and she blindly reached for something to lean against. Unfortunately, that happened to be Kody, as he moved swiftly to her side.

'Don't you dare bloody faint on me,' he muttered, leading her to a chair at the oak dining table in the corner. 'Sit. Breathe.'

Feeling increasingly stupid, Tash sat and took several steadying breaths. Only then did she risk looking at him, propped against the island bench, looking like a model channelling sexy rock star on holiday.

'What are you doing here?'

His upper lip curled in a sneer, like she had no right to ask him anything. 'Taking a break, not that it's any of your business.'

'Out here? Why aren't you sunning yourself in St Moritz or Barbados or Bora Bora?'

'Because being stuck in the arse end of the earth ensures anonymity.'

She stifled a guffaw. She'd been guilty of labelling Brockenridge the same when she'd wanted to escape it after high school and her parents had insisted she could do nursing at a country hospital rather than at university in Melbourne. They hadn't been impressed. Maybe that had been the beginning of the end for them. Then again, her parents had never understood their only child; partially her fault for being too agreeable.

'The fame getting to you?'

Something dark and painful shifted in his eyes. 'You still don't watch the news?'

He'd teased her about her lack of current affairs knowledge when they'd been dating. She hated the news, every boring, depressing second. Yet the fact he remembered something so small about her sparked something deep inside, a memory of shared intimacy.

'No. Why should I? It's always bad.'

'Yeah, I guess.' He looked away, but not before she glimpsed something akin to fear in those dark depths. 'There was an accident with fireworks at one of our concerts in Wellington. It caused a stampede.' He dragged his gaze back to meet hers and the depth of his agony snatched her breath. 'Seven people were killed.'

'I'm so sorry,' she said, her apology sounding trite in the face of his devastation. She wanted to go to him, to take him in her arms and ease some of his pain. But she'd given up that right many years ago, around the time she'd convinced him she'd given up their baby.

And just like that, the wooziness was back, making her clutch at the table. Kody had met Isla. Now Tash had showed up on his doorstep, it wouldn't take him long to do the maths and figure out she'd lied to him and stolen something major from him: the chance to raise his daughter.

She had to tell him the truth. Now.

But he looked so ... broken. The deaths of those concertgoers must be weighing heavily for him to hide out here. She had to be smart about this and ease into the news of Isla's paternity rather than blurting it like she wanted to.

'Was anybody else injured? Everyone in the band okay?'

He glared at her like she had no right to ask and the depth of his animosity towards her made her chest ache. His opinion of her shouldn't matter after all this time but it did. An opinion that would get a hell of a lot worse in the next few minutes.

'Twenty-three others were taken to hospital, minor casualties from broken wrists to cuts and abrasions. The band is fine.'

Except him. She could see it in the devastation he tried to hide by blinking. 'Are the guys joining you out here?'

'Rock Hard Place are on hiatus,' he said, a haunting edge under-lying his icy tone. 'I've walked away from the only thing I ever loved.'

Ouch. But she'd always known music was his first love—his only love—which is why she hadn't made it hard for him to choose between her and their child or stardom.

'How long are you in town for?'

He shrugged, drawing her attention to the breadth of his shoul-ders. Stupid, to notice a thing like that at a time like this. He'd been lean back in Melbourne, wiry, but he looked like he'd been work-ing out since and she irrationally missed being alongside him to see the changes over the years.

'Don't know.' He tapped his temple. 'As long as it takes to get my head back in the game according to the boys, but that may never happen.'

'You'd seriously walk away from your music?'

'I have no frigging idea,' he snapped. 'I can't face touching a guitar let alone singing.'

The urge to go to him was stronger this time and she stood, eager to escape. 'I'm really sorry you're going through some tough stuff. And I know me showing up on your doorstep is a shock for both of us, but Isla mentioned she'd invited you round for dinner and when I heard your name I thought it couldn't be you but I couldn't take the chance of us meeting in front of her for the first time.' Damn it, she was rambling like an idiot. 'I need to tell you something.'

'I'm not really interested in what you have to say, Tash.' He pinched the bridge of his nose, a familiar gesture that made her breath catch. 'For however long I'm stuck here, you stay out of my way, I'll stay out of yours.'

Bitterness radiated off him, and she didn't blame him. How much worse would he despise her when she confessed?

'This is important,' she said, her voice quavering, and she cleared her throat. 'It's about Isla, my daughter. She's almost thirteen.'

His eyes widened in shock. 'Thirteen ... but does that mean ... is she ...'

Every self-preservation mechanism in her body insisted Tash turn and run. Divulging the truth would have far-reaching consequences for them all. She'd never envisaged crossing paths with Kody ever again but somehow he was here, now, and she couldn't lie to him, not again.

'Yes.'

That one loaded syllable hung in the air between them as their gazes locked, his stunned, hers apologetic.

'She's mine?' He sounded furious and hopeful and wondrous.

She gave a brief nod, watching the colour drain from his face as he staggered and sank onto the nearest chair.

'She's mine,' he murmured, a statement this time, not a question, as a lone tear trickled down his pale cheek.

Tash had never felt so bereft. She reached out a hand to comfort him but when his head snapped up and she glimpsed his fury, she took a step back.

'Get out,' Kody said, his tone cold and lethal.

When she didn't move, he yelled, 'Get the hell out!'

Nothing Tash said now would make the situation any better so, with a final, regretful shake of her head, she turned her back on him and walked out.

CHAPTER

8

Betty's Bakery had been Jane's go-to place since she'd been a kid, despite her mum's insistent warnings that 'once past the lips forever on the hips'. Jane hadn't cared back then, she'd been a sporty kid and burned off the calories from Betty's amazing baked goods. These days she had to be more careful, but she'd always had curves no matter what she ate and nothing would soothe her like a prize-winning vanilla slice.

After ducking home to change, she parked near Nancy's op shop, the scene of the infamous incident where she'd framed Ruby for stealing a necklace, all because she'd been green with envy that the handsomest guy in school, Connor Delaney, had asked Ruby to the graduation ball and not her. She'd done some shitty things in her life since, but that had been a particular low point. Ruby had left town that night and hadn't returned until her mum died and she'd taken over the roadhouse. If she were in Ruby's shoes she wouldn't have been so forgiving. Maybe Ruby understood however many apologies Jane uttered, there was nothing she could do that would truly make up for her blunders over the years. That was something she had to live with every damn day.

Her decision-making had gone downhill since she'd discovered the truth about her parents. Foolish, considering no amount of disrepute she brought on Gladys Jefferson seemed to make the slightest difference. Her mum continued to swan through life, pretending that her marriage had been perfect, that she didn't lie like everyone else. Jane hadn't hurt her mum with her shoddy behaviour over the years. The only person still hurting was her and she was done.

Needing that custard-filled slice of heaven more than ever, she picked up the pace and had almost made it to the bakery when a man stepped out of a doorway directly into her path. She tried to sidestep him but her foot tangled with his and she would've gone down in an ungraceful heap if he hadn't grabbed her arms.

'Watch where you're going,' she muttered, brushing off his grip as she straightened, only to lock eyes with a startlingly handsome guy. He looked familiar ... probably one of the guys she'd gone to high school with who had left town and only visited family occasionally. He hadn't been one of the cool crowd—she would've remembered him. He was tall, about six-four, with wavy dark blonde hair, brown eyes and the kind of chiselled jaw that usually adorned superhero movie posters.

'You're the one who ran into me.' The deep voice, filled with censure and disapproval, made her bristle and step back. 'So an apology wouldn't go astray.'

That voice—the moment she heard him speak she recognised Mason Woodley, because his gruff voice used to hurl insults at her on a regular basis.

Jane had been popular in high school—with everybody but Mason. She'd enjoyed being the centre of attention back then. Everybody liked her and she thrived on it. So when Mason didn't fall for her charms, she'd taken it as a personal challenge. But no matter how hard she tried to sweet-talk him, he'd cut her down with snarky comments that never failed to rile. She'd hide her chagrin behind saccharine smiles that he saw right through and it annoyed the crap out of her. She couldn't wait to see the back of him at the end of year twelve.

Yet she adored his mum now. The few times Betty had mentioned her son and how proud she was of him, Jane would change the subject and Betty soon got the message. She'd rather not remember the many times Mason had laughed at her expense.

'An apology?' Her nose crinkled like she smelled something bad. 'You expect me to say sorry for something you did?' She folded her arms, annoyed that a flicker of heat shot through her body as he stared at her. She'd just spent the last half-hour chastising herself for hooking up with a stranger yet here she was, noticing how hot Mason was, from the golden stubble dusting his jaw to the deep tan that set off hair naturally lightened by the sun. He must take really bad selfies because he looked nothing like the photos Betty occasionally showed her on her mobile.

'Still the same supercilious princess, I see,' Mason said with a dismissive shake of his head. 'Some things never change.'

Supercilious princess? He was right about one thing, though. Some things never change. Still the same old Mason: a judgemental prick. Before she had a chance to tell him exactly where he could stick his unwanted opinion, he pinned her with a withering stare.

'You don't even know who I am, do you?'

In that moment Jane knew how to get back at him for his holier-than-thou attitude: wound him in his precious ego. Besides, if she pretended she didn't recognise him the sooner she could get that vanilla slice.

She peered at him, forcing a confused frown. 'Uh, no.'

'That's because you only deigned to notice the pretty boys.' He snorted in disgust. 'Too bad for you, because the geeks were the smart ones who actually made something of themselves.'

It irked that he was partially right; she did only notice the kids like her back then: rich, popular, cool. But they'd left high school a long time ago and she didn't deserve this level of vitriol, so she mustered her best blasé mask and quirked an eyebrow.

'Bitter much?'

'Just stay out of my way,' he growled, his frown doing little to detract from his exceedingly good looks.

'I will if you get out of mine.' She pointed over his shoulder. 'I have a date with Betty's sublime creations.'

Some of the tension pinching his mouth eased but his frown didn't. 'I'll make sure to tell Mum to lace whatever you buy with arsenic.'

Her incredulity at his overt rudeness must've shown on her face because a faint pink stained his cheeks. 'Remember me now?'

'Yeah, but you haven't changed a bit, Mason Woodley.' She rolled her eyes. 'I recognised you earlier and was pulling your leg, but looks like your sense of humour is the same as it was back in high school. Pretty damn crappy.' She blew a raspberry.

She hoped he might laugh. She really liked Betty and having to fraternise with the enemy during however long he was visiting wasn't something she looked forward to if he couldn't lighten up.

'Still a game-player, huh?' Disapproval radiated off him. 'For the record, I'll be helping Mum run the bakery for a while, so if you want to feed your sweet tooth, you better be a hell of a lot nicer than you were in high school.'

Maybe it was her plummeting blood sugar levels, maybe it was the morning she'd had, or maybe it was yet another person in a long line of people judging her, but Jane wanted to slug him; tiny pinpricks of black danced across her vision as anger made her hands shake.

'I can't believe you're dredging up the past.' She stepped in closer, hating that he smelled so good, an enticing combination of citrus and freshly showered male. 'For the record, high school was a long time ago and some of us have matured, so why don't you grow up?'

She pushed past him and strode towards the bakery, her desire for one vanilla slice morphing into a desperate need for three.

CHAPTER
9

Tash had no recollection how she made it home from next door. She must've traversed the path automatically, one foot trudging in front of the other as she tried to hold herself together.

Kody Lansdowne was her neighbour. He now knew the truth.

Which meant she had to tell Isla before he did.

A wave of nausea swept over her and she staggered to the bench in their backyard. She collapsed onto it, dragging in deep breaths that did little to settle her roiling stomach. She'd always instilled honesty in her daughter, so how could she turn around now and admit to a monstrous lie?

Isla would never trust her again ... A sob clogged her throat and she hung her head, unable to stop the tears from falling. She'd learned to live with the guilt of not telling Kody the truth, but had never imagined it would come to this.

'Mum? Are you okay?' Isla sat next to her and rested a tentative hand on her shoulder.

Her daughter's concern only served to make the tears fall faster but she had to pull herself together to get through this.

'Mum, you're scaring me.' Isla tugged on her arm this time and Tash lifted her head, dashing a hand across her eyes. Isla's big hazel eyes were filled with worry and Tash hated that her daughter's concern would soon give way to derision, maybe even hate, once she learned the truth.

'I'm okay, sweetie.' She wrapped her arms around Isla and squeezed tight, wishing she could infuse her with strength to help her cope with what she was about to hear.

Isla hugged her back but all too quickly wriggled out of the embrace. 'You never cry—what happened?'

Tash's chest tightened and her feet and hands tingled, like she was on the verge of a panic attack, so she took a deep breath and blew it out, then repeated the process under the wary gaze of her daughter.

When the tingling and tightness abated, she said, 'I need to tell you something important and it may be hard for you to understand at the start, but know that whatever I've done, I did to protect you.'

Isla's eyes filled with suspicion and Tash reached for her hand, surprised when her daughter allowed her to clasp it.

'What have you done, Mum?'

Lied to the man she loved. Deliberately drove him away. Kept secrets from her daughter for almost thirteen years.

She settled for: 'This is probably the oddest timing considering Swap Day at school and what happened with Dennie, but your father's in town.'

Isla froze, eyes wide, mouth open, so Tash hurried on: 'I didn't know. I thought I'd never see him again—'

'Who is he?' Isla gripped her hand so tight Tash's went numb. 'Can I see him?'

'He only just found out about you so we need to give him time and space, then I'll discuss it with him.'

Tash knew she'd made a blunder when Isla snatched her hand away. 'What do you mean he only just found out about me? You said he knew but he chose to walk away.'

'I—I left him in Melbourne and I returned here to have you.'

'So you lied to him, and me.' Isla leapt to her feet. 'Why would you do that? Why?'

Her plea reached deep into Tash's bruised soul and tweaked it, hard. She'd never seen her daughter so angry and she didn't blame her. Her greatest fear, that Isla would hate her for withholding the truth all these years, was coming true. And there wasn't a damn thing she could do about it. Tears burned her eyes but she couldn't cry again, not when Isla needed her.

She hadn't lied about one thing: she'd hidden Kody's identity to protect her daughter and she hoped to god that Isla would understand.

'Things got complicated between us. Your father was about to launch his career and I didn't want to force him into making a choice between us and that.'

'You still should have told him.'

Relieved her daughter was mature enough to understand life's hard choices, Tash nodded. 'Maybe I should have, but I made the decision I thought was right at the time. Now he's turned up in Brockenridge and we all have to figure out where we go from here.'

'I want to meet him.'

'You already have.'

Isla's brow furrowed in confusion for a moment before understanding lit her eyes. 'Kody?'

Tash nodded. 'Kody Lansdowne is your father.'

Isla whipped her mobile out of her pocket, brought up the search engine and typed in the name. When the screen filled with results, Isla looked up, stunned all over again.

'My dad is *the* Kody Lansdowne?'

'Uh-huh.'

'No shit.'

Tash didn't tolerate swearing but in this case, she let it slip. The situation warranted it.

Isla's stunned gaze moved back and forth from her mobile to Tash, so Tash stayed silent, giving her time to assimilate the revelation, knowing there'd be plenty of incoming questions.

'There's millions of hits on him,' Isla said, her voice tight with emotion. 'This is so surreal.'

'I know it's a lot to take in—'

'I'm really mad at you.' Isla's glare was hostile and a small piece of Tash's heart splintered. 'All those times I asked you about my dad and you fobbed me off with a bunch of BS.'

Tash bit her lip to stop from blubbering. 'I know, honey, and I was wrong. I should've trusted you enough to deal with the truth.'

'You should've.'

The resentment in Isla's eyes made Tash want to bundle her into her arms again. But this wasn't one of those times when a simple hug would make everything better.

'I made a mistake, and I know it's going to take time to adjust to this, but whatever you need, I'm here.'

Isla grunted in acknowledgement but the anger in her eyes faded as she glanced at her mobile again. 'Having a rock star at Swap Day is going to seriously shut up every one of those cows at school,' Isla eventually said.

Considering the mood Kody had been in when Tash had dropped her bombshell on him, she had no idea whether he'd be up for parenting Isla, let alone spending a day with a bunch of high school kids. But they'd deal with that problem when it eventuated. For now she wanted to ensure Isla was okay.

'Do you have any questions, honey?'

'Stacks, but is it okay if I go chill in my room for a while?' She waved her phone around. 'I want to look him up on my laptop. This screen is too small to read all the stuff on.'

'Okay, I'll be in the kitchen when you're finished.'

Isla shuffled her feet, shifting her weight from side to side, before finally eyeballing Tash. 'I guess I should thank you for finally telling me the truth.'

Tash's throat tightened and she managed a brief nod.

'But if Kody hadn't moved in next door, would you have told me?'

Tash had lied enough so she shook her head, hating herself when Isla's face fell. 'Probably not, sweetie. Like I said, I wanted to protect you—'

'I think you wanted to protect yourself, Mum.'

With that, her wise, mature tween stalked back into the house and slammed the door.

Half an hour later, Isla stomped into the kitchen. Tash had prepared nachos, one of Isla's favourites. The tantalising aromas of roasted tomatoes, capsicum and melted cheese hung in the air, and Tash hoped the meal would tempt her daughter to sit down and talk this out.

'You're bribing me with food,' Isla muttered, snatching up a corn chip and dunking it in sour cream before popping the laden triangle into her mouth.

'Guilty as charged.' Tash placed the piping hot tray between them before laying out plates and serviettes. 'A little comfort food never goes astray.'

'I guess.' Isla plonked onto the seat opposite and used the metal tongs to help herself to a giant, gooey wedge of nachos. She avoided eye contact and her jaw jutted slightly, like she was clenching her teeth. 'I'm going to eat this before asking you stuff, okay?'

'Okay.'

They sat in silence, a first when it came to her garrulous daughter. Tash hated the tension between them but it was to be expected. At least Isla's bitterness hadn't diminished her appetite. Tash forced a few chips past her lips while Isla had no problem demolishing half the dish. Tash even had to replenish the guacamole after her daughter scooped up as much as she could fit onto each chip before stuffing the lot into her mouth. It heartened Tash to see Isla eat like that. Maybe she hadn't scarred her for life.

'Nachos are so good.' Isla wiped her mouth with a serviette before patting her stomach. 'Thanks.'

'You're welcome.'

They lapsed into awkward silence again. Tash could practically see a million questions bouncing around her daughter's head so she waited, hoping she could answer them. She loved being a mum but nothing had prepared her for parenthood. Her folks had been crappy role models—controlling, reserved, emotionless—and she'd vowed to be the opposite in every way. Yet while there were countless books and online articles on how to breastfeed/wean/potty train, there weren't many manuals on dealing with the fallout after revealing a life-changing secret.

'Kody's really famous. Can you tell me about him? How you met? How you ended up dating? That kind of stuff?' Isla flung the questions out casually, but Tash saw the way she plucked and twisted the serviette in her hands, almost shredding it.

'We met in Melbourne. I was studying there, doing a nursing degree, and we met at a pub one night.' An understatement for the instantaneous connection they'd shared when Kody swaggered up to her, leaned down and murmured in her ear, 'That last song of our final set was for you.' It was a line, one he'd probably used on countless girls before, but Tash had been naïve and lonely and living in a big city far removed from her sheltered upbringing, so she'd responded with, 'In that case, you better sit and let me buy you a drink.'

They'd talked well into the night, and every time his knee brushed hers or his fingers touched her arm, she lit up, as though an electrical current surged through her and made her come alive for the first time ever. And when he invited her back to his studio apartment, she threw her usual reservations to the wind, and ended up losing her virginity and her mind to the sexiest guy on the planet. He owned her from that moment, body and soul, and she'd loved him wholeheartedly, unreservedly.

'We fell in love, shared our hopes and dreams. He had an amazing talent and his band was going places. When I fell pregnant, I didn't want to force him into making a really hard choice, so I broke up with him.'

Isla's eyes screwed up, as if she were pondering a particularly difficult maths problem. 'So he knew about me but chose to go anyway?'

'I gave him no choice. I drove him away deliberately so he wouldn't think he had to stay out of guilt.' The reality of how she'd driven Kody away was something she could never discuss with her daughter. Tash patted her chest. 'This was my fault, Isla. I didn't want him resenting me if he stayed to be with us so I was really mean and made sure he left.'

'How?'

She should've known Isla wouldn't let this go easily. 'The specifics aren't important. But what is important is that by some strange twist of fate, your dad's here and living next door for a while. How do you feel about that?'

Isla's gaze dropped to the shredded serviette in her hand and she put it on her plate. 'I want to meet him properly. As his daughter, not just some kid he bumped into by the fence.'

'Would you like me to arrange it?'

Isla bit her bottom lip and nodded, and once again Tash had to clamp down on the urge to haul her in for a comforting hug.

'Do you want me to be there?'

Isla remained silent for a moment then said, 'Maybe at the start? Then you could leave us to talk?'

'That sounds like a plan.'

Isla fell silent again, her expression a mix of fear and hope, propelling Tash around the table to lean down and wrap her arms around her daughter's shoulders. Isla stiffened but she didn't shrug her off and Tash was grateful for that.

'This is a lot to handle and I'm incredibly proud of you.' Tash dropped a kiss on Isla's head and straightened. 'And I think this calls for me to ditch my anti-soft-drink rule for a day and pour us both a cola.'

'You let me swear before too,' Isla said, the return of her sass giving Tash hope they could cope with whatever challenges came their way when Kody entered their family unit. Hope they could move forwards with a suitable arrangement that had Isla's best interests at heart. Hope that whatever the future held, they would never lose this incredible mother–daughter bond that was Tash's life.

CHAPTER

10

Fury surged through Kody after Tash left, making his hands shake and his head pound. He kicked out at a stool, upending it, before his gaze landed on the guitar in the corner and bile rose in his throat at his utter helplessness. Yelling at Tash to get the hell out hadn't put a dent in his anger. He needed to get out of here, to blow off steam, and he knew just the way to do it.

Grabbing keys off the labelled row of hooks above the entry table, he stormed into the carport and headed for the quad bike. Yanni loved any kind of all-terrain vehicle and the band had gone ag-biking in Nevada, California and New Zealand. Yeah, a fast ride would clear his head and calm him down so he could think this through logically.

What did he know about fatherhood? Nothing.

What did he know about mentoring young girls? Nada.

What did he know about patience and commitment and being a role model a child could look up to?

'Fuck,' he muttered, snagging a helmet from a storage cabinet and jamming it on his head before climbing onto the bike.

It started after several attempts and he revved the engine before letting out the clutch and accelerating out of the carport. He followed a roughly hewn path across a paddock towards a dam. He let the throttle out once he cleared the first paddock, picking up speed. The wind in his face, the roar of the engine and the blur of trees in his peripheral vision served to distract. He needed this, needed his rage to abate. Back in the house it had nowhere to go but out here, he could contemplate Tash's shocking revelation without wanting to break something.

He'd never dealt with frustration well. As a kid, he'd throw the biggest tantrums, which was probably why his father dumped him into foster care when he was six. As a teen, he'd acted out: fights; alcohol; dabbled in drugs. But he'd hated the blackouts and had steered clear of any kind of stimulant since, despite being offered the high-end stuff all around the world. It had been his love of music and meeting Yanni and his mates at sixteen that had turned his life around and since then he'd dealt with problems by losing himself in composing and singing.

Today, that wasn't an option. Not that he hadn't considered it, but every time he so much as glanced at the guitar propped on a stand in the corner of the rumpus room, he broke out in a cold sweat. It scared the shit out of him that he may never get past this. His career could be over.

But for now he had other things to worry about. Namely, being a father when he had no idea how. The father figures he'd known had ignored him, tortured him or belted him. He'd pretended he didn't care, grew tougher with each beating, learned to hide the pain beneath a veneer of arrogance that only incensed his torturers further. It served him well, hiding his true feelings, because his 'stage face' came in mighty handy when he'd been sick or exhausted or not given a fuck but still had to perform.

Ironic that, in all the beatings he'd suffered at the hands of sadistic bastards, he'd never felt this flayed open, like his chest had been split and his heart laid bare.

How could Tash do it to him? How could she lie about aborting the baby then keep his daughter a secret for almost thirteen goddamn years?

An ache like nothing he'd experienced before spread through his chest. He'd adored Tash once, had loved her so much he would've done anything. Her deception made him want to down enough bourbon to pass out for a week.

A bad thought, because in the next moment the bike hit something hard, sending a powerful jolt up his spine and propelling him into the air. He flew one way, the bike another, and as he came down he heard the distinctive crack of a bone breaking the second before excruciating pain in his left ankle made him cry out.

He woke to find himself flat on his back, staring at a cloudless sky, terrified to move in case he'd broken more than his ankle. He gingerly pushed up onto his elbows and glanced at his legs, instantly wishing he hadn't. His ankle protruded from the bottom of his jeans at a right angle to his leg. A wave of nausea made him lie back down.

Gritting his teeth against the agonising throb in his ankle, he fished his mobile out of his pocket and dialled 000. The operator put him through to the ambulance service and after he gave his location he closed his eyes, listening to the soothing voice of the emergency service worker, trying to picture himself anywhere but here.

He should never have come to this godforsaken town. His shitty life had turned shittier since he'd arrived at Wattle Lane.

But a small, stubborn part of him refused to join the pity party, because if he hadn't come here he never would've discovered he had a daughter. Isla.

He may know jackshit about parenting but once he got his ankle sorted, he had to pull his finger out and start acting like a responsible adult and not some whiny, woe-is-me kid.

'Kody, are you still there?'

'Yeah, not going anywhere,' he muttered, his dry response earning a chuckle.

'You should hear the chopper any minute now.'

Chopper? Of course. He'd come off in a paddock in the middle of nowhere; a car couldn't traverse this terrain.

The *whoosh-whoosh-whoosh* of helicopter blades broke the silence and he watched the chopper grow closer until it landed about five hundred metres away. He tried propping himself up on his elbows again then wished he hadn't when breath-stealing pain ripped through his leg, like someone had skewered him from foot to hip.

The next thirty minutes passed in a blur: being strapped onto a portable gurney; loaded onto the chopper; a short flight to the nearest hospital in Echuca; examination in ER. Several nurses recognised him, a doc too, but even in his pain haze, he implored them to keep his identity confidential and they agreed. With X-rays done and a break confirmed, his ankle was plastered, but not without a lecture about the dangers of quad-bike riding. He now lay in a single bed in a quiet room, waiting to be picked up.

That had been the kicker. When the discharge nurse asked who she should call to pick him up, he'd had to give the name of the only person he knew in the area: Natasha Trigg. The nurse had cast him a suspicious glance when he couldn't give her Tash's number but said she'd look it up when she got back to the nurse's station.

Tears of frustration burned his eyes and he blinked them away. Tears were for sissies, he'd been told many times growing up. They served no purpose other than to make a person look weak.

But right now, with the guilt of those concertgoers' deaths on his hands, the fear he may never sing again, the revelation he had a daughter, and a broken ankle that hurt like the devil, he didn't care about weakness.

He felt like bawling.

CHAPTER
11

Tash had been reluctant to drop Isla off at a friend's place after the big discussion they'd had earlier in the afternoon, but her daughter had been insistent. Tash understood; Isla needed some space, more time to process, and Tash didn't want to hover. She'd always been a bit of a helicopter parent when Isla had been younger, for the simple fact she only had one child and couldn't foresee having any more. Not that she was closed off to dating, per se, but the availability of single guys in Brockenridge was low. Those who moved away tended to meet women and marry elsewhere, whereas the few who remained tended to be hard-working farmers perpetually under the pump who rarely had time for a relationship.

While she had no intention of hanging out with Kody for how-ever long he was in town, it was kind of sweet Isla had thought to invite him over because she didn't have a boyfriend. It looked like her daughter had been borrowing one too many young adult romances from the library.

'Can I get another beer, love?'

Tash nodded at Bazza, the octogenarian farmer who popped in to The Watering Hole for a late lunch once a month. 'Sure thing, but you know two's your limit.'

'You sound like the old ball and chain,' he muttered, along with something that sounded suspiciously like 'nag'.

Tash bit back a grin as she slipped behind the bar to pull him a beer. Bazza and Shirl had been married for sixty years and bickered whenever they came to the roadhouse. Considering her longest relationship—with Kody—had only lasted a few months, she couldn't imagine living with someone and tolerating their foibles that long.

'Here you go.' She placed the beer in front of him. 'Go easy on that one, it's your last.'

'Yep, you could be Shirl's double.' Bazza glared at her, before tempering it with a wink. 'Remind me to find another place to whet my whistle.'

'Come on, Baz, 'fess up, you'd miss my nagging.'

'Women,' he muttered with a roll of his eyes, before grinning at her and taking a giant draught.

She'd done the right thing by popping in to work. An hour or two of an extra shift was guaranteed to take her mind off things. But with Bazza savouring his beer and no other customers, her mind inevitably wandered to Kody and what had brought him to Brockenridge. She grabbed her mobile and slipped into a quiet corner near the bar. It had been many years since she'd typed 'Kody Lansdowne' or 'Rock Hard Place' into a search engine and it felt plain weird doing it now. Yet she needed to know what she was dealing with when it came to Kody's mental state, so she could protect Isla if necessary. There was no way the tough guy she'd known would have walked away from his band and his career over an accident.

The concert accident popped up as the third item in a long list of hits. The report didn't tell her anything more than what Kody had: seven people at a Rock Hard Place concert in Wellington, New Zealand, had been killed and another twenty-three injured in a stampede when patrons had been spooked by a fireworks mal-function and the resultant fire. Sorrow for those poor people who'd lost their lives and their families squeezed her chest. It must've been horrific for all involved, including the band. Had Kody witnessed some of the carnage? Is that why he was hiding out? She assumed the band would've been whisked to safety first, but in a situation like that who knew what could happen? Whatever he'd seen, being witness to a tragedy could seriously mess with his head.

'Someone's got a crush,' Ruby said, peeking over Tash's shoul-der. 'Kody Lansdowne is seriously hot.'

Tash whirled around, cheeks burning as she slipped her mobile back into her pocket.

Ruby hooted. 'Look at you, all hot and bothered over a rock star—'

'Kody is Isla's dad.' The truth tumbled from her lips before she could consider the wisdom of telling one of her closest friends a secret she'd kept hidden for over a decade.

Ruby's eyes widened and she burst out laughing. 'You had me there for a second—'

'It's true. We were a thing in Melbourne before he got famous, and now he's here in Brockenridge and he's moved in next door, and I had to tell Isla the truth and everything's a bloody mess ...' Tash trailed off, almost relieved to get all of that off her chest.

Ruby grasped Tash's arm, led her to the nearest seat, and pushed her into it. 'Be right back.'

Now she'd told her friend the truth, Tash had the distinct urge to unburden herself. Silly to have kept this inside for so long, because

Alisha and Ruby were the least judgemental women on the planet, and when she'd told Alisha years ago, her friend had said nothing beyond urging her to tell Kody the truth. Then again, not so silly after all, because Tash knew if she'd told all her friends about Kody she would've been tempted to look him up again and no way did she want to end up back in that spiral of doubting her decision and wishing for things that couldn't be.

She'd done enough of that when Isla had been a toddler, when Tash had come home from a long shift at The Watering Hole, tucked her daughter into bed, and spent way too much time online, analysing every aspect of Kody's glamorous life. The parties, the awards, the women … it had driven her crazy, imagining the kind of life she could've had with him. Then she'd tiptoe into her adorable daughter's room, stare at her innocent, cherubic face lax with sleep, and know she'd made the right decision. Dragging a child from one city to another, dealing with intrusive paparazzi, not having a real home— that was no life for a child. Tash had definitely done the right thing, but in those early years it hadn't stopped her wondering what if and yearning for something, or someone, she could never have.

'Here. Drink this.' Ruby placed a glass of port in front of her. 'This aged tawny will go down easier than whiskey or brandy. It's super sweet.'

'I'm not drinking that, I have to pick up Isla in a few hours.'

'Fine, then. I will. I need it more for shock than you do anyway.' Ruby downed the port in three gulps, slamming the glass down hard and making them both jump. 'Damn, girl, you're full of surprises.' She leaned in close and said, in an exaggerated whisper, 'You shagged *the* Kody Lansdowne?'

'Many times.' Tash winked, relieved she could joke about this now. She hadn't felt like laughing earlier when she'd told Kody the truth and seen the devastation mixed with fury in his eyes.

'Wow. Go you.'

Tash knew her friend. She'd want to ask a million questions but wouldn't want to pry either. 'It's okay. Go ahead and ask. I know you're dying to.'

Ruby grinned, leaned over and poked her in the shoulder. 'You actually dated him? What happened? Who ended it? Does he want you back? Is that why he's here? And what about Isla? How will you two parent—'

'Whoa, slow down.' Tash held up her hands. 'But in answer to your questions, yes, we dated for a few months in Melbourne. I fell pregnant around the time he was offered his big break in America and I didn't want him to stick around because of the baby, so I told him I was coming home.' Not the entire truth but nobody knew about the abortion lie except her and Kody, and she intended on keeping it that way. The more who knew, the more risk Isla would find out, and she couldn't have that. There were enough people hurting; she didn't want to complicate it. Her daughter would never understand. And Tash would never put her in that position.

'So what's he doing here now? Pure chance?'

'Apparently.' Tash shrugged. 'The drummer in his band owns the place next to me and Kody's crashing there for a while.'

Ruby's forehead crinkled in confusion. 'He's really slumming it if he's in Brockenridge for time out rather than Monte Carlo or Bintan Island or some remote hotspot in the Caribbean.'

'That's what I thought too.' But Tash understood. Kody would be instantly recognised in any of those places whereas hiding out on Wattle Lane meant anonymity when he probably needed it most. That concert accident had to be playing heavily on his mind and until he was ready to re-join the tour he could enjoy some rare quiet time.

There were a few die-hard rock fans in Brockenridge, and Tash knew them because they attended every rock night at The

Watering Hole. They punched in the same songs on the jukebox and requested the same songs from visiting bands. Those people would recognise Kody, but the younger generation, not so much. Isla was a perfect example. She knew every hot band in the world at the moment, it's all tween girls talked about apparently, and had extensive playlists on her phone and laptop. But she hadn't recognised Kody, so that meant none of her age group would either.

Perhaps Tash could offer to help Kody out, run his errands in town so he wouldn't be at risk of exposure? It was the least she could do.

Yeah, like that could make up for depriving him of the joys of being a father for the last twelve years.

'What's the frown for? I take it Isla's okay with the truth?'

Tash nodded. 'She's been amazing, took it all in her stride.'

'And Kody?'

'Not so much.'

'He wants to be a part of Isla's life, right?'

'I think so, though we didn't really talk about it much ...' Tash cleared her throat as it tightened with worry. 'But we will. He's in shock. He needs some time to process.'

'Yeah, I guess.' Ruby eyed the empty port glass. 'Wish I could have another of those. I'm like Mr McHottie Rock Star. This is a lot to process.'

Tash barked out a laugh and Ruby joined in.

'Does anyone else know?'

'Alisha,' Tash said. 'The truth popped out after a few drinks one night years ago, but she's respected my request for privacy and hasn't bugged me about it since.'

'What about Harry?'

Tash shook her head. 'Though it wouldn't surprise me if he knows. Those two tell each other everything. Just like you and Connor—way too romantic.' She mock gagged.

Ruby opened her mouth to speak but Tash beat her to it. 'Yeah, you can tell him.'

'I'll make sure he knows to keep it secret.'

Damn secrets. Tash had had a gutful of them. Her mobile rang, the impersonal tone of an incoming call from an unidentified caller, and she wished her stomach wouldn't flip-flop with nerves that something could be wrong with Isla. She hit the answer button and held the phone to her ear.

'Is that Natasha Trigg?'

Her gut twisted at the official tone and she clenched the mobile tighter. 'Yes.'

'This is Babs McCalp from Echuca Regional Hospital.'

Tash's stomach went into free-fall before common sense kicked in. Isla was nowhere near Echuca.

'We have a Kody Lansdowne here with a fractured ankle, and he asked us to call you to pick him up. Is that possible?'

Relieved Isla was fine, she said, 'Yes, I'll be there in forty-five minutes.'

'Good, I'll let him know.'

Kody had to be desperate to ask for her. When the nurse hung up, Ruby leaned forwards and laid a hand on her arm. 'What's wrong?'

'Can you cover the rest of my shift? I have to go.'

Ruby nodded. 'Is it Isla?'

'No, thank goodness. It's Kody.'

With that, she gave Ruby's shoulder a quick squeeze, grabbed her bag from behind the bar and made a dash for the car park.

CHAPTER

12

Kody had enough painkillers rattling around inside him to take the edge off his pain, but they did nothing for his temper because the minute he laid eyes on Tash striding into the hospital short-stay waiting area, he wanted to kick something with his good leg.

Damn her for looking so attractive. She'd always favoured denim and her skinny jeans were moulded to legs he remembered all too well. Her red T-shirt was plain but highlighted curves he'd explored in intimate detail. In that moment, he wondered how it had all gone so wrong.

He'd always been a stubborn bastard, born from years of self-preservation as a kid growing up in places no child should have to live, but on the odd occasion, usually after a gig and a few beers, he'd pondered if he should've chased after Tash the night she'd ended it. She'd never know why her decision to abort had gutted him but he could've been a man and stood up to her. Demanded she give him more of a say. Instead, he'd let her walk away and, if he were completely honest, a small part of him was glad. Would he have had the career if he'd had a child?

He'd seen what life on the road did to families. Daz's wife had divorced him two years after Rock Hard Place hit the big time and he rarely saw his kids. Roger and his wife had an open marriage, meaning the bass guitarist slept with as many women as humanly possible—guilt free—so why stay married? Blue and Yanni were confirmed bachelors, but both had had serious relationships when the band first arrived in LA, relationships that didn't last under the strain of long days, long nights and long-legged women.

Ultimately, it had been Kody's decision to let Tash walk away. But she'd robbed him of almost thirteen years of his daughter's life and for that, he'd never forgive her.

She shot him a tentative smile as she stopped in front of him. 'Are you okay?'

'Just peachy,' he muttered, brandishing a crutch. 'Can we go?'

'Sure. Do you need anything—'

'I've signed the discharge papers and organised a follow-up orthopaedic appointment, so there's nothing you can do.'

She stiffened and a sliver of guilt wormed its way into his angry heart. But then he remembered Isla and how she'd made him laugh for the first time in forever and the guilt faded. He had to hang onto his anger against Tash because if he didn't, he'd be right back to where he was while lying in that paddock: feeling sorry for himself. He'd wallowed in pity the last four weeks, used it as a shield against anyone, including his best mates when they got too close. No way in hell he'd let the woman who'd deceived him so badly get anywhere near him.

To her credit, Tash didn't bug him with questions, nor did she hover as he struggled to master the crutches. Instead, she waited until they reached the front door before saying, 'Give me a minute and I'll bring the car around into the pick-up area.'

He grunted but even then she didn't respond, giving a slight shake of her head instead.

It was going to be a long forty-five minute drive back to Brockenridge.

The last thing he needed was to be holed up in her car while he craved a hot shower and a bourbon chaser. He was dusty, dirty and sweaty, and the alcohol would mix nicely with his painkillers. Sadly, both the shower and the bourbon were a pipe dream, as he couldn't get the plaster on his lower leg wet and getting blotto might result in him damaging more than his ankle. He'd been in a foul mood since he arrived in Brockenridge and no amount of alcohol would change that.

An old blue Holden sedan pulled up in front of him and he struggled to hide his surprise. She still owned the same car. That's when it hit him. While he'd been swanning around the world in the lap of luxury, indulging in the best of everything, it looked like Tash had been doing it tough raising his child. He knew nothing about her life now. Was she working as a nurse? Did she have the support of her parents? Had some other guy raised his kid? Was money a problem?

Shame burned his cheeks. He'd been so wrapped up in his fury that he hadn't given her a second thought. They had a lot to talk about but now wasn't the time. He'd wait until he had a clear head, not this weird cottony feeling from the painkillers.

She left the car running and came around to the passenger side to open the door for him. He hopped towards her, gritting his teeth against a sharp stab of pain as the end of a crutch knocked the plaster.

'Careful,' she said, and got a filthy glare for her warning, so she compressed her lips and waited with folded arms while he reached the car, swivelled and backed up towards the seat.

She waited until he'd sat and got both legs in the car before taking his crutches and storing them in the boot.

When she got behind the wheel, he said, 'Thanks for picking me up.'

'Not a problem.'

But it was. The taut silence between them as she navigated back to the highway headed for Brockenridge held a multitude of untold problems and the thought of addressing the main one, her thirteen-year lie, made his head ache more than his ankle.

'What happened?'

Small talk he could do, just. 'I was pissed at you, so after you left I took a quad bike out to blow off steam.'

'Are you nuts? You shouldn't be riding those things if you're inexperienced.'

'I don't need a lecture from you,' he said, hating that she saw him as some pampered, clueless rich boy. 'I've done my fair share of ag riding.'

She muttered something unintelligible under her breath but it sounded suspiciously like 'dickhead'. 'I'm surprised the hospital contacted me to pick you up and you didn't hop all the way back to Brockenridge.'

It was a direct jibe at him wanting nothing to do with her and he didn't blame her, not after the way he'd yelled at her to get the hell out of Yanni's place.

'If you expect me to apologise for shouting at you, you'll be waiting a long time,' he said. 'I was so bloody mad at you. Still am, but despite what you think, I'm not an idiot. I want to get to know Isla and you'll be part of facilitating that.'

A soft sigh escaped her lips. 'I've told her the truth and she wants to get to know you too.'

'All of it?'

'Of course not,' she snapped, the hint of vulnerability beneath her anger making him feel like a bastard for pushing this issue. 'How do you think she'd feel if she knew I'd lied about aborting her?'

'As shitty as I do for you lying to me about it?' He wasn't the bad guy here, and he'd be damned if he sat back and let her off the hook.

'Touché,' she muttered. 'I told her it was my fault, that I deliberately drove you away because I didn't want you missing your big break, so I'd appreciate if you kept the abortion lie out of it if she asks you what happened. It would devastate her to think she wasn't wanted.'

'Of course,' he muttered, hating that she thought him so heartless she had to spell it out.

He wanted to ask so much but the faint rose fragrance she'd always favoured befuddled his head with every breath he inhaled. It catapulted him straight back to those days and nights in Melbourne when they couldn't get enough of each other. He'd been an ambitious, cocky upstart, hiding his insecurities behind a microphone. She'd been a shy, innocent introvert who'd stared at him with wonder in her eyes from the moment they met. He'd wanted to warn her off him back then—he'd never be any good for a girl like her—but they'd clicked in a way he'd never anticipated and every second spent in her company made him feel a foot taller. Like he could do anything.

He'd shared more of himself with Tash than with anyone, even his best mates in the band. And she'd crapped all over him. Which brought him back to being stuck in this car with a bung ankle and a smouldering resentment he'd never get over.

'When can I spend some time with her?'

Tash shot him a quick sideways glance and he saw so much in her eyes in those few seconds—fear, hope, regret, sadness—before she blinked and re-focussed on the road.

'She's had a lot to absorb today, and you've had a big day too. I'll check with Isla and see if she's okay with catching up tomorrow.'

It made sense, considering the painkiller fog hadn't lifted, but he hated having her make presumptions about him; just like she had thirteen years ago when she'd ripped away any choice he had about his child.

'I may have had a "big day" but if I want to get to know my daughter, I will.' He sounded like a sulky brat and expected her to call him out on it.

Instead, she laughed, a short burst of amusement that shocked the hell out of him. 'At the risk of exacerbating your wrath, you look pretty rough and you smell worse, so wouldn't you like to get cleaned up and hold off on seeing Isla until tomorrow?'

She made perfect sense, damn it. 'Way to go with the flattery,' he said, earning another laugh.

'I get that you hate me right now, Kody, I really do. But Isla is my world and I'll do anything to protect her, so I suggest you lighten the hell up before you spend time with her because she's smart and will pick up on how much you loathe me. And that won't help.'

'I don't hate you,' he said, surprised he actually meant it. He couldn't hate Tash, not when she'd once been his everything. They'd only dated for a few months but in that time he'd fallen hard, so hard he'd contemplated asking her to accompany him to LA. He'd been torn over it, knowing how much her nursing degree meant to her but wanting her by his side as he embarked on a huge adventure that could result in his dreams coming true. In the end, she'd made the decision for him and it had taken a while to get over her.

'Is there a medical centre in Brockenridge or do you work at the hospital in Echuca?'

She took too long to answer. 'I'm not a nurse. I work at a local roadhouse as a waitress.'

Surprised, he glanced at her. Her chin was tilted, her jaw clenched. If being famous had been his dream, being a nurse had been hers. He'd assumed she would've completed her degree, even if she'd kept Isla. The thought of this smart, caring woman serving people meals rather than dispensing meds or offering comfort really irked.

'It's rude to stare,' she said, sounding cold and haughty.

'Why didn't you finish your degree?'

'Because I had a daughter to raise, no money and minimal support, Einstein.'

'But what about your parents—'

'Turns out religious zealots don't take too kindly to having their only child return home pregnant and unwed, so they disowned me and moved several hundred kilometres away to make sure my evil didn't taint them.'

'Fuck,' he said, unable to stop the pity sneaking under his guard. 'So you've done it tough.'

'I've done what I've had to do to raise my daughter, who I adore.' Her chin tilted higher. 'And I'd do it all again in a heartbeat because Isla's an amazing kid, and I'd like to think I've had something to do with that.'

The right thing to do would be to thank her for bringing up his kid right, but the way she'd said 'my daughter' rammed home yet again how she'd deprived him of so many years. He knew nothing about Isla and it made his chest ache in a way he never could've anticipated. He'd interacted with people from all walks of life over the years: eager fans; swooning teens; parents who'd eye him with suspicion like the mere fact he sang rock songs made him the devil.

But he'd never spent a lot of time with kids and he hoped he'd get a clue before he interacted with his daughter, because he wanted her to like him.

'She seems like a good kid, but you had no right to keep her from me all these years.'

Tash flinched at his bitterness and blinked several times.

'You better not cry—'

'Shut up,' she said, the quiver in her voice ensuring he did exactly that for the remainder of the ride back to Brockenridge.

CHAPTER

13

Jane had consumed her second vanilla slice and was feeling the effects, surreptitiously sliding open the top button of her jeans before reaching for her skinny latte. The juxtaposition never failed to amuse her, how she sought comfort in sugar-laden baked goods while forgoing sweetener and full cream milk in her coffee. Story of her life really—over-indulging in some areas, skimping in others. Seeking comfort in the wrong things—withholding her true self from the people who mattered.

'You look like you could use another vanilla slice.' Betty sat on the chair opposite. 'You can't sit here with a sour expression. You'll scare away the customers.'

'Sorry.' Jane forced a smile. 'By the way, your vanilla slices get better every day.'

'Tell me something I don't know.' Betty's wide grin warmed Jane's heart. The baker was one of the few people in town Jane could honestly call a friend. She'd poured her heart out to Betty on more than one occasion while drowning her sorrows in sugary treats and the older woman had never judged, just been supportive in a way Jane treasured. Pity her son hadn't inherited his mother's sunny personality.

'Actually, I'm glad you popped in today. I want to get your opinion on something.' Betty pointed at the wall behind them. 'We're expanding. I've already instigated proceedings to buy the empty shop next door and want to knock down this wall to open the place up.'

'That's great.'

'I'm really excited about the expansion.' Betty pressed her palms together in a begging motion. 'Would you mind taking a quick squizz and giving me suggestions about the refit? Your interior design skills are legendary around here.'

Heat crept into Jane's cheeks. She'd completed a six-month interior design course at a small college in Echuca when she left school because she'd always loved prettying up rooms. It had been her thing, something she'd wished she could share with her mum but their relationship had always been shit. She loved the feel of fabrics, the splashes of colour, the art of arranging furniture for good feng shui. Because Gladys had spent an inordinate amount of time making every room in their mansion perfect, Jane's idealistic teen self had envisaged opening a small business with her mum one day, doing something they both enjoyed.

That dream, along with several others, had been ripped apart courtesy of Gladys's callousness after her dad's death that had driven a wedge between them permanently. Since then, Jane had helped out a few folks in town. She'd had a hand in redesigning the CFA's meeting room, the main hall and the boutique in Main Street. They'd wanted to pay her, but she'd refused. It had been her way of giving something back to the town she'd always loved, a way to show them she wasn't the spoilt entitled brat many of them assumed.

Another thing townsfolk didn't understand: why she stayed around. Having a substantial trust fund meant she could've escaped to Melbourne and beyond when she turned eighteen, but Jane had never craved freedom like so many others in her year at school.

What Jane wanted was the one thing that remained elusive.

Security.

She wanted a partner, a strong, silent type who would provide her with more than money could buy. A stoic, dependable man like her dad, who she missed every single day. And if she couldn't have the man, at least staying in the town she'd grown up in gave her some semblance of the security she craved.

'Hey, where did you go?' Betty snapped her fingers in front of Jane's face. 'You totally checked out for a while.'

Jane grimaced. 'Rehashing memories I shouldn't.' She stood. 'Shall we check out this new space?'

'Great. The real estate agent left me a key so we can do some preliminary planning.' Betty led the way out of the bakery. 'The advantage of living in a small town, huh?'

Betty was one of the most recognised faces in Brockenridge so it didn't surprise Jane that the realtor trusted her with a spare key.

'Here we are,' Betty said. 'I've got a few ideas already, but I'm sure Mason will have more.'

Jane stiffened, not wanting to have anything to do with Mason Woodley after the way he'd stared down his snooty nose at her earlier. But before she could beg off helping Betty, the door to the empty shop opened and the man himself appeared.

'Glad you're already scoping out the shop, Mason.' Betty squeezed her son's arm as she bustled past him. 'I was just telling Jane you'd have some ideas for this place but I really want her opinion.'

'Why?' He stared at Jane like he'd stepped into a bucket of paint and she resisted the urge to flip him the finger.

'Don't be rude.' Betty's sharp rebuke had Jane biting back a grin as Mason glowered. 'Jane's got a good eye when it comes to interior design and I want her input.' A loud beep emitted from Betty's smart watch and she groaned. 'Damn, I forgot about the flourless orange cake. Why don't you two get started and I'll pop back soon? Besides, this place is going to be Mason's baby so it's only fitting he has more input than me.'

Jane's heart sank. The last thing she wanted to do was give advice to a rude guy who wouldn't value it.

But Betty touched her arm as she left, murmuring, 'Thanks for doing this, Jane, you're a gem,' leaving her no choice but to stick around.

As if reading her mind, Mason said, 'You don't have to stay, I've got this.'

She tilted her chin. 'So you're an interior designer like me?'

'I'm a patissier who's trained with the best in Paris,' he said, managing to sound condescending, patronising and cocky all at the same time, reminding her so much of his teen self she wanted to laugh. 'So I have a vision of what I want this place to look like.'

'And you don't think I have anything to offer? Your mum's a friend. She asked for my opinion so I'll give it.'

He stared at her for a few tension-fraught seconds before giving a brief nod. 'Okay.'

Surprised by his capitulation, she swept her arm wide. 'What do you envisage here?'

'I want to recreate a Parisian vibe, cosy yet chic. A touch of luxe. High-end pastries and coffees. Something different. I think townsfolk are interested in seeing expansion and development, so why not give them something new? Most haven't been to France, so why not bring France to them?'

Jane stared, surprised by the transformation in Mason as he talked about his vision for the café. The frown disappeared, as did the lines bracketing his mouth, and his brown eyes almost sparkled with enthusiasm. This is what he'd been like in high school with his friends, a group of geeks who somehow managed to fit in with everyone but her. He'd been fine with Louise and Bec, and they'd been popular girls too. It seemed like he'd reserve his special brand of snark just for her, and she'd hated it. She wanted to ask him why he did it, but that would lend credence to it and she didn't want to show him she'd once cared.

When their eyes locked and he raised an eyebrow in provocation, she cleared her throat. 'So you're thinking white wrought-iron tables and chairs, pastels everywhere, artisan posters on the walls, that kind of thing?'

'Exactly,' he said, the admiration in his gaze making her feel warm. 'Uh, look, I want to apologise for how I behaved earlier.' His cheeks reddened and his gaze slid away before refocussing on her. 'You're right. High school was a long time ago and I acted like an idiot.'

'It's okay,' she said, wondering what he'd think if he knew she'd done a lot of stupid things since.

'I'd like to get this place up and running sooner rather than later ...' He glanced around, pride straightening his impressively broad shoulders. Must be all that dough kneading. 'I know we were enemies in high school and the way I reacted when we bumped into each other earlier wouldn't have changed your impression of me, but would you be interested in acting as our interior design consultant?'

While Jane remained silent, struggling not to gape at his offer, he continued. 'I mean, it's obvious Mum trusts you, otherwise she wouldn't have asked for your opinion in the first place, and the way you just articulated my vision so clearly means we're on the same wavelength.'

He smiled, it wouldn't be the first time, and all the air whooshed out of her lungs at its potency. If he'd smiled more often at her in high school she wouldn't have been so bitchy and they might have stood a chance at becoming something resembling friends.

'So what do you think?'

Jane thought she was completely bonkers for agreeing to undertake anything alongside this guy, but she found herself nodding regardless.

CHAPTER

14

Tash shouldn't feel anything other than anger towards Kody. Anger that he'd chosen this town to heal his wounds, anger that he'd forced her hand when it came to Isla, anger that he had the potential to turn her tight-knit family upside down. But as she pulled into his driveway, killed the engine and glanced at the soundly sleeping rock star, she knew some of that anger should be directed at herself.

She'd done the wrong thing in keeping Isla a secret from him all these years and because of her, he'd missed out on so much. Like the time eighteen-month-old Isla had tumbled headfirst into a bucket of apple peels at the roadhouse, making Tash, Harry, Alisha and Clara laugh. And the time she'd aced her two-times tables in prep. And the first time she'd shot a goal in netball. And several months ago, when she'd rocked the year six play by breaking into a surprising rendition of an Aussie pop classic. Tash had experienced a particular twinge of guilt that night, realising Isla must get her strong voice from her father. But she'd learned to subdue those twangs over the years because no good could come of it.

She'd never believed in karma or fate or any of that crap, but Kody turning up here and taking away her choice to divulge the truth was the cosmos having a belly laugh at her expense.

Kody snuffled in his sleep, a cute snorting sound that had her biting her bottom lip. Watching him slumber brought back a host of memories she'd spent thirteen years trying to forget. She'd lain next to him so many nights doing this very thing, watching him, marvelling that an incredibly sexy guy liked *her*. He'd been larger than life back then and she'd had no doubt he'd make it big. When Kody Lansdowne strutted into a room, people—especially women—took notice. He'd never told her anything about his past. Then again, she hadn't revealed much about hers either. She'd liked the fact they never discussed their pasts so all that mattered was the present. They'd been so caught up in each other, so blissfully happy, she'd never anticipated her future being twisted into something unrecognisable. But Isla was a by-product of their self-absorbed love and Tash would never regret that, no matter how much her heart ached for all they'd lost and what could've been.

Kody blew out a small puff of air and it drew her attention to his lips, the bottom one fuller than the top, and for a scant second she allowed herself the luxury of remembering exactly how sensational they felt trailing over her body—

His eyes snapped open and she jolted, heat scorching her cheeks.

'That's creepy,' he mumbled, straightening. 'Quit staring at me.'

'You were drooling and I didn't want it getting on my window.'

A half-smile quirked his lips. 'Thanks for bringing me home.'

'No problem,' she said, opening her door and all but tumbling out in her haste to escape his too-knowing stare. She almost preferred him angry because the softer Kody, the guy with a killer sense of humour who used to love teasing her, had the potential to undermine her.

By the time she grabbed the crutches from the boot he had the passenger door open. Their fingers touched as she handed them over, a fleeting brush that lasted less than two seconds, but long enough for Tash to know she needed to focus on Isla and not memories of Kody's lips or hands or any other damn thing.

'I'll be going if you don't need anything else—'

'Actually, I do need a hand.' He steadied himself on the crutches, his expression carefully blank, but she could see how much it annoyed him to have to ask for help. Kody had always been stubborn and if having her pick him up weren't bad enough, asking her to stick around would be the pits. 'I really need a bath, seeing as you said I stink, but I can't get the plaster wet and it would help if you could rustle up some plastic bags, ties, that sort of thing.'

His mouth may be set in an unimpressed line but she glimpsed vulnerability in his eyes and that's what ultimately made her stay.

'Fine, but only because you reek,' she said. In reality, Kody didn't smell. She'd only said that earlier to buy some thinking time about how to ask Isla if she was ready for the big face-to-face with her father now she knew the truth.

She had the sense not to offer assistance as Kody hopped to the front door, unlocked it and struggled to push it open. It must've cost him big time to ask for help with the bath and she didn't want to rub his nose in it.

'Why don't you head on through to the bathroom and I'll rummage around for bags and ties in the kitchen?'

'Okay.' He paused. 'Thanks for doing this.'

'No worries,' she said, heading for the kitchen before she could blurt how much she liked this unguarded side of him. Even when they'd been dating she'd never seen him anything other than confident and in charge. She'd liked that alpha side of him because she'd been so ridiculously naïve and having him take control of their relationship made her feel treasured. It wasn't until she'd returned to Brockenridge, been abandoned by her folks and endured the birth of her baby alone had she realised how much she'd come to depend on Kody. Isla's birth had been the wake-up call she'd needed, because as a single mother with a newborn to care for, she'd realised the only person she could rely on was herself and now she had to be the strong one for the both of them.

She hoped Isla admired her independence and that she'd taught her daughter the value of self-reliance. She might have the support of her pseudo-family at The Watering Hole, but she'd done it alone for a long time. Which brought her full circle back to Kody and that rare glimpse of vulnerability. Gone was the cocky guy she'd dated, or the furious man she'd hidden the truth from all these years. Instead, for a few fraught moments, she'd seen a ... broken man. A man pushed to his limits. A man defeated.

Blinking back the sting of tears, she rummaged through the drawers beneath the island bench, discovering what she needed in the last. She snapped an extra large garbage bag from a roll and grabbed some ties, then dragged in a few breaths. She could do this. She could help get Kody sorted for his bath, then make a run for it.

However, as she followed the sound of running water to a room at the end of the hallway, she knew she couldn't abandon him. He'd need food and maybe a top-up of painkillers. She'd make sure he was okay before bolting because he was a man in need.

'Hey, I found what you were after ...' she trailed off as she reached the bathroom, completely gobsmacked by the sight that greeted her.

Kody. Naked.

Well, not completely naked. He still had his jocks on—she didn't know whether to be grateful or disappointed—but his chest and legs were on full display where he sat on the edge of the bathtub. He'd always been lean but sported more muscles than she remembered: clearly defined pecs and abs, impressive biceps, delineated quads ... wowza.

'You're staring at me like you used to, but you don't have the excuse of studying anatomy anymore.'

His amused drawl snapped her back to attention. She should say something, make light of the fact she'd been blatantly perving on his impressive body, but her brain wouldn't work in sync with her mouth and she couldn't think of one damn thing to say.

With a knowing grin that did strange things to her insides, he turned off the taps, giving her time to reassemble her wits. Hating how discombobulated he made her feel, and channelling her old nursing training in which bodies were nothing more than something that had to be healed, she barged into the bathroom and squatted in front of him.

'Here. Stick your leg in this,' she said, holding open the garbage bag.

'Damn, this plaster is heavy,' he said, grunting as he lifted the lower half of his leg and slid it into the bag.

'Depending how bad the break is, you could make do with a fibreglass cast, or even a walking boot,' she said, focussing on securing the top of the bag with the ties. 'Did you get an opinion from the orthopaedic surgeon?'

'No. The registrar on duty read the X-rays, said I had an ankle fracture, and plastered it.'

'You should get a second opinion,' she said, standing and backing away a few steps so she wasn't so close to all that tempting skin on offer. 'It'll be much easier for you to move around in a boot.'

'And miss out on having you help me like this?'

He was laughing at her. She could hear it in his voice and when she finally raised her eyes to meet his, what she saw took her breath away.

Awareness. Not anger. Not loathing. Recognition of what they'd once shared.

She swallowed and backed up some more. She couldn't do this, let down her guard, for him to revert to disdain tomorrow. Because she had little doubt the painkillers were responsible for blunting the edges of his pain—emotional and physical.

'I'll fix you something to eat while you take a bath,' she said, only stopping to close the door on his soft, taunting chuckles.

Kody hated baths. Growing up in foster homes, he'd barely have a shower because being naked in a houseful of sadists, even with a lock on a door, left him uneasy, so no way in hell would he ever take a bath. Besides, he could never see the attraction in sitting around in one's filth. But Tash had loved baths and he remembered her squeezing into the tiny tub in his studio apartment, covered in strawberry-scented bubbles, poring over textbooks. He wondered if that's what her stunned expression had been about as she stared at him earlier.

The painkillers may have taken the edge off but he wasn't a complete idiot. She'd been staring at him, not the tub, and by the high colour in her cheeks and the way her lips parted, she'd liked what she'd seen. It had been the damnedest thing, because in those moments when she'd been devouring him with her eyes, he'd forgotten that he'd been responsible for the deaths of seven innocent people, forgotten that she'd deprived him of almost thirteen years of his only child's life, and forgotten that she'd turned his life upside down with the revelation he had a daughter. He'd felt ... something.

He daren't label it because he knew acknowledging he still found Tash attractive on a visceral level could only end badly. He didn't want to like her. He couldn't let her in, not again, not after all this time. Not after what she'd done. But all the logic in the world couldn't stop him from closing his eyes as he towelled off and remembering exactly how he used to feel when she looked at him like that.

He struggled into clean clothes before grabbing the crutches, taking care not to slip. She'd been right; the sooner he got out of this cumbersome plaster the better. He'd seek a second medical opinion tomorrow. After spending time with his daughter, that is.

He had a daughter. A child of his own. A feisty, confident girl. His kid.

Equal parts trepidation and hope expanded in his chest until he could barely breathe. He'd spent his adult life on the road, living lavishly, partying hard. He'd enjoyed the spoils of his success and, until the accident, he'd been unapologetic for being self-centred. But those concertgoers dying had shattered him, and discovering Isla's existence had the potential to undo him completely.

What if he wasn't good enough?

What if he wasn't enough?

A light knock sounded at the door. 'You okay in there?'

'Be right out,' he barked, instantly regretting it. Tash had been nothing but helpful and the fact she'd stuck around to make him a meal after driving all the way to Echuca to pick him up spoke volumes. She'd always been a caring person and he should make an effort to shelve his resentment. Because no matter how mad she made him, she was the mother of his child—they had an irrevocable bond. Besides, he knew he'd need her help traversing the parenting minefield, considering he knew nothing about it.

He had so much to catch up on. What was Isla's favourite colour? Favourite band? Favourite dinner? Did she like sport? Did she have ambitions to leave town like her mum had? And the biggest of them all: Did she really want a father she'd never known intruding in her life?

Cursing under his breath, he opened the door to find Tash nibbling her bottom lip, concern etched in the lines between her brows.

'I thought you'd drowned,' she said, her flippancy not disguising the worry in her eyes.

'You couldn't be that lucky.' He hopped past her, gritting his teeth against the urge to apologise. Damn it, he should, because she'd been a real trouper. But it somehow stuck in his throat as he made it to the kitchen and saw what she'd done.

A place for one had been laid at the dining table in the corner, complete with a pitcher of water and a steaming bowl of pasta. The scene irritated him. She had no intention of staying. Then again, had he given her any indication she should? He'd been surly and disgruntled and dismissive since she'd picked him up, and he didn't blame her for wanting to escape as soon as possible. But the least he owed her was a meal after all she'd done for him today.

'Do you have to rush off to pick up Isla?'

'No, she's having dinner at her friend's place.'

'Then why don't you stay?'

He glimpsed the refusal in her eyes but before she could speak he rushed on: 'That looks like a lot of pasta for one person and I wouldn't mind a hand sorting out my meds when we're done.'

Okay, so that was sneaky. He knew perfectly well how many painkillers he had to take and how often, but appealing to her medical side was guaranteed to make her stay. And he really didn't want her to leave.

She gnawed on her bottom lip again, indecisive, before finally nodding. 'Okay.'

He took a seat and watched her move around his kitchen with ease. It struck him then that she might've eaten in this very kitchen, might've even known Yanni, and a ridiculous surge of jealousy twisted his gut at the thought.

'Have you been here before?'

'No. I don't have time to socialise, what with my shifts at the roadhouse and being a taxi-mum to Isla.' She grabbed a fork from the top drawer and added it to the plate in her hand. 'This place is rarely occupied so I figured it was a holiday home.'

'That would've been a spin out, if you'd met Yanni here one day.'

'Yeah,' she said. 'How long are you planning on hiding out here?'

'For as long as it takes.'

'Want to talk about it?' She sat opposite him and dished out a healthy serve of the pesto pasta. Another of her go-to meals when they'd practically lived with each other in Melbourne and she'd insist he load up on carbs before a gig.

'Talking won't help,' he muttered, picking up his fork and stabbing at the spaghetti, twirling it around and around. 'I have to get my shit together on my own.'

Roger, Blue, Daz and Yanni had all seen a counsellor afterwards, but he had an aversion to blurting his innermost fears to a stranger who would potentially judge him. If he couldn't face empathy from his best mates, no way in hell did he want to blab to anyone else about his fear that he'd never pick up a guitar again let alone sing.

'Uh-huh,' she mumbled, pushing her pasta around the plate. 'But just so you know, kids pick up on moods, so you might want to rethink bottling everything up inside if you're going to spend quality time with Isla.'

His fork slipped from his fingers and clattered against the plate. 'Give me a break, Tash. We don't know each other anymore and you want me to pour my heart and soul out to you? And when I don't want to, you bring up Isla as some kind of stick to beat me with?'

She widened her eyes before lowering her gaze. 'I'm sorry. I thought it might help.'

Feeling like a bastard for snapping at her, he reached across the table to touch her hand. 'I'm the one who should be apologising.'

To his surprise, she didn't snatch her hand away. Instead, she turned it over so their palms aligned. Her acceptance of his touch after the way he'd treated her made his throat swell. She'd always been like this, quick to forgive, caring, intuitive. He'd loved so much about her and she'd gutted him.

But he was here, now, and by some strange twist of fate they were neighbours for the foreseeable future. And he shared a child with her. He really needed to pull his head out of his arse and stop being so touchy around her.

'I can't talk about what happened at that concert yet.' He patted her hand before removing his. 'It's still too raw. But I'm getting a handle on it and if I need to talk, I know where you live.' He managed a half-hearted smile. 'As for Isla, I'll do my best not to inflict my moods on her. I want to get to know her, to spend time with her.' He dragged in a breath, determined to get the rest out. 'And I might need your help in learning how to be a good parent.'

Tears filled her eyes and stricken, he fumbled for the right words to say. But she didn't give him a chance to say anything. She stood, moved around the table and dropped a kiss on his forehead.

'You're a good guy, Kody, and something tells me you're going to be a great dad.'

CHAPTER

15

Tash had thirty minutes before she had to pick up Isla and she used half that time to wash her face and apply a bit of make-up. She'd always been an ugly crier and, after barely touching her dinner and ensuring Kody knew his meds schedule, she'd bolted for the sanctity of her car where she let the tears she'd been battling fall. She didn't know why she was crying. For Kody, stoic and hurting? For Isla, who would pine when Kody eventually left? For herself, who'd spent a few hours in his thorny company and realised she still had a major soft spot for him?

Whatever the reason, she had to pull herself together because she'd been right about one thing: Isla picked up on the slightest shift in her mood. They had enough to talk about tonight without her daughter zeroing in on the fact she was upset.

As she drove the short distance into town, Tash tried to rehearse what she'd say to Isla about spending time with Kody tomorrow. But every time she tried to formulate a plan, the image of an almost-naked Kody would intrude on her thoughts, making her heart pound and her palms grow clammy. It had been a long time since she'd been that turned on, so long in fact she couldn't remember the last time. She'd had sex a total of five times since Kody. By her calculations, that equated to a shag every two-point-six years. Little wonder she'd almost combusted when she'd caught sight of her ex's muscled, tanned body. How did a guy who spent most of his time indoors get a tan like that anyway? Then again, he probably spent his downtime in hotspots like Nice or Barbados or Cancun. As for the muscles, they were new, and her fingers had tingled with the urge to see if they felt as good as they looked.

Tash rarely allowed herself to dream but for those few seconds after his bath, when they'd sat across from each other at the dining table and he'd placed his hand over hers, she'd wished she did. The kind of dream that featured her and Isla as part of Kody's life, a dream where the three of them were a happy family. If spending only a short time with him had that kind of effect, she'd need to be more careful moving forwards. She'd help Isla get to know her father but would make herself scarce as soon as she felt Isla was comfortable.

Too much time with Kody wouldn't be good for her peace of mind.

When she reached Isla's friend Ellen's house, she pulled over and shook out her hands. Her cheeks felt hot. This wouldn't do, not at all. She had to be cool and calm when she talked to Isla, not hot and bothered over a man she had no future with other than as a coparent.

The front door opened and Isla stepped out. She watched her daughter give her friend a hug before trudging towards the car as though spending time with her mother was the last thing she wanted to do. Isla never looked this reluctant to see her so Tash knew her daughter still harboured resentment about the Kody fiasco.

The passenger door flung open and Tash pasted a welcoming smile on her face. 'Hey, did you have a good time?'

'Yeah.' Isla's response was cool, dismissive, as she slid onto the seat, placed her phone on the console and snapped her belt into place. 'Ellen's always cool to hang out with. We listened to music.'

Tash inadvertently stiffened but she needn't have worried as Isla continued, 'I didn't tell her about Kody, if that's what you're worried about. I'm not telling anyone until I get to know him, see if he's a good dad.'

Isla's honesty and insight impressed Tash. 'That sounds like a plan.'

'When can I see him?'

'That's entirely up to you, sweetheart.' Tash knew how eager Kody was to meet Isla for real but this whole process had to be guided by their daughter. She felt guilty enough for lying to them both for so long and didn't want to force anything.

'How about tomorrow?' Isla wriggled in her seat, excitement and trepidation warring across her expressive face. 'Could you ask him if that's okay? I mean, tomorrow is great but it's soon. Does he want to see me?'

'He can't wait to spend time with you,' Tash said, glad to hear some of Isla's usual verve in her voice. 'I actually spent the last few hours with Kody. He wanted to see you sooner but he took a tumble off a quad bike and broke his ankle—'

'What? Oh my god, is he okay?'

'He's in plaster but he's fine.'

'How come you spent time with him?' A hint of anger underlined Isla's question, like she resented not being the one to do it.

'Someone needed to pick him up from the hospital in Echuca and he gave my name.'

'Oh.'

Tash heard the reservation in that brief syllable. What was going through her daughter's mind? 'He wanted to see you tonight but he's pretty sore and is dosed up on painkillers, so he's resting. And

I wanted it to be your decision to see him, but I reckon he'll be thrilled about tomorrow.'

'I can't wait. What do you think I should wear? Should I straighten my hair? What do I call him—'

'Hey, slow down.' Tash reached out to squeeze Isla's hand, relieved when her daughter didn't avoid the contact. 'You don't have to get tizzied up to see your dad. Just be yourself.'

'But he's so famous and I'm … ordinary.'

Tears prickled Tash's eyes and she blinked several times before replying. 'You are amazing and don't you ever forget it.'

A glimmer of a smile twitched Isla's lips as she rolled her eyes. 'You have to say that, you're my mum.'

'And proud of it.' She leaned over the gearstick and hauled Isla into her arms, grateful when her daughter relaxed into the hug rather than pulling away. 'You're incredible, Isla, and I can't wait for your dad to discover that for himself.'

Isla snuggled into the hug and those damn tears Tash had been battling were back, making her eyes smart.

She dabbed at her eyes before easing away and flashing a bright smile. 'Did you eat much at Ellen's? Because I have a sudden hankering for some of Harry's fajitas.'

Isla's eyes lit up. 'Ellen's mum serves a lot of healthy stuff like carrot sticks, celery and tzatziki, so I'm still hungry.'

'Great, the roadhouse it is.' She wouldn't normally head back to her workplace on a Saturday night, especially when she had a rare evening off courtesy of the emergency with Kody, but with the turmoil of the day she had a sudden hankering to be surrounded by people who loved her.

Tash fired off a text to Kody saying Isla would love to spend some time with him tomorrow, and his speedy response confirmed what she already knew: he really wanted to get to know his daughter. It made her feel bad all over again for keeping them apart this long.

She had never been more relieved when Isla kept up a steady stream of conversation on the drive to the roadhouse, most of it centred around various events for the newest batch of year sevens at high school, leaving her to murmur the occasional agreement while pondering the upcoming meeting with Kody tomorrow.

Sunday mornings were her special time with Isla. They'd sleep in, whip up a batch of blueberry pancakes, then go for a long walk before curling up on the couch to watch reruns of their favourite sitcoms together. That would all change tomorrow and she couldn't help the flicker of fear that made her stomach twinge. She faced so many uncertainties with letting Kody into Isla's life. What would happen if they didn't bond as she hoped? What were his expectations beyond his stay in Brockenridge? Or the worst of them all—what if he filed for shared custody?

She'd built a stable life for her and Isla here, with a good support network and people who genuinely cared. How would sharing Isla with Kody even work? Having her daughter travel the world for six months of the year with a father who'd be busy with rehearsals and recordings and concerts seemed unfeasible and inappropriate for a girl her age. Not that Isla would see it that way. She could only imagine her impressionable daughter's reaction at the thought of being part of a rock star's entourage. Isla could end up seeing Kody as the fun parent who took her on worldwide adventures while she would be the opposite, stuck in Brockenridge, supervising home-work and playing taxi-mum.

A headache started pulsing at her temples as the welcoming neon sign of The Watering Hole came into view. She'd pop a few paracetamols and try to put on a brave face, because no way in hell would she dampen Isla's enthusiasm for a proper introduction with her father.

'I'm starving,' Isla announced theatrically as Tash pulled in behind the roadhouse. 'Really, really hungry.'

'If that's your way of hinting for one of Harry's famous lemon curd mini pavs after the fajitas, you might have twisted my arm.'

'You're the best, Mum,' Isla said, opening the car door and slamming it shut.

Tash hoped Isla would always feel that way. She was glad her daughter's earlier resentment had faded. She followed Isla at a sedate pace and entered the kitchen, not surprised to find her already popping treats into her mouth while Harry looked on fondly.

'You spoil her,' Tash said, snaffling one of the arancini balls for herself.

'They're yum, aren't they, Mum?'

Tash nodded and murmured her appreciation.

'We'd like to order your chicken fajitas please,' Isla said, shooting Harry her best buttering-up look before adding, 'and four of those delicious lemon curd pavs.'

'Two,' Tash said, trying to sound disapproving and failing when Harry beamed at Isla like she'd awarded him a Michelin star.

'Coming right up.' He waved them towards the dining area.

Saturday nights at the roadhouse were bustling and Tash didn't feel like interacting with patrons, though if they sat at the small table reserved for staff they should be able to eat unobserved. But as they slipped from the kitchen and headed to the table, Alisha spotted them and waved Tash over.

'Take a seat, honey, I'll be back in a sec,' Tash said to Isla.

Isla nodded and already had her phone in hand to scroll through whatever was the best social media site of the day, while Tash joined Alisha near the bar.

'How did you go today? Is Kody okay?' Alisha slid a half-glass of chardonnay towards her without asking.

Tash took a sip before answering. 'He's fine. A broken ankle is the worst of it.'

Alisha shot her a sly look. 'So, are you dusting off the old nurse's uniform? Because I'm sure he'd love a sponge bath or two.'

'You're sick,' Tash said, her cheeks heating.

'Well, well, will you look at that? Harry could fry eggs on your cheeks.'

'Drinking wine on an empty stomach always makes me hot.' As if to prove it, Tash sculled the rest. 'Now, can we change the subject please?'

'Why, when the fact you're blushing over a guy for the first time in years is so much fun?'

Tash and Alisha had confided in each other forever, but could she tell Alisha about that tense moment with Kody in the bathroom and expect objectivity when her loved-up friend was planning a wedding? Alisha had been the most practical person Tash knew until she'd hooked up with Harry and begun walking around with hearts in her eyes like a love-struck cartoon character. Not that she begrudged them happiness, but if Tash told her what had happened with Kody, Alisha would give her all sorts of crazy advice, like: 'Flirt with Kody and see what happens'.

So she settled for: 'I blush at the slightest glimpse of that hot farmer from Mildura who pops in here once a year, so it means nothing.'

'Keep telling yourself that, babe.' Alisha's grin stretched from ear to ear. 'What are you doing here on a night off?'

'Isla had a hankering for fajitas.'

'Like everything Harry cooks, they're the best.' Alisha's grin turned goofy. 'You know how much I hate exercise but if I don't start taking those local Zumba classes soon I won't fit into my wedding dress.'

'You have a dress?'

Alisha nodded, her eyes glittering. 'I found it when I was in New York a few months ago. It's simple but stunning and I love it.'

'I'm so happy for you.' Tash gave her an impulsive hug, thrilled for her friend, but unable to ignore the niggle of discontent that she may never find the same happiness. The dating pool in Brockenridge was a minuscule pond and until Isla was older and independent, Tash had no intention of leaving.

Alisha released her. 'Looks like your fajitas are ready. You better get over there before Isla demolishes the lot.'

'I'll just grab a water jug and two glasses—'

'You go eat, I'll get it.' Alisha hesitated, as if she wanted to say more, before blurting, 'I know how hard it must be for you, having Kody back in your life. And you're probably worrying about what kind of impact he'll have on Isla, but I'm here for you, sweetie, whenever you need to talk.'

'Thanks, Lish.' Tash touched her arm in gratitude and managed a wan smile. 'When I feel like chatting, you'll be the first to know how I saw him almost naked in the bathroom today.'

With a smirk at Alisha's shocked expression, Tash headed back to the table.

CHAPTER

16

Jane arrived ten minutes early for her meeting with Mason. She told herself it was to see his reaction when he walked into the road-house but in reality she couldn't bear second-guessing her choice of outfit for another minute. She'd already changed five times, swapping dresses and skirts and tops until she'd flung the lot on her bed and grabbed skinny black jeggings, a free-flowing paisley blouse and her comfortable crimson ankle boots. She never dithered over what to wear on a date these days. Then again, meeting Mason to discuss interior design plans for his new café was far from a date. This was business and nothing like going out with guys over the years, when she'd been searching for ... something. A connection. A bond. A way to feel cherished.

She'd never got that from her mother, though it hadn't mattered how non-maternal Gladys was because her dad lavished enough attention on her for the both of them. But he'd been dead for over a decade and there wasn't a single day that went by when she didn't mourn him and remember who drove him to it.

Nobody in town understood. They saw Jane with a beautiful mortgage-free house, exercising a lot because she didn't have to work, filling her spare time with a variety of hobbies from pottery to bowling, and labelled her a privileged brat at best, a rich bitch at worst. Throw in her healthy dating life and she'd been judged and found lacking for years. She pretended not to care that the one person who should be her greatest confidante was her greatest disappointment.

Regret expanded in her chest and she dragged in a few deep breaths. Her mother had inadvertently driven her to make many mistakes. Then again, she should own the crappy things she'd done. She'd been responsible for driving Ruby away and if she could take back every bitchy thing she'd done or said to her, she would. Although she'd apologised, it didn't seem enough. To Ruby's credit, she'd forgiven her when not many would.

Frequenting the roadhouse was Jane's way of saying sorry and as she glanced around the retro interior, she wondered if offering her design services would be another way to make up for the past. Then again, this place was often packed, so it probably didn't need changing. Patrons loved the old-style charm just the way it was.

She spied Tash eating with her daughter and something Ruby had said, about the single mother being judged yet turning her life around, resonated. They had another thing in common too: Tash's parents had abandoned their pregnant daughter and Gladys had virtually done the same to her but for different reasons known only to her mother. As Tash laughed at something her daughter said, hope expanded in Jane's chest. Tash had definitely come out the other side after shoddy treatment from her parents and she could too.

With one eye on the door, she ordered a sav blanc from Aldo, the young guy behind the bar who always tried to flirt with her, before finding a table towards the back of the room. She'd barely sat when Ruby appeared from her office near the bar, caught sight of her and waved. Jane acknowledged the greeting with a wide smile, hoping Ruby could read her sincerity behind it. She really wanted to put the past behind them. That had been another reason Jane had chosen The Watering Hole for her meeting with Mason tonight: she wanted to confront her shame from earlier that morning rather than running from it. If she wanted to make changes, she had to face up to her failings and coming here tonight was a start.

Ruby wound her way through tables and stopped next to her. 'Hey, how are you?'

'Better than I was this morning,' Jane said, gesturing to the seat opposite. 'I want to say thanks again for making me brekkie and being a good listener.'

Ruby sat. 'No worries. You look great.'

'Thanks. I'm meeting Mason Woodley here to discuss his ideas for revamping the bakery.'

'Mason's back? Last time I chatted with Betty she said he loved Paris and wouldn't return in a pink fit.'

'They're expanding, apparently. They're buying the empty shop next door and plan on knocking down walls and creating a French vibe for the whole place.'

'It'll be a shame to see the old bakery go.' Something akin to regret flickered in Ruby's eyes. 'It was one of my go-to places.' A wry smile twisted her mouth. 'Nothing a good sugar fix can't cure.'

Guilt peppered Jane anew at the angst she'd caused Ruby in high school, but she didn't want to dwell on the past, not when she intended to take charge of her future. 'I know the feeling. Betty's been a good friend to me over the years—always supportive.'

If Ruby wondered why a woman old enough to be Jane's mother was one of her closest friends, she didn't show it. Instead, she fixed her with a curious look. 'Have you seen Mason yet? As I recall, you two didn't get along too well.'

'He had very poor judgement back then.'

Ruby laughed. 'More like he was the only guy in school who didn't fall at your feet and you hated it.'

'That too.'

'I wonder if he's the same geek who used to help me with physics occasionally.'

'He's not,' Jane said, trying to sound nonchalant—and failing, if Ruby's widened eyes were any indication. 'We bumped into each other at the bakery earlier today and he's … changed.'

'How?'

How indeed. Jane could wax lyrical about his broad shoulders, strong arms, dark chocolate eyes, tousled blond curls and chiselled jaw. Instead, she settled for a less telling, 'He's more mature.'

'Aren't we all? Is he still good looking?'

'You thought he was good looking?'

Ruby nodded. 'Yeah. He was quiet but had that whole smouldering look down pat.'

Jane hadn't noticed. She'd been too hung up on the footy players and, in year twelve, she'd only had eyes for Connor. Mason had been an annoyance, a pest who wouldn't worship her like the rest. For that, she deliberately didn't pay him much attention. Perhaps if she had she would've seen more beyond her own shallow interests and made better choices.

She made a noncommittal sound of agreement anyway, considering she'd just spied Mason stroll into the roadhouse and didn't want to acknowledge that his teen smoulder had morphed into outright sexiness. They were about to have a business meeting. She had no right noticing how his navy T-shirt moulded to his chest or how his beige chinos elongated his muscular legs. He may have changed physically but his reaction to her during their first meeting after all these years still showed he didn't think much of her. Sure, he'd apologised, but that's only because he wanted her to design the interior for his precious new bakery.

'He's just arrived,' she said, feeling increasingly antsy as Mason spotted her and his handsome face broke into a smile.

With a knowing grin, Ruby stood. 'I'll leave you to it.'

Almost panicked at the thought of being left alone with the gorgeous guy strolling towards her, Jane said, 'Stay. He'll want to say hi.'

'Okay, just for a minute.'

They watched him cover the last few feet and Jane could've sworn she heard an echo of her sigh in Ruby's.

'Ruby?' To Jane's chagrin, Mason leaned down and brushed Ruby's cheek with a kiss, an easy greeting far removed from their fraught first encounter. 'Long time, no see.'

'Ain't that the truth.' Ruby laughed and Mason seemed unable to take his eyes off her.

For a moment Jane experienced a stab of jealousy so potent it took her breath away.

Stupid, because she and Mason were frenemies, acquaintances thrust together for business purposes, but the fact she noticed his attractiveness and didn't like the ease with which he interacted with Ruby compared to her meant she wanted to impress him, shake up his opinion of her.

Bad girls like her had no right showing interest in good guys like him.

'Mum told me about Clara.' He touched Ruby's arm. 'I'm sorry for your loss.'

'Thanks. I still miss her every day.' Ruby gestured around the room. 'She left me this place and keeping her legacy alive is my way of acknowledging her.'

'She would've been proud of you.'

Ruby smiled. 'Jane tells me you're lending a French flair to the bakery? Good for you.'

'It's a pet project.' Finally acknowledging Jane's presence, he turned that warm chocolate stare onto her. 'And Jane's being kind enough to lend me a hand.'

'Great. On that note, I'll leave you to it.' She pointed at the kitchen. 'If you're hungry, Harry's whipped up a mean butter chicken as the special and I highly recommend it.'

'Thanks,' Jane and Mason said in unison, followed by an awkward laugh.

As Ruby walked away, Jane held her breath, wondering if Mason would kiss her in greeting, and couldn't help a little twang of disappointment when he didn't, and took the seat Ruby had just vacated.

'That was a blast from the past,' he said, resting his tanned, muscular forearms on the table. Jane had a thing for guys' arms. You could judge a lot by the strength in a forearm and it looked like Mason spent a lot of time preparing dough. She stopped staring at his arms to find him studying her with blatant curiosity.

'Yeah, it's great Ruby's back in town,' she said. 'Most of our year left after school so it's nice to have some of you return.'

'So does that mean you're happy to see me? Because when we bumped into each other you had that same look in your eye you had back in high school.'

'What look's that?'

'The one where you'd like to push me into the Murray River and hold my head under.'

She laughed. 'You were a pain in the arse at school.'

'Why? Because I didn't grovel like the rest of your minions?'

Harsh, but true. 'You didn't put up with any crap.' She shrugged. 'I guess that's a good thing.'

'I hated that you and your friends never looked twice at me,' he said, with a sheepish wince.

'Are you fishing for compliments?'

He chuckled. 'What if I am?'

'You don't need to. You'll be turning enough heads in town.'

'Is that right?' He arched an eyebrow, lending a rakish quality to his face. 'Does that apply to you too?'

Jane wanted to tell him his flirting was wasted on her, that she didn't want to stuff this up for Betty considering how supportive she'd been over the years when not many had. But when Mason looked at her with that intense stare, like he wanted to see beneath her deliberately cultivated façade, she knew she liked this new flirtatious Mason way too much to be good for her.

'I've lived here my whole life, so trust me when I say the local spinsters will pounce on any new guy with a pulse.'

This time, he laughed out loud, the deep timbre rippling along her skin like a physical caress. 'I'm not sure if you insulted or complimented me.'

'Let's just say if you attend the blues night here in a fortnight, you won't be short of dance partners.'

'I'll make sure to stay away.' He winked and in that moment Jane wished she could go back in time and tell her younger self to wake the hell up. She'd tell young Jane to not want to be a people-pleaser so much, especially with her mum. She'd tell her to not worry about designer clothes or hanging out with the richest kids or being considered the prettiest and most popular. She'd tell her to change before it was too late, to acknowledge kids like Mason and Ruby at school, to embrace friendship rather than considering life as a giant competition.

But she couldn't turn back time so the best she could do was ensure she didn't screw up now.

'Shall we get down to business?' She sounded brusque and softened her abruptness with, 'I'm buzzing with ideas.'

'As much as I admire your enthusiasm, I'm starving, and that butter chicken Ruby mentioned sounds mighty fine. How about you? You hungry?'

Jane didn't want to eat because sharing dinner with Mason reeked of this being a date and her overactive imagination didn't need the encouragement, but her stomach betrayed her with a loud rumble.

She could tell he was biting back a smile as he stood. 'I'll order two,' he said, making his way to the bar to order, leaving her to study how fine his butt looked in those chinos.

Damn it, she always did this, check out a guy for his physical assets, deliberately not seeing beneath the exterior because it could never go anywhere. The guys she hooked up with were transient, despite her yearning for security.

The thing was, Mason would be transient too. If he'd lived in Paris for so long she couldn't see him hanging around once the bakery revamp was done—he'd hit the road again, live in Melbourne or Sydney or beyond. So technically a fling with the hot baker wouldn't be entirely out of the question. Once they got business out of the way, that is.

But there was something about Mason that appealed to her on a deeper level, beyond his obvious attractions. When he looked at her, she didn't feel an urge to take a shower to rinse off the sleaze like with other guys. Instead, he looked at her like he knew she had half a brain. Heady stuff for a girl whose intelligence had been undervalued her whole life.

When he returned, he placed a bottle of chardonnay and two glasses on the table. 'The kid at the bar said this wine goes well with the butter chicken so I took his recommendation.'

'Perfect.'

As he poured the wine she studied his fingers and suppressed a shiver of longing, imagining them caressing and stroking—

'Jane?'

She blinked and refocussed on the glass he held out to her. 'Thanks.' She flashed a smile, took the glass and clinked it against his. 'To bringing French flair to Brockenridge.'

'I'll drink to that.'

She gulped half her wine before setting the glass on the table, eager to concentrate on business. 'Can I ask you something?'

'Sure.'

'Why Brockenridge? I mean, I get that your mum's bakery has been a fixture here for decades, but you've worked in *Paris*. Why not open your own patisserie in a chic city like Sydney or Melbourne?'

Shadows clouded his eyes and she mentally cursed, hoping she hadn't hit a sore spot. 'Because I owe Mum. Every cent she saved from the bakery went towards me doing my apprenticeship in Melbourne and later funding my life in Paris. If it weren't for her, I wouldn't be where I am today, so this is my way of giving something back.'

'That's sweet,' Jane said, her admiration for him increasing. 'So does that mean you'll be staying around once it's up and running?'

'What's with the twenty questions?'

Nice deflection. As if someone like him would stick around in backwater Brockenridge when he'd lived in Paris.

'Just curious.' She shrugged. 'Betty's been a good friend to me over the years, almost like a second mum, and I want what's best for her.'

'What about your mum? You're not close?'

And just like that, Jane shut down. She couldn't talk about Gladys without wanting to blurt the whole sorry truth or thump something.

'Not so much,' she said, and changed the subject. 'When Betty initially mentioned the expansion she said something about knocking down the wall between the two shops. But I actually think it'd be nice to keep the current bakery and spruce it up with a retro theme, adding a few French touches, then having an archway flowing into the new space. What do you think?'

Mason bought her distraction, and they launched into a detailed discussion of his vision and what that entailed. They only stopped to eat, oohing and aahing over the butter chicken served with rice and naan bread, before resuming their shoptalk.

Jane couldn't wait to get their ideas down on paper. 'I'll start work on this tonight. It'll take me a day or two to input our preliminary ideas into the software I use, so maybe you can pop over Monday evening and take a look?'

'Great,' he said, glancing at his watch. 'I actually have to run.'

'Hot date?' The words popped out before Jane could censor them and she wanted to crawl under the table.

'No.' His mouth quirked into a roguish smile. 'Besides, I've just had that.'

Flustered, Jane searched for something witty to say and came up blank, but was saved when he took pity on her and stood. However, her relief was short-lived when he held out his hand. It would appear churlish to refuse so she placed her hand in his, liking the curl of his fingers over hers way too much.

'Why don't I cook us dinner when you come over?'

When he squeezed her hand, she hurried on: 'I mean, it makes sense. I'll be busy finessing our ideas for the next few days and you'll be running around sourcing contractors and the rest, so that only leaves us the evening to work. And it's only fair, after you paid for dinner tonight.'

'That sounds good,' he said, and she practically sagged in relief that she hadn't made a complete fool of herself. 'But only if I can bring dessert.'

He was dessert enough but she wisely kept that gem to herself and nodded.

'What's your number?' He took out his mobile and after she rattled off her number he pocketed it again. 'I'll text you later for your address.'

'No worries.'

Jane braced as he leaned down to brush an all too brief kiss on her cheek. 'See you then,' he said, before releasing her hand and striding away, too tall, too gorgeous, too much.

Jane didn't fall for guys, not anymore, but in that moment she came mighty close.

CHAPTER
17

Doing so many late gigs, Kody was used to sleepless nights. Often after a concert he'd be so wired he'd stay awake until morning then crash early the next night. However, having to spend time with his daughter after minimal sleep didn't seem the brightest idea. Not that he hadn't tried, but every time he closed his eyes, the last twenty-four hours would play like some goddamn movie, leaving him restless and on edge. His ankle had throbbed intermittently all night and the painkillers had done little. So he'd face his daughter tired and grumpy. Great.

A knock sounded at the door and trepidation strummed his spine. What if he screwed this up? He didn't care so much for himself—he'd never had a real family and had closed off his heart to one a long time ago—but what about Isla? She deserved better than some deadbeat dad who'd leave sooner rather than later.

The knock came again, louder and more insistent, and with a hearty sigh he hopped to the door and opened it.

Before he could say anything, Tash said, 'Sorry, I forgot it would take you longer to answer.'

He heard the words but for all he knew Tash could've been talking Mandarin because his gaze had zeroed in on Isla. His daughter.

She had his eyes. Big, with the slightest tilt upwards at the outer corners, though hazel whereas his were brown, but her smile was all Tash. Isla stared at him with a mix of hope and fear, and all he wanted to do was reassure her everything would be okay. But he had no right making promises like that, not when he remained clueless as to how this would pan out.

'Hi.' Isla pushed past Tash, who appeared rooted to the spot and wore the same deer-in-the-headlights look he was sure he did. 'How's your ankle?'

'Okay.' He flashed Tash a silent 'help' glance and that seemed to wake her up as she followed Isla in. 'Would you like something to drink?' Damn, he sounded stilted and formal, but he needn't have worried, as Isla took charge of the situation with an ease that surprised him.

'I'll make us iced chocolates,' she said, a tiny frown marring her brow. 'You do have cocoa, right?'

'Check in the pantry,' he said, in sudden need of a seat that had nothing to do with his ankle. With his daughter bustling around like she owned the place and Tash subtly wringing her hands, he felt decidedly wobbly.

Tash sat next to him and pulled her chair close. 'In case you hadn't noticed, she's a bit of a dynamo.'

'She's amazing,' he said softly, and meant it. He'd expected this first official meeting to be awkward and silent, but Isla had taken charge with aplomb.

'Will you be okay if I leave you?'

His panicked expression must've returned because she chuckled and laid a hand on his forearm. 'Isla's really keen to spend time with you alone and I think that's the only way for you two to really bond.'

'Yeah, okay,' he mumbled, so out of his depth something akin to terror gripped his chest. 'I hate to be a pain but do you think you could give me a lift back to the hospital tomorrow? I've got an orthopaedic outpatient appointment at ten.'

'Sure. I don't start work until two so that'll give us plenty of time.'

'Thanks, I appreciate it.'

Their gazes locked and held, and Kody experienced the same deja vu as he'd had last night in the bathroom. They may not have seen each other for thirteen years and it hadn't ended well but there was a hint of ... *something* still between them and whatever it was scared him almost as much as the prospect of getting to know his daughter.

'I'll pick you up tomorrow morning at nine,' she said. 'Isla, I'll see you later,' she called as Isla emerged from the huge walk-in pantry brandishing cocoa in one hand and a can of whipped cream in the other.

'Okay, Mum, bye.'

She didn't seem at all fazed when Tash let herself out, leaving them alone, and once again he was struck by her self-confidence. However, when she placed the supplies on the bench and turned to face him, he glimpsed a hint of nerves in her eyes.

'Where are the glasses?'

'Top cupboard, last on the right.'

'Thanks.'

She remained silent as she bustled around the kitchen, spoon-ing cocoa and sugar into two glasses, adding a dash of hot water to dissolve it, topping up with milk and stirring vigorously before adding whipped cream and an extra dusting of cocoa. He didn't particularly like chocolate but if she'd served him outback dust mixed with dam water he would've drunk it, that's how much he wanted to impress her.

'Here you go,' she said, placing a glass in front of him before sitting on the chair Tash had vacated. She didn't seem fazed it was a tad too close. Instead, she held up her glass and waited for him to pick his up before clinking it. 'I'm making a toast to us, because I think it's really cool I have a dad.'

She stared at him wide-eyed and with so much hope that his throat tightened. 'And I think it's even cooler I have a daughter,' he said, clinking his glass to hers.

She seemed satisfied by his lame response and drank half her chocolate milk before placing the glass on the table, regarding him through slightly narrowed eyes because he hadn't touched his. To make her happy, he drank the whole thing, and was surprised when she giggled—an innocent sound that warmed his heart.

'What's so funny?'

She pointed at his top lip. 'You have a milk moustache.'

'Oh.' He swiped at it with the back of his hand, glad he'd made her laugh without intending to.

An awkward silence descended as he racked his brains for something to say.

Isla saved the day by asking, 'Do you want to know stuff about me?'

'I want to know everything,' he said, meaning it.

It irked that Tash had deprived him of so much but he'd come to a decision in the wee small hours of the morning; regretting the past thirteen years and blaming Tash wouldn't be conducive to moving forwards with Isla. He had to stop lamenting all he'd lost and focus on gaining so much: a relationship with his daughter.

'Okay.' She tapped her bottom lip, thinking for a moment. 'Well, I'm really good at history and English at school. Though it's been a big jump from primary school to secondary school and year seven is pretty hard overall. And I hate maths because I'm no good at it, though the teacher is cool and wants to help.' She snapped her fingers. 'I'm ace at netball and it's my favourite sport. Though I like drama too ...' She trailed off, hesitant. 'I really like being on stage. Maybe I get that from you?'

'Maybe,' he said, that damn tightness in his throat not easing up. 'Can you sing?'

Her mouth quirked into a cheeky grin. 'Only in the shower.'

'I do my best work there too.'

'No, you don't. I looked you up on the internet. You're awesome.' A faint blush stained her cheeks. 'I can't believe my dad is a rock star.'

Hearing her say 'my dad' almost undid him completely and he inhaled slowly, determined not to cry.

When she didn't seem inclined to say anything else, he filled the silence. 'I've always loved singing.'

'Since you were a kid?'

He shook his head. 'I started when I was older than you, about sixteen, when I met some guys at high school and we formed our own band.' Yanni, Blue, Roger and Daz had stood by him all these years and he hated that he'd let them down so badly since the concert accident. They were the family he'd never had and he owed them, big time. He tried not to think about what would happen if he never picked up a guitar again, if he never wrote another song, if he never stepped behind a mic. He'd justified his funk by telling himself they'd understand, that they only wanted the best for him. Besides, Rock Hard Place could always find another lead singer. But the thought of his best mates playing on without him left him oddly breathless.

'That must've been cool. Did you play mainly at school?'

'Uh, we gigged everywhere.' Mainly because they'd lied about their ages and played pubs while they'd been underage.

'Were your parents okay with that?' A light dawned in her eyes. 'Do I have grandparents?'

He hated having to dash her hopes. 'Sorry, kiddo, I was raised in the foster system.'

'Oh.' Her shoulders sagged. 'I don't have a gran or pop from Mum's side either. Mum said they're really religious and didn't approve of her having me without a husband, so they moved away and don't want anything to do with us.'

At least Tash had been honest about something, though he immediately felt disloyal, since he'd decided to move forwards and not dwell on recriminations.

'It's their loss, because you're an amazing kid.'

Isla practically glowed. 'Thanks, but you've only just met me, so how do you know?'

'Because I've always had the best instincts for reading people and I'm so proud of how you've reacted to all this. And I'll be honest with you, kiddo, I'm out of my depth here. I have no idea if I've got what it takes to be a good dad but I'm going to try my best.'

Isla hurled herself at him and wrapped her arms around him, snuggling her head into the crook of his shoulder. He stiffened for a second before sliding his arms around her and hugging tight. The strawberry fragrance of her hair tickled his nose but he inhaled deeply, savouring it and the warmth of his daughter in his arms.

Kody had no idea how long they hugged for. It felt like an eternity—yet like nothing at all—when they pulled back and stared at each other with surprise. Had the hug been too much too soon? He hoped he hadn't made her uncomfortable. But as she continued to stare at him with approval, her smile shy, he knew it was okay. Emotions he never knew existed ricocheted through his chest, pinging off his ribs like tiny bullets.

He needed a distraction before he blubbered so said the first thing that popped into his head. 'Do you have a favourite band?'

'Not yours, if that's what you're asking.'

He laughed at her blunt honesty. 'Too old, huh?'

'Yeah, sorry. Rock Hard Place isn't my thing.'

'No offence taken.'

Isla screwed her eyes up slightly as she thought; it was the cutest thing he'd ever seen and reminded him so much of Tash when she'd been poring over her nursing textbooks that his throat tightened.

'I'm more into indie music, though most of the kids at school like pop.'

He liked that she knew her mind and didn't follow the crowd, even though he couldn't stand the eclectic sounds of some of the indies doing the rounds now. Give him a thumping bass and strong lead vocals belting out a rock classic any day.

'Speaking of school, there's this lame Swap Day where parents take the place of kids in their classes for a day, while we get to do jobs around the school.' She screwed up her nose. 'It's not for a while yet but I know a lot of dads are doing it and I thought maybe you'd like to?'

So much for keeping his identity under wraps while he was in town. Spending a day in a classroom was bad enough as a kid; doing it now would be pure torture. Besides, he didn't even know how long he'd be in town for, but as Isla continued to stare at him with expectation he knew he had to give her an answer.

'If I'm around, absolutely. But I'll be honest, kid, I'm not sure what my schedule's going to be like over the next few weeks, so let's see how we go.'

Damn it, he'd disappointed her. He could see it in her eyes, which now stared at him with disillusionment. But he didn't believe in bullshitting anyone and the sooner his daughter learned that the better.

'It's no biggie. Besides, if enough parents don't want to take part it'll get cancelled anyway.' She shrugged, playing it down, but he could see the Swap Day meant a lot to her. For the first time since he'd come to this godforsaken town, he wondered if he should do more than let time heal his wounds—he could seek professional help. He couldn't be around a bunch of kids if his head wasn't in the game, because kids saw right through crap. And if Swap Day was important to Isla, he wouldn't want to screw it up for her, especially if it was the first time he got to meet her friends.

'If I do it, will I need to do any science? I'm terrible at all those push–pull forces and periodic table elements.'

'Me too,' she said, her expression clearing and her smile returning. 'It's cool to have things in common.'

He managed a lame 'Yeah.'

He wanted to spend endless hours learning what else about his daughter made them alike and he would have that time. Because now he knew of her existence, no way would he walk away from Isla the way Tash had walked away from him.

CHAPTER
18

Tash had been home ten minutes and had alternated between peeking out the window in the direction of Kody's place and making half-hearted attempts at cleaning out the kitchen cupboards. She'd got as far as stacking old plastic cups Isla used as a kid to donate when Alisha knocked on the door. Her friend knew Isla would be spending time with Kody this morning so rather than let Tash wallow, she'd texted to say Harry had made extra vegetarian lasagne and she'd bring it over.

'Special delivery,' Alisha said, brandishing a picnic basket, when Tash opened the door. 'With love from the greatest chef this side of the border.'

'Thanks.' Tash took the basket out of Alisha's hands and placed it on the bench before sliding a still-warm lasagna out of it. 'Harry cooked this fresh?'

'Uh-huh.'

'So let me get this straight. Rather than you two *sleeping in* on a Sunday morning, your only day off for the week, he's cooking lasagna?'

Shame-faced, Alisha smiled. 'I might have coerced him into it with the promise of *sleeping in* when I get back, because I wanted to come see you.'

'I knew it.' Tash snapped her fingers. 'Though you never need an excuse to visit.'

'So how are you?'

'Okay.' Tash's shrug may have been nonchalant but she felt anything but. 'At least, I'm trying to be.'

'She'll be okay. Isla is a good kid.'

'I know, but what if—' She stopped, unable to articulate her deepest fear: *What if he breaks Isla's heart too?*

'What if?' Alisha prompted.

Tash shook her head. 'Nothing. I'm being silly. Kody has every right to get to know his daughter and Isla's over the moon at having a dad.'

'So why the face?'

'I'm feeling all over the place, guilty and sad and more than a tad angry at myself,' Tash said, flicking on the kettle. 'Seeing them together this morning, even for a few minutes, rammed home that maybe I did the wrong thing all those years ago.'

'You did what you thought was right at the time.' Alisha pulled out the nearest chair. 'Sit. I'll make tea.'

'Okay. Choc-chip cookies are in the container above the stove.' Tash watched Alisha prepare the tea, hoping a good cuppa would ease the churning in her stomach. Doubtful, as nothing would help until Isla waltzed through the back door and told her everything that had transpired.

Alisha placed a plate of biscuits between them and their cups of tea on the table.

Tash reached for hers. 'Thanks, Lish, I needed this.'

'My pleasure.'

They sipped their tea in silence but Alisha kept casting her curious glances.

Tash put her cup down. 'Whatever's on your mind, Lish, spit it out.'

With a sigh, Alisha said, 'Have you considered seeing a lawyer?'

Tash shook her head. 'Not yet, but I know I'll need to book an appointment shortly.'

'Kody's mega rich and I think you need to protect yourself.'

'He'd never sue for full custody. He'd want what's best for Isla.'

'You lied to this guy and kept Isla a secret for thirteen years. It's natural he'd resent you, and who knows where that could lead?'

Tash didn't like Alisha's pitying stare. 'He's not like that,' she said, wishing the fear gripping her heart would ease. 'There's no room in his life for a child. Which is why I didn't tell him in the first place.'

Alisha shrugged. 'People change. Hell, look at Harry and me. If you'd told me a year ago I'd be marrying a confirmed hermit, I would've laughed.'

'You and Harry were always destined to be together. It just took you longer to figure out than most.'

'Better late than never.'

Tash laughed. 'Speaking of Harry, how are the wedding plans coming along?'

'Surprisingly well. Keeping it low key is helping.'

'I'm so happy for you both.' Tash reached across the table and squeezed Alisha's hand. 'Let me know if you need anything.'

'Now that you mention it, how would you feel about throwing a bridal shower? I'm not into all that palaver, especially at my age, but Ruby keeps hounding me about it and she's sweet to offer to host, but you and I've been friends for years—'

'Consider it done.' For the first time all morning, excitement replaced worry. 'Do you have anything special in mind?'

Alisha rolled her eyes. 'If I had my way we'd be sneaking off to the registry office in Melbourne to avoid all this, but you guys plus Mum and Dad are my family and I want to celebrate with you all, so whatever you want to do is fine by me.'

'One stripper or two?' Tash deadpanned, biting back a laugh at Alisha's startled expression.

'Mum would have a heart attack.'

'I think Brenda might surprise you. Doesn't she devour those racy novels by the carload?'

'Good point.' Alisha chuckled. 'But this is a bridal shower, not a bachelorette party, so no strippers.'

'But there'll be cake and party favours so there will be penises.'

They laughed and it felt good for Tash to take her mind off what was happening next door.

As if reading her mind, Alisha said, 'How long do you reckon she'll be?'

'I don't know.'

Tash wanted Isla to bond with her dad but a small part of her hoped Isla would rush home to tell her all about it sooner rather than later. She'd raised Isla to be confident and articulate, and to that end her daughter rarely had a quiet moment. But while Kody may have thawed since their fraught reunion yesterday, Tash couldn't help but wonder if some of his residual resentment would spill over and affect their daughter.

Not that Isla would stand for it. She never had any trouble voicing her opinions. What Tash wouldn't give to be a fly on the proverbial wall over there right now.

'What's he like? Has fame changed the guy you dated?'

Tash thought for a moment, before slowly shaking her head. 'Not really. He's angry at me for withholding the truth, but overall he seems the same.'

Alisha's eyebrows rose. 'Really?' She flashed a sheepish grin. 'Because I did an online search this morning and he's one of the most famous rock stars this country's ever produced. Gorgeous too.'

Tash had to agree he hadn't changed much in that regard. Apart from the lines creasing his forehead and the corners of his eyes, Kody looked better than she remembered.

'Speaking of which, are you going to tell me about that cryptic comment regarding seeing him naked in the bathroom?'

Tash mimicked zipping her lips and Alisha reached across the table to slug her on the arm.

'Come on, now that I'm virtually an old married woman I need to live vicariously through your dating exploits.'

'But we're not dating,' Tash pointed out, a sliver of something akin to excitement shimmering through her at the thought.

'Tell me. Pretty please.'

'I should've never mentioned it.'

'But you did, so spill.' Alisha waggled a finger in her face and Tash swatted it away.

'Not much to tell. When we got back from the hospital yesterday I offered to make him something to eat because he was struggling on the crutches. He needed a bath and when I went into the bathroom to cover the plaster with plastic bags, he was sitting there in his jocks.'

Alisha gaped a little, before a mischievous twinkle lit her big, brown eyes. 'Let me get this straight. He knew you were coming back into the bathroom but he stripped down regardless?'

'He had to. How else would I get the plastic bags over the plaster, and how would he take his pants off after it?'

'You could've left the bags for him. Then he could've undressed after you'd left and put the bags on himself. Instead, he strips off, which means he wanted you to see him in all his bare-chested glory. Pity he left the jocks on.' She wiggled her eyebrows sugges-tively. 'So how was it?'

Heat burned Tash's cheeks. 'The bod?'

'Yeah.'

'Phenomenal.' A soft sigh escaped Tash's lips. 'I mean, I know it's been a while since my last shag but wow ...' She fanned her face and Alisha wolf-whistled.

'That good, huh?'

'Better,' Tash admitted, wishing she could erase the image from her mind.

Alisha's smirk faded. 'I'm going to ask a tough question, honey, and I want you to be honest with me.'

'Yeah?'

'Do you want something to happen between the two of you?'

Tash wanted to refuse but she'd always been upfront, most of all with herself.

Predictably, Alisha took her hesitancy as a yes.

'Just be careful, okay? I don't want to see you hurt.' Alisha reached across and squeezed her hand. 'Rock stars aren't keepers, and after he leaves, you'll always be in contact because of Isla—that could pose a problem for you.'

'I'm not the pining type,' Tash said, hating how her heart leapt at the thought of any kind of relationship with Kody beyond a parental one.

'You're also not the wham-bam type, so any kind of fling with your old flame, who happens to be the father of your child, may end badly if you can't separate your emotions from the physical stuff.'

'Thanks for the advice, mama bear.' Tash tempered her words with a smile. 'But my priority right now is helping Isla adjust to the idea of having a father in her life. Anything else doesn't enter the equation.'

Alisha's lips compressed in a stubborn line and she knew her friend wouldn't let this go. 'What if Hot Stuff wants to start something up with you? What then?'

'I'm the last woman he'd want to get involved with,' she scoffed. 'He hates my guts and is masking it with a veneer of polite indifference.' Discounting those few sizzling looks they'd shared when neither of them had been prepared ...

'There's a fine line between hatred and love, that's all I'm saying. And I know you. I know why you walked away from him in Melbourne all those years ago: you put his needs above your own. You loved him but you didn't want to tie him down, not when his star was taking off. So you deliberately pushed him away, shelved your dreams, and came back here to do the right thing for your child.' Alisha made a soft tut-tutting sound. 'By some twist of fate your past is back, and if I'm correct, neither of you are prepared for it.'

Alisha's words only served to exacerbate Tash's regrets. What if she'd told Kody the truth back then? What if she'd given him a choice? What if she hadn't walked away?

But she had and if she'd learned one thing over the years it was to never look back.

'I'll be okay, honest.' Tash stood and leaned down to hug Alisha. 'And I appreciate your concern, but let's focus on sourcing a phallic-shaped cake, okay?'

Alisha laughed as Tash intended but it didn't detract from the concern in her eyes.

Tash knew the feeling. All she'd done since discovering Kody had lobbed next door was worry, and she had a feeling it wouldn't let up anytime soon.

CHAPTER
19

Kody couldn't believe how well the morning had gone with Isla and was surprised to discover it was almost lunchtime when his stomach growled. 'Are you hungry?'

She stared at him with those all-seeing eyes and nodded. 'I can make toasted cheese sandwiches if you like.'

'That'd be great. Want some help?'

'Nah, I'm good.'

He hated feeling this helpless while he watched his daughter move around the kitchen with ease. The sooner he got out of this damn plaster and became more mobile, the better. He hadn't taken any painkillers today and his ankle throbbed.

'Are you okay?' She eyed him with concern, knife poised above the butter, and he inwardly cursed his inability to hide his feelings. The last thing he wanted was her worrying about him.

'Yeah, my ankle's a bit sore, but it'll be fine.'

'Okay.' She resumed buttering the bread.

He loved how kids took everything at face value. At least, his kid did. Compared with some of the tweens and teens he'd encountered over the years, Isla still seemed innocent. All the band members were smart enough not to mess around with jailbait but that didn't stop young girls trying anything to get it on with a rock star. They'd received questionable fanmail including undies and bras, and fended off inappropriate groping during organised photo ops. One industrious young lady had wangled her way backstage during a concert in New York and had been lolling around naked in his dressing room after he came offstage. That had shocked him, and he'd seen enough of the world to deem himself unshockable.

Maybe it was growing up in a quiet country town, but Isla appeared genuine and guileless and comfortable in her own skin, not entirely typical for a girl on the brink of her teen years.

'Quit staring,' she said, glancing up from the bread.

'Sorry. I still can't believe you're here.'

Appeased by his honest response, she smiled. 'Do you like tomato sauce in your cheese toasties?'

'Love it,' he said, remembering how Tash used to slather it on, a culinary peculiarity he'd come to enjoy. 'Your mum used to make them like that.'

She stilled and he hoped he hadn't done the wrong thing in bringing up a snippet of the past. They'd avoided talking about Tash for the last few hours, not by any deliberate act on his part, but because he wanted to know everything there was to know about his daughter.

'I'm still a little peed off at Mum for not telling me the truth about you all these years,' she said, sounding young and lost.

He heard the hurt in her voice and he didn't want her feeling that way, not because of something he'd stupidly said. He got to his feet and grabbed his crutches to hop over to her.

'It's okay to be annoyed but your mum made a decision she thought was best at the time.' He stopped two feet away. 'Like you, I'm pretty upset about it, but your mum's a good person and while I don't agree with what she did, I can understand why she did it.'

'I guess.' Isla shrugged, but he saw the doubt in her eyes. 'It still sucks I haven't had a dad around all these years when I did actually have one.'

Man, she was breaking his heart. But he had to be careful not to disparage Tash no matter how much he agreed with Isla. He wouldn't do that, despite his gut churning with anger and regret and bitterness that he'd missed out on so much with this amazing kid.

'The thing is, kiddo, even if we'd known about each other, I probably wouldn't have been around all that much.'

Her gaze narrowed, coolly appraising. 'I get it. You're famous. But you wouldn't want to spend time with me now if you didn't care, so I reckon you would've made time for me.'

His heart twanged again, like she'd aimed an arrow and shot a bullseye. He couldn't believe this no-nonsense, blunt, sensible child was his. He'd been the opposite at her age, getting by on cunning and lies in the various foster homes he'd been dumped in. He'd been wily and street-smart but non-confrontational, nothing like his daughter. It made him admire her all the more.

'I do care, more than you know.' He laid a hand on her shoulder, glad when she didn't shrug it off. 'But it doesn't change the fact my life's on the road. And it's hectic. When I'm not on a concert tour I'm in the studio, writing and recording. I move around—a lot— and that means I may not see you as much as I'd like.'

'I could come with you.'

Hell. Of course she'd say that. What kid wouldn't find a transient lifestyle appealing? He needed to backpedal, fast. Tash would kill him otherwise.

'We could work something out with your mum so you could spend some time visiting me, but your life is here.' He squeezed her shoulder. 'You're a smart kid. I bet you've got dreams and to follow those you need to finish high school.'

Her expression turned sullen. 'Heaps of kids do school by correspondence, so I could do that too. Or I could have tutors wherever you are.'

Man, this situation had gone from bad to worse, because she was actually making sense and for an instant he could see the scenario she painted. If it were up to him, Isla could spend months travelling, maybe longer, because no amount of classroom teaching came close to life experience.

But Tash would never go for it.

Unless she had no choice …

He could hire the top custody lawyer in the country and put forward a strong case: she'd deprived him of parental rights; he deserved time to get to know his daughter; and he could provide Isla with the best of everything. But that would fracture their relationship as parents forever, and drag Isla through a potentially nasty custody battle that would result in bad press.

And that's the last thing he wanted. Like many musicians, his manager had crafted a carefully fanciful history that appealed to the masses and hid the seedier side of his upbringing. He'd thought the reality of his childhood would give him cred but his manager hadn't agreed so he'd gone with the fabricated story circulated when he'd first made it big in LA.

But it was more than that holding him back from pursuing a custody battle. He may not know what fatherhood entailed but he knew he wanted to be the kind of dad Isla admired and wanted to emulate, not some dropkick who lobbed into her life and tore it apart.

No, he couldn't do it, but maybe if he presented his case to spend more time with Isla rationally to Tash, she'd understand.

Yeah, and he'd be playing a gig on top of the pyramids soon.

'What are you thinking?' Isla cocked her head to one side, studying him.

'That I'd like nothing better than to spend as much time with you as possible, so how about we make that happen for as long as I'm staying here, then think about the rest later.'

'Mum will never go for it,' Isla muttered, shaking her head. 'Because she's a waitress she wants more for me and that means getting good grades and trying really hard at school.'

'Your mum's a smart woman and I happen to agree with her.'

Isla rolled her eyes. 'Now you're ganging up on me.'

'Get used to it, kiddo, parents often agree to disagree with their kids.' He ruffled her hair, eliciting a rueful grin. 'Now, those sandwiches aren't going to make themselves and I'm starving.'

'Slave driver,' she said, elbowing him away, and he marvelled anew at the ease between them.

'I'll hop back to the table and issue orders from there,' he said.

She laughed. 'It's amazing you've been all around the world.' She placed the buttered bread in the sandwich maker and it sizzled. 'What's your favourite city?'

'Vancouver.'

'Why?'

'The people are laid back, like Aussies.' And because the beautiful Canadian city reminded him of Melbourne, which he'd never returned to after Tash broke his heart.

Isla didn't speak while she carefully placed the cheese slices on top of the bread, before squirting tomato sauce in zig-zags over the lot. 'Where do you live?'

He'd been hoping to avoid this question because saying he didn't have a house made him sound like a flake. In fact, he'd have to rectify that situation, because if it came to a custody battle, he'd need to show he could provide a stable home environment for Isla. But how could he explain to his daughter that he'd never had a real home and preferred moving around because that's what he'd done his entire life?

So he settled for partial honesty. 'I move around a lot so it doesn't make sense for me to pay a housekeeper and bills for a place I'm never at.'

'Fair enough.' She topped the cheese with slices of bread and closed the sandwich maker, before looking up. Kody didn't like the cunning glint in her eyes. 'So, basically, if we're going to spend time together I'd have to move around with you too, yeah?'

He should've known she'd capitulated too easily a few minutes earlier. She wasn't going to let this go. Life on the road would appeal to a teen as much as no curfews.

'Probably, but like I said, this is something we'll need to discuss with your mum.'

She pinned him with a stare that implied she wouldn't back down and he'd never been more relieved than when the light on the sandwich maker turned green.

'Our sangers are ready,' he said, pointing at the maker. 'There's something about the smell of melted cheese that makes me want to stuff the whole sandwich in my gob in one go.'

'Yeah, me too,' she said, switching off the sandwich maker before placing the toasties onto plates. 'I hope you've got one of these in your tour bus because we're going to be eating a lot of toasted cheese sandwiches when I hang out with you.'

He laughed because he couldn't help it, her tenacity a thing of wonder. 'I like your determination, kid.'

'It's one of my best qualities,' she said, matter of factly, as she handed him a plate.

They lapsed into comfortable silence as they ate but Kody wasn't looking forward to discussing Isla moving around with him if he returned to his previous lifestyle with Tash, not one bit.

CHAPTER
20

Jane decided to keep the menu simple for her dinner with Mason: bruschetta with oven-roasted tomatoes and fresh basil for entrée, roast lamb for main and one of Betty's famous custard tarts for dessert. He said he'd bring dessert but she had an ulterior motive: baking wasn't her forté and she hoped that by serving one of his mum's creations he might appreciate her more. Her work, that is. He'd been nothing but pleasant since they'd got over their initial hiccup yet her insecurities ran deep and she couldn't help but feel inferior somehow, just like he'd made her feel in high school.

Mason had a worldliness she had no hope of emulating and a small part of her wondered if he'd taken pity on the hick country chick when he'd asked for her help in decorating the bakery's expansion. In reality, Betty probably had more to do with him wanting her onboard than any confidence in her skills, but whatever the rationale, she wanted to ensure she did a great job. The fact she harboured a surprising crush on the handsome baker had nothing to do with it.

She picked up a nice lean shoulder of lamb and popped it into her trolley. But as she headed in the direction of the vegetable section at the supermarket, her trolley collided with another, pushed by her mother. Jane's spine stiffened as it always did when she ran into Gladys, an old habit from countless lectures on the importance of posture in attracting a man.

Gladys looked immaculate as usual, wearing a designer suit in the deepest plum, with an ivory silk blouse underneath and patent pumps that would have cost enough to feed a farmer's family for a month.

'Hello, Jane.' Her mum's well-modulated tone was so familiar yet held a world of secrets. Jane had only heard Gladys lose her cool once, her screeches as she divulged the truth about their family a far cry from this practised façade. Her mother had never given a damn about her but almost eleven years had passed since she'd heard the proof that Gladys was nothing more than a soulless drone.

'Hey, Mum. How are you?'

'Fine.'

Gladys glanced into her trolley, saw the lamb, and wrinkled her nose in disapproval. Jane knew what her mother would say before she opened her filler-injected lips.

'Meat is fattening. You know that.'

Jane resisted the urge to ram her trolley over her mother's feet. 'Everything in moderation.'

The nose crinkles increased. 'I can't understand why you refused to convert to veganism when I did.'

'I was sixteen and liked hanging out with my friends, who all liked burgers.'

'What's your excuse now?' Gladys arched a perfectly etched brow. 'From what I hear, you don't have many friends.'

Jane gritted her teeth and composed a more suitable response than *eff off*.

'It seems this needs reiterating, even though I've told you several times before.' Jane lowered her voice when a septuagenarian carrying an overflowing basket of fennel and carrots cast a curious glance their way. 'I gave up caring what you think of my dietary habits, my choice of wardrobe and anything else involving my life a long time ago.'

Hating how the old familiar hurt spread outward through her chest, she disengaged her trolley and backed up a few steps. But she knew Gladys would get a last barb in. She always did.

'Apparently you're sniffing around the Woodley boy.' Gladys's upper lip curled in a sneer. 'He'll tire of you like all the rest once he realises you're only good for one thing.'

It never failed to amaze Jane that her own mother believed the rumours circulating about her. Not once had her mother asked about any of her relationships. Instead, she chose to believe the worst. Jane had been tempted to come clean to Gladys once, to tell her why she deliberately played into people's wrong opinions of her, that it was a stupid warped way to punish her mother. But what would be the point? Gladys only heard what she wanted to hear and if she'd had a little faith in her daughter they never would've reached this stage of their relationship, where insults were the norm and they rarely saw each other.

Tired of all the bullshit, all the years of passive-aggressive put-downs, all the disappointments at the hands of this callous woman, Jane said, 'At least my life's real, Mum. Pity you can't say the same.'

As a comeback, it didn't have the vitriol Gladys deserved, but it made Jane feel good. As did her childish angling of her trolley so it ran over her mother's pinkie toe as she sailed past.

However, the encounter had soured her mood and as she selected veggies for the roast lamb, she contemplated sending Mason a text and calling off dinner. She hated the way Gladys looked down her snooty nose, like Jane was a mound of cow dung she'd stepped in.

She'd had many years to deal with what she'd learned that fateful day twelve months after she'd finished school, years to try to rationalise the lengths to which her mother had gone. But going by the churning in her gut as she paid for her groceries, it still bothered her more than was good for her. The townsfolk assumed their falling out had been because of Jane's behaviour, when nothing could be further from the truth.

Gladys had virtually killed Jane's dad and Jane would never forgive her for it.

After paying for her groceries, Jane pushed her trolley through the sliding glass doors and almost ran over Louise.

'Sorry,' she mumbled, flashing a tentative smile.

Louise didn't return it but she glanced at the recycled bags filled to the brim in Jane's trolley. 'Roast lamb for one? If I didn't have to feed my hungry horde I'd be over in a jiffy.'

'Actually, Mason Woodley's coming over,' she said, regretting it when Louise's eyebrows shot up.

'To discuss business,' Jane said, but she could tell Louise didn't buy her clarification. 'He's expanding the bakery with his mum and they want my input for the interior.'

'Sounds like a fun job. Better than cleaning motel rooms for a living.'

Jane didn't know what to say to that. If she said the wrong thing, Louise would think she was being patronising or condescending. She had to change the subject, fast.

'Did you end up ringing that lawyer?'

'Yeah. He was really helpful. But I need to get my ducks in a row before I kick Ed out.'

'It's a start,' Jane said. 'Don't forget to text me when you want to have a coffee, okay?'

'I haven't forgotten.'

They lapsed into an awkward silence Jane felt compelled to fill. 'Better get home to start dinner,' she said, pointing at the groceries in her trolley.

'Yeah, and I better buy half the store to feed my ravenous lot.'

Jane smiled and moved forwards an inch before Louise laid a hand on her trolley to stop her.

'I appreciate you being honest with me about what happened with Ed. It helped me take the next step in getting rid of him. So … thanks.'

'My pleasure,' Jane said, grateful that they were taking small steps to renewing their friendship after so long.

'It got me thinking about how I misjudged you. How a lot of others have too. So I want you to know I feel really bad about believing what your mum said, because I know you two were estranged at the time and she's got some weird vendetta against you.'

Jane froze, her fingers gripping the trolley so tight her knuckles stretched the skin taut. 'What did she say?'

Louise flushed, her gaze darting sideways before she spoke. 'I bumped into her after we had that argument over Ed in the main street. She heard it all and wanted to "apologise" for your behaviour.' Louise made inverted comma signs with her fingers. 'She said you were jealous of my marriage and had always got whatever you wanted so if you'd set your sights on Ed, I'd better watch out.'

A wave of nausea swamped Jane at how low her mother would stoop to discredit her. They'd never been close but to say that stuff about her … it defied belief.

Louise grimaced. 'I'm really sorry, because we'd been friends for a long time and I shouldn't have believed her. I think I already knew my marriage was in trouble at that point and it was easier to blame you than look in the mirror.'

'It's okay, Lou.' She reached out and squeezed her friend's hand. 'And thanks for telling me.'

'Do you think you and your mum will ever reconcile?'

'Not bloody likely. Heads up, the she-devil's in the supermarket, so beware.'

Louise laughed, the unique snorting chuckle bringing back a host of memories: the two of them, along with Bec, sleeping over and watching rom-coms, or borrowing daring romance novels from the library and snickering over the naughty bits. She'd pretended not to miss their friendship over the years, but that was the old, stupid Jane.

Here went nothing. 'Hey, when you text me for coffee, maybe we could invite Bec too? I really miss you girls.'

'Me too,' Louise said, so softly Jane had to lean forwards to hear it. 'It'll be good for the three of us to get together again.'

'It's a date,' Jane said, smiling. 'I better go. Take care.'

'You too.'

And despite the nasty confrontation with Gladys and hearing about the awful lies she'd told Louise years earlier, Jane felt lighter than she had in ages.

Eternally grateful her father had set up a trust fund that enabled her to come home to her own cosy slice of Brockenridge every day, Jane pulled up outside her cottage and lugged her groceries inside. She loved every inch of this place, from the tiny ornamental

Japanese garden leading to her front door, to the hot tub on the ele-vated back deck that had views of the Murray River if she squinted hard enough.

She'd bought the cottage at a steal and had redecorated the inte-rior with polished ash floorboards, pale mint green walls and ivory plantation shutters. The white, grey and green theme continued throughout, with artfully arranged pictures on the walls, throw rugs over the suede sofas, and lush indoor plants. She liked to think of it as her private oasis, a shelter from the prying eyes of folks who only saw what they wanted to see. She could've left judgemental Brockenridge far behind a long time ago but with every run-in with Gladys, no matter how unwelcome, she was reminded of the reason she stayed: to ensure her mother, who thought she had an entire town fooled, never forgot Jane knew the truth.

Popping an antacid to stop the churning in her gut, Jane set about prepping for dinner. Slow-cooking the lamb would ensure it fell off the bone, just the way she liked it. She hoped Mason appre-ciated a good roast.

Once she had everything in the crockpot she took out her port-folio and lost herself in planning for the new bakery, only looking up an hour later when the tempting aromas of garlic and rosemary filled the air. She had plenty of time to shower and get ready, but found herself reaching for her laptop to do an online search.

Feeling a little stalkerish, she typed 'Mason Woodley, patissier' into the search engine. Her research had everything to do with being professional, and nothing at all to do with womanly curiosity about a guy she'd once hated who she might now fancy a tad. She kept telling herself that as she clicked on the first few hits, which showcased his work in an upscale patisserie in Paris, praised him for catering an exclusive event for a prominent European royal fam-ily and labelled him one of the most eligible foodie bachelors in

France. Ooh la la. The rest of the links were more of the same and proved what she already knew.

Mason Woodley was way out of her league.

She attributed her battered self-esteem to Gladys but she'd always been insecure. She'd hidden it well, behind designer clothes and immaculate make-up and snarky putdowns. It's why she'd gone after Ruby in high school: Ruby had been smart and when she stared at Jane, she felt like Ruby saw beneath her poised surface to the quaking girl inside. Mason had seen right through her too, and she pushed him away to ensure he never got too close.

Her residual lack of confidence was silly, really, because she shouldn't need the validation these days. She was thirty, owned a house, secretly donated money to a lot of charities and liked where she lived. She didn't harbour grandiose plans or pie-in-the-sky dreams. She was … content.

So why did she care what her mother said or getting Gladys to own up to what she'd done?

Annoyed at herself for dwelling, she closed her portfolio and laptop and headed for the bathroom. But not even a long, hot shower, a leisurely application of subtle make-up and dressing in her favourite casual sundress could shake off her funk.

The sooner Mason got here and they got down to business, the better.

She set the table, uncorked the wine and had just finished making the gravy when the doorbell rang. After a quick wipe down of the surface she'd been working on, she rinsed her hands and dried them on a tea towel. The bell rang again. Ridiculously flustered, she slipped her bare feet into low-heeled wedges and headed for the door. After dragging in a deep breath that did little to steady her nerves, she opened it.

And her mouth went dry. Mason stood on her stoop, freshly showered, by the look of his wet hair curling around the collar of his sky-blue polo shirt, faded jeans elongating his legs, and golden stubble accentuating his strong jaw. But it was what she spied in his hands that really had her salivating: the signature silver-embossed Betty's Bakery paper wrapped around a rectangular box.

'Dessert as promised,' Mason said, holding the box out to her.

'I love everything your mum bakes, so thank you.' She took the box and stepped back to let him in. 'I'm there practically every day, as you can probably tell from my waistline.'

'Your curves are beautiful,' he murmured, his fingers brushing the dip of her hip for a second, sending heat streaking through her body. 'But Mum didn't bake any of that, I did.'

The way to her heart was definitely through her stomach and as she kicked the door shut, their gazes locked, sending another sizzle through her.

'Come in,' she said, her voice a tad squeaky as she led the way to the kitchen. 'I can't wait to see what you've made.'

'A little of everything. Mini chocolate croissants, apple strudel and plaited pastry dusted in cinnamon sugar.'

'Sounds divine,' she said, placing the box on the counter and tearing a corner of the paper to take a peek, blown away by the detail of his pastries. 'Wow, they look amazing.'

'What can I say? I'm good with my hands.' As if to emphasise the point, he waved them at her while wriggling his eyebrows suggestively, making her laugh and dissolving some of the tension she'd been harbouring all afternoon.

'That's good to know, considering you'll be holding up a lot of swatches and colour samples in the new bakery.'

His smile faded. 'Speaking of the new bakery, there may be a problem.'

Her heart sank. She knew this whole thing had been too good to be true. He didn't want her designing the interior; had probably found some upmarket firm in Melbourne to do the job.

'Apparently the owner is reneging on the deal.'

'Why?'

'Mum's been negotiating through the real estate agency in town and assumed the sale would go through easily, seeing as the place has been empty for years. But the owner's stalling before signing on the dotted line.'

A long-buried memory surfaced of her parents arguing about the deed to one of the shops. Jane knew her father had owned a few shops in Brockenridge, along with extensive land holdings and factories in Melbourne. When her dad had been alive, he'd sold most of the Brockenridge holdings and she assumed her mum had sold the rest. Was Gladys the owner of the empty store beside the bakery? Could she be deliberately stalling on the sale because she thought Mason and Jane were involved? Gladys rarely did anything by chance, and now that throwaway comment about Jane sniffing around Mason made sense if Gladys wanted to sabotage this deal to make her look bad by association. Could her mother really be that petty?

She couldn't say anything, not until she'd confronted her mother. Presenting a professional front to Mason did not include airing her family laundry, so she settled for, 'That's weird.'

'It's bloody annoying, because if we can't secure that extra space I can't see the patisserie idea taking off.'

And he'd leave town ASAP. It shouldn't bother her. They were nothing more than work colleagues who'd flirted a little. But it did, because for the first time in a long time, she felt something beyond attraction and, once the redecorating was done, she wouldn't have minded exploring exactly what that was.

Maybe it was for the best. She craved a stable, secure relationship and a guy likely to return to France once his project was complete wasn't a good bet.

Tell that to her stupid, impressionable heart.

'When will you know?'

'Mum was meeting with the agent as I left so I'm expecting a call when she's done.'

'Shouldn't you have been at that meeting?'

'And miss out on having a beautiful woman cook for me? Not bloody likely.'

She laughed. 'So what's the real reason?'

His lopsided grin made her heart leap. 'I'm an outsider so it wouldn't bode well for me to blow into town and try to negotiate. Mum's much better equipped to handle the locals than I am.'

Jane didn't point out that he seemed pretty darn adept at handling the locals himself—at least, one of them, and he was looking straight at her.

'Something smells amazing,' he said, inhaling deeply. 'I hope that's roast lamb.'

'Sure is. You sit and I'll dish up.'

'Anything I can do to help?'

'Pour the wine, please.'

As she plated up the lamb and veggies, Jane couldn't ignore a niggle of worry. How far would Gladys go to prove how little she thought of her?

'Here you go,' she said, injecting gaiety into her voice as she placed a plate in front of Mason. 'There's gravy and mint jelly coming up.'

'Thanks.'

When she placed the condiments on the table between them and sat, he raised his wine glass. 'To our design collaboration.'

She clinked her glass against his and forced a smile, but that nasty thought about her mother's vindictiveness had wheedled its way into her brain and she couldn't dislodge it. She'd confronted Gladys once, a few months after her dad had died, hoping her mother would reveal the truth. Rather than being honest her mother had completely withdrawn, before steadily undermining her every chance she got. That's when she'd stopped caring what her mum thought of her. She'd retreated behind a brittle shell of faux cheerfulness and overt brashness, not giving two craps about anybody, yet hoping her mother would make some kind of overture to broach the gap between them. Instead, the gap had widened and Jane lamented the loss of both parents.

As Mason forked the first mouthful of lamb past his lips, she toyed with hers and watched for his reaction. She'd always loved cooking but didn't do it often enough, as whipping up meals for one wasn't much fun. But this meal was one of her favourites and by the blissful expression on Mason's face, he liked it too.

'This is incredible,' he said. 'The lamb is tender and juicy, and the veggies cooked to perfection.'

'Thanks,' she said, forcing a forkful past her lips when she noticed him staring at her untouched food.

'A woman of many talents.' He raised his wine glass again and she smiled, hoping it didn't come across as a grimace.

Mason demolished his food in record time and she'd managed to clear a quarter of her plate when his mobile rang. He slid it out of his pocket and glanced at the screen. 'It's Mum. Do you mind if I take this?'

'Go ahead,' she said, clenching her hands under the table, bracing for the worst as he answered.

His responses were short, and when his eyes narrowed and locked on hers, she knew. Damn it, she knew.

'Don't worry, Mum, we'll get this sorted. Bye.' He hung up, stood and slipped his mobile into the back pocket of his jeans. 'I have to go.'

'But we haven't discussed the plans—'

'Why are you doing this?' He stalked a few steps away before spinning back to glare at her. 'Is this some kind of sick joke? Making me pay for being a dickhead in the past? Demanding top dollar on a shop that has been empty for years?'

Hating that he thought so little of her, she shook her head. 'I have nothing to do with this. I'm assuming my mother owns that shop and—'

'You're assuming?' He snorted. 'Like you wouldn't know.'

'We're not close, haven't been for years.'

'This is bullshit. I thought you'd changed but it looks like you're still the game player you were in high school.'

Of all the things he could've said, that hurt the most, because she *had* changed. She'd spent a decade trying to distance herself from the airs and graces she'd assumed in school to emulate her mother. If he'd known her better back then he would've given her the benefit of the doubt now rather than accusing her of playing games.

'It's a shame you're so quick to jump to conclusions when you don't know the first thing about me,' she said, her tone icy. She pointed at the hallway, hating that her hand shook. 'Please leave.'

'Like I need to be asked twice,' he sneered, his disdain almost palpable. 'If you have the slightest shred of decency, you'll make sure the sale of that shop goes through.'

Jane had as much chance of influencing her mother as she did of doing the interior design for the new bakery: absolutely none.

'You're wrong about me,' she said softly to his retreating back.

He paused in the doorway to glance over his shoulder, his expression thunderous. 'Am I?'

CHAPTER
21

Tash had a feeling Isla was still mad at her, because her daughter hadn't said much about the time spent with Kody yesterday and it hurt that the one person she loved most in this world wasn't communicating.

This morning, with Kody in her passenger seat as she drove him to Echuca for his follow-up appointment at the hospital, Tash played an audio book to stop herself interrogating him. By the time they reached Echuca, she had no idea whether they'd listened to a thriller, a rom-com or a memoir, thanks to the effort it took not to ask him about Isla's visit.

When she pulled over near the hospital's front entrance, he said, 'You've been quiet.'

'Didn't sleep well.' The truth, considering Tash had ruminated over Isla's reluctance to talk to her all night. 'Needed to focus on the road.'

'Uh-huh.'

She huffed out a breath. 'Isla didn't say much when she got back from your place yesterday and I didn't want to grill her, so I left her alone. But I really want to know how it went and I'm conscious of giving her space to assimilate all this and—'

'Hey, slow down, take a breath.' He reached across and laid a hand on her arm, a perfectly innocuous gesture that made her pulse race more than it should. 'We can discuss this after my appointment, if you like?'

Damn him for sounding so calm and rational.

She nodded. 'That would be good.'

'Okay, see you soon.'

She got out of the car, grabbed the crutches from the boot, and handed them to him, waiting until he'd hopped inside before driving away. She parked in a spot with a clear view of the front door and waited. A bad move, because it gave her too much time to think about her daughter. Isla had practically bounced through the back door around four yesterday, after spending an inordinately long time with Kody. Tash had expected their first time together to last two hours max and the fact Isla had hung around for most of the day made Tash feel guiltier for keeping Kody a secret all these years.

Tash had asked how it went, Isla had answered with a generic 'good'. She'd offered to answer any questions Isla may have but her daughter had responded in the negative. They'd had an early dinner and while they'd made small talk Tash could sense a gap between them, as if Isla had withdrawn from her.

It had hurt like the devil.

It was natural Isla would blame her for keeping Kody from her all these years. But could one of her greatest fears—that Isla would prefer Kody as a parent—be in danger of coming true? After all, what kid wouldn't find a rock star parent more appealing? Kody led a glamorous life and Isla had never been out of Victoria. Tash could count the number of times they'd been to Melbourne on one hand. Kody could give Isla anything she wanted and while her daughter had never been greedy or demanding, Tash wouldn't blame her for wanting more than she could give her.

She didn't think Kody would buy Isla's affection; he seemed too genuine in his desire to get to know his daughter on a deeper level to do that. But if Isla's behaviour towards Tash after only one day with her father was any indication, the more time they spent together, the more Tash was in danger of losing Isla. That was another fear: that Kody would want to take her away. He had the resources and Tash didn't. It meant she had to be proactive and make informed decisions rather than worrying about custody issues. She needed to seek a legal opinion—the sooner, the better—because the thought of not having Isla around made her chest ache.

It also meant she had to establish some kind of rapport with Kody beyond frigid politeness, because she didn't want the situation to come to a custody battle. She'd robbed Kody of so many years with Isla. What if he wanted to make them up by gaining full custody?

Exhausted by her sleepless night and the tension of dwelling on what happened between Isla and Kody, Tash rested her forearms and head on the steering wheel. In keeping the truth from her daughter all these years, had she ultimately lost her to Kody?

She wanted to know what had happened yesterday. Had they connected beyond the superficial? Had they felt a real bond? Had they laughed like Tash and Isla did over crazy cat videos and reality TV and celebrity makeovers? And the kicker of them all: did Kody feel one-tenth of the love that she did for their bright, bubbly, gorgeous girl?

Her mobile buzzed and she lifted her head from the steering wheel to reach for it. Looking at the screen, she sighed.

Ready to go.

She glanced up and saw Kody waving from the hospital entrance. Great. How long had he been standing there, watching her with her head slumped like some sad sack?

She'd like nothing better than to flip him the finger and leave him standing there and for a fleeting second she contemplated gunning the engine and screeching out of the car park. But that wouldn't be conducive to fostering the cordial relationship she needed to ensure he wouldn't fight her for custody, so she started the engine and drove back to the entrance.

He'd lost the crutches and the plaster and was sporting a black walking boot instead, just as she'd suggested. Much better for mobility and bathing, as she remembered from her days doing rounds on the orthopaedic outpatient wards.

A tiny pang of regret flickered through her but she clamped down on it like she always did when she saw the latest medical breakthrough on the news or passed the doc's surgery en route to The Watering Hole. Nursing had been her dream since she'd received her first toy first aid kit as a six-year-old. Her devout parents had fostered her dream, believing nursing to be a highly respectable profession. She didn't know what disappointed them more when she returned home to Brockenridge: the fact she'd been pregnant or the fact she'd walked away from her degree before finishing.

Tash never regretted her choice to have Isla but not completing her nursing degree made her wish she'd made wiser decisions during her uni days, like avoiding sexy rockers and focussing on her studies. But then she wouldn't have Isla and she couldn't imagine her life without her darling daughter.

Pulling up outside the hospital entrance, she fixed a smile on her face. She couldn't let Kody see how maudlin she felt.

But as Kody got in the car, he took one look at her and said, 'What's wrong?'

'Nothing.'

'Still lying to me, huh?' He shook his head, and Tash bristled. He had no right to be disappointed. They weren't close anymore, so what did he expect, for her to unburden herself to a virtual stranger?

'Quit hassling me.' She pulled away from the entrance and headed for the highway. The faster they got back to Brockenridge, the sooner she could ditch him and his prying eyes.

But he scuttled that plan when he said, 'Do we have time to stop for a coffee in town?'

She wanted to lie, to tell him she had to get to work. But they had plenty of time to get back before her shift started, though the last thing she felt like doing was sitting across from him and making small talk. Then again, this would be the perfect opportunity to ask him about Isla's visit, and easier than trying to get a read on him while driving.

'Sure.' She drove into the heart of town. 'Have you been here before?'

'No, I didn't travel much as a kid and I haven't been back to Australia since I headed to LA.'

He spoke without rancour but she read so much in his calm response. Of course he hadn't travelled as a kid. He'd told her he'd been raised in various foster homes growing up, but he'd never elaborated even when prompted. As for not coming back to Australia after hitting the big time, she had no idea if that meant he'd grown out of his homeland or he didn't want reminders of a past he'd rather forget.

'I love this town,' she said, parking outside a café that channelled the fifties. She adored the duck egg–blue painted weatherboards and red-trimmed windows, and the daffodil-yellow door that welcomed patrons. Bright and cheery, exactly what she needed at the moment. 'Isla used to come here for excursions in primary school and I'd always find an excuse to tag along as a helper.'

He glanced at her in surprise, probably because she sounded wistful and not snappy for once, but before he could question her, she said, 'Come on, they serve the best Devonshire teas here.'

As they walked up the brick path, he said, 'Aren't you going to mention my new footwear?'

'Considering I advised you to get it, not particularly.'

'Smugness doesn't become you.'

She chuckled. 'Bet you were glad to ditch those crutches.'

'Yes and no.'

They paused at the doorway and when he looked at her, the twinkle in his eyes surprised her.

'Yes, because I can move around better,' he said. 'And no, because I won't need your help in the bath.'

His comment flustered her. 'I didn't help you in the bath,' she managed.

'Yeah, you did.' He grinned and tapped his temple. 'Last night, when I was sitting in that tepid pool of my own filth, I closed my eyes and imagined you helping me just fine.'

Her body prickled with an awareness she daren't acknowledge. 'You're an idiot,' she muttered, ignoring his taunting chuckles as she strode into the café. What the hell had happened in that hospital to change him from reserved and wary to charming and flirtatious? Had they removed his reservations along with the plaster?

'You looked like you could use some cheering up, that's why I teased you about the bath,' he said, as they chose a table. 'It won't happen again.' He held up his hands like he had nothing to hide and she couldn't help but smile at his guileless grin.

'I hate that you can still read me so easily,' she said, hoping a waitress would appear pronto to prevent her from blurting too much.

'We were pretty close.'

'But that was a long time ago. And to be honest, I don't want to rehash the past.'

He fixed her with a steely glare, all hint of teasing gone. 'Then what do you want?'

'I want to know how yesterday went,' she said. 'Isla stayed with you for a really long time and I've been torturing myself about it ever since.'

'Why? Don't you want us to get to know each other?'

'Of course I do,' she snapped, immediately regretting it when he recoiled. 'It's just that we've always been super close and having her not confide in me—practically avoid me—last night has left me feeling … unsettled.'

'How the hell do you think I feel? I've been unsettled since the moment you told me I had a kid.' He drummed his fingers against the table, the habit so familiar the back of her eyes burned with unshed tears. He'd done that all the time when they were dating. At first she'd thought it signalled impatience but later she'd learned he did it because he often had new melodies floating through his head that made his fingers itch to jot them down. 'And to be honest, I'm not sure how I feel being interrogated about what went down with Isla and me.'

'I'm not interrogating you,' she lied.

Thankfully, the waitress arrived, giving her time to gather her thoughts. They ordered cappuccinos, deciding they didn't have an appetite for scones. When the waitress left, Kody fixed Tash with that penetrating stare again.

'Look, Isla and I had a good time. We talked. Actually, she talked, mostly.' His goofy grin told her exactly how smitten he was. 'She's a great kid.'

She wanted to say 'Tell me something I don't know' but didn't want to sound like a smart arse so she waited for him to continue.

'I have to admit, yesterday went a lot better than I hoped. Once we got past the initial awkwardness, we just chatted. About school stuff and music and life on the road.' His gaze shifted away, furtive. 'She brought up that she'd like to spend more time with me.'

A chill swept over her. 'What does that mean?'

'Life on the road is appealing for any kid—'

'No.'

How she managed to stop at one short sharp syllable and not scream a resounding 'hell freaking no' Tash had no idea.

He shook his head. 'Contrary to what you think of me, I'm not a complete idiot. I told her it wasn't a good idea, that her place is in Brockenridge.'

Kody's reassurance should've made her feel relieved. It didn't, because if Isla had broached the subject of leaving, she wouldn't let it go easily.

'Thanks for that,' she said, hating how quivery her voice sounded. 'A solid education is important.'

'But I also think it would be good for her to spend some time with me when I tour, to get some life experience beyond a small country town.'

The chill that had swept over Tash a few moments ago turned into a full-on freeze that made her want to clench her jaw to stop her teeth from chattering. She wanted to yell her disapproval, to thump the table—or him—to express her horror at the idea of her sweet, innocent daughter touring with a rock band.

But while she had some say in this, she didn't have the right to forbid it, not when there was two of them now parenting Isla.

'Anyway, you asked what we discussed, so that's what was mentioned. And we're not making any rash decisions but I thought you should know.' He gave a self-deprecating laugh that sounded harsh. 'Besides, I doubt I'll tour ever again, so you may not have to worry about it.'

'What does that mean?'

'I still can't pick up a guitar or sing.' He shrugged, like the loss of one of the most sought-after voices in the world meant little. 'I don't have the inclination any longer and, surprisingly, I don't give a shit.'

'But that's wrong,' she said, glimpsing the pain shifting in his eyes. 'You have an incredible gift and creating music is everything to you.'

'It used to be,' he said, pushing a crumb around the table with a fingertip. 'I just … can't.'

'You weren't responsible for those people dying—'

'How the hell would you know?' He sat back and folded his arms, his jaw rigid. 'Every time I even glance at a guitar I break into a cold sweat and feel like vomiting …' He raised his eyes to her and his anguish made her want to hold him tight. 'I still have nightmares, hearing their screams, and it's like I'm back there, smelling the smoke, not being able to see or do anything …'

Her heart broke a little. She had no idea he'd been suffering this badly and it made her feel more helpless than ever. According to her mum, Tash had always had a saviour complex. From the time she could walk, she'd rescue caterpillars and crickets, and later

wounded magpies or stray cats. She guessed that's where the desire
to nurse came from too, helping those in need. Maybe that had
been part of her initial attraction to Kody? He'd been cocky and
charming but she'd seen beneath his exterior to a vulnerable young
guy trying to make ends meet.

Regardless of their past, what could she do for Kody now beyond
listening? Would suggesting professional help only anger him more?
She couldn't afford to alienate him.

'Have you chatted with the boys since you've been here?'

He shook his head. 'No. I've sent Yanni a short text thanking
him again for letting me use his place, and the other guys have
wanted to chat or video conference, but I've fobbed them off.'

'Are they as affected by the accident?'

'We all deal with stuff in our own way. I couldn't handle being
around them because they'd want to rehash what happened or try
to distract me by coming up with new material and I couldn't face
any of it.'

The waitress appeared with their coffees and placed them on the
table.

Tash wanted to say so much, but she settled on: 'I think it
wouldn't hurt to chat to a professional about what you're going
through, but if you ever need to talk, I'm here for you.'

'Thanks,' he muttered, staring at the foam on his cappuccino as
he stirred in the sugar.

Her hand itched with the urge to touch him, to offer some kind
of reassurance. Instead, as she sipped at her coffee, searching for the
right thing to say, she wondered if spending time with a fragile,
broken man was good for Isla.

CHAPTER

22

After Tash dropped him home, Kody spent half an hour sitting on the sofa and glaring at the guitar in the corner. He'd been doing it ever since he'd arrived in Brockenridge, staring at the inanimate object like it might sprout wings and fly around the room at any moment. It felt weird, loving an instrument so much his entire life but being unable to touch it now. He knew why, of course. He'd been strumming his favourite acoustic guitar and singing a slow version of the band's first song when the fire had broken out at the concert. When the fireworks had gone off prematurely he'd been annoyed but slip-ups happened on the road all the time. But the resultant fire and panicked stampede was a nightmare branded into his subconscious he doubted he'd ever get over.

The stupid thing was, when the warning sirens initially went off, everything halted, playing out in slow motion. The flames spreading from the pit beneath the stage out into the front rows of the venue, the panic of security staff desperately trying to usher patrons towards the nearest exits, the screams of terrified people, and his feet being rooted to the stage while staff tried to drag him to safety. He'd shrugged them off initially, dithering over whether to make a death-defying leap to help those below. Of course the decision had been taken out of his hands when three roadies had tugged him off-stage. Another had managed to rescue his precious guitar, but seven people had lost their lives and he'd never forget it. Their screams, along with the smell of burning flesh, would haunt him forever.

'Fuck,' he muttered, swiping a hand over his face, only to refocus on the guitar again. Not his—Yanni's, who'd dabbled in strings back in high school, before realising drums were his dream. It had scratches etched into it from being dragged between school and band practice in Daz's parents' garage. Its pine colour had faded over time, appearing almost bleached now. And the plectrum, a funky green opal design that teenage Kody had coveted, was tucked into the bottom strings.

He knew why Yanni kept the guitar—sentimentality. Kody's first guitar travelled with him everywhere even though he rarely played it. He may have hated school but thanked the big guy upstairs every day that his year seven music teacher had seen his potential and given him an old guitar. He knew every inch of that instrument: the feel of the strings; the rough wooden surface; the precise tuning required. It had grounded him like nothing else in his crappy teen years and he'd taken it around the world as a lucky talisman, a reminder of how far he'd come.

Kody blinked, the moisture in his eyes annoying him as much as the invisible band constricting his chest. He'd never been the sentimental type, so tearing up over an old guitar was plain idiotic. But he knew that his maudlin mood stemmed from so much more than an inability to pick up a guitar and he needed to get out of this funk before Isla picked up on it.

From their day together yesterday, Isla was way too smart for him. She'd see right through him. If she knew about the concert accident she didn't say but the fact she hadn't asked why he was in town hiding out in this house or how long before he returned to touring spoke volumes. She must've looked him up on the internet like any kid would and figured out he hadn't done any gigs since Wellington.

He'd explain it to her if she asked. Then again, what could he say? That he had no inclination to play music of any kind? That the thought of getting up on a stage again made him want to barf? That he'd be letting down the only real family he'd ever known but seeing the disappointment in his band's eyes when he froze on stage would gut him further? How could he explain any of it to his daughter when he'd barely processed his feelings himself? The guilt, the pain, the regret, was wrapped up in a tight bundle of nerves lodged in his gut and refused to budge no matter how much he willed it away.

He owed the band an explanation. But for now, he'd touch base with Yanni and lay the groundwork for his big reveal: that he'd be leaving Rock Hard Place.

He flipped open the laptop on the coffee table and stabbed at the button to video conference. The wifi took longer to connect out here so he waited, relieved when Yanni's face appeared. Apart from the lines fanning from his eyes and the deeper grooves either side of his big nose, Yanni looked the same as he had in high school: curly black hair, big brown eyes and a grin that made you want to smile back at him. He'd been Kody's first real friend, someone he could depend on when he'd started high school and realised being a sulky, grouchy introvert wouldn't get him far. They'd bonded over their love of music, and when Blue, Roger and Daz had started hanging around the music room at lunchtime too, Rock Hard Place had been born and they hadn't looked back.

'Mate, good to hear from you,' Yanni said, holding up his hand in a wave. 'How you doing?'

'Okay.' He hefted his walking boot into the air. 'Apart from this.'

'What the hell happened?'

'I battled your quad bike and lost.'

'Dickhead. Bad?'

'Fracture.'

'I was talking about the bike.'

Yanni never failed to make Kody laugh, even when he didn't feel like it. 'I'll replace it.'

Yanni waved away his offer. 'So how are you, apart from a bung ankle?'

'Not bad.' *Not good* hung unsaid between them. Evading the truth was much easier than flat-out lying to his best mate. 'The damnedest thing has happened.'

Yanni waited for him to continue. Another thing Kody liked about his friend: he didn't waste words. Some guys blathered for the sake of it, spinning bullshit as naturally as breathing, but not Yanni. He was a good listener.

'Have you ever met your neighbour here?'

'Nah. I keep a low profile when I'm in Brockenridge. That's the whole point of having a place out there: to decompress.'

'Fair enough.' Kody inhaled a breath and blew it out. 'You're not going to believe this but … remember Tash?'

'*Your* Tash? From back in Melbourne when we were gigging at the Princeton?'

Kody nodded. 'Turns out she's your neighbour, and she has a kid, Isla, who's mine.'

Yanni's jaw dropped. 'Tash had your kid and you didn't know?'

Kody didn't want to get into Tash's lie so he said, 'Biggest surprise of my life, but in a good way.'

'You've got a kid …' A slow grin spread across Yanni's face. 'I'll be damned.'

'Yeah, it's a real spin out.'

'So that would make her … what? Thirteen?'

'Yeah, almost.'

'That's great news, mate. I'm happy for you.'

'Thanks.'

Kody wanted to ask so much. *Do you think I'll make a good dad? What happens if I can't get my shit together? What will happen to my new relationship with my daughter once I leave town?* But no use asking Yanni questions he might not want to hear the answers to.

'Uh … how's Tash? Are you guys getting on okay?'

'Yeah, she's been helping me out since the ankle. And she's facilitating my relationship with Isla.' Only Yanni knew how gutted he'd been when she'd walked away from him all those years ago. Yanni had been the one to watch over him as he'd downed enough tequila shots to pickle his liver three nights in a row, who'd given him a pep talk about bucking the hell up before they got to LA, who'd taken him on a double date with two American cheerleaders the first week they'd landed in the City of Angels. Yanni had his back and always would, which meant revealing the real intent behind this call.

'Anyway, I wanted to talk to you about something.'

Yanni nodded and pointed to his face. 'I knew you weren't calling just to look at this mug.'

'As handsome as you think you are, you're right.' Kody huffed out a breath then rushed on. 'I know all of you saw shrinks after the accident, but how are the boys coping these days?'

'At the risk of you biting my head off again: better than you.'

'Really?'

'Yeah. Being back in Melbourne, killing time until you're ready to join us, has been good.'

That may never happen hovered on the tip of Kody's tongue. He didn't want to stuff his mates around and now that he had Isla, he had to make careful decisions and not rush in.

'Any idea when that's going to happen?'

Kody shook his head. 'Not a bloody clue. I still can't pick up a guitar, let alone sing a note.'

'Fuck,' Yanni muttered, concern clouding his eyes. 'Still that bad?'

'Yep and it shits me.' Kody thumped the table in frustration, causing the screen to pixellate for a second. 'I want to get past this but I can't.'

'You need professional help.'

'So I've been told.' He hesitated. 'Tash virtually said the same.'

Yanni's eyebrows shot up. 'You opened up to her about all this?'

'A little.' A lot—he hadn't anticipated telling her any of it but she'd always been a good listener and he'd fallen into old habits. Or maybe she'd got under his skin? Because as angry as he may be that she'd withheld Isla from him all these years, spending time with his daughter had shown him exactly what kind of a person Tash was: a caring, loving mother who'd raised an amazing kid, a resilient, well-adjusted girl who took major surprises like meeting her dad in her stride.

It had softened his stance towards Tash to the point he'd found himself teasing her. Her blush about his bath comment had catapulted him straight back to the time they'd first met and she'd blush at the slightest innuendo. Her innocence had been a huge turn-on and he'd loved unveiling her hidden sensuality. But that couldn't be his intention now. He had more important things to worry about, like getting to know his daughter and figuring out how he'd let his mates down if he ultimately couldn't return to his role as front man of Rock Hard Place.

'So are you two ... getting reacquainted?'

Kody snorted. 'Not in the way you're implying. I'm too bloody furious with her for keeping Isla from me all these years.'

'Why did she?'

'Protecting the kid, mostly.'

'From you?'

'No—more from the lifestyle, I guess. And not wanting me drifting in and out of Isla's life while the band was travelling constantly and doing so well.'

'That wasn't her decision to make.' Yanni's lips flattened in disapproval. 'You're a father, for fuck's sake, you should've had the chance to see your daughter grow up.'

For a second Kody wished he'd never told Yanni about Isla. But he valued his friend's opinion and had to tell someone the truth. 'Yeah, I know, but I'm moving past the bitterness for the sake of Isla. Tash and I are bound now, so no use alienating her when it's easier if we work together for the sake of Isla.'

Yanni deflated a tad. 'Yeah, you're right. Ignore this grumpy old man.'

'You're my age, dickhead, and we're not that old.'

Yanni laughed. 'Want me to come up there and hang out for a few days?'

'No!' Kody yelled, earning another laugh. 'Thanks for the offer, but the whole point of me being up here is to get my shit together.'

'That was before you discovered you had a daughter, though. You sure?'

'Yeah.' Kody made a grand show of looking at his watch. 'Gotta go.'

'Hot date?'

He flipped his middle finger in response, before smiling and hitting the disconnect button. He'd done the right thing in calling Yanni. Telling him about Isla and Tash made him feel lighter somehow, but as his gaze fell on the guitar again, the band of anxiety around his chest constricted. Revealing he had a daughter to his mate was easy compared with telling him the rest: that he feared he'd never play music again.

A loud banging on the back door roused Kody. He had no idea how long he'd been asleep—the last thing he remembered was drifting off to the sounds of a raucous kookaburra, but as he hobbled to the door he noticed dusk had descended.

As the banging intensified he called out, 'Hold your horses,' glad for the increased mobility of the walking boot but wishing he didn't need anything at all. The doc said he'd be in this damn boot for at least six weeks, but because the fracture in his fibula was hairline he could ditch the crutches. He reached the door and flung it open, to find Tash on the other side holding a casserole dish.

'Isla made you dinner,' she said, holding it out like an offering. 'She would've loved to share it with you but she had dance class.'

Through his sleep-clogged mind, he wondered if Isla sending Tash over with a meal was her version of matchmaking, before dispelling the thought. He already knew Isla enough to guess this was a genuine attempt to look after him.

'She's a good kid,' he said, opening the door further. 'Come in.'

Tash hesitated before stepping in. 'Were you asleep?'

'Guilty as charged.' He dragged a hand through his hair in a half-hearted effort to tidy it. 'What gave it away? My bleary eyes or the tousled do?'

She smiled and something deep inside twanged when it had no right to. 'You look pretty rumpled.'

'I wasn't expecting company.' He eyed the casserole dish and his stomach rumbled loudly, making her laugh.

'It's mac and cheese, Isla's speciality.' She moved around the kitchen as if it were the most natural thing in the world to bring him dinner. 'I'll dish up for you then get out of your way.'

'Stay,' he said, the invitation slipping from his lips before he had a chance to suppress it.

She paused, plate in one hand, ladle in the other, fixing him with a curious stare. 'You sure? Because you were already stuck with me in the car earlier, then at the café. I'm fine to drop this off and go.'

'Have you eaten yet?'

'No. I have to pick Isla up in an hour so I was going to grab a souvlaki in town.'

'There's enough for two in there, yeah?'

She glanced at the dish and nodded.

'Then join me. Please,' he added as an afterthought when she still seemed reluctant. 'So she dances?'

'Yeah.' Tash grabbed another plate and ladled mac and cheese on it, about a quarter of his portion. 'She loves it almost as much as drama. When she's on stage, she's a natural.'

Kody couldn't help but feel chuffed that maybe his daughter inherited her stage presence from him. As if sensing his thoughts, Tash stole a quick glance at him.

'She's like you in so many ways.'

'Yeah?' His throat tightened with emotion and he gratefully took the plate she held out to him.

'Uh-huh.' Tash grabbed some cutlery before sitting opposite him at the table and it struck him that if they'd stayed together, they would've done this kind of thing all the time. Sharing a simple dinner when he returned home from tour, hanging out, comfortable with each other.

He'd always felt like this around her, even when they'd been sitting cross-legged on the floor in his studio apartment in Melbourne, sharing a small pizza because they couldn't afford anything else. She'd never made him feel second best because he didn't have a lot of money. Back then, he'd fully expected his first real relationship to be his last, they'd been that in sync. Before she'd gutted him and stole almost thirteen years of his daughter's life from him.

Scowling, he picked up a fork, stabbed at a glob of macaroni and shoved it into his mouth to stop from bringing up the past.

Oblivious to his deteriorating mood, Tash said, 'There's this way Isla has of tilting her head when she's listening to music that reminds me of you. And she picks the sultanas out of anything. And she likes to lie in bed for at least thirty minutes after waking to ease into the day—'

'I wonder if she can sing like me,' he blurted, desperate to change the subject because the longer Tash waxed lyrical about how like him Isla was, the angrier he got that he hadn't been around to witness it firsthand.

'She has a great voice,' Tash said. 'But she's never been interested in lessons or anything. Maybe that'll change now?'

'Maybe.' He shoved the macaroni around his plate, his appetite gone. He hated this roller coaster of emotion whenever he was around Tash. He wanted to shelve his resentment for Isla's sake but realising he had to learn so much about his daughter made him want to thump the table and rail at this woman who had deprived him of so much.

Tash laid her fork down and only then did he notice she'd barely touched her meal too. 'What's up? I thought we were okay after that coffee earlier today?'

He could lie, but opening up to Yanni earlier had been cathartic. Maybe if he lay it all on the line for Tash they could finally move forwards without the residual bitterness eating away at him?

'We are, mostly,' he said, gruff and abrupt. 'And I want to learn everything about Isla, I really do, but hearing you talk about her gets me here.' He thumped a fist over his heart. 'I want to get past the fact you lied to me all those years ago, and that you've kept lying for thirteen years, but it may take time because it's bloody tough to deal with.'

Her eyes held so much hurt and it pissed him off, because he was the injured party here, not her.

'Tell me something. Is my name even on Isla's birth certificate?'

She flinched, before tilting her chin up. 'You're her father—of course it is.'

'Guess I should be grateful for that,' he said. 'This whole situation is doing my head in, thinking about how much I've missed out on.'

'I'm so, so sorry. And I know an apology doesn't cut it, but I need you to understand I never intended to hurt you. I was in a tailspin when I discovered I was pregnant and I didn't want you to sacrifice your dreams for me—'

'I should've had a say!' he yelled, making her jump. He hated himself for it. But his latent resentment didn't take much to ignite. Damn it.

'You're right,' she murmured, and when she gave the barest of nods and a tear trickled down her cheek, something inside him broke.

They were both hurting for different reasons but all the rehashing in the world wouldn't change facts. He had a choice to make: wallow in the past, caught up in regret and retribution, or learn to forgive her and move forwards. It wouldn't happen overnight, but he wanted to have more friendly moments and not have to watch what he said every second around her for fear of exploding.

'We need to find a way to make this work,' she murmured. 'For Isla's sake.'

'Don't you think I know that?' Weary to his soul, he rested his forearms on the table. 'My foul mood isn't all about you. I spoke to Yanni earlier, told him about Isla and how I'm still avoiding music of any kind. It's got me in a funk. He thinks I should get professional help too.'

She nodded. 'Can't hurt.'

The thought of opening up to a stranger left him cold. But maybe seeking help would be different now? He couldn't see things changing unless he got a handle on how to deal with the debilitating guilt from the accident and all his bottled-up bitterness against Tash.

'How is Yanni?'

'Okay. Him and the rest of the boys are in Melbourne, waiting for me to get my shit together.' He straightened. 'He was bloody surprised to discover you were his neighbour.'

'I bet.' She managed a rueful chuckle. 'I can't believe I've lived here for so long and didn't know he owned this place.'

Curiosity about Isla's early years prompted him to ask, 'How long have you lived on Wattle Lane? Since you came back from Melbourne?'

She snorted, but sadness clouded her eyes. 'Next door isn't my parents' house, if that's what you're asking. They lived a lot further out of town.' She made inverted comma signs with her fingers. '"Away from the temptations" in town apparently.'

From the few trips he'd made through Brockenridge, the only places where a person could be led astray were the run-down pubs.

'You didn't talk about them when we were together. They were super religious?'

She nodded and glanced away. 'They met in Shepparton through one of those churches that spring up overnight. Got married, bought a cheap block of land here, had me. They taught outback kids online.' She barked out a harsh laugh. 'But they saved their special brand of fervent teaching for me. I was the dutiful daughter but I worked my arse off to get good grades to do nursing in Melbourne. So you can imagine their reaction when I returned home pregnant ...'

She bit her lip and he scooted his chair around next to hers, unsure whether to hug her or pat her shoulder. Her upbringing was obviously a sore spot and he wished he'd never brought it up. He knew the feeling. It made sense now, why she'd never spoken about where she came from and why she'd accepted his reluctance to do the same.

'I knew they wouldn't be happy but I never imagined they'd disown me. They sold up and left town when I was about seven months pregnant.' She blinked rapidly. 'I thought after Isla was born they might come around. I didn't know where they were living so I texted them photos and an invitation to come see her. They changed their mobile numbers.'

He reached for her, unable to bear a moment longer of the pain radiating off her, and hauled her into his arms. She stiffened, tough and unyielding, until he stroked her hair and murmured, 'It's okay, Tash.'

The sobs started then and as he held her, gritting his teeth against the urge to bawl with her, he wondered if they'd ever resolve the pain of their pasts and find a way to move forwards, together.

CHAPTER

23

Jane sulked for an hour after Mason left. She muttered under her breath like a crazy woman while she ladled leftovers into containers and stacked them in the fridge, calling him some not-so-nice names he thoroughly deserved for misjudging her. She then overloaded on sugar by cramming the mini chocolate croissants, apple strudel and plaited pastry dusted in cinnamon sugar into her mouth in quick succession. It didn't help her mood. If anything, with every bite of the delicious flaky pastry, with every burst of perfectly stewed apple and cinnamon on her tongue, she cursed him a little more.

She'd never tasted anything like it. The guy could bake. The buttery, melt-in-the-mouth pastry, the rich, dark chocolate, the tartness of the apple perfectly combined with the sugar and spices ... He created magic with an oven and a few ingredients. If she'd thought Betty was good, Mason was in a league of his own—if this was the kind of fare he intended on serving to the good folk of Brockenridge she'd be first in line every day.

But that might not happen now, courtesy of her witch of a mother, and Jane knew she wouldn't sleep until she confronted Gladys.

With sugar making her blood fizz and her head spinning with the implications of why she cared so damn much what Mason Woodley thought of her, she drove ten minutes out of town to her childhood home.

After her father died, she'd expected Gladys to leave Brockenridge in favour of Melbourne or Sydney, to live her fake life in a glamorous city better suited to a phoney like her. She should've known better, because Gladys needed the adulation of those around her and it would've taken her too long to build up an audience of minions in a new city. Here, she could lord it over everyone: hosting the best book club; donating the most to local charities; opening her famed garden to the public to raise money for drought relief. Revered, adored Gladys Jefferson, a pillar of the Brockenridge community.

What a crock.

Jane pulled into the circular driveway of her old home with a spray of gravel, quashing the childish urge to do a few burnouts. The only thing stopping her was that it wouldn't affect her mother anyway, she'd just get one of the staff to clean up the mess in the morning.

She'd barely parked and stepped from the car when the ornate front door opened. Anger made her shake as she stalked towards her mother, silhouetted in the doorway like some villain from a classic movie.

'It's awfully late for dropping in—'

'Cut the crap, Mum. We need to talk.'

As Jane caught a glimpse of Gladys's smug smirk, she knew this was her mother's intention all along: to get her to come home, on her terms.

Jane stalked into the nearest room, a lavish library that housed floor-to-ceiling mahogany bookshelves filled to capacity. She'd always considered this room her dad's space because she'd often find him in here, behind the desk, poring over something on the computer. She later wondered if it had been his coping mechanism, a way to hide from Gladys, some much needed me-time. Whatever his rationale, it hadn't worked, because her dad had been compelled to find the ultimate way to escape Gladys. And the suspicion surrounding the lack of skid marks before his car slammed into that tree at one hundred and forty kilometres an hour told Jane all she needed to know. Her dad's death hadn't been an accident. Gladys had driven him to it.

'What's this all about, Jane?'

Gladys perched on the edge of a brown Chippendale sofa, her hands clasped in her lap, her smile serene. It didn't surprise Jane that even at this late hour her mother wore a designer pantsuit in the palest of pinks. Gladys never let anyone see her as anything other than polished and perfectly made-up. Jane couldn't remember ever seeing her mother without make-up, or in pyjamas for that matter. Every morning Gladys would appear in the kitchen fully clothed and made up, and would maintain her façade until she closed her bedroom door at night.

Jane had once done everything in her power to present the perfect image Gladys wanted in the vain hope it would get her mother to acknowledge she actually had a daughter; it hadn't been enough, so she'd stopped caring about her mother's aloofness towards her. She'd put it down to the lack of a maternal gene or two. While her mother's indifference hurt, it hadn't mattered as much because her dad had adored her and they'd been a tight-knit twosome.

Bitterness tightened every muscle in her body but Jane had to relax. She needed to get this sorted out. 'Why are you stalling the sale of the shop next to the bakery?'

'Oh, that.' Gladys waved her hand like she was shooing a bother-some fly. 'I'm an astute businesswoman so there's nothing wrong with wanting top dollar for my investments.'

'It's been empty for years. Why not settle quickly?'

A glint of smugness lit Gladys's steely blue eyes. 'Why would I do that when this is so much more fun?'

Jane had known this was about her mother yanking her chain all along, wanting to see her grovel or dance to some warped tune, damn her.

'Mason and I are not involved. He's hiring me to assist with the interior design. That's it. So whatever you think you're doing, it's not going to work.'

'Yet you're here.' A self-righteous smile spread across her moth-er's face and Jane's hand itched with the urge to slap it.

'If all you wanted was to get me to come home, Mother, you could've asked.'

'I could have, but I doubt you would've responded because you persist in this weird vendetta.'

'No vendetta, Mum, I'm just tired.' She pinched the bridge of her nose; it did little to ease the pressure building between her eyes. She never got migraines but any clash with her mother always resulted in a headache. 'During our last conversation many years ago, I gave you the option of salvaging something out of our bro-ken relationship. Instead, you chose to pretend nothing was wrong, then proceeded to make my life miserable.' She tilted her chin up, defiant. 'Newsflash, Mum, I've wasted enough time trying to get you to acknowledge me let alone open up to me, and I'm done.'

A flicker of remorse flickered in Gladys's eyes before she blinked, and Jane wondered if she'd imagined it. 'During our last confronta-tion, that day when you yelled at me and wouldn't hear reason, you made it more than clear what you thought of me.' Her lips thinned.

'You said you wanted nothing to do with me and if you know me at all you know I never grovel to anyone, least of all my spoilt brat daughter.'

Jane could say so much but what was the point? The yawning gap between them was growing wider every day and it would take a miracle for them to reconcile.

'I'm not the one with hidden motives, never have been.' Jane eyed the door, desperate to escape. 'Stop toying with decent people in this town. Betty's Bakery is an institution and she's a good woman.' And more of a mother to Jane than Gladys had ever been. 'Their proposed expansion can only be good for Brockenridge, so why would you want to interfere with that?'

Gladys stood slowly, poised and elegant and poisonous. 'Because I heard you were involved in the revamp and I knew this would get your attention.'

Confused, Jane shook her head. It did little to clear it. 'Why? You could've picked up the phone to do that.'

'Would you have answered?'

'This is ridiculous. What's really going on, Mum?'

Gladys waggled a finger in Jane's direction. 'That's always been the problem with us. You have no idea what makes me tick when I know you better than I know myself.'

Jane glared at her mother, who regarded her with that infuriatingly serene gaze. A small part of her wondered if this *was* some warped cry for attention. Her mother had already said she'd never grovel. Was this her way of wanting to thrash out their problems after all this time?

'You need to stop believing the worst about me, Jane. I wish you could understand I'm not the bad guy here.'

Jane had given up trying to figure out what went through her mum's head a long time ago so she had no hope of understanding what had motivated her mother's latest showdown. For now, she wanted Betty's plans to come to fruition and that meant Gladys needed to back down and butt out.

'Get that sale done,' she said, her tone frigid.

The woman she'd once idolised stared at her with indifference, then had the audacity to chuckle. 'Or what?'

Jane could say so much but she swallowed her threats. Antagonising Gladys was not the way to go. 'Please, Mum, it's important.'

By her haughty expression, Gladys thought she'd won this round and Jane let her have her victory. If it meant Betty got to build her new bakery, it was worth it.

Jane should've waited until the morning to speak to Mason but she wanted to sit down with him and Betty and convince them she'd had no knowledge of her mother's tactics. Before she could change her mind, Jane parked around the back of the bakery, in front of a quaint cottage where widowed Betty lived. She assumed Mason would be staying with his mum. Nobody returning home would choose to bunk down at the hotel over the pub or the motel behind The Watering Hole. Local folk valued family. Pity her mum had never got the memo.

She marched to the front door, shaking out residual tension like a dog drying off after a bath, and took a deep breath before stabbing at the doorbell. She hoped Betty would answer the door. But when it swung open, Mason stood there, wearing nothing but a towel.

She shouldn't look, not when she'd come here determined to set things right between them, but she had a pulse and the sight of the tall, blond baker wearing next to nothing pretty much ensured she couldn't *not* look. He wasn't buffed or overly muscly but his chest, covered in a smattering of hair several shades darker than on his head, had definition. His shoulders looked broader without clothing and the strength in his arms was testament to many hours spent kneading. As for his legs, she didn't go there. She had no intention of glancing below his waist, considering the heat surging through her body.

'Uh ... sorry to interrupt your evening—'

'What the hell do you want?'

'To let you know I've tried to fix things.'

Wariness flickered in his eyes, as if he didn't trust anything that came out of her mouth. She didn't blame him. She felt the same way about her mother.

'Can it wait until morning?'

She shook her head. 'I want to set your mum's mind at rest.'

'She's gone to bed already.'

'Oh.' She hadn't taken into consideration that bakers were up before dawn to prepare and would go to bed earlier than most. But she wouldn't be deterred. 'Then can we talk?'

A deep, disapproving groove slashed his brows, his glare formidable as he edged the door shut. 'I'm tired.'

'It'll only take a few minutes. Please.' Jane hated how needy she sounded but she had to make him understand she had nothing to do with her mother stalling on the sale. In the past, it wouldn't have mattered what he thought of her but she believed they'd moved past their tense teen years, and if she was serious about reinventing herself, she didn't want to revert to not caring. When he'd accused her of still being a game player like she was in high school, she'd been too mad at him to consider his insult. But now she really wanted to know what he meant. She'd been uppity and condescending to him back then, but they hadn't interacted all that much. They'd never liked each other and she preferred kids who enjoyed having a laugh, not ones like Mason, who stared at her like a speck of dirt. He was looking at her now in almost the same way. But school finished long ago—what had she done to make this guy dislike her so much?

After what seemed like an eternity, Mason stepped back and opened the door. 'Lounge room is on the left. Wait there while I get dressed.' When she hovered on the doorstep, he stomped away, leaving her with a rather impressive view of shifting glutes beneath the towel. Hot damn.

Pressing her hands to her cheeks, she entered the cottage. With a little luck, Betty might wake and save her a guaranteed unpleasant confrontation with Mason.

After closing the door, she wandered into the lounge room and took a seat on a bottle-green velvet armchair. Betty had always been lovely to her and Jane had occasionally offloaded to the older woman when she'd visited the bakery, but she'd never been inside the cottage. It channelled the warm-hearted baker perfectly: floral rugs over red gum floors, comfy sofas covered in vivid throw rugs, oversized cushions and bookcases stacked with cookbooks warring for space alongside novels of every genre. The entire room exuded cosy warmth, far removed from the pristine frigidness of the home she'd grown up in.

Before she had a chance to check out Betty's literary tastes, Mason entered the room. He hadn't lost the formidable glower but she could handle it better now that he'd put some clothes on. In fact, he looked almost normal in navy trakkie pants and a grey cotton T-shirt. The few times she'd seen him he'd been immaculately dressed, which she'd attributed to his time in Paris. Funny, in the past that would've mattered to her, but after learning the truth about her parents she'd realised that appearances meant nothing.

He folded his arms and leaned against the doorframe, keeping as far from her as possible. 'What's so important that it can't wait till morning?'

'I wanted to explain about the shop you're trying to acquire—'

'Nothing to explain. You're stalling, trying to up the price, despite the place being empty for years.' He shook his head. 'Pretty shitty, if you ask me.'

'Who asked you?' She leapt to her feet, her determination to keep the discussion calm deserting her. 'If you shut your big trap for one second and let me speak, you'd learn that I have nothing to do with those shops. They're owned by my mother, who's a bitter cow who'll do anything to get me to dance to her tune, and she's turning the screws because she somehow thinks I like you ...' She trailed off, mortified she'd said too much.

'Why does she think you like me?'

He'd asked the question she had no intention of answering. 'Who knows? Anyway, I've just come from her place. I told her she has to sell to you and Betty.'

Some of the tension holding his shoulders rigid dissolved as he crossed the room to sit in the armchair next to hers. 'Do you think she'll listen?'

'Honestly?' Jane screwed up her nose. 'I have no idea. That's the first time I've been home since I stormed out ten years ago, vowing never to return, and we rarely talk. But I tried. And I want you to know I'd never screw you over like that, not when you're giving me a chance to decorate the place.'

He swiped a hand over his face; it did little to erase the sheepishness. 'I jumped to conclusions. Sorry about that.'

'Why did you?' She hesitated, not sure if she wanted to hear the rest. 'What did you mean about me being a game player?'

A surprising blush stained his cheeks. 'When you're not a cool kid at high school, you hate the ones that are.'

'That's it?'

'You don't remember, do you?'

'Remember what?'

'Home ec. Last day of first term, final year.'

She shook her head, embarrassed to admit the only thing she remembered from her last year at high school was trailing after Connor Delaney, doing everything in her power to make him like her. 'Sorry, I don't remember.'

'Figures,' he muttered. 'At the risk of sounding like a dickhead for bringing up something that happened over a decade ago, I'll tell you. I was a guy who preferred to cook rather than play cricket or footy, so you can imagine the shit I copped.'

'Yeah, but I didn't give you crap about that.'

'You gave me crap about everything else though.' He huffed out a sigh. 'That last prac session, we had to work in pairs to make a lemon meringue pie. You were assigned to work with me. You said you'd buy the ingredients if I did all the cooking. When you didn't show up in the home ec room at the time we arranged, I went looking for you. I found you at the oval, watching the footy team train. You'd bought the stuff but when I asked you to come make the pie with me, you accidentally-on-purpose dropped the bags at my feet. And you laughed like an idiot along with the dickhead players who made my life enough of a misery.'

Mortification flooded Jane, both at her actions and the fact she couldn't remember the incident. Something that had been a blip on her radar had made a lasting impression on this great guy.

'You really don't remember?'

She shook her head. 'I'm so sorry, Mason, I don't. I know you and I used to butt heads over other stuff but that was a shitty thing to do. One of many shitty things I did to people back then because I was a self-absorbed bitch.'

'Harsh but true,' he deadpanned, making her smile a little.

'I guess that explains why you thought I was screwing you around over the sale of the shop.'

He nodded. 'But I jumped to conclusions and that's almost as shitty as what you did.'

'Not really, but I appreciate the comparison.'

Their eyes locked and the ever-present hint of heat shimmered between them, unexpected and untenable. She couldn't do anything about her attraction—considering he already thought poorly of her, he might think any kind of flirtation was part of her repertoire to distract him from securing the shop and expanding the bakery.

'So what's the deal with your mum?'

'Trust me, you don't want to know,' she said, the familiar sorrow gripping her heart. 'Suffice to say we don't get on and that's enough of a reason for her vindictiveness to taint you too if she thinks we're friends.'

Confusion clouded his eyes but she didn't give him a chance to ask anything else. 'Thanks for hearing me out. Let me know what happens with the shop, okay?' She stood.

'Sure,' he said, standing too. 'You're still keen to decorate, despite my childish behaviour?'

'If you still want me.'

His enigmatic stare bored into her as he touched her arm. 'Absolutely.'

Before she could overthink his response, she did the only sensible thing she'd done all night.

She fled.

CHAPTER
24

With Isla's thirteenth birthday coming up, Tash had to face facts. She may have been fiercely independent since she'd returned to Brockenridge and had encouraged Isla to be the same way, but sobbing her heart out in Kody's arms a week ago had given her a much needed wake-up call. Now she'd faced her greatest fear—letting Kody into Isla's life—maybe it was time to confront her parents.

Once Kody returned to the limelight the news he had a daughter would break and despite the cruel way her parents had shunned her, she didn't want them hearing about Isla's paternity via the media. Not that her folks had ever paid much attention to the news, but the small part of her that harboured guilt she'd disappointed them felt compelled to tell them face to face. So with one of the part-time wait staff covering her shift at the roadhouse, Tash drove two hours to the tiny town of High Ridge, a dot on the map south of Swan Hill. She'd never been there before but she'd researched her parents online. They weren't hard to find considering they'd set up a Christian school for kids in remote areas. Their website boasted thirty students of varying ages, with a wide range of subjects on offer. Though Tash knew firsthand the primary form of education would be religious indoctrination.

She'd timed her visit to coincide with the end of the school day and as she parked opposite the small hall and watched kids trudge out, jostling each other and scuffing their shoes in the dirt, she hoped they had a better time being educated by her parents than she did. Predictably, a giant white cross took pride of place on the roof above the front door. She believed in a higher power, always had, but the sight of the cross brought back memories she'd rather forget: being dragged to mass despite having a temperature bordering on forty degrees; having to recite the rosary repeatedly until her throat ached because she'd been caught with a young adult paranormal novel deemed unsuitable; being grounded for a month because a boy in her class had asked her out on a date.

Blinking back tears, Tash waited, watching the deserted schoolyard for another ten minutes before getting out of the car. Crazily, she'd contemplated bringing Isla along to soften the confrontation, in the vain hope her parents might take one look at their incredible granddaughter and fall in love. But if this went the way Tash expected, she'd be glad she'd never exposed her precious daughter to her parents' special brand of hate. She could take it—she had in the past—but it wasn't fair to ask Isla to accept such awful treatment.

Steeling her resolve, she squared her shoulders and marched across the yard and up the steps to the front door. It was open, giving her a clear view into the hall. They'd set it up like a normal classroom, with two seats at each of the rectangular tables. A whiteboard took pride of place at the front, bookshelves lining one wall and stackable tubs emblazoned with children's names on the other. But that's where the similarity to other classrooms ended. There was no artwork on the walls, no colourful posters or newspaper articles featuring current affairs. As for computers, one screen with an ancient hard drive attached to it sat in the corner at the front of the room with the screen angled so that everyone could see it. It rammed home the fact that her folks still viewed art as frivolous and self-indulgent, and media as the devil's work.

Determined to get this over with, Tash knocked on the door and entered, almost jumping out of her skin when her father appeared seemingly out of nowhere from behind her.

'What can I do for—' The colour leached from his face as he gasped in shock.

He'd aged—a lot. Her parents had been in their early forties when she'd been born, so they'd always seemed old to her, but her dad looked older than seventy-six. Lines covered his forehead and cheeks, deep crevices surrounded his mouth and his tan emphasised the leathery appearance of his skin.

She wanted to say so much to him but settled for taking a step forwards and half-lifting her arms in the hope of a hug.

He scowled and took a step back.

She let her arms fall to her sides and dragged in a deep breath. 'Hi, Dad.'

'What are you doing here?'

'I came to talk to you and Mum,' she said, hoping her mother might soften once she heard more about Isla and saw the photos on her phone. Then again, she'd looked to her mum for sympathy many times in the past but she'd stood resolute, backing up Tash's tyrannical father in every outlandish decision.

'Your mother's not here. She's in Mildura doing outreach work for the church.'

Tash's heart sank. She had no hope of getting through to her father but she'd come all this way, she had to try.

'Listen, Dad, I need to tell you something—'

'Not having another bastard child, are you?' He glared at her stomach with ill-concealed distaste and Tash resisted the urge to turn tail and run.

'Isla is wonderful, thanks for asking.'

His eyes narrowed at her sarcasm, malevolence radiating off him like a toxic cloud. 'Leave. Now.'

'I will, but I thought I'd give you the courtesy of hearing about Isla's father from me rather than the media.'

When he remained silent, she said, 'Kody Lansdowne is a famous rock star. He's Isla's father and he didn't know about Isla's existence until recently, and it stands to reason you might hear her name in the press associated with him once the news breaks. He's making an effort to get to know her—' *unlike you* '—and I thought I'd extend the same courtesy to you and Mum. Isla's almost thirteen and a lot of years have passed since you shut me out, but she's a wonderful girl and maybe you'd like to get to know her too—'

'No.' When he lifted his hand to point at the door behind her, it shook a little. 'You're dead to us, so we don't have a granddaughter.'

A pain Tash had thought she'd conquered a long time ago blossomed in her chest, making breathing difficult. Ridiculous, to feel this crushed when she'd expected it, but the reality of her father's heartlessness far exceeded the way this scenario had played out in her head.

'I feel sorry for you.' Tash turned away and headed out the door, only letting her tears fall when she reached the last step.

'And I'll pray for you.'

Tash froze for a moment before forcing her feet to walk at a sedate pace towards her car when she wanted to run from this place and never look back.

CHAPTER
25

With Isla due to pop in any moment, Kody set out after-school snacks. He'd been thrilled when Tash had asked him to mind Isla because she wouldn't be home until late. Like he'd ever say no to that. He'd scarcely seen his kid over the last week, what with her busy extra-curricular activities schedule and massive homework load. He'd rattled around this place for seven long days.

Not that his time alone had been all bad. After his revealing chats with Tash and Yanni, he'd taken steps towards confronting his demons by utilising a website for mental health issues to chat via keyboard with a psychologist. He'd been wary at first, reluctant to reveal anything, but that was the beauty of remote contact: he could remain anonymous and divulge his innermost doubts without fear of being judged. Ironically, once he'd started talking he couldn't shut up and all three sessions had run over two hours. The anonymity definitely suited him, because no way in hell could he confide in anyone face to face. Shrinks had a legal duty to patient confidentiality, but the last thing he needed was to be spotted visiting a psych by some overzealous local. He'd been in that position before, caught sneaking in to appointments or a rendezvous by relentless paparazzi, and he hated having his private life plastered across the tabloids. It was the one downside of fame he'd never gotten used to.

Chatting to a faceless psychologist had another bonus: the session could happen at a time that suited him. He'd always produced his best work late at night, when he'd sit in a low-lit room, pencil and notepad in hand, jotting down lyrics and melodies at will. Having the freedom to chat to someone any time he liked helped him divulge thoughts he'd otherwise be reluctant to.

The psych had helped him re-evaluate priorities and what letting go meant. Because once he started delving beneath his guilt—for those deaths, for not being around for Isla, for not fighting hard enough when Tash walked away—he realised how much his pent-up resentment was holding him back.

Knowing he'd let Tash walk away had particularly bugged him, because after he'd left Melbourne and landed in LA he'd spent several weeks bagging her, both in his mind and to his mates. It made him feel better to be the injured party, the guy who'd been robbed of a say in the future of their unborn child: poor Kody. But a small part of him had known, even back then, that he'd been secretly relieved Tash had made the choice for both of them. He hadn't wanted to be saddled with a kid, not when his career had the opportunity to take off. And he sure as hell hadn't wanted to make the tough decision whether to stay and be a father or head overseas for a chance at the big time. So he'd channelled those shameful feelings of relief into resentment and anger towards Tash. Easier to deflect than face the hard truth: that she'd made the right call in letting him off the hook.

Being older, wiser and having enough money to give Isla the life she deserved was a far cry from that stubborn, self-centred idiot he'd been back then. Time to stop blaming Tash for something he'd secretly wanted all along and be thankful for what she'd given him: a second chance at fatherhood.

A melodic knock at the back door signalled Isla's arrival and he called, 'Come in.'

The door opened and Isla appeared, grinning. She dropped her backpack, kicked the door shut and made a beeline for him.

'Hey, Dad. School sucked but it's good to see you.'

He laughed and accepted her hug, loving her demonstrative nature, amazed that she didn't seem awkward when they were still establishing some kind of relationship.

When he released her, he said, 'Good to see you too, kiddo. Tough day?'

She rolled her eyes. 'Double period of maths, and no PE or drama.'

'Will a banana milkshake and choc-chip cookies improve your day?'

'Only if you add extra ice-cream in the shake,' she said. 'How's the ankle?'

'Not so sore.'

'What have you been up to?'

Kids asked a lot of questions. He'd witnessed it firsthand with Daz's two and when the band had done impromptu high school visits. Kids never held back, and their bluntness was a blessing and a curse. You can't bullshit kids; they see right through you. But still, there was no way he'd reveal how he'd spent his week to Isla.

'Not much,' he said, scooping ice-cream into a blender, adding milk, a banana, and a dash of cinnamon. 'Watching TV, reading, looking at the view.'

She wrinkled her nose. 'That sounds almost as boring as all the homework I've had to do for some stupid tests.'

'Homework is important.' He held back a smile at his hypocrisy—he'd barely done a night's homework in his entire schooling life and the plethora of Es and Fs on his reports proved it.

'Sport and drama are important, the rest of that stuff like algebra will never be used in real life once I finish school.'

Her cute pout was so reminiscent of Tash he had to flick on the blender to stop himself mentioning it. That's another thing the psych had helped him with: confronting his jealousy that Tash held pride of place in their daughter's affections because of the time he'd missed out on. Crazy, because Isla had been nothing but keen to welcome him into her life. But that didn't mean he'd release all his resentment towards Tash at once.

Switching off the blender, he said, 'Do you have any idea what you want to do after school?'

'Not really.' She perched on a stool at the island bench and rested her chin in her hands. 'I've got plenty of time to decide, though I'd like to go to uni in Melbourne.'

Kody forced a smile even as he felt like yelling, 'No! You'll meet too many young guys who'll take advantage of an innocent country girl.' Which was crazy, considering he'd never taken advantage of Tash. Sure, he'd been more street smart than her, but their attraction had been mutual. The thought of his daughter encountering the big, bad world beyond Brockenridge scared the shit out of him.

'Or maybe I'll be a muso like my dad?'

She'd said it to test him; he saw it in the mischievous glint in her eyes. Once again, he wanted to warn her off, to explain the nebulous nature of the music industry, the constant rejections, the pitfalls of unscrupulous agents, the effort required for little return. He was one of the lucky ones, he knew that, but for every success story in this business there were another hundred talented musicians who'd never make it.

He unscrewed the blender lid and poured the milkshake into a glass. 'I reckon you could be anything you want to be.'

A faint blush stained her cheeks as she accepted the glass from him. 'Thanks.'

He'd heard this parenting gig could be tough but, boy, he was enjoying the early stages—every time Isla looked at him he felt like a god.

She downed the shake like she hadn't had a drink all day, and followed it up with three cookies. Then she tilted her head to the right, another gesture reminiscent of Tash. 'Can I ask you something?'

'Shoot.'

'With all the stuff you said you'd been doing over the last week, how come you're not playing music?'

Shit. The one question he had no answer for. At least, not one he wanted to reveal to her. 'I'm taking a break. That's why I'm here, getting away from that whole scene for a while.'

'Are you taking a break because of what happened at your last concert?'

Bloody internet. A godsend for promotion but way too revealing. He could hedge around the truth, come up with a lame excuse, but what sort of message would that send? That it was okay to lie?

'Partially,' he said eventually. 'It was rough having people die at one of my concerts and I needed to get away for a while.'

She eyed him with respect and he was glad he'd responded with partial honesty. 'I read about it online. Must've been awful for everyone there.'

'It was.' He sounded curt and needed a change of subject. 'Have you listened to any of Rock Hard Place's songs?'

'A few.' A cute crinkle appeared between her brows. 'Don't take this the wrong way, Dad, but rock isn't really my thing.'

He laughed, releasing the tension he'd been holding since she'd started quizzing him. 'You've already told me you listen to indie, but I bet you like pop too, preferably sung by a boy band.'

She poked her tongue out at him. 'It's called pop for a reason. It's *popular*.'

He held up his hands. 'Hey, I won't hold it against you.'

'But it's cool you're so famous and lots of people like rock.'

A fact he was thankful for every day. The band hadn't looked back once their first album had taken off and everything they'd released after that went platinum. Their last song held the record for the most downloads in the first twenty-four hours of release. Not bad for a bunch of rockers in their mid-thirties competing against every young up-and-comer.

'Yeah, I'm pretty lucky I get paid to do what I love.'

The moment he uttered the words, he realised how much he missed it: the creative freedom of writing songs; setting the lyrics to music; jamming with his mates. He needed to get out of this funk or risk losing his one great passion.

'I know I've already mentioned this but I'd really love to learn the guitar,' she said, looking at him with so much blatant adoration he had a hard time not reaching out to hug her. 'Can we start now?'

Hell no, not when he hadn't had the guts to pick up the instrument since he'd arrived. But the longer Isla stared at him with hope and adoration, the harder it would be to fob her off. Besides, hadn't he just said how lucky he was to have a dream job, a job he had no hope of returning to if he didn't take baby steps to confront his demons? And what better motivation to pick up a guitar again than teaching his daughter?

'Okay.'

Did she hear the angst in those two syllables? The fear? The reluctance? Considering how she practically leapt off the stool and raced to the lounge room where Yanni's guitar was propped in a corner, it was doubtful. He hobbled after her.

When he entered the room, she already had the guitar propped on her knees, holding it like a natural.

'Have you ever played before?'

'No.' She strummed her thumb across the strings and the jarring twang did little to dispel his initial assessment: she held the guitar with such ease he knew she'd be a quick learner.

'I asked because you've got a great posture,' he said, dragging a footstool closer and sitting on it in front of her. 'Firstly, it's all about finger placement.'

He had no idea how long he spent showing her the basics, how to tune, guiding her fingers onto certain strings, outlining chords, but when she wanted to take a break to grab a glass of water he was shocked to find dusk had descended. He'd been so immersed in teaching her he hadn't once panicked about touching the guitar. Either that psych he'd been chatting to was a miracle worker or his daughter's zest for learning had been a major distraction.

Whatever the reason, he found himself reaching for the guitar. His hands trembled a little as he settled it on his knee but as he started plucking at the strings, playing the melody from Rock Hard Place's first hit, a song as natural to him as breathing, he found his nerves settling. He closed his eyes and let the notes flow, one into another, a flawless transition from the fear holding him back to reawakening his soul. The music soothed him as much as the feel of the guitar in his hands, his fingertips sliding over the strings with innate memory. Comforting.

When he played the last note, loud applause rang out and he opened his eyes to find Isla kneeling in front of him, wonder in her eyes.

'Wow, Dad, you're amazing. You're so much better than those videos I watched online.'

'Thanks, kiddo.' He managed to smile through the sting of tears. 'Your mum should be home soon. Should we make some dinner so she doesn't have to?'

'Okay.' Isla stood and headed for the kitchen, leaving him battling the urge to cry.

What was it about this kid that cut straight to his core?

CHAPTER
26

Tash had been deluded thinking her parents might've mellowed with time. They hadn't reached out in thirteen years so she should've known nothing she said now would make a difference. She thought she'd got over their callousness years ago, deliberately steeling her heart. But seeing her dad reopened old wounds and the hurt poured in, stinging in a way she hadn't anticipated. So the last thing she felt like doing now was having dinner with Isla and Kody. But when she'd seen Isla's enthusiastic text before she'd left High Ridge, she didn't have the heart to say no. At least with Isla there the evening couldn't end like the last time she saw Kody, with her sobbing in his arms. That hadn't been one of her finer moments so she'd avoided him all week. Childish, maybe, but having him hold her and comfort her resurrected too many feelings she preferred remained buried.

He'd always been great at hugs, damn him. Every time he'd come off stage at the Princeton he'd hug her tight, like performing had been irrelevant and his entire focus was her. She'd revelled in the attention and had occasionally preened when she'd seen the envious glances cast her way by groupies. Kody had been her man and he'd never given her any reason to doubt him. Which made her wonder, not for the first time, how much of a disservice had she done him by removing his choice to be a parent?

Weary to her bones, she stopped at the bakery to pick up dessert. One of Betty's chocolate mousse cakes and rhubarb crumbles would hit the spot. Loads of sugar, perfect comfort food. Kody had a wicked sweet tooth when they'd dated in Melbourne, back when they'd been young and blessed with the fast metabolism of youth. Lucky, because Kody insisted on visiting every gelateria in the city. It had been their thing on the weekends when she didn't have classes: late nights at his gigs; rushing back to his apartment because they couldn't keep their hands off each other; sleeping in late then strolling along Acland Street or Brunswick Street or one of the many Melbourne laneways to sample ice-cream. He'd been a rum'n'raisin or pistachio kind of guy, she was mint choc-chip or boysenberry swirl all the way. Not that it mattered which flavour they chose because they'd end up tasting each other's.

As she drove along Wattle Lane and spotted the lights on at Kody's, a pang of longing shot through her. What would it be like to come home to him every night, into his welcoming arms, with their daughter happy to have her parents cohabiting? An outlandish dream considering his lifestyle, but it was nice to fantasise for a moment.

Parking under the carport, she killed the engine and got out, balancing the desserts carefully. She'd cried enough tears after seeing her dad, no point risking more over mangled desserts if she dropped them. She'd made it halfway to the back door when it flung open and Isla ran out.

'Hey, Mum, what have you got there?'

Tash forced a smile. 'I swear you can sniff out Betty's creations a kilometre away.'

Isla called out, 'Told you she'd bring dessert,' before relieving Tash of the mousse cake.

'You know me that well, huh?'

'Duh.' Isla rolled her eyes, her smile radiant, and Tash knew spending time with Kody had a lot to do with that.

They had a great relationship and Tash counted herself lucky to have a daughter who liked to hug or chat with her. But Isla had been distant the last week and Tash knew why: she'd put her foot down about Isla trying to squeeze in evenings with Kody during the school week. It had been a decision purely based on concern for her daughter because she didn't want her falling behind in her studies, but Isla still viewed her as the bad guy.

Tash hated feeling like an ogre but it was her responsibility to be the voice of reason in this whole unexpected scenario. She was prepared to be lenient to a certain degree but she didn't want Kody getting the wrong idea: that once he left he'd have this same freedom of access to his daughter. Bad enough he'd be seen as the entertaining parent, taking Isla on grand adventures around the world. Tash had no hope of emulating that and she suspected Isla would want to spend more time with her cool dad. They'd have to draw up some kind of custody agreement to formalise coparenting arrangements and while the thought of not seeing Isla for a day let alone a week when it was Kody's turn for access turned her stomach, she knew it had to be done.

'Mum, are you okay?'

Tash blinked and shoved her thoughts aside, annoyed she'd started dwelling on stressful stuff again. 'Long day, sweetie,' she said, falling into step beside her daughter.

'Hope you're hungry, because we made pasta and salad.'

Isla bounced ahead of Tash and through the back door, oblivious to how that 'we' sent a stab of fear through her mother. It would be the first of many and logically Tash accepted that, but it didn't make hearing it any easier.

Bracing for a dinner filled with polite small talk and faux cheer, Tash stepped into the kitchen. She caught sight of Kody at the dining table dressing the salad and her sedate pulse immediately kicked. She remembered the normal range from her nursing days, between sixty and eighty beats per minute, and hers usually sat around the seventy-two mark. But she knew if she pressed her fingertips to her opposite wrist now that reading would be in triple figures.

As if sensing her stare, Kody raised his head and their eyes locked. And just like that her pulse shot from racing to catastrophic. He flashed her a tentative smile and she returned it, not surprised by their newfound shyness. He'd revealed a lot of himself last week and she wondered if he regretted it. She may have been avoiding him the last seven days but he'd done the same, which spoke volumes.

'I brought dessert,' she said, brandishing the crumble in her hands to break the deadlock between them.

'Great, thanks.' He was still hobbling but he moved with more ease than previously. 'What is it?'

'Rhubarb crumble,' Tash said, as Isla added, 'Chocolate mousse cake.'

'I'll have a double helping of both.' Kody smacked his lips and Isla laughed.

'You'll have to fight me for it, Dad,' she said, completely oblivious of the impact that one little label had on him.

But Tash saw it: the way his shoulders straightened a tad; the goofy softening of his mouth; the tenderness in his eyes.

He must've caught her staring at him because he mouthed, *Are you okay?*

She nodded, hating how astute he was but appreciating his intuition at the same time. He'd always been attuned to her moods, knowing when she had an exam coming up and her stress levels shot through the stratosphere, knowing when she needed to take a break, knowing when she wanted to lose herself in him.

The only time he hadn't guessed what she was thinking was when she'd revealed her pregnancy to him. A small part of her resented him for that. For a guy who could usually read her so easily, who'd spent countless evenings in her arms, who'd whispered shared confidences during the nights, the speed with which he believed her lie left her relieved yet disappointed. She'd wanted to drive him away, and she'd succeeded, but she'd assumed he knew her better than that.

'I'm starving,' Isla said, taking a seat between them and reaching for the bowl filled with steaming pasta. 'We kept it simple, Mum. Olive oil, garlic, bacon, sundried tomatoes.'

'Sounds good.' Tash held out her plate and Isla ladled a large serve of penne onto it, then some salad. She watched her do the same for Kody, inordinately proud of her daughter, who politely served her parents first. At home, they often had informal dinners curled up on the couch, cradling bowls of risotto or pasta while watching their favourite reality show. Tash knew the experts would frown upon that, citing family dinners should always be at a table. But Tash loved those nights on the couch and from what she could see, Isla had turned out just fine.

She stabbed at the penne and forked it into her mouth. Her appetite had fled around the time her father had yelled at her, but she'd have to make some show of eating to avoid an interrogation.

'I'm auditioning for a play at school,' Isla said. 'The drama teacher wanted us to do *Macbeth* or *Romeo and Juliet*, but our class said we want to write our own.'

Kody's eyebrows shot up, pride shining in his eyes. 'That's a big undertaking.'

'Yeah, I know.' Isla shrugged. 'But we want to ditch the usual and do something different.'

'Is it a musical?'

Isla rolled her eyes. 'Everything doesn't revolve around music, Dad.'

'Yeah, it does,' he said, and as they laughed, Tash felt more of an outsider than ever. Stupid to feel jealous when she'd had Isla all to herself for twelve years.

Sensing her discomfort, Kody shot her a concerned glance. As their gazes locked, her disquiet gave way to something else as heat filtered through her body like slow-moving lava. She clenched her thighs to stop herself from squirming under his intense gaze, wanting to break the deadlock but unable to look away.

'Coach says I should keep training so I can slot back into the netball team when my suspension is over,' Isla said, oblivious to the tension simmering between her parents. 'Pretty stupid though, training on my own, and I told her so.'

That caught Tash's attention and she turned to her daughter. 'Why would you do that?'

Isla's lips compressed in a mutinous line and she gave a slight shake of her head.

Kody opened his mouth but before he could say anything Tash jumped in. 'Isla, I asked you a question.'

Isla's fork hit her plate with a clatter as she glared at her. 'Because I was mad at you, okay? It was a few days after you told me about

Dad and I was angry you'd kept him from me and everything was topsy-turvy.'

Tash's heart sank. She'd been afraid of this, Isla bottling up her anger then letting it spill out. And as her daughter slouched in her chair, arms folded and looking anywhere but at her, she wondered if she'd been fooling herself by believing things would ever be the same between them again.

Kody shot her a sympathetic glance. 'What did the coach say after that?'

Tash watched her daughter revert to normal as she looked at Kody with open adoration.

'She told me off and extended my suspension for a week. Harsh, but I guess I shouldn't have spoken to her like that. I get it now.'

Tash swallowed, hating that Isla had taken so long to reveal this, hoping when she spoke her voice wouldn't reveal how damn miserable she felt at causing her daughter so much angst. 'Did you apologise?'

Isla nodded. 'Anyway, can we forget about it? I'm not mad anymore, Mum, and I'd really like dessert now.'

'I'll get it,' Tash said, eager to escape the table and Kody's all-seeing stare. Did he blame her for causing their daughter pain as much as she blamed herself? Did he know how truly crappy she felt?

As she sliced the cake and stuck a spoon into the crumble, she let Isla and Kody's chatter wash over her. They were so at ease with one another, so incredibly comfortable after knowing each other such a short time.

'When can I have another guitar lesson, Dad?'

Tash stilled. Isla's innocuous question reinforced the yawning gap between them and the close relationship her daughter had quickly built with Kody. The last time they were together he'd told her about being unable to touch a guitar let alone face anything to do with music, so for him to teach Isla how to play he'd undergone a massive shift. Had he sought professional help? Had he come to terms with the concert accident? She hoped so, because the world didn't deserve to be deprived of his talent. No other rock star had a voice like Kody's: deep, powerful, raw, with an underlying guttural edge that never failed to send a shiver down her spine. After he'd first approached her that fateful night at the pub, she'd been mesmerised by his voice and the bad boy on stage.

'How about you check your study schedule and get back to me?' He pointed at his walking boot. 'Because I'm not going anywhere.'

'Okay.' Isla swivelled on her seat to face her. 'Dessert ready, Mum?'

Tash quashed her feelings of being left out and nodded. 'Sure is.'

Tash placed the cake and crumble in the middle of the table, followed by bowls and spoons. When she passed Kody's chair, she resisted the urge to give his shoulder a reassuring squeeze to indicate she understood how huge teaching Isla guitar was for him. Instead, she resumed her seat and forced a chuckle as Isla and Kody tried to outdo each other in fitting the biggest spoonful of dessert into their mouths.

After finishing her tiny serve of chocolate mousse cake—turns out a sugar hit didn't ease the hurt inflicted by her father or the feeling of being ostracised in this pseudo family of three—she sent a pointed glance at the clock on a nearby wall. 'Isla, do you have homework to do?'

Isla rolled her eyes. 'Yeah.'

'Hey, kiddo, the more homework you get done every night, the more time you'll have to practise.'

'But I don't have a guitar.' Isla slouched in her seat, channelling every moody pre-teen on the planet.

'It's better to have a few lessons, see if you're really into it, before investing in an instrument,' Kody said.

Tash nodded her agreement.

'I guess.' Isla shrugged and straightened, eyeing another piece of cake. 'If I get to take some of that mousse cake home, I'll go now and get started on my homework.'

'Deal,' Tash and Kody said in unison, and this time, when Tash joined in Kody's laughter, she didn't have to force it.

'There are plastic containers in the cupboard over the sink,' Kody said, standing to help clear the table. 'Make sure you leave some for me, though.'

'No worries.'

To Tash's surprise, Isla made quick work of dishing the remaining cake and crumble into containers and snaffling one for herself before she picked up her backpack from near the door.

She waved. 'Great hanging out with you, Dad. See you at home, Mum.'

And with that she was gone, a whirlwind in her navy school uniform, jogging across the five hundred metres that separated their houses.

'She's in an awful hurry to get started on that homework,' Kody said.

'Yeah,' Tash said, wondering what Isla was up to and hoping her rush to leave the two of them alone wasn't some lame attempt to match-make. Dinner had been fine, but if Isla hoped to make it an ongoing thing she'd be sorely disappointed. Despite Tash's physical reaction to Kody, he'd be leaving sooner rather than later and no way would she encourage Isla to build false hope where her parents were concerned.

'I'll help clean up then I'll leave too,' she said, bustling around the table, stacking plates and bowls with expertise mastered at the roadhouse.

Kody smiled. 'Just how many of those can you carry without the whole lot tumbling to the floor?'

'This is nothing,' she said, giving a little jiggle that set the crockery clanking. 'You forget, I've been doing this for thirteen years.'

His lips compressed into a thin line. 'So you've waitressed all that time?'

'Yep,' she said, as she rinsed off the plates and stacked them in the dishwasher. 'I got a job at The Watering Hole not long after I returned to town and have been there ever since.'

'Do you like it?'

'I like having a job that pays the rent, the bills and whatever Isla wants to do.' She wondered if he heard a hint of resentment in her voice and rushed on: 'Plus it's rare to find a job where your co-workers are more like family and that's what Ruby, Alisha and Harry are.'

'You're close to them all?'

For a second Tash thought she glimpsed jealousy, but that probably had more to do with her overactive imagination than any real caring on Kody's part. Besides, even if she were involved with anyone, it was none of his business.

'Ruby is the new boss—her mum, Clara, gave me the job in the first place, but she died unexpectedly last year. Alisha is my best friend. And then there's Harry.' It was wrong of her to torment him but she wanted to see if her suspicions were correct. If his clenched jaw was any indication, she was spot on.

'You two are close?'

'Very.' She bit back a smile as she entwined her index and middle finger. 'Like this.'

'Right,' he said, sounding like it was anything but as he snatched up the salad bowl and stomped towards the sink.

'Then again, we're all close, considering Harry is Alisha's fiancé.'

Kody deliberately bumped her with his hip as he deposited the salad bowl in the sink. 'You think you're pretty funny, don't you?'

'As a matter of fact, I do.' She pulled an exaggerated frown. 'With you looking like this, I almost thought you were jealous.'

He carefully blanked his expression before speaking. 'Stands to reason I'd be curious if you were dating anyone, considering they'd be in Isla's life too.'

'I'm not,' she said, pinning him with a stare that conveyed she didn't believe his BS about Tash letting a man into Isla's life for a minute. 'What about you?'

'I've been on tour for the last fifteen months. It doesn't leave time for relationships.'

'So we're both single and loving it.' She rinsed off cutlery and separated the forks, spoons and knives into their respective dish-washer compartments to avoid looking at him in case he saw right through her lie. She may wear her single status like a badge of hon-our but she didn't love it. Every time she served happy couples at the roadhouse she experienced a tiny stab of envy, and attending school functions as a single parent drew the inevitable pitying glances. But there were few partner prospects in Brockenridge; none she'd want Isla close to, that is. Though the last thing she wanted was Kody thinking she was a sad spinster.

'Not sure if I love it so much,' he said, rinsing off the last of the bowls and standing way too close to her at the sink. 'It gets pretty lonely living on the road.'

Surprised by his honesty, she said, 'It's lonely here too, some-times, but I keep busy.'

'Busy doesn't keep you warm at night though.'

Tash turned to find herself almost toe to toe with him. She could see the widening of his pupils, the flecks of caramel in the chocolate, and the tiniest of scars beneath his right eye that she'd kissed many times before. She shouldn't have thought about kissing because that drew her focus to his mouth. The full, sexy mouth that could coax the most amazing responses from her, the mouth that crooned soulful rock ballads or belted out bangers, the mouth that had slayed her from their first hello.

As he moved infinitesimally closer, Tash had a second to put a stop to this madness. To back away. To make a joke. To laugh it off as an awkward moment between two old friends.

Instead, she stood there, frozen, as Kody's lips claimed hers.

CHAPTER
27

Kody had always been impulsive. Running away from a foster home for the first time age nine, punching a kid for calling him a snivelling bastard at ten, stealing his first bike at eleven. Stupid, rash decisions.

Those had nothing on giving in to the impulse to kiss Tash.

The moment his mouth fused with hers, he wondered how such a foolish action could feel so right. Her soft, pliable lips melded to his, warm and sensual, making him groan deep in his throat. Increasing the pressure, he savoured the way she met him halfway, challenging, demanding, giving as good as she got. Then her lips parted and he was a goner. He cupped the back of her head, raking his fingers through her hair, deepening the kiss until he could barely breathe. Their tongues tangled, slow and sensuous, the sexiest damn thing he'd done in a long time.

Eager for more, he backed her up against the island bench and plastered his body to hers, leaving her in little doubt of how much he wanted her. But the moment their pelvises aligned, she wrenched her mouth from his and stared over his shoulder, unable to meet his eyes.

Their ragged breathing echoed in the silence of the kitchen. They didn't speak. And when she finally raised her eyes to meet his, he knew her confusion and excitement and trepidation matched his.

'Don't expect me to apologise for that,' he said, sounding stupidly gruff when all he wanted to do was kiss her senseless again.

'I gave up expecting anything from you a long time ago.'

He didn't deserve her retort and the stricken widening of her eyes told him she knew it.

'That was way out of line and I'm sorry,' she said, placing a hand on his chest directly over his heart. 'You took me by surprise and I lashed out.'

'Took me by surprise too.' He couldn't help but grin. 'But that kiss was pretty damn amazing.'

She blushed, the slight upturning at the corners of her mouth making him want to kiss her again. 'As good as I remember.'

'Not better?'

'Now you're just fishing for compliments.' She patted his chest and lowered her hand, leaving him yearning for her touch. 'Let's chalk it up to an impulsive gesture at the end of a long day.'

He understood she didn't want to talk about it. No way in hell he wanted to analyse what had prompted him to give in to temptation, not when their lives were already complicated enough.

'Are you sure you're okay? You looked pretty shell-shocked when you first arrived.'

She ducked her head to close the dishwasher, but not before he glimpsed real sorrow in her eyes. Indignation flared swiftly; he wanted to throttle whoever had hurt her.

'I visited my parents today,' she said, with the slightest quiver in her voice. 'At least, that was the plan. But my mum was away so I only saw my dad.'

'And it didn't go well?'

She shook her head. 'I thought after all this time he might've softened, that he might even want to get to know his granddaughter ...'

'But?'

She blinked rapidly and he waited until she composed herself, his fingers curling into fists by his sides. He knew if he reached out to comfort her on the heels of that kiss, he might be tempted to do it all over again. That's the last thing she needed, not when she trusted him enough to offload about her crappy parents.

'He said I was still dead to them, so they didn't have a granddaughter.'

She sounded so forlorn he had to hold her. Outrage at her shitty father made him squeeze too tight and she quickly pulled away, casting a quizzical glance at him.

'Sorry. I don't know your dad but I'm bloody angry he'd treat you that way.'

'I should've known ...' She gave a little shake of head and squared her shoulders, as if coming to a decision. 'At least I tried and it's their loss. Isla's an amazing kid and if they don't want to find that out for themselves, too damn bad.'

'Absolutely.' He squeezed her arm. 'Are you okay with me teaching her guitar?'

'Of course.' A small smile played about her lips. 'I think it's great she can share that with you.'

'Have you given much thought to how this coparenting will work after I leave?' He didn't want to bring this up, not when they were getting along much better than a week ago, but at some point he'd be leaving and he wanted to get their custody arrangement locked down.

Predictably, the shutters descended, darkening her eyes, wiping her expression. 'Not really. We've got another month at least?'

He wanted to call out her blatant lie—as if she wouldn't be thinking about how custody would work. She loved Isla and, from what he'd seen, was a brilliant mother. Which probably explained her brush-off: she was scared about how sharing custody would work. Rather than push, he backed off a little.

'Yeah, but I don't want to leave it till the last minute to get something concrete in place.'

Her heartfelt sigh shot straight through his chest. 'Logically, I know we'll need lawyers to draw up some kind of agreement. But the sentimental part of me wants to give it more time to see how things go between you and Isla.'

He had no idea what she was implying. Did she think he'd turn his back on his daughter once he left? If so, she didn't know him at all and never had. He wouldn't have abandoned Isla if he'd known about her back in their dating days and he sure as hell wouldn't now.

'She's a part of my life, Tash, and that's not going to change.'

She must've heard the anger in his tone because she slipped her hand into his. 'I know, but I'm scared.'

'Of what?' He wanted to wrench his hand away. He didn't need her comfort. He needed her to see him as a responsible parent, a good father who'd do anything to make his child happy now he knew of her existence. But he didn't, because he needed to hear what she had to say, to reassure her that she could depend on him.

'I'm scared of letting Isla travel with you because she'll find living with you more appealing than staying here with me.' She swallowed, like the admission stuck in her throat. 'And I'm afraid of feeling redundant and alone when she's with you.'

Hell. He hadn't expected her to be so blunt but a part of him was glad she'd opened up. It meant they had hope, that they both had Isla's best interests at heart and would do whatever it took to ensure their daughter came first.

'You'll always be her mum and this town is her home. Travel will be glamorous for her but I'd never try and sway her to live with me permanently. You have to know that—right?'

After a long pause, she said, 'I don't know anything anymore. The moment you showed up here my life turned upside down and I'm still spinning because of it.'

'Are you sure that's not because of my kiss? Because I'm damn good at it, apparently.'

'Idiot.' She whacked him on the arm with her free hand, but at least her eyes had lost their haunted look. 'So exactly how many recommendations have you had over the years?'

He released her hand. They were nothing more than friends now. Who'd kissed. Once. And it couldn't happen again.

'I'm on the road most of the year and I'm the lead singer in a well-known band, so suffice to say I haven't been a monk.' He wiggled his eyebrows, determined to make her laugh. 'Jealous?'

Her gaze swept him from head to toe. 'Been there, done that.'

He laughed. 'You haven't lost your sense of humour. I like that.'

He liked a lot more than that but it wasn't the time or place to pursue whatever interest he may have in reigniting the spark between them. Because that kiss, and her response to it, suggested it would take little for them to fall into bed together and the last thing he needed was a fling before they'd settled their custody issues.

'I know we're joking around,' she said, her expression suddenly guarded, 'but I worry about Isla being exposed to … uh … the kind of lifestyle you lead.'

'And what kind of lifestyle is that? A healthy sexual relationship where both parties know the score?' He shook his head. 'I'm not an idiot. I wouldn't be parading women through my dressing room right in front of her. And that's even if I get back to touring.' His voice had risen and he hated the pity he saw in her eyes. He'd rather have her staring at him with interest, curiosity, even passion, than feeling sorry for him.

'You're playing guitar again, that's a start.'

'I wouldn't have done it for anybody but Isla,' he said, sounding grouchy and out of sorts and needing to rein it in. 'But I took your advice, and Yanni's, and have been chatting to a professional online.'

'That's great.'

'Anyway, I'm due to check in with the boys—' He didn't want to get into a discussion about it and he sensed that's exactly what she wanted.

'I'll get out of your way.'

A flicker of hurt crossed her face but he couldn't be swayed by it. Tash couldn't be his confidante, no matter how easy it was to talk to her. She'd always been a good listener and revealing his dreams to be a rock star hadn't seemed so ludicrous when spoken out loud to her. Ironic that, in telling her the truth about his ambitions, she'd chosen to not tell him the truth about her pregnancy because of how badly he craved success.

'No worries,' he said. 'I really enjoyed spending time with Isla today so if she could check her study schedule and squeeze me in more often, that'd be great.'

'Okay.' She paused. 'See you later.'

When she reached the back door, he said, 'Tash?'

She turned, hand on the doorknob. 'Yeah?'

Here went nothing. 'I like hanging out with you too. For Isla's sake, we need to be friends and if you can squeeze me into your busy schedule, I'd like to spend more time with you.'

'As friends.'

'That's what I said. Friends.' He winked. 'Who kiss occasionally.'

'You've always been a bad influence on me.' Her smile warmed his heart. 'But okay. What's the worst that can happen?'

He didn't want to contemplate that because he knew deep down spending time with Tash in a *friendly* capacity had the potential to morph into so much more. And damned if he was ready for it.

CHAPTER
28

'I'm really glad you wanted to meet for a coffee.' Jane raised her latte to Louise. 'Here's to many more catch-ups.'

Louise hesitated, before tapping her mug against Jane's glass. 'We've got a lot to catch up on.'

Jane agreed but she didn't know where to start, which is why she'd asked Louise to meet her at Betty's Bakery. Here they'd have stuff to talk about, at least, like the work she was doing with the redecoration.

'Shame Bec couldn't join us but she's parent helper in the classroom this morning and couldn't get out of it. She said she'll join us next time though.'

'That's great.' Jane wanted to make a fresh start in this town and what better way than getting reacquainted with her former best friends?

Louise placed her cup back in its saucer, eyeing her with wariness. 'You know the last time we bumped into each other at the supermarket and you warned me your mum was inside?'

Jane dropped the pistachio macaron she'd reached for, her appetite gone. 'Did you run into her?'

'Yeah. No offence, but your mum's a bitch.'

'Tell me something I don't know.' It had been over a week since Jane had seen her mother. Gladys had capitulated forty-eight hours after their conversation and the sale of the shop to Betty and Mason had proceeded without a hitch. Though Jane still wasn't clear on why her mother had given in.

'You two haven't been close since your dad died?'

Jane nodded. She didn't want to resurrect bad memories, but Louise was making an effort to reconnect and she couldn't shut her down immediately without appearing insensitive. 'Yeah, we had a falling out back then and haven't been able to patch things up since.'

'Do you want to? I mean, you reached out to me and I think it's great. And while Gladys seems horrible, maybe she's lashing out at you because she's hurt?'

Lashing out for a decade? Mighty long time to hold a grudge. Jane settled for a shrug. 'Maybe, but the one time I tried to set things right she pretended nothing was wrong and ignored me for a month. In the end, I gave up.'

'That's tough. My mum's been a godsend, helping me with the kids because Ed's a useless arsehole.' Louise gave a little shake of her head. 'Anyway, tell me about the work you're doing here.'

Grateful to her friend for changing the subject, Jane said, 'I'm loving it. Over the last few days I've confirmed colour schemes, sourced materials and contacted suppliers for furniture. It's going to be amazing.'

Mason had been pleased and signed off on her plans yesterday, giving her a sizeable budget to complete the redecoration. They'd agreed to meet here today to finalise preparations. She was relieved when he suggested they consult at the bakery, a perfectly safe environment where she couldn't spring him practically naked. That towel fiasco had stayed with her, the image of all that bronzed, bare skin popping into her mind when she least expected it. Very distracting if not unwelcome. Tall, blond guys weren't her type but there was something about Mason that rattled her on a level beyond the physical. And she knew what the attraction was: he expected the worst from her, but still had the capacity to tease her. He disarmed and terrified her, because she thought she could really like this guy given half a chance.

'You practically glow when you talk about interior designing,' Louise said. 'I remember your folders being perfectly colour coordinated in high school, depending on the subject.'

'Pity I spent more time decorating my folders than opening them to actually study.'

'You and me both, babe.'

They laughed like they had many times in the past. At least Jane could appreciate this change in her life. Reconnecting with her bestie was the smartest thing she'd done in a long time.

Louise's mobile buzzed and she glanced at the screen. Her face fell. 'That's the school. I dropped my three off this morning but looks like my eldest is wagging again. The school sends a text if they're not there for roll call.'

'Go,' Jane said. 'We'll catch up another time.'

Louise stood and grabbed her bag. 'Sorry about this.'

'Don't worry.' Jane stood and hugged Louise, and for the first time since they'd started talking again, Louise hugged her back properly. 'I know your life is way more hectic than mine, so text me when you're free again, okay?'

'Thanks, and I'll make sure to drag Bec along too.'

As Jane watched Louise hurry out the door, she didn't envy her friend the stress of dealing with three kids and an inept, cheating husband. But she had enjoyed catching up, however briefly, and valued the distraction. Because now she'd have too many hours to mull her upcoming meeting with Mason.

When Jane arrived home, she spied a box on her doorstep. She was expecting colour samples for the bakery walls and Tom from the local hardware shop had said he'd deliver some swatches to her today. However, when she got out of the car and strode up the path to her door, she noticed the package was wrapped in Betty's Bakery's distinctive paper. Intrigued, she lifted the box to her nose and inhaled, savouring the sugary vanilla aroma.

She took her mystery delivery into the kitchen and laid it on the table. The box weighed a tonne and when she tore off the paper she saw why: a large vanilla sponge topped with pale pink icing took pride of place in the centre of the box, the ornate turquoise lettering making her smile.

I DECORATE CAKES, YOU DECORATE ROOMS.

Mason. An unexpectedly sweet, corny gesture, but she couldn't figure out why. They'd been nothing but professional with one another since she last saw him and this cake reeked of sentimentality. It reminded her of her dad, who'd regularly bestowed flowers and chocolates on Gladys, trying to show how much he cared.

And it had been a lie, all of it.

She swiped a finger through some of the frosting and popped it into her mouth. Creamy and smooth, with a hint of rosewater. Delicious. As tempted as she was to cut herself a giant piece and eat the lot, she had to finish the last of her presentation and head back to the bakery. She had a job to do and impressing Mason had become incredibly important. Not because she wanted to make up for her shoddy behaviour towards him in the past, but because, for the first time in forever, she valued what a man thought of her.

Not that she was under any illusions. She didn't expect them to have a relationship beyond professional. And if she were foolish enough to succumb to his obvious charms, it would end like all the other 'relationships' she'd ever had: short-term gain, long-term pain. She was tired of flings. She deserved better.

After a solid ninety minutes of work, she slid her laptop into its case, gathered her portfolio and headed for the door, pausing briefly in front of the hall mirror to check her appearance. She hadn't dyed her hair in months and darker strands wound through the blonde, giving the appearance of artfully applied highlights. She wore it in a ponytail most days but had blow dried it into a sleek, glossy curtain today—for professional reasons, of course. Yeah, she had to keep telling herself that and forget seeing him in that damn towel.

Today would get them back on track. Work focussed. Business-like. Minimal flirting. She repeated that mantra for the ten minutes it took to reach the bakery, park her car and strut in like a woman on a mission. The vanilla and cinnamon aromas in the air always comforted her. But today, not even the familiarity of those sweet smells could quell her nerves as Betty caught sight of her from behind the counter and pointed at the shop next door.

Of course Mason would be waiting there for her, prompt and professional. She could handle that. What she couldn't handle was imagining things that weren't there, like the desire in his eyes when she'd asked if he still wanted her for the job and he'd replied 'abso-lutely'. She'd pondered that response for days, mentally chastising herself for being foolish and reading too much into it. Heck, the guy had lived in France for five years, stood to reason he'd be a flirting expert. For the next hour or so, she would have to remind herself of that and not try to interpret every glance or comment.

She entered the empty shop with a giant red 'sold' sticker on the window and spotted Mason standing behind the counter. Jane could barely remember what this place had been used for—possibly a dry cleaners? It had been closed since her early teens. Had Mason harboured a dream of expanding his mum's bakery since then? Driven to fulfil his potential while she'd been strutting around high school pretending she owned the world? It irritated, knowing so little about him. The one person she could ask, Betty, would get the wrong idea if Jane started delving into what made Mason tick.

'I see you've come prepared,' Mason said by way of greeting, gesturing at her portfolio and laptop.

'I'm keen to get started.' She placed her stuff on the counter and stood beside him. 'Thanks for the cake, by the way.'

'I was experimenting and Mum said you loved vanilla so I thought you might like to be a guinea pig.' He grinned. 'I tried to come up with a better message but "I decorate cakes, you decorate rooms" seemed fitting.'

'Yeah, poetry isn't your strong suit, so keep your day job.'

He laughed and leaned against the shelf behind the counter, making his biceps bulge nicely. 'If you decorate as well as I bake, this place will be spectacular.'

'Confident, much?'

'I know when I'm good at things,' he said, his gaze challenging her, daring her to imagine all sorts of scenarios where he'd be better than good.

Damn it. Time to get back on track.

'Now that you've approved the budget, I'll get onto the tradesmen who specialise in the fancy cornices we want. Some may be between jobs, others may be working, so I might have to outsource to Echuca and that may involve higher costs. Are you okay with that?'

'Absolutely. I want this place up and running ASAP.'

Her heart skipped a beat. He wanted to get out of town sooner rather than later. Considering the cosmopolitan lifestyle he must lead in Paris, she didn't blame him. She shouldn't care but a small part of her did, the part that had developed a wee crush on the sexy pastry chef.

'Any particular reason?' She tried to sound blasé but, going by his knowing smirk, had failed miserably.

'Go on, admit it. You'll miss me when I leave.'

Her brain latched onto one word: *when*. Of course he was leaving.

'You've done nothing but misjudge me since you've come back to town, so yeah, I'm going to miss that a whole lot.' She rolled her eyes and he laughed.

'Butting heads can be fun,' he said, lowering his voice. 'Nothing like a bit of strenuous discussion as foreplay.'

She stilled. He was thinking about sex? With her? As tempted as she was to clamber all over him, she knew sleeping with him before the job was done would be misconstrued. People in this town would say she'd slept her way to the decorating job. They'd say she'd reverted to type. And they'd make sure her mother heard about it. That's the last thing Jane wanted, to give Gladys any ammunition to say, 'I was right.'

So she ignored his innuendo when every cell in her body wanted to spar with him a little longer.

'Want to see the final plans?'

He hesitated and she silently willed him not to push her; there was only so much willpower a girl had to hold out against his charms. When he gave a little shake of his head, as if telling himself to snap out of it, she breathed a sigh of relief.

'Sure.' He patted the counter in front of him so she slid the port-folio and laptop out and opened her presentation.

For the next fifteen minutes he scrutinised and questioned and argued a few points but she held her own and by the end they'd agreed on everything. This would be a good job for her and would go a long way to highlighting her skills. Her website needed a revamp so updating it with this job front and centre would be excellent promotion. Though what sold anything in this town was word of mouth and once happy patrons flocked to the new patisserie, she had little doubt her own interior design dreams would flourish. With a little luck, more people would trust her to decorate their places and she could start up a business. She was tired of not working. Donating anonymously to charities hadn't won her any favour with the locals, and while she'd given money without expecting kudos, she now wanted to be recognised in this town rather than ridiculed.

After she wound down her presentation, Mason said, 'Good job. Now that's out of the way, I want to mention something to you, but I don't want you thinking I'm prying, okay?'

'Okay.'

He looked positively uncomfortable and she wondered what on earth he had to say.

'While the deal went through the real estate agent, once I'd signed the papers I got a call from the owner.'

Jane's heart sank. 'My mother.'

He nodded. 'She warned me against working with you.'

'What did you say?'

'That your work is flawless and I'm looking forward to seeing your talents showcased in the new patisserie.'

To her mortification, tears stung her eyes. She didn't need anyone defending her, least of all some guy who probably thought gallantry was part of his assumed French persona, but the fact he had made her want to hug him all the same.

'Thanks.'

'That's it?'

'What do you want me to say?'

'A little insight into why your mother has a vendetta against her only child might be nice.'

'Why?' She gestured at the empty space around them. 'Her opinion has nothing to do with my work here, as you so kindly reiterated to her.'

An awkward silence stretched between them, before he finally said, 'Because I can't fathom why a mother would go to such lengths to badmouth her daughter.'

'Betty is an amazing mum, sweet and non-judgemental. In fact, I've offloaded to her at the bakery more times than I can count and she's been more supportive than Gladys. So you wouldn't understand what it's like to grow up with a mother who doesn't care about anybody but herself, who only values appearances, who thrives on the adulation of those around her and if she doesn't get it ... let's just say it's not pretty.'

'I'm sorry,' he murmured, taking a few steps towards her to bridge the distance between them. 'It's none of my business, but I didn't want her sabotaging your work here.'

'Because it's all about the patisserie, right?' she snapped, immediately embarrassed, because he didn't deserve her bitter retort.

'You're wrong,' he said, reaching up to cup her face with his hand.

Her breath hitched as his thumb swept along her jaw, then her cheek, before coming to rest at the corner of her mouth.

'This is about you,' he whispered, a moment before his mouth covered hers in a searing kiss that scorched any lingering sadness and made her reach for him, clinging onto his polo shirt for purchase so she didn't slither to the floor in a swooning heap. She may have fantasised about the way he'd kiss after seeing him in that towel but her imagination didn't do justice to the reality.

He kissed like a dream. Strong and commanding, sensual yet tender. Alternating the pressure, sweeping his tongue into her mouth, challenging her to meet him halfway. And she did. For a blissful few moments she gave herself over to the pleasure of having a guy she lusted after fancy her right back.

But this was wrong. She couldn't fall into old habits. She wouldn't. Rebuilding her self-esteem depended on it.

So she broke the kiss with reluctance, opening her eyes to find him staring at her with a startling mix of desire and pity.

That's when it hit her.

He hadn't kissed her out of any grand passion—he'd felt sorry for her.

And the realisation made her knees wobble more than his damned kiss.

'I need to go,' she said, gathering up her things. 'I'll be in touch about the contractors.'

He tried to grab her arm. 'Jane, wait—'

'No.' She spun out of his grip and strode to the door, determined not to cry in front of him. 'We've got work to do, so let's forget that damn pity kiss and move on.'

He stared at her, open-mouthed, before she barged out and slammed the door.

CHAPTER
29

'I'm really glad you girls talked me into a bridal shower.' Alisha held up a champagne flute filled to the brim. 'Here's to me being pampered like a maharani.'

'To you,' Tash and Ruby echoed, clinking glasses with the bride to be. 'Though technically this isn't a shower, with only three of us,' Tash added.

Alisha waved away her concern. 'I don't want a bunch of hangers-on who don't really know me celebrating my upcoming nuptials. It's better with just us.'

'I agree.' Ruby tipped half the champagne down her throat in one go. 'Though I can't believe you wouldn't let us organise a stripper, especially after Brenda couldn't make it because she's unwell.'

'And a penis cake,' Tash said, tut-tutting. 'What's a bridal shower without some crass weenie paraphernalia?'

Ruby laughed and Alisha rolled her eyes. 'I'm getting married at forty-three. That corny stuff's for innocent young things with hearts in their eyes, blinded by unrealistic expectations and dreams of happily ever after.'

'Cynical, much?' Tash slugged Alisha on the arm, spilling her champagne in the process. 'We see the way you look at Harry and there are definitely hearts in your eyes.'

'Maybe.' Alisha's goofy grin belied her tough words. 'Doesn't mean I want to see any fake dicks.'

The three of them laughed until tears streamed from their eyes. Tash needed this, some bonding time with her friends, far from rock gods and the memory of a kiss she couldn't forget no matter how hard she tried.

Ruby held her stomach. 'I haven't laughed this hard in ages.'

'Same here,' Tash said, reaching for the salt and vinegar chips to pass around. 'Are you sure this is enough, Lish? Don't you want to go out dancing or something?'

Alisha shook her head. 'Having a spa day, relaxing with my best buds, is perfect.' She raised her glass in another toast. 'To a bridal shower filled with laughter, champagne and gossip.'

Ruby clinked her glass. 'And to a phallic-free zone.'

'I'll drink to that,' Tash said, clinking her glass with the others before downing her champagne in a few gulps.

When she reached for the bottle to top up, Alisha covered her glass with her hand. 'Hey, slow down, missy. I want you conscious for our rom-com marathon.'

'I'm fine,' Tash said, accentuating her false declaration with an ill-timed hiccup.

Ruby giggled as Alisha pinned her with an astute stare. 'What's going on? You rarely drink and certainly not that fast.'

'Can't a girl enjoy her bestie's bridal shower without getting the third degree?' To her chagrin, however, she blushed and her friends pounced.

'Ooooh, what's going on?' Ruby asked at the same time as Alisha said, 'Something's up with you.'

Knowing they wouldn't let up, Tash gave a small nod. 'Okay, I'll tell you, if I can top up my glass.'

'Done.' Alisha removed her hand and Tash filled her glass to the brim. She'd have a mighty headache tomorrow but how long had it been since she'd done this, let loose with friends, secure in the knowledge that Isla was with someone who loved her as much as she did? Though she couldn't think about that, because the speed with which Kody had bonded with their daughter terrified her, especially when he seemed determined to sort out their custody arrangement sooner rather than later.

She wanted him to recover from his accident, and to heal from the trauma of witnessing those deaths in Wellington, but she knew every day that passed brought her a step closer to losing Isla. Not permanently, but the thought of rattling around her house on her own whenever Isla spent time away with Kody made her stomach clench with dread. Stupid, because she'd known it would come to this when Kody first arrived next door. That didn't make it any easier to accept.

After downing another healthy slurp of champagne that left her head spinning slightly, Tash blurted, 'Kody kissed me.'

Alisha let out a loud 'Woo hoo!' while Ruby gave a maniacal laugh like she'd already imbibed too much champers.

'It's not funny, guys, I'm confused and worried and thoroughly bamboozled.'

'So I take it you told Rubes about Kody being Isla's dad.' Alisha poked her in the arm.

Tash nodded. 'Nice to know you two don't gossip about me, otherwise you would've already known that.'

'I've been a bit preoccupied with all this wedding hoopla.'

'Plus I never gossip,' Ruby said, pretending to be affronted. 'But if I did ...' Ruby fanned her face. 'Man, I love Connor, but you've had sex with a rock star and I'm so bloody jealous!'

They broke into champagne-fuelled giggles.

'Does he pluck at your heartstrings?' Ruby imitated playing a guitar.

'I bet he strums real good,' Alisha said, complete with suggestive hand movements.

'Does he have a large plectrum?' Ruby guffawed at that one and attempted to pat herself on the back.

'Stop.' Tash held up a hand while pressing the other to her side where she had a stitch from laughing so hard.

'I can't believe this.' Ruby shook her head. 'It's like something out of a soap opera, but it's happening right here in Brockenridge, to someone I know.'

'And love,' Alisha added, leaning over to sling an arm across Tash's shoulder and hug her.

'Yeah.' Ruby nodded. 'We love you, Tash, but I'm still a little green about you bonking Australia's rock god.'

'Many times.' Tash tilted her chin in the air, trying to channel haughtiness, and ending up spilling more champagne.

Alisha righted her glass. 'Tell us more about the kiss.'

'And don't leave out a thing,' Ruby added. 'We want to know everything.'

But Tash couldn't tell them everything. She couldn't divulge the shame that haunted her in the wee small hours when she lay awake in bed, regretting how she'd lied to Kody about having an abortion. She couldn't reveal her terror at the prospect of coparenting with someone as wealthy as Kody because she could never compete and she feared Isla would come to love him more. And she sure as hell couldn't articulate one of her greatest fears: that she'd fall for him all over again and he'd break her heart.

It had nearly killed her to walk away from him thirteen years ago. Letting him in this time around would be a sure-fire way to ensure he shattered her heart once and for all.

Intuitive as ever, Alisha gave her a gentle nudge. 'You don't have to talk about it if you don't want to, but it might help to get our impartial take on it?'

'You're not impartial, you're on my side,' Tash said. 'I hope.'

'Of course we are, sweetie.' Ruby squeezed her hand. 'But you look kind of shell-shocked so it might help to talk about it.'

Where to start? 'Kody was furious I hadn't told him about Isla all those years ago and I don't blame him—I robbed him of her entire childhood. But he seems to have made his peace with it and we've been getting along better, like friends. Then a few nights ago he'd been looking after Isla and they invited me over for dinner too, and after Isla went home to do homework ...' She shrugged, like that momentous kiss meant little. 'He kissed me.'

'How romantic.' Ruby sighed, while Alisha simply tilted her head to one side, studying Tash.

'That's a complication waiting to happen.'

'Don't listen to her.' Ruby whacked Alisha on the arm. 'She's the least romantic bride I know.'

'That's because I'm a realist,' Alisha said. 'How do you feel about it, Tash?'

'Honestly? The kiss was amazing, better than I remembered. And it made me fall for him a little all over again. But you're right, it's complicated.'

Ruby snapped her fingers. 'Because you'll have to sort out custody issues, yeah?'

Tash nodded. 'And the whole thing terrifies me.'

'Is he fair?' Alisha asked, worry clouding her eyes. 'Or do you think he's cosying up to you to screw you over?'

'I didn't before but I do now,' Tash said drily, as Ruby glared daggers at Alisha.

'Don't listen to her,' Ruby said. 'She's just bitter because we didn't get her those penis cookies she secretly craved.'

'Again with the dicks.' Alisha rolled her eyes. 'Seriously, Tash, what are you going to do?'

'Well, I'm not going to kiss him again for starters.' Then again, she shouldn't make any promises she couldn't keep. Because she wanted to kiss him again, desperately. Maybe more. The moment he'd pressed his lips to hers, he'd rekindled embers she'd thought long doused. She still felt something for him.

So yeah, whatever happened between them was one giant complication waiting to happen.

'How's Isla handling all this?' Alisha asked, as Ruby frowned at her for steering the conversation away from the juicy stuff. 'I take it she doesn't know about the kiss?'

Tash choked on a sip of champagne at the thought. 'Hell, no. I don't want her getting her hopes up that her parents would ever reunite when that's not going to happen.' She sighed. 'She's head over heels for Kody, understandably. He's a pretty good guy and he's a rock star, so stands to reason she'd be gaga over him.'

'And he's good with her?' Alisha sipped at her drink, her expression thoughtful. 'Then again, that's a dumb question, because she wouldn't be with him now if he wasn't.'

Tash nodded. 'I love seeing the two of them bond and the relationship they're developing, but it hurts here too.' She pressed a hand over her heart. 'I did the wrong thing keeping them apart and I can never take it back.'

'Oh, sweetie, no use looking back and wishing things were different,' Ruby said, leaning in for a quick hug. 'I regret not coming back to Brockenridge before Mum died, but I try to focus on the roadhouse and keeping her legacy alive. Maybe you should focus on the future too?'

A sound plan, but how did Tash do that when all she could see in her future was too many empty days while Isla was swanning around the world with her dad?

Catching sight of Alisha's worried expression, Tash knew she had to lighten the mood. It wasn't fair, hijacking Alisha's special day, when she wanted her friend to have fun.

'I think we've had enough Kody talk and it's time to do those honey facials now.'

Their conversation turned to Alisha's wedding plans as they slathered masks on their faces, painted each other's nails and teased Alisha endlessly about the wedding night, which the couple had chosen to spend on a luxury houseboat on the Murray. There was lots of banter along the lines of 'if this boat is a rockin', don't come a knockin'', which kept Tash suitably distracted.

Until Ruby swiped her finger over her phone screen, scrolling through something, and let out a squeal. 'Oh my goodness, I can't believe I didn't think of this before. We still don't have a band for that blues night and you know how feral locals get if we don't have live music on those nights. So why don't you ask Kody if he could fill in? Nothing major, just a few songs ...' Ruby trailed off as she noticed Tash's stricken expression. 'Not a good idea?'

Tash fiddled with the seal on a box of chocolates, trying to come up with a refusal that wouldn't entail betraying Kody's confidence.

'Tash?' Ruby touched her arm and took the box out of her hands. 'It was just an idea.'

'And a good one, but Kody's taking some time out from the hectic touring life and that's why he's in Brockenridge.'

Ruby nodded. 'I get it. Being on the road all the time would be tough. And I read about the accident at Rock Hard Place's last concert in Wellington so it stands to reason he'd want to take some time out. But do you think you could ask him?' Ruby faked puppy dog eyes. 'For me?'

Playing to a packed house at The Watering Hole would be the last thing Kody would want, not when he valued his anonymity and was hiding out to preserve it. But Ruby was her boss as well as her friend and she couldn't refuse.

'Okay, I'll ask, but expect the answer to be no.'

'Maybe you can sweeten your request with a kiss or two?' A sly glint lit Ruby's eyes as she made smooching noises.

Alisha stifled a laugh and Ruby pointed at Tash's face. 'You should see your expression, it's priceless.'

'I'm never telling you two anything ever again,' she said, miming a zipping action across her lips.

'We'll just ply you with alcohol and drag all your secrets out that way.' Ruby reached for the second champagne bottle. 'Starting now.'

CHAPTER
30

Kody had never considered himself an emotional guy. He'd learned from a young age to close off, not get too close to people, and never trust easily. He'd put up metaphorical barriers to keep hurt at bay and retreated behind a wall of practised indifference or deliberate cockiness. He'd been labelled everything from smart-arse to dickhead to emotionally stunted and he'd never let it bother him.

So what had happened to make that guy feel like his chest had been split open every time he looked at his wondrous daughter?

He'd jumped at the chance to have Isla stay overnight when Tash had asked if he could mind her while she threw a bridal shower for her bestie, and had looked forward to it. Considering Isla had been practising guitar for the last hour without any signs of stopping, she seemed to be having a good time too.

'Hey, it's bedtime soon, so do you want a snack?'

'Mum lets me stay up till eleven so we've got plenty of time.'

He didn't buy that for a second. 'Eleven, really?'

Isla looked away, suitably shame-faced. 'Ten at the latest and that's only if I've got home late after drama or netball practice and have a stack of homework.'

'That's better,' he said. 'So how about that snack?'

'Okay. Though I could play guitar all night, I love it that much.'

He did too and the fact his daughter had inherited his talent made him choke up every time he listened to her. This was their fourth session; Tash had been surprisingly accommodating. Then again, she seemed in a rush whenever he'd rung, like she didn't want to talk to him and would agree to anything if it got him off the phone quickly. Looked like that kiss had shocked the hell out of her too. Neither of them had the guts to bring it up again but he would, eventually, because after several more sessions with the online psych he'd come to a few decisions, the major one being forgive and forget.

Not that he could ever forget Tash's decision to keep him oblivious to Isla's existence, but he could forgive. He would. And he needed to tell her that in person. He had it all planned out. A lunch, maybe a picnic, so he wouldn't be tempted to kiss her again and drag her into the nearest bedroom. Nothing overtly romantic, because he wasn't in the right headspace to start any kind of relationship, least of all with the only woman he'd ever truly had feelings for. Just a tension-free lunch where he could bring up topics they'd rather avoid: like setting the past to rest once and for all, and making a start on the custody discussion. Spending more time with Isla reinforced how badly he wanted to be in her life.

He still had no idea how it would work. She couldn't be dragged out of school regularly, which meant he'd be reduced to school holidays with her. Three term breaks of two weeks each and the six-week summer holidays—it seemed not nearly enough. Depending on his schedule, he could squeeze in trips to Australia and spend time with her here, but he didn't want to disrupt her life any more than he had to. Would she be distracted by brief visits? Would she resent him constantly leaving her? Would she hate Tash for keeping them apart?

That was another decision he'd come to over the last week. Hiding out here indefinitely, leaving his band mates hanging, wasn't good. Picking up a guitar again hadn't made his head implode. The grief at the senseless deaths of those concert-goers was still fresh, and may never leave him, but what kind of example would he be setting Isla if he gave up his passion altogether? Walking away from Rock Hard Place would gut him, and cause a massive stir in the music industry. Questions would be asked. Fans and paparazzi would demand answers. His past would be dug into. Tash, and in turn Isla, would be exposed to muckraking. He wouldn't put them through that. So he'd have to go back. Back on the road, on tour, thrust into the limelight he adored but which now seemed somewhat hollow after this quiet time with his daughter.

Isla played a loud, jarring chord that gave him a jolt.

'Dad, what about that snack you promised?'

He gave a mock bow. 'Coming right up, princess.'

She chuckled and went back to strumming as he headed to the kitchen. Along with his psyche, his ankle felt stronger every day and he couldn't wait to get rid of the walking boot. He laid out crackers and was slicing cheese to top them when his phone rang where it lay on the bench top. One glance at the screen had his heart beating faster: Tash.

Wiping his hands, he reached for the phone and hit the answer button. 'Hey.'

'Hey yourself,' she said too loudly, her words slurred slightly, and he heard giggling in the background.

'Are you drunk?'

'Pleasantly tipsy.'

He bit back a grin as he heard a muted belch. 'Everything all right?'

'Never better. How's Isla?'

'She's great. I'm making her a snack.' He heard collective sighs. 'Do you have me on speakerphone?'

'Noooooo ...' More laughter and he smiled, glad she was having a good time with her friends. 'Okay, yes, but that's only because Alisha and Ruby are bugging me to ask you something and they won't let up until I do.'

'Okay, shoot.'

'Uh ... it's okay to say no ... and I don't even want to ask you this ... but ...'

'Oh, for goodness sake,' he heard someone mutter, followed by a loud 'Ow!' from Tash that he assumed came from being poked in the ribs.

'Okay, I'll ask him,' Tash muttered. 'Ruby owns the roadhouse where I work and she runs these great theme nights that locals flock to. We can't get a band for one of the blues nights and she's already sold a shitload of tickets, so she was wondering if you could play instead.'

Fear, swift and potent, shot through Kody and he broke out in a cold sweat. Stupid, because he'd just been thinking of returning to the touring circuit, but thinking about it and taking the first step towards actually doing it were poles apart. What if he froze the first time on stage? What if he couldn't squeeze the words past his tight throat? What if he had a panic attack in front of everyone as the memories of clogging smoke and terrified screams overtook him?

'It's dumb, I know, because you're on hiatus. But Ruby is hassling me and she says she'll prank call every old geezer in the district from my phone unless I ask.'

'Let me think about it, okay?'

That stunned them into silence. It even shocked Kody a little. He should've said no. Playing in a country roadhouse would bring a ton of attention he didn't want. It would ruin the rest of his quiet leave and infiltrate what precious time he had left with Isla. But at least it would answer the question of whether he could still perform.

'Wow, thanks,' Tash said, sounding like she couldn't believe he'd practically agreed.

'I haven't said yes yet, but maybe I could check out the place before I make a decision?'

'Absolutely,' someone yelled, while another woman let out a whoop.

'Ruby and Alisha are stoked,' Tash said. 'Just give me a minute, okay? I want to talk to you without an audience.'

He heard a yelled 'Spoilsport!' before the background noise shut off.

After a few moments, Tash said, 'Sorry to ambush you like that.'

'No worries.' Though there were plenty, most of them centred on his fear of performing and making an ass of himself.

'Listen, I know how tough this will be for you, so take your time deciding.'

'Actually, I want to talk to you about a lot of stuff. Can we have lunch together some time soon?'

'Uh, sure. I'm rostered on to work the next five days so how about next Friday?'

He hated having to wait that long; it left him too much time to stew. But it would have to do. 'That's fine.'

'Great. Kiss Isla goodnight for me.'

'Will do.'

For some inane reason, he didn't want her to hang up. Tash grounded him, always had, and chatting to her made him more relaxed.

'So how's the bridal shower going?'

'Good, but I'll have a headache in the morning.' She groaned.

He laughed. 'Keep the paracetamol handy.'

'Hopefully if I drink a litre or two of water before bed I'll be right.'

He remembered another time long ago when she'd tried the same remedy. They'd been high on the rush of the band's first sold-out gig at a pub not far from the Princeton and had done tequila shots. Tash had been a lightweight with alcohol so had been hilariously tipsy after three shots and a beer chaser. But she'd sworn that drinking copious glasses of water before bed would help. It hadn't. She'd spewed twice when they got back to his studio and had ended up making several trips to the loo overnight.

He shouldn't bring up the past, not when so much had happened—not all of it good—since. But he couldn't help himself. 'That theory didn't work so well for you the last time. Remember the tequila shots?'

'Don't remind me.'

Silence stretched between them before she added, 'We had some fun times together.'

'Holding back your hair as you barfed wasn't so much fun for me.'

She chuckled. 'I meant the rest. The dating. The gigs. The dinners.'

'Yeah, we were good together.' The admission came out of nowhere. Tash had hurt him badly when she'd walked away from him, and it had taken him a long time to get over it. He'd thrown himself into a party lifestyle in LA, sleeping with women the antithesis of her in order to move on, and writing a stack of ballads filled with heartbreak and bitterness. But he couldn't hold onto the past, not when a product of their relationship sat in the next room playing a song he'd taught her earlier tonight.

'I miss us ...'

At first he thought he'd imagined it, but then Tash rushed on, 'Don't listen to me. Alcohol makes me maudlin, which is why I rarely drink these days.'

Kody wanted to say, 'I miss us too' but he didn't want this conversation heading down a track of reminiscing and false promises. Because he couldn't give Tash anything beyond being a father to Isla, no matter how much a small part of him yearned otherwise.

'See you in the morning,' he said, hanging up before he changed his mind and blurted exactly how much he wished things were different between them.

CHAPTER
31

Jane always hibernated when life got too much for her. Back in high school, after she'd driven Ruby out of Brockenridge on the night of the graduation ball, she'd spent a week holed up in her room, listening to music and bingeing on chocolate. Gladys hadn't cared. She'd only checked on her once in that time to warn her against consuming too much sugar because her skin and hips would bear the brunt. Because heaven forbid any child of perfect Gladys Jefferson spoil her appearance.

These days, she wallowed in peace. Any time her self-esteem took a hit, usually after hooking up with the wrong guy, she'd hide away at home with a well-stocked freezer of ice-cream and as many rom-coms as she could physically watch in a day—or three.

After that disastrous kiss with Mason she'd stopped at the supermarket on the way home and stocked up on ice-cream and family-sized chocolate blocks. Now, with her favourite rom-com of all time, *Notting Hill*, ready to roll, she pulled a fleece throw rug over her legs and cradled a bowl of strawberry swirl. However, she'd barely swallowed her first spoonful of ice-cream when her doorbell rang.

She ignored it. What was the point of hibernating if you answered the door? But it rang again, several times. Then she heard Mason's booming voice.

'I know you're home, Jane, and I'm not going away until you open the door.'

Damn it. She could ignore him but she didn't want their first meeting after the kiss to be at the bakery with contractors looking on.

Calling him unsavoury names under her breath, she stomped to the door and opened it a fraction. 'I'm busy.'

'It's four o'clock and you're in your pyjamas.'

'I'm tired,' she said, angling her body behind the door. The most important part of hibernating was lounging around in the oldest pair of PJs she owned, which happened to be covered in emojis.

'Okay.' He didn't sound convinced, but worse—he didn't budge. 'Can I come in?'

'No. I'm not dressed for company.'

'I can see that.' He grinned, as his gaze dropped to her visible pyjama sleeve. 'Is that poop emoji reserved for me?'

Damn him for pulling out the big guns. She'd always been a sucker for a sense of humour.

'What do you want?'

'To clear up a misconception,' he said, leaning closer. 'And unless you want your neighbours hearing all the reasons why I'd never kiss you out of pity, you better let me in.'

She didn't want to have this conversation. She wanted to wallow for an evening then front up at the bakery to get started on the interior design and pretend that kiss, and her over-the-top reaction, never happened. She'd expected him to do the same; what man wanted to rehash anything remotely connected to emotions? Though considering his occupation, maybe Mason was more in touch with his sensitive side than she wanted him to be.

'Fine,' she said, swinging the door open and letting him in. 'But you're interrupting my movie.'

'What are you watching?'

'*Notting Hill.*'

She expected him to scoff but to her surprise, his eyes lit up. 'I love Julia Roberts and Hugh Grant in that.'

'Now you're just sucking up,' she said, trudging into the lounge room ahead of him.

'No, I'm being honest,' he said, taking her arm and swinging her around to face him. 'Just like I'm being honest when I say I kissed you out of many things, and pity wasn't one of them.'

She shrugged. 'Whatever.'

'I mean it, Jane.' He lifted his other hand so he held both her arms, not giving her much room to move let alone look anywhere but directly at him. 'I like you. And I kissed you because I like you. That's it.' An embarrassed flush crept into his cheeks. 'I probably shouldn't have because we're sort of working together and I don't want to mess with that. But you're nothing like I remembered in high school and I feel like an idiot for judging you without getting to know the real you. You're sweet and sexy and I want to get to know you better.'

What could a girl in hibernation say to that, other than, 'Do you want ice-cream while we watch the movie?'

'Hell, yeah.' He placed an all-too-brief kiss on her lips. 'You sure it's okay if I stay?'

'Shut up and press play on the remote,' she said, slipping out of his grasp before she did something foolish, like drag him into her bedroom instead.

She'd always been a sucker for sweet talk and while she didn't think Mason was doing a number on her, she didn't trust her judgement these days; she'd been burned too many times. In trying to upset her mother, she'd done herself a disservice. She wanted to be adored, to have a guy accept her, faults and all, and the more time she spent in Mason's company the more she wondered if he could be that guy. But she couldn't overthink it. He'd come here to set the record straight and to make sure she was all right. He liked her. That kiss hadn't been about pity. For now, that would have to do.

'I want a triple scoop,' he called from the lounge room and when she glanced over her shoulder, he'd slipped off his shoes and was wrapped up in half of the throw rug.

After filling a bowl with ice-cream—and adding a fourth scoop because he'd wormed his way into her heart a little with his declaration—she padded back into the lounge room. Acutely aware of her attire, but not wanting to give him the satisfaction of changing, she sat on the opposite end of the couch.

'Thanks,' he said, glancing into the bowl she handed him. 'I must be back in your good books if you gave me an extra scoop.'

'Just finishing off the container.'

'Whatever works.' He brandished the remote. 'Ready to start?'

Jane nodded and picked up her bowl. It had turned to sludge, but she didn't mind. It felt nice to have company while she watched her favourite movie and as the familiar tune signalling the opening scene filtered through the room, she snuck a peek at him.

His gaze was glued to the TV as he spooned ice-cream into his mouth and a funny ache resembling indigestion filled her chest. What would it be like to have a guy like Mason in her life on a permanent basis? A good guy, who appreciated the finer things like ice-cream and romantic comedies and chilling in your PJs for the hell of it?

She'd never watched a chick flick in her home with a guy before. The men she'd chosen had been too transient, too shallow, not the type she'd let into her life. But seeing Mason curled up on her couch with the throw rug draped over his legs gave her hope.

Could they have a future if she let her guard down?

'You're not watching the movie,' he said, without shifting his gaze from the screen.

'That's because I've seen it a hundred times and it's more fun watching you demolish ice-cream.'

'It's rude to stare,' he said, shooting her a quick wink. 'Especially when a guy's got a sweet tooth.'

'Do you really want to watch this movie?'

'I wouldn't still be here if I didn't. Can we watch or are you one of those annoying people who have to chatter through a movie?'

'Just watch,' she muttered, and they did exactly that. For the two hours she pretended to watch the screen, acutely aware of his feet a few inches away from hers beneath the rug, of his booming laughter when Hugh Grant's roommate posed in his underwear for the paparazzi, of the way his breathing mellowed during the romantic reunion at the end.

She may have loved having someone to share her favourite movie with but it was torturing her to be this close to a hot guy and not jump him. She wanted to, there was no question. But she didn't want to fall into old habits, thinking sex equated with affection. This time had to be different. No use reinventing herself in other aspects of her life only to fail at this.

When the closing credits rolled, he switched off the movie and turned to face her. 'So what's next? A mani-pedi? Braiding each other's hair? Playing truth or dare?'

'Time for you to leave.' She laughed as she pointed at the door. 'Because I have a feeling you're dissing my girly time.'

'No dissing here.' He held up his hands. 'Though if I sit under this blanket with you for one second longer and you don't make a move on me, I'll start to seriously question my manliness.'

Her heart *ka-thump*ed at the thought of exactly how she could make a move on him. Her skin flushed with anticipation. But she wouldn't, no matter how much she wanted to throw caution to the wind and do exactly that.

'Can't two people watch a movie without making out at the end?' She managed to sound calm when inside she was anything but.

'I don't know. But if the two people you're referring to is you and me, I'll say no.' He snaked a hand under the rug and snagged her foot. She gasped as he tugged it onto his lap and started kneading it, hitting all the right pressure points with his powerful thumbs.

'You don't play fair,' she murmured, unable to stifle a groan as he dug into her heel. 'Wow, you're good at that.'

'I'm good at lots of things.' He wiggled his eyebrows and she laughed.

'Haven't you heard that self-praise is no recommendation?'

He grinned. 'That's one of my mum's favourite sayings.'

'I know.' She grinned back at him, trying to keep things light-hearted and not imagine what he could do with those magical hands on other parts of her body.

'Give me your other foot,' he said, and she did as she was told, letting her head loll back on the couch a little as he turned her body to mush under his ministrations.

She might've dozed off, or she might've been in a pleasure stupor, but when he stopped it took her a few seconds to come back down to earth.

'Hey, are you awake?'

'Mmm,' she mumbled, blinking several times and stretching. 'That was … something else.'

They locked gazes and she could've sworn the air sizzled between them.

'Jane, I—'

'You give the best foot rubs on the planet but you have to go,' she said, her resistance wavering the longer he stared at her with desire in his eyes.

'Why?'

She could've lied or come up with some flimsy excuse but what was the point? If she wanted to do things differently with Mason, it was time to come clean.

'Because I like you too and I'm sick of mistaking lust for something more.'

His eyes widened at her bluntness, but before he could say anything she continued, 'That doesn't mean I sleep around, but a lot of my behaviour in the past has been fuelled by poor judgement and I don't want to be that person anymore. And don't worry, I'm not saying I see us having a full-blown relationship and living happily ever after, but whatever this is, I don't want to rush into anything.'

She blew out a breath and flopped back on the couch, suddenly weary. She'd never been so honest with a guy before and, going by Mason's edginess, maybe she should've kept all that to herself.

When he cleared his throat, she braced for his response.

'I'm okay with taking it slow,' he said, throwing off the rug, slipping his shoes on and standing. 'I've waited long enough.'

With that cryptic comment, he dropped a quick kiss on her lips and let himself out, leaving her wondering if he'd had a crush on her since high school or if he meant something else entirely.

CHAPTER
32

By the time Tash made it to Kody's the next morning, bleary-eyed and needing the loo yet again after drinking litres of water first thing, he'd already got Isla onto the school bus and had her things packed and waiting at the back door.

'Fancy a coffee?'

'You're talking too loud,' she muttered, taking careful steps into his kitchen. Any sudden movement could be her downfall considering Rock Hard Place and every other band in the world had taken up residence in her head and were having one giant jam session.

'Coffee it is,' he said, his smug grin making her want to grab Isla's bag and run.

'I'll be back in a minute.' She made it to the toilet and splashed water on her face after she washed her hands. She felt a little more human as she returned to the kitchen, where Kody had coffee waiting.

'Do you fancy a hangover breakfast? A big fry-up with bacon, eggs, the works?'

Her stomach churned and she pressed a hand to it.

'I'm guessing that's a no.' He chuckled and took her coffee over to the dining table. 'Come and sit, get this into you.'

'Thanks,' she said, taking a sip of the powerful espresso and savouring the caffeine hit. 'You were right. The water trick didn't work.'

He laughed and she winced. 'Still too loud.'

'You are such a two-pot screamer,' he said, sipping his coffee and eyeing her with amusement over the rim of his mug. 'But as long as you had a good time.'

'Yeah, we did. Thanks for looking after Isla.'

'My pleasure. She's a fast learner on the guitar.'

'Takes after her dad.' She managed a tentative smile and in that shared moment of mutual affection, she wished it could be like this all the time. That they'd never need to have a difficult conversation, that they'd never have to resolve custody issues guaranteed to tear them apart all over again.

'On that note, I wanted to ask you if it's okay I buy her a guitar? I'd like to surprise her with it.'

'That's a great idea. She'll love it.'

Isla had been babbling about how cool it was to learn guitar from someone as famous as her dad so she'd be over the moon. Tash was genuinely pleased for their daughter, but a small part of her couldn't deny a sliver of fear that this would be the first of many amazing gifts Kody could afford to give Isla that Tash could never match.

'There's a great place online that stocks the best in Melbourne, so I'll put in an order and get it delivered.'

'Okay.' Tash had no intention of bringing up the topic of him playing at the blues night, but Ruby had bugged her about it again this morning and Kody mentioning the guitar gave her the perfect in. 'Speaking of guitars, have you given any more thought to Ruby's request?'

A shadow passed over his face, dark and foreboding, but he didn't shut down as she expected. 'I have.'

'And?' She held her breath, waiting for the inevitable refusal.

'I meant it when I said I'd like to take a look at the roadhouse without a lot of people around.'

'Really?' She exhaled in relief.

He nodded, a small frown creasing his brow. 'Yeah, I've been thinking a lot about the band and what effect this is having on them. I've needed this time to work through some stuff but I can't hide out here forever and if I'm to have any chance of getting back on stage, maybe I should start small and see how I go.'

'That's great. But have you thought about the implications? If you perform at the blues night, word will get out and media will descend on the town like a plague of locusts.'

'Yeah, I know.' He pinched the bridge of his nose. 'It's not fair bringing all that down on Brockenridge but the last thing I want is to freeze on stage in front of thousands, and that's a real possibility. This way, I can ease back into it and if I make a fool of myself, so be it.'

He shrugged like it meant nothing but she knew Kody, knew how much he'd dreamed of taking centre stage his entire life, knew it would kill him to have to step aside from the band and let his mates down.

'How about I arrange to take you to the roadhouse after hours? That way you can get a feel for the place, maybe bring your guitar along, see how you go being on a stage without an audience?'

'That sounds good. Can you make it happen?'

She nodded, unable to quell the worry that she'd pushed him into making a decision about his future when he may not be ready for it. 'I'll speak to Ruby and set something up.'

'The sooner the better, I think. Before I lose my nerve.'

'Would tomorrow night be too soon?'

He stiffened, almost imperceptibly, but she'd once known this guy better than she knew herself and the way his shoulders bunched beneath his worn navy T-shirt told her exactly how nervous he was.

'That'll be fine.' He looked her straight in the eye. 'Even if tomorrow night goes okay, I'll only agree to do the performance on one condition.'

'What's that?'

'That you consider following your dream.'

Bemused, and wondering if too much alcohol had made her incapable of comprehending the basics, she said, 'What are you talking about?'

'Your nursing degree.' Tash had no idea where this was coming from but before she could ask, he said, 'You've pushed me out of my comfort zone the last few weeks, making me confront my fears, and now I'm doing the same for you.'

She wanted to tell him she didn't need a shrink, but that would hurt him and he didn't deserve it. He thought he was doing the right thing, giving her a nudge towards nursing, but he didn't know how damn inadequate she felt whenever she pondered her incomplete degree.

'That has nothing to do with you.'

'Like my hiding out here had nothing to do with you, yet you suggested I get professional help,' he said. 'At least I did you the courtesy of listening.'

She rolled her eyes. 'Nothing you say will change my mind. I don't have time to finish my nursing degree.'

'You will if I coparent Isla.'

'What does that mean exactly?'

'I'll be around for another month at least, and I'm happy to spend as much time as possible with Isla, so that should give you time to at least look into what it would take to complete your degree.' He quirked an eyebrow. 'What have you got to lose?'

Damn him. Tash had always put off completing her nursing degree because she didn't have time: she had to work long hours to support Isla and her daughter needed her. But here was Kody offering her the precious gift of time. Should she take it? She knew he wasn't being entirely altruistic, that he probably wanted to spend as much time as possible with Isla, but she'd like to think his heart was in the right place.

'What's the point of me looking into it when I can't do anything about it?'

'You're still a stubborn mule,' he muttered, with a shake of his head. 'How about this? I won't consider performing at your blues night unless you investigate your degree options.'

'You're blackmailing me. Nice,' she said, shooting him a scathing glare.

'If that's what it takes.'

She contemplated what she had to do: an online search or two, contacting universities, talking to admission offices, researching learning by correspondence, tasks she'd avoided for so long because she wanted to devote time to Isla when she wasn't working. She'd been resigned to finishing her degree some time in the future. But what if that timeline had been brought forwards because she'd let Kody into their lives?

When he continued to stare at her, she sighed. 'Fine. I'll look into it.'

'That's my girl.'

Before she knew what was happening, he'd leaned across and kissed her. On the mouth. A quick kiss and nothing like their steamy pash last week, but enough to resurrect the memory of how damn good it had felt.

'You need to stop doing that,' she said, no sting in her words.

'And you need to stop telling me what to do.'

This time when they grinned at each other, Tash sensed the deeper bond they'd once shared slowly but surely growing between them.

It terrified her.

CHAPTER
33

The Watering Hole was nothing like what Kody expected. He'd envisioned a small, grungy venue similar to the dive bars the band had played in around the States. Back then, Rock Hard Place had been trying to cement the success of their first song climbing the charts by playing as many gigs as humanly possible. They'd done a road trip from LA to San Fran, across to Las Vegas, down to New Orleans and back to the City of Angels. By the end of those six months, they were being labelled a band to watch, courtesy of a big-name rock star in Vegas asking them to open his show when another band pulled out.

Their first song had done okay, their second hit the top twenty and their third shot to number one, catapulting them to the kind of fame he'd only ever dreamed about. Being so busy those first six months had been a godsend because it gave him little time to dwell on Tash walking away from him and the heartless way she'd done it. He'd drowned his sorrows in bourbon, women and song. Many songs, penned in the dead of night when the rest of the band members had crashed from partying hard and he'd be left alone to ponder their rapid rise to fame and what that meant for his future.

Never in a million years had he anticipated factoring a kid into that future. He'd worn his single status like a badge of honour, intent on never stringing a woman along. Sure, he'd slept with his fair share, but they'd all known the score. And while those encounters had been fun, he'd never had the deeper connection he'd had with Tash. A connection that was still there, if he dared admit the truth to himself.

He didn't want to delve into his reawakened feelings for her. He didn't want to give her false hope. It could only end badly between them and considering he'd be in touch with her for years to coordinate parenting Isla, he couldn't afford to screw this up.

His logical plan wavered when Tash locked the front and back doors of the roadhouse, leaving them alone in a dimly lit room that smelled of barbecue wings and beer, the exact aroma of the Princeton when they'd first met and fallen for each other many moons ago.

'Did you mention to Isla we were doing this tonight? Because she didn't say a word when I dropped her off at Ellen's for a sleepover.'

He shook his head. 'No, I didn't want her asking a bunch of questions I have no idea how to answer until I actually make it up onto that stage so I haven't texted her.' He jerked his thumb at the corner. 'Just looking at it makes me want to puke.'

'You sure you want to do this?'

He nodded, despite the tension that held his spine stiff and made his palms grow clammy. The thought of picking up a guitar and stepping onto the stage terrified him.

Crazy, because there was nobody here to witness his humiliation if he couldn't do it. Tash would give him complete privacy if he asked, she'd said as much on the drive over. Better here, on a small stage, than at a Rock Hard Place gig where he'd let down thousands.

Tash eyed him warily, as if she expected him to bolt any second. 'Do you want me to wait in the kitchen?'

'No, but I'd love a bourbon.'

'I'll make it a double,' she said, slipping behind the bar, leaving him to study the stage.

Though small, the stage could hold a four-piece band, five at a squeeze. It was elevated by a few inches, made from the same pocked mahogany boards as the rest of the floor. The roadhouse may look a little worn in places but everything gleamed and he could imagine it housing several hundred when packed.

'Do bands perform here often?'

'There's a blues night monthly, and since Ruby took over we have regular theme nights too. Eighties, Elvis, rock 'n' roll, that kind of thing.' Tash approached him and he tried not to ogle. There was nothing remotely seductive in her outfit—faded denim jeans, tan suede ankle boots and grey tank top—but her body rocked it, making her sexy as hell.

'Here you go.' She thrust a glass at him, filled over halfway.

'I take it you don't man the bar,' he said, raising his glass in a salute. 'Because if you call this a double, this place would be out of business damn quick.'

She smiled. 'I thought you needed it.'

'I do.' He downed half the bourbon in one gulp, the burn in his throat a welcome distraction from his nerves.

'Better?'

'Not really but, hey, I'll try anything at this point.'

He didn't mean it to sound like a come-on but maybe she felt the simmering attraction between them as much as he did, for she took a step closer and laid a hand on his chest.

'You can do this. And if you can't, it's okay.' She brushed a soft kiss on his cheek and damned if he didn't feel like crying.

He'd never been emotional. He'd learned that the hard way in his first foster home; tears equated with weakness and that got you picked on. He'd honed his impassivity over the years, preferring to bottle up his reactions than give anyone the satisfaction of seeing him hurt. Not entirely healthy, considering the way every god-damn emotion he'd ever had bubbled out in a toxic torrent after the concert accident, and the online psych had helped him see that.

It didn't mean he could change his ways all at once and letting Tash see his vulnerability would only undermine his stance to keep things friendly between them. Letting her too close, opening up to her, could produce a wave of emotion he may not recover from. Getting back on stage would be traumatic enough.

'You can stay,' he said gruffly, tossing back the rest of the bourbon. 'But if I ask you to leave, you need to do it quick, okay?' The last thing he wanted was for her to see him break down.

'Sure.' She touched his cheek, the barest graze of a fingertip across the stubble, but it sent a stab of longing through him. 'Take your time.'

Rather than sitting at the front table nearest the stage, she walked across the room and perched on a stool near the kitchen, as if expecting him to ask her to leave. But if he couldn't do this in front of an audience of one, with a woman he'd once loved, he had no hope of braving a larger crowd.

Kody picked up the guitar case and laid it on a table. A fine sheen of sweat broke out over his forehead and his fingers trembled slightly as he unzipped it. He took a few deep breaths, swiping the sweat away with the back of his hand. That's another thing the psychologist had suggested, to check out a few meditation and mindfulness techniques. Kody had thought it was a bunch of hooey at first but every now and then, usually when he woke from a nightmare of clawing at faceless monsters, he'd slow his breathing, forcing it deep into his belly, taking time to readjust.

The distant howl of a wild dog punctuated the silence as he slipped the guitar from the case and caressed the wood from the headstock to the bridge. It was a ritual he did before every concert, even if he wouldn't be playing any acoustic numbers. And while Yanni's guitar was a superb example of fine craftsmanship, he couldn't help but wish he had his.

Slinging the strap over his shoulder, he took a step towards the stage. And stopped, as panic swamped him, strong and potent, leaving him gasping for air, drowning.

The psych said he didn't have PTSD but that gave him small comfort as he stared at that rectangular platform as though it would devour him whole if he stepped onto it.

Frozen, he risked a glance over his shoulder. Tash hadn't moved; she perched on the stool, her hands clasped in her lap, her expression carefully neutral. Then she flashed him an encouraging smile and it catapulted him straight back to the Princeton where she'd do this very thing, wait for him on a bar stool off to the side of the stage, smiling encouragement whenever he glanced her way.

It helped, and he willed away the tension holding his muscles rigid, taking one step, another, until he stood in the middle of the stage. He didn't implode, the roof didn't fall in and when he reached for the microphone stand, it felt like the most natural thing in the world.

Kody stroked the guitar again, along the neck and frets, lingering over the sound hole, before positioning his fingers to play the first chord. He had no idea what song he'd sing. His goal had been to make it up on the stage and he hadn't thought much beyond that. But as he plucked at the strings, a familiar melody flowed through him and he found himself humming the first few bars.

Their song, the one he played at every gig for her. Of course it would be, when he needed comforting. And as the lyrics flowed seamlessly with his strumming, a sense of peace enveloped him. His eyes closed as he sung his heart out. And when he played the final chord, his head dropped forwards as exhaustion made him want to curl up in a corner.

He heard Tash's heels on the floorboards but when he opened his eyes and her boots appeared in his line of vision, he couldn't look at her. He didn't want to see pity or gratitude. It would undo him completely.

So he waited while he got his emotions under control. When he raised his head, their gazes locked and the admiration in hers blew him away.

'You did it.' She took a step forwards, hesitated, staring at his guitar like she wished it would vanish.

So he made that happen, slipping the strap over his shoulder and propping the guitar to one side. He stepped off the stage and she moved into his arms like it was the most natural thing in the world, her arms wrapped around his neck tight, her face buried in the crook like she used to. They still fit and as he hugged her close, he wished they could somehow recapture the magic of the past.

In that moment, he finally let go of his residual anger towards her.

She'd always been good for him. His rock. His voice of reason. They hadn't dated for long in terms of time but it had felt like forever when he'd had her by his side, supporting him. Removing any say he might've had in having Isla had been another way of shouldering the burden and letting him off. She'd supported his career to the extent she'd given up hers. He had no right judging her.

She was the most beautiful woman he knew, inside and out. When Tash looked at him, he felt like he was invincible and while that was far from the truth, she made him want to be a better man.

He kissed the top of her head and she stilled, the faintest shiver racking her body as she snuggled in closer. His arms tightened, melding her to him in a way that made him wish they were somewhere more private.

As if sensing his thoughts, her fingers weaved through his hair, moving his head away so she could press her mouth to his. The kiss started gently, a tender, repeated grazing of her lips against his, almost teasing.

Kody didn't want to complicate their relationship and he had no idea if it was the adrenalin coursing through his body at conquering his fear of performance, or the feel of having Tash in his arms so completely, but whatever it was, he wanted more. He deepened the kiss, expecting her to pull away. When she wrapped her leg around his hip and ravaged him back, he had all the answer he needed.

Lifting his mouth from hers, he whispered against the corner of her mouth, 'Nobody's coming in here tonight, yeah?'

'Yeah, we've got the place to ourselves,' she said, desire making her eyes glitter in the semi-darkness. 'But do we want to do this—'

He silenced her doubts with a scorching kiss that proved exactly how much he wanted her. She responded by pushing him onto the nearest chair and straddling him. Damn she was sexy, writhing in his lap, her hair tumbling loose from its ponytail, draping their faces as they kissed like they couldn't get enough.

They didn't speak—the sound of soft panting and moans mingling in the air with unzipping and tearing of foil. She had to dismount for a moment to take off her shoes, jeans and underwear, and it gave him the perfect view of how beautiful she was. The familiarity of her made his chest ache. And then she was back, sliding onto him, engulfing him in heaven.

There was nothing remotely tender about the way she rode him. She slid up and down with abandon, her head thrown back, the column of her neck exposed to his greedy lips. Lust engulfed him as the tension built. He reached between their bodies, found her clitoris, pleasured her until she came apart. He followed moments later, tumbling into welcome oblivion, the kind of release that obliterated everything but being with this incredible woman in this cataclysmic moment.

He held her tight, savouring her warmth, lost in memories of the two of them in the past, and how being with Tash like this now felt like coming home.

CHAPTER
34

Tash had to stop grinning like an idiot. She'd seen her reflection several times—in the microwave, in the window overlooking the backyard, in the glass cabinet housing her crockery—since she'd arrived home after having spontaneous sex with Kody at the roadhouse and each time, she sported the inane grin of a well-satisfied woman who wanted more from the man currently sitting in the lounge room waiting for her to rustle up some drinks.

She shouldn't be feeling this euphoric. Having sex with Kody before they'd sorted custody issues was foolish. But she couldn't help herself. Seeing him struggle with his performance anxiety, watching him conquer his fears, made her heart swell with admiration. She'd once loved him and having him lay himself bare like that … His vulnerability made her want to hold him and never let go.

She couldn't afford to indulge in crazy thoughts like that but the moment he'd opened his arms to her and she'd stepped into them, she knew there was no other place she wanted to be. The mistakes of the past had faded, along with the complications of the present, leaving her with him to just … be.

She'd never felt so alive.

Sex with Kody had always left her wanting more but this time was different. Back then she'd been young and naïve, revelling in the discovery of her body and the way it responded to his. She may not have had a hell of a lot of sex since but what had happened in that roadhouse defied belief. It was frantic and hot. Scorching, melt-her-into-a-puddle hot.

Pressing her cheek against the fridge didn't cool her off much so she opened the freezer and stuck her head in a little. Of course, that's the moment she heard him clear his throat. She straightened so fast she clunked her head on the top shelf.

'You okay?'

'Sure.' She winced and rubbed her head. 'Just searching for ice cubes.'

'But I asked for a beer?'

'I felt like a bourbon.'

'Then why are there two beers on the counter?' His wide grin made her heart skip a beat. Sexy as hell. 'And why are your cheeks so red?'

'Shut up,' she muttered, biting back a smile as he burst out laughing.

'Hey, I'll take it as a compliment.'

'Whatever.' She grabbed the beers and flounced past him, to the sound of more laughter. She loved this, swapping banter with him like they used to. He'd always made her laugh back then, saying her studies made her too serious. She had been too staid, and he'd been the perfect distraction, preventing her from turning into a nerd who put her degree above everything else. His ability to bring out her lighter side had been one of the many things she loved about him. He complemented her in a way she hadn't expected. No prizes for guessing why she'd reverted to a hermit when she walked away from him.

Then again, having a baby with no family support didn't leave a lot of time for a social life. Maybe if she'd dated more, had a relationship after Kody, she mightn't be this gaga all over again. Because that's exactly how she felt at the moment, like he'd dazzled her and she couldn't resist.

She'd invited him back here to get past potential awkwardness after riding him like a bronco at the roadhouse. But there hadn't been any and that had surprised her more than anything. Once she'd got her gear back on and he'd visited the men's room, they'd held hands and walked out, only pausing to lock up. It had all seemed so ... natural. It should've terrified her, but it didn't. This was Kody. And he'd always had a piece of her heart even if he didn't know it.

'Come here.' He sat on the sofa and patted the cushion next to him. 'I want to hold you.'

Her heart fluttered like a bird trapped in a cage as she did exactly that, fitting into the crook of his arm. She handed him his beer and they clinked bottles, content to sip on the boutique brew in silence. Leaning her head back against his shoulder, she stretched out her legs next to his. They fit on the sofa as well as they'd fit together at the roadhouse. Natural. Meant to be.

'Thanks for standing by me tonight,' he murmured, pressing a kiss into her hair.

Her heart swelled but she wanted to keep this light. 'You know Ben E. King already did a song about that, right?'

He chuckled. 'Yeah, I know. But I just want to let you know I couldn't have faced my demons if it hadn't been for you.'

Now she knew why he'd wanted her in his arms like this, her back to him: so she couldn't see his face. His voice sounded tight with emotion and she wondered if this was the right time to ask him about those demons. She didn't expect him to answer. He'd fob her off, change the subject, get back to banter.

'I know how much performing means to you. It's your life. So … what really happened at that concert?'

His arm flexed where it rested on her shoulders, tension coiling through his body. 'It's my fault those people died,' he said, so softly she thought she'd misheard. 'We have a designated fireworks expert on tour who really knows his stuff. The band just wants to play music, but our managers and promoters insist on the whole shebang these days so we have fireworks as part of our second set.'

He blew out a breath and continued, 'Our guy was sick with gastro and a few of the guys wanted to scrap the fireworks. But I insisted we deliver for our fans, so agreed for the lead stagehand, supposedly a local expert, to set everything up. There was a malfunction apparently—an accident, and not his fault but …'

He shuddered and silence stretched between them before he spoke again. 'That malfunction caused a mini-explosion and a fire. The fans panicked and there was a stampede.' His voice hitched. 'If I hadn't insisted on those bloody fireworks, seven innocent people would still be alive.'

Tears burned the back of her eyes. He'd been shouldering the blame for those deaths. No wonder he'd walked away for a while.

She half-swivelled in his arms, not surprised to find his face pale and tension pinching his mouth. Laying a comforting hand on his chest, she said, 'That firework malfunction could've happened any time, at any concert. You're not to blame for it.'

He gave a half-nod, but his lips still compressed into a line. 'That's what the online psych said. I poured a lot of crap out and he helped me work through it.' He covered her hand with his, pressing it against his chest. 'But you did too.'

'I didn't do anything.'

'Yeah, you did. You let me into Isla's life. You didn't judge me for being an angry, bitter guy doing his best to push you away. You trusted me with our daughter—' He gulped, the sheen in his eyes matching hers when their gazes met. 'You've always been special, Tash, I hope you know that.'

She could say so much. She could let every wild emotion bubbling inside spill over and terrify him as much as they petrified her. But nothing had changed between them. Now that he'd conquered his stage fright he'd leave sooner rather than later, but with a watertight custody agreement in his guitar case. An agreement they had to nut out before that could happen. Better to keep things light between them. Besides, it would make Isla happy to see her parents getting along. Though the part where they'd got physical would be kept under wraps. No point confusing the poor child or giving her false hope for some kind of reunion.

'You're an incredible man,' she said, slipping her hand out from under his to cup his cheek. 'And I'm glad you're confronting your fears. But Isla will be home in the morning and I have a feeling we won't be able to recapture the closeness of tonight, so let's make the most of it.'

He arched an eyebrow as she wriggled down the couch and slid to her feet. Holding out her hand to him, she waited. Surely one night of wild, wanton sex for old times' sake wouldn't be so bad?

When he placed his hand in hers, she had her answer.

She'd make tonight count.

CHAPTER
35

Jane worked alongside Mason for two days. Forty-eight excruciating hours when she channelled a professional persona and tried not to remember how it had felt having him curled up under a throw rug on her couch. The upside being she'd been so hell-bent on focussing on work that the bulk of the interior design was done. The shop had been in good nick and only needed a coat of paint, which the contractors did on the first day, and revamping the counter to include a glass display case. The rest of the work had been window dressing, her domain, and she'd thrown herself into it with gusto.

The wrought-iron tables and chairs in pristine white had been delivered and set up, and French movie posters hung in strategic places on the walls. She'd carried a pastel theme of mint and lemon throughout, lending the place a bright, airy feel. Once the stencilling had been done on the front glass and a sign hung, her part of the job would be complete.

The great thing about designing the interior was not bumping into Mason very often. He'd been supervising the kitchen revamp and had been on his phone for much of the week, contacting suppliers for new ovens and utensils. Betty had insisted she could get the best price from a local guy in Echuca but Mason had wanted to investigate for himself, so Betty had rolled her eyes at Jane and left him to it.

Jane stood back, surveying the room, proud of what she'd achieved. Once the electrician finished installing and wiring the new light fittings later today, she could take photos and update her website. She'd forgotten how satisfied doing a good job could make her feel. And with a little luck, when townsfolk saw what she'd done with this place they'd be more inclined to give her more work. Not that she could ever make a living out of interior design in a town this small but that wasn't the point. She wanted to feel valued in a way she never had. Gladys had seen to that.

There'd been no more calls from her mother to Mason; or if there had been, he hadn't told Jane. The thought of Gladys trying to sabotage this job before it had begun made her want to throw something. She had tolerated her mother's shoddy behaviour too long, tried to shame her into having a conscience and it hadn't worked. Which meant they needed to have the confrontation Jane had been putting off for a decade.

Not that it would change anything. She wasn't that naïve. But saying what had to be said might go some way to soothing the disquiet within.

She'd wait until the patisserie opened then she'd arrange a meeting, for no other reason than she wanted to enjoy the happy occasion. Betty deserved all the success in the world and so did Mason. He'd given up a glam life, even if it mightn't be for long, to return home and do this, and she wished him all the best.

Gathering her things, Jane's breath hitched as Mason strode from the kitchen, barking orders into his mobile, before hanging up with a muttered, 'Dickhead.'

When he caught sight of her his frown cleared. 'You done for the day?'

'Uh-huh. I'm done, period.'

He blinked and looked around, as if seeing it all for the first time. Crazy, because he'd been popping in and out and had given his approval for everything. But this was the first time he'd see the finished product of her labours and she yearned for his approval.

'Wow.' He stood in the middle of the patisserie and did a slow three-sixty. 'It's perfect.'

Heat flushed her cheeks at his praise. 'I love how it turned out exactly as we envisioned.'

'Don't do that.' He wiggled a finger at her. 'This was mostly you. You had an idea, you presented it to me, we agreed and you did it.'

'Thank you.' Silly that she craved his praise so much but now she had it she burned with embarrassment. Then again, she hadn't been praised for much in her life. The uncharacteristic feeling of accomplishment was foreign to her.

'My pleasure, though you're paying me enough, so I had to produce something of value.'

He laughed. 'Stop underselling yourself. You've got real talent.'

Increasingly uncomfortable, she leaned on a table. 'I've always loved colour matching and the course I did years ago opened my eyes to how much I actually enjoy bringing a room together.'

'Why haven't you done more projects?'

His curiosity was natural but she couldn't give him an honest answer. Instead she said, 'How many people in Brockenridge do you think would want to hire an interior designer and how often?'

He grimaced. 'Good point.' He hesitated, as if unsure whether to continue. 'Why did you stick around? Of all the kids at school, I thought you would've hit the highway as soon as the graduation ceremony finished.'

'What does "of all the kids" mean?'

He smiled, rueful, as if she'd caught him out. 'Come on, Jane, you were the most popular girl and owned every room you strutted into. You were confident and gorgeous—you would've taken any city by storm.'

Flustered and incredibly flattered, she flashed him a coy smile. 'Gorgeous, huh?'

'You still are, but you don't need me to tell you that.' His gaze swept over her from head to foot like a physical caress, leaving her feeling vulnerable, as if he'd stripped away her jeans and T-shirt so she stood naked in front of him.

'Actually, I do,' she said, mentally chastising herself for flirting but unable to resist after his flattering appraisal. 'It never hurts to get a confidence boost.'

His smile faded and she could've sworn the air, heated a moment ago, actually cooled. 'What happened to you?'

Uh-oh. He'd seen through her. How did he do that?

She'd have to fake it like she'd done her whole life, pretending everything was fine when on the inside she died a little every day because she had no one to depend on. No real friends, no family. It sucked.

'What do you mean?'

'You've changed a lot. You've lost confidence.'

He took a few steps towards her and she wished she'd left when she'd first intended to. Having this man strip away her defences could only end badly. He wasn't a keeper. He'd leave, and she could handle that, but it meant getting a grip on her stupid crush and stop wishing things could be different.

He stepped in front of her, concern darkening his eyes. 'Did some guy do a number on you?'

'No.'

'This can't be all about your mum.'

'You know nothing about me,' she said, holding up a hand when he looked like he wanted to hug her. 'So please don't try to psychoanalyse.'

He stiffened, his expression frosty. 'I'm not doing that.'

'Then what's this about?'

'I just want to get to know you better, damn it. I know you feel the attraction between us and now that your work here is done, why are you still determined to hold me at arms' length?'

'Because no good can come of you and me getting involved.' She straightened, picked up her things, and held them to her chest like a shield. Then she turned on her heel and strode towards the door, but he didn't let her get far. His hand clamped down on her shoulder and he spun her to face him.

'Have dinner with me.'

Her heart leapt at the thought of a real date with Mason but she'd been right a moment ago: no good could come of this. She needed to stop creating fanciful notions in her head, scenarios that involved the two of them together for longer than a fling. Because that's all she could ever be for him. That's all guys were ever interested in with her. They saw blonde hair, blue eyes, big boobs, and instantly thought 'easy lay'. The fact she'd played up to the stereotype for a while to embarrass her mother was all on her. She'd done herself no favours and in trying to reinvent herself in a town this size she knew it would be tough.

People gossiped about her. Even though she'd never been as bad as they thought she was, and no matter what she did now they still judged and found her lacking. Maybe it was time to move away? Have the final confrontation with her mother and move on? She hadn't done it before now because she wouldn't give her the satisfaction of winning. Because that's exactly how Gladys would view Jane leaving Brockenridge; that she was the victor.

'If you have to think that long and hard about having dinner with me, I'm guessing the answer is no?' He didn't sound put out, more amused.

'Isn't the electrician finishing the light installation tonight?'

'We can be back in time for that.'

'We?'

He rolled his eyes. 'Here's a newsflash for you. Just because your job here is done doesn't mean you don't get to be a part of it. You're responsible for this. You're friends with my mum. Don't you want to see the whole thing come to fruition?'

She'd love nothing better but the longer she spent in his company without the excuse of business between them, the more likely she would be to fall for him.

'This is your dream, but we're done here, and I don't want to complicate things by hanging around because I like you.'

His lop-sided grin infused her with warmth. 'You like me?'

'Yeah, go figure.'

'As it so happens, I like you too. A lot. But I thought you already knew that? I don't sit through *Notting Hill* under a throw rug with just anybody, you know.'

'Actually, I don't know, and that's half the problem.' She sighed. 'I have no idea what's going on here, Mason, but I'm done with flings. So if that's what you're after—'

'Stop. We haven't even been on a date yet so aren't you jumping ahead a little?'

'I don't want to set up false expectations.' Because if he did put the moves on her she knew she'd be powerless to resist. Tall, blond, rugged and the guy could bake—resistance was futile.

'Dinner. Tonight. You and me. No expectations. You choose the restaurant.'

She should say no. She already liked him too much to be good for her.

But they'd worked well together and deserved a treat, so she found herself reluctantly nodding. 'I know just the place.'

Jane took Mason to the roadhouse because it was the least romantic place in town and guaranteed to be packed. After his probing questions and insight earlier she didn't feel like facing any deep and meaningful conversations, so the raucous vibe of the The Watering Hole would be perfect.

He didn't seem fazed by her choice of venue and, as they entered, he greeted several familiar faces like long-lost relatives. People flocked to men like Mason because he exuded a genuine charm; no BS, no ego, just one of their own returning to Brockenridge to start a new business. Many asked him about the patisserie and he invited them all to the grand opening the following week.

Several people cast Jane curious glances. She'd tried to slip away to organise a table but Mason wouldn't allow her, taking hold of her hand instead, leaving inquiring minds in little doubt that they were more than friends. Not entirely true, but it was easier to go with the flow than make a big deal out of it.

By the time they made it to their table, her face ached from smiling so much, something she rarely did when interacting with townsfolk these days. Then again, she never mingled with people the way Mason had just done. Because she expected judgement, she kept any chatting to a minimum, offering nothing more than a nod of acknowledgement and an occasional smile. Maybe if she shrugged the chip off her shoulder and started opening up a little more, people wouldn't stare at her with wariness.

'You okay?' He touched her hand across the table, a brief graze of his fingertips against the skin on the back of it, and her body flared to life. Ridiculous.

'Fine.' Her response came out high-pitched and he raised an eyebrow.

'Just hungry,' she clarified, snatching up a menu she could hide behind.

Mason didn't call her out on the lie. But after they'd placed their orders, mushroom risotto for her, honey-glazed lamb rack for him, he studied her with that all too astute stare.

'Interesting choice of venue,' he said, his lips curved in amusement. 'We've already eaten here so I was hoping for something different.'

'Harry serves the best food in Brockenridge, so why go anywhere else?'

He leaned forwards, resting those strong forearms on the table. 'For a little privacy? So we could actually hear our conversation without having to shout it?'

'This place is great. Maybe you're too used to posh Parisian cafés and restaurants?'

He waggled a finger at her. 'Stop making me out to be a snob. Brockenridge will always be home to me.'

The guy had to be crazy. Paris or Brockenridge? No comparison.

'How long do you think you'll stay?' Inquiring minds wanted to know, mostly hers, as his gaze darted away, almost furtively, before he refocussed on her.

'If it wasn't for Mum busting her arse, I never would've made it to Melbourne let alone Paris so I owe her, and I want this patisserie to be a successful adjunct to the bakery. That means I'll be around for a month or two until it really gets off the ground and I can show her how to make the fancier stuff.'

Jane's heart sank. Four to eight weeks and he'd be gone. While she'd known he wouldn't stay, it hurt more than it should to hear him say it.

'And after that?'

He shrugged. 'I might seek out a new challenge.'

'Sounds like you have it all planned out,' she said, hoping he didn't hear the disappointment in her tone.

A tiny frown dented his brow. 'What's with the twenty questions regarding the patisserie and my plans?'

Jane could hedge around this. She could bluff her way out of it. But if she'd decided to finally confront her mother and expose all the lies, maybe she should stop lying to herself?

'I'm trying to ascertain whether you're worth taking a chance on.'

Mason's eyes widened in surprise, before his mouth eased into a grin. 'Have you come to a decision?'

'Not yet, but I'm working on it.'

'Don't take too long.' He crooked his finger and she leaned forwards until their faces were only inches apart. 'Because being a master pastry chef means I can do wicked things with honey.'

How was a girl supposed to respond to that?

CHAPTER
36

Kody whistled under his breath, a nameless tune he wanted to get down on paper. His muse had fled that night in Wellington and for the first time since then he itched to grab a pencil and some blank sheet music and get creative. Though if he were honest with himself, he hadn't felt inspired for a long time before the New Zealand leg of the tour. He'd been stagnating, going through the motions of performing, craving some R&R. Hiding out here hadn't been what he'd envisaged but the isolation had forced him to confront a lot. Including his feelings for Tash, feelings he'd thought had been destroyed thirteen years ago.

She'd dropped him home after their incredible evening together and he'd been wandering aimlessly through the house since. He knew he should contact Yanni and the boys to tell them the good news—as soon as the walking boot came off he'd be heading down to Melbourne to jam with them—but it felt too soon to be making that call and facing Yanni's astute stare when he was still floating.

Yanni would take one look at his smug face and know exactly what had transpired between him and Tash.

Kody could hardly believe it himself. Their sizzling encounter in the roadhouse had been impulsive, born of the adrenalin surge from conquering his stage fright. But later at her place, in her bed, they'd had the best sex. Several times. Their connection left him reeling. How easily they'd slipped back into being comfortable with each other, like they'd never been apart.

Usually, he never looked back. Once he'd broken off with a casual partner, he'd never return. It didn't bode well to build false hope. With Tash, it was different. Comfortable. Not the sex, that had been mind-blowing, but the aftermath. He'd even opened up to her about the concert and it had felt okay. She'd always had that effect on him, the ability to soothe without trying.

When they'd first met in Melbourne it had been a bit of a lark for him to get her to lighten up. She'd been so staid, so studious, that he'd played up his bad-boy angle and she'd loved it. But she'd grounded him too in a way he never knew he needed. Losing her had set off a chain reaction. Personally, he'd spiralled: drinking too much, screwing as many women as he could. Professionally, he'd shot to the top. When he'd eventually got tired of drowning his sorrows and revenge sex, he embraced the fame and all that came with it. But he'd never forgotten the man he'd been with Tash, if only for a short time. The other night, he'd felt that same sense of calm being with her again.

It almost made him regret not telling her about the appointment he had scheduled for later today. But he hadn't wanted to ruin things and he knew any mention of lawyers would've done exactly that. He'd made the appointment after that first time they kissed because he'd known then things could get complicated and he didn't want anything happening between them to interfere with the custody agreement. But they'd done a whole lot more than kissing now and it seemed imperative they institute rules when it came to Isla's future.

He doubted Tash had any expectations where he was concerned. She knew he was leaving town so their night together could only ever be a spectacular one-off—unless Isla had another sleepover scheduled in the next few weeks. But he couldn't contemplate it. The night with Tash had been special but a repeat could give her ideas, namely there was a chance they'd reunite when nothing could be further from the truth.

He couldn't have a long-distance relationship. He hated the thought of Tash waiting for him in this tiny town, expecting him to visit during his downtime to dole out scraps of affection. He wouldn't do that to her, because she deserved so much better. Now that he'd be sharing custody of Isla, maybe she'd have more time for a relationship with someone local, someone who could give her what he couldn't: stability, permanency, adoration.

So why did the thought of her hooking up with some country yokel leave Kody feeling like he'd been dunked in an ice bath?

This is what happened when sex entered the equation. It screwed with his brain and made him overthink. Which was why the appointment this afternoon was so important. It should be simple: meet with the lawyer; get the custody agreement sorted; contact the band; make plans for the future.

With Isla in his life, he'd have to curtail the touring, which he'd already been hoping to scale back anyway. And he'd have to buy a place in Melbourne, a house maybe, with a backyard and a pool, somewhere she'd enjoy chilling when she visited.

His first real home.

Perhaps Isla would like to help him choose? It made him feel like a god, being able to give his child anything she wanted when his own childhood had been so shitty. He'd do anything to make her happy.

At the risk of making her mother unhappy?

He scowled, wishing his voice of reason would shut the hell up. He knew what Tash would think once he started lavishing Isla with possessions: she'd think Kody was buying her off. But he wasn't. He wanted to make sure his child wanted for nothing, the way he'd often yearned for a gaming console or a smartphone or the latest sneakers. He'd have to be careful, because he didn't want Tash to feel like it was a competition between them for Isla. And he didn't want Isla to undervalue the many important life lessons her mother was teaching her, the kind money couldn't buy.

Yeah, this coparenting thing would be a minefield, one potential explosion after another, but by getting the legalities sorted out he'd have one less thing to worry about.

As he headed for the shower, whistling the same tune he had to flesh out later, he had a feeling there'd be plenty to worry about when he delivered the agreement to Tash.

CHAPTER
37

As much as Jane would've liked to invite Mason back to her place after dinner, she'd resisted, because she couldn't quite shake the feeling that sleeping with him too soon would set her back. He was the first guy she'd really liked in a long time and she wanted to do this right, so as soon as dinner finished she insisted he head back to the patisserie to supervise the installation of the light fittings and she'd headed home. To spend the night tossing and turning with erotic dreams of a tall, blond baker with particularly strong hands brandishing honey.

But it wasn't broken sleep making her cranky this morning. The minute she opened her eyes, Jane knew she had to see her mother. If she was even considering getting serious with Mason for however long he was in town for, she wanted to confront her insecurities and that meant a chat with Mummy dearest.

After a quick call that Gladys picked up—meaning she was home—Jane hung up and drove out of town. As a kid, she'd never noticed the poverty of some farms on the outskirts of Brocken-ridge, or the barren brown land that became drier by the day. She'd been too absorbed by online shopping, ordering the latest designer jeans and T-shirts and make-up. Her father had indulged her and Gladys hadn't cared what she bought as long as she looked good. She hadn't forgotten being young, stupid and selfish, which is why she donated so freely to local causes now.

She tried to mentally rehearse what she'd say. *I know the truth about you yet I wanted to give you the benefit of the doubt regardless. I have a reason to be mad at you because you drove Dad to his death, what's your excuse? Why do you hate me so much?*

All valid questions but she knew when she came face to face with Gladys, her calmly rehearsed questions would mean nothing unless her mother actually wanted to listen to reason for once.

As she turned into the circular driveway, her hands gripped the steering wheel tighter so she wouldn't be tempted to keep going and drive out the other side. Every muscle tensed and she broke out in a sweat, a typical fight-or-flight reaction she'd had since she was a kid and Gladys would glare at her like she was a giant inconvenience.

Gladys must spend her entire day looking out the window because Jane had barely parked and stepped from her car before the front door opened. Today her mother wore a bottle green jump-suit that made her look like she'd stepped off a catwalk. Her hair was styled in a chignon, showing off the emerald studs in her ear-lobes. And she wore heels, three-inch stilettos. Who did that when lounging around at home? Gladys Jefferson did, because life was all about looks for her. She didn't care about anybody else.

'Jane, what a lovely surprise—'

'Save your pleasantries,' Jane said, pushing past her. 'I've got something to say and it's long overdue.'

'By all means, make yourself at home,' Gladys muttered, her sarcasm something Jane was well used to.

Jane stomped into the study because it was the nearest room. When Gladys entered, Jane slammed the door.

'These theatrics are beneath you—'

'I know!' Jane yelled, immediately regretting the outburst. She'd vowed to be calm for this, knowing indifference would hurt Gladys more than drama. 'I know why you never bonded with me and why you drove Dad to his death.'

'I don't know what you think you know—'

'I heard that last argument you had with Dad before he drove into that tree.'

'That's nonsense. Your father didn't kill himself. It was an accident.'

'Was it?' She pinned her mother with a disgusted glare but, predictably, Gladys didn't flinch. She'd put in too many years presenting a perfectly poised front to let her mask slip now.

Her mother waved her away like a bothersome fly. 'I don't know why you're bringing up all this pointless speculation now.'

'Because this is the end, Mother. I'm done playing your game.' She snorted, an unladylike sound she knew Gladys hated. 'Haven't you ever wondered why I never moved away? Why I stay in this dead-end town where everyone knows everyone else's business?'

Gladys opened her mouth to respond and Jane held up her hand. 'I'm not interested in anything you have to say. I stayed because the moment I heard that argument between you and Dad, I knew I couldn't leave.' Jane jabbed a finger at her mother, surprised when she flinched. 'Because I wanted to make your life a misery, exactly like you made mine and Dad's.'

For the first time in a long time, Gladys appeared uncertain. Her gaze darted away, only to return to Jane, before sliding away again. Jane supposed she was trying to come up with some plausible excuse for what Jane had heard on the day her perfect world came tumbling down.

'Even after that awful night, I gave you a chance. I thought you might need time to grieve, to get past your guilt, so I left you alone out of respect. Then I came to you later, thinking it was long enough for you to deal with everything, hoping you'd open up to me. I wanted you to confide in me, to say it had all been a horrendous mistake, an argument that had gone horribly awry. And what did you do?' Bitterness tightened Jane's throat. 'You made me feel bad for staying away. And you blamed me for the crappy relationship we've had since I could walk.'

Gladys blanched, her pallor more startling than before. 'You're right, I did feel guilty.'

'So why did you take it out on me? I heard everything. How you only had a child as an adjunct to secure your perfect life. As a way to keep your rich husband, when you'd never wanted a child in the first place. How I meant nothing to you. How you despised Dad for fawning over me. That you hated him and wished he was dead.'

Even now, all these years later, Jane couldn't bear thinking about the depths of her mother's dislike for her. The shocking truths she'd overheard that night explained why, when Jane had been growing up, nothing she ever did pleased Gladys, why her mother treated her like an annoyance, why Jane had tried so hard to be like her but always fell short.

'You don't know everything,' Gladys said, her docility as shocking as the pain in her eyes. 'In fact, you know nothing.'

'I know enough, Mum. I heard everything.'

The remaining colour leached from Gladys's face, the blush on her cheekbones looking almost clownish. 'Your father was gay.'

Jane stared in disbelief at her mother, horrified by the lengths Gladys would go to in order to disparage her father even now.

'He was,' Gladys said. 'I had you via artificial insemination.'

Jane swayed and clutched the nearest bookshelf to steady herself. Of all the outlandish excuses, this one was a doozy.

'I knew he was gay when we married, but he needed a wife to stay in his parents' good books and inherit their sizeable fortune. And I needed money. We were housemates in Albury, we got along well, it seemed like a plausible story to tell everyone that we fell in love.'

Gladys bit her bottom lip, smearing fuchsia lipstick across her teeth. 'Your father was a good man and a marriage of convenience wasn't the worst thing in the world. It suited our purposes. But you're right about one thing. I needed a child to ensure I wouldn't lose everything if he ever decided to come out of the closet and cast me aside. So yes, you were a calculated decision born out of my need for financial security.'

Jane expected having her mum confirm the truth to hurt but she never anticipated the burning pain cleaving her chest in two.

'That day you heard us arguing, your father had told me he'd met someone. That he was tired of living a lie. That he wanted to end our marriage …' She shook her head, the trembling of her lower lip the only time Jane had ever seen her mother near tears. 'Could you imagine what kind of laughing stock I would've been?'

Her mother's eyes narrowed, their nasty glitter more like the Gladys Jane knew. 'I wouldn't let him do that to me, so we had that massive row you overheard … I said some harsh things—'

'Like how he'd be better off dead?' Horrible words Jane couldn't fathom at the time and now she knew the truth could never forgive her for. 'You ultimately drove Dad to his death.'

Gladys's shoulders sagged like she bore a huge invisible weight. 'I didn't think he'd actually do it … I was angry. And terrified that the life I'd built would come crumbling down around my ears.'

'Would it have been so bad? Coming clean with the truth rather than living a lie for so long?'

'If you have to ask that, you don't know me at all.' Gladys tilted her head up in defiance and reassembled the mask she wore with aplomb. 'I love my life, Jane. I put up with a sexless marriage and lived with a man who could never be more than my friend for twenty years. And I wasn't about to throw it all away because your father wanted to prance on a float in the Mardi Gras.'

Appalled at her callousness, Jane said, 'Dad was a good man. I adored him and I'm sad he had to hide his sexuality for so many years. Knowing the truth would've changed nothing for me. I loved him.'

Gladys wrinkled her nose. 'The way he doted on you made my decisions easier to bear. Because every time he indulged you, I saw it as a reward for the lengths I'd gone to in order to have the kind of life I deserved.'

'Money can't buy happiness, Mum.' Jane took a step closer, feeling nothing but pity for this empty shell of a woman. 'Are you happy?'

'Of course,' Gladys said, flashing a bright, brittle smile. 'I have everything I want.'

'But you don't have me anymore, Mum. I'm done.'

Gladys's smile faltered. 'Don't be ridiculous. I'm your mother—'

'You've only ever been a mother in name only. I never understood why you didn't like me when I was growing up. So I copied you, hoping you'd acknowledge me, but you didn't, even when I swanned around school, flaunting myself, making sure everyone

knew I was so much better than all of them …' Jane's throat tightened with disgust but she had to finish this so she could walk away
once and for all. 'I hated the way you treated me. Then when I
heard your argument, and how the lack of skid marks on the road
cast doubt as to whether Dad's death was an accident or not, I
blamed you. So I did the one thing guaranteed to pay you back. I
let people believe the worst about me, and did my utmost to disrupt
your perfect bloody life.'

Breathing ragged, Jane held up her hands and backed towards the
door. 'So now you know why, when I walk out of here, I'm never
coming back.'

Jane had finally realised it wouldn't matter how many places she
redecorated around here, how many old friendships she rekindled,
how much she tried to revamp her image, people would always
know her as Gladys Jefferson's daughter, the woman who'd frittered
away the last decade.

The only option for a fresh start was to leave.

'I'm leaving town,' Jane said, liking the sound of those decisive
words. 'I'm so tired of this.' She waved a hand between the two of
them. 'Of us.'

Gladys took a step forwards, halted, something akin to sorrow
in her eyes. 'Jane, now you know the whole truth, maybe we can
get past this—'

'You honestly think it's that simple?' Weariness seeped through
Jane's body, and she sagged against the nearest wall. 'Even now I
know Dad was gay, I still don't understand any of this. Why you
hated me when it was your choice to have a child, albeit for selfish
reasons? Why you chose to make life harder for me all these years?
Why you told Lou those lies about Ed and me? Why you tried to
sabotage my work with Mason?'

'I was horrible to you, Jane, and I'm sorry.' Gladys spoke so softly Jane had trouble hearing her. 'I blamed you.'

Incredulous, Jane shook her head. 'For what?'

'When he was alive, for tethering me to him and later, after he was gone, for reminding me of him every damn day.'

'But you just said that's the only reason you had me, to bind you to Dad for the money.' Jane pressed her fingertips to her temples, confusion making her head ache. 'As for me reminding you of him, that's bullshit—your way of projecting your guilt of driving him to his death onto me.'

'You may be right.' Gladys shook her head. 'I know my rationale doesn't make sense and I'm a terrible person for taking my problems out on you, but I sat back and watched you and your father for years, closer than close, with me being on the outer. Stupidly, I resented you for tying me to him yet was jealous at the same time. Then when he died I thought things would change, that you would turn to me like you depended on him, and when you stayed away instead I hated you for that.'

'I was giving you time to grieve because you were ignoring me anyway!' Jane threw her hands up in exasperation. 'And when I eventually came to you, hoping you'd tell me the truth about what I'd overheard the night Dad died, you left me in little doubt that I meant nothing to you.'

All her life, Jane had never seen her mother cry, so to see tears pooling in her eyes and dripping down her cheeks was almost as shocking as learning of her dad's homosexuality.

'I've never known how to love,' Gladys whispered. 'Your grandparents were cold, nasty people who sent me to boarding school from the time I commenced school. They lived in Western Australia and sent me to Victoria, that's how far they wanted to get away from me.' She barked out a harsh laugh. 'They died when I was seventeen, so I left school and started working. Odd jobs along the Murray, fruit picking mostly.'

Jane's jaw dropped. The thought of her mother doing manual labour was completely outlandish.

'That's when I met your father—in Albury. He came from a rich family but wanted to rebel, so took a consultancy job for a small irrigation firm and that's how we ended up as housemates.' Gladys shrugged. 'The rest you know. But what I'm trying to say is I always knew I'd make a lousy mother. I hoped things would change after you were born and while I tried, I was hopeless, while your father was a natural parent. You seemed to hate me more after he died, which I can understand now because you heard us arguing that horrible night … and every time I saw you, you reminded me of him and the mistake I made, telling him he'd be better off dead … I took out my guilt on you and for that, I hope you can forgive me.'

Jane didn't know what to say. She'd never seen this human side to her mother before but it didn't change facts or erase the awful things she'd done. But as tears continued to trickle down Gladys's cheeks, she knew she had to give her something.

'I appreciate you telling me this, but I think it's going to take a while for me to work through it. Give me time to process it all.'

'It's a start.' Gladys managed a watery smile. 'And more than I deserve.'

'Thanks for finally opening up. I'll let you know my plans.'

Gladys nodded. 'Where will you go?'

'Melbourne, probably.' Though in reality she could start afresh anywhere, an incredibly liberating thought she'd allow to flourish now she'd made the decision. 'I'll tell you before I leave.'

As she headed for the door, Gladys called out, 'Jane?'

She paused. 'Yes?'

'I truly am sorry.'

Jane wanted to say words were cheap and her mother's actions spoke volumes, but in coming here she'd gained the closure she'd wanted so she swallowed a bitter retort. She managed a tight smile of acknowledgement before closing the door behind her.

CHAPTER
38

Isla's coach had relented and let her back on the netball team a week early from her extended suspension, but only if Isla put in extra training every night after school, which left Tash with a luxurious forty minutes to herself at home tonight before she headed into town to pick up her daughter. She'd just settled on the couch and opened her novel when a loud knock sounded at the front door. Nobody came all the way to Wattle Lane unannounced so as she padded to the door, she hoped it wasn't bad news.

Opening it, she got a pleasant surprise. Kody on her doorstep was definitely good news but he'd usually use the back door.

'Can I come in?'

'Sure.' She held the door wider. 'How did you get here?'

'I've been in town. Asked the taxi driver to drop me off here.'

Something had changed between the time she'd taken him home this morning and now. Earlier, there'd been a softness to him when he looked at her: a spark in his eyes, the way he'd once looked at her all those years ago. Now, he could barely meet her gaze as he hobbled past her without a kiss.

Disappointment made her slam the door a little harder than intended and he jumped before spinning around to face her. Only then did she notice the large yellow envelope by his side, his fingers clutching it so hard it crinkled.

'What's that?' Though the moment she asked the question she knew. His downcast expression, his inability to touch her after he'd done nothing but, all night. Those had to be custody papers. But why the moroseness ... unless ...

'Are you trying to screw me over custody?'

He startled, his eyes wide. 'Of course not. But in these situations where the parents don't live close together it's difficult to keep everybody happy.'

Tash's blood chilled. She may be naïve but she'd envisioned them doing this together, especially after the way they'd reconnected. A visit to the lawyer as coparents, trying to come to a mutually beneficial agreement for all involved, mostly Isla. But Kody wouldn't be acting like this if he didn't think she'd be okay with it. Which meant she could be in trouble.

'Let me see.' She held out her hand and he gave her the envelope. She didn't offer him a drink or a seat, her lack of hospitality indicative of how much he'd rattled her. 'Guess I should be grateful you took it upon yourself to deliver these in person,' she said, sliding the papers out of the envelope.

'I want this to be as painless as possible, for everyone,' he said, dragging a hand through his hair, in the same way he'd done last night after she'd messed it up. 'I care about you, Tash—'

'Oh my god.' Her eyes were drawn to one thing: the time Isla would spend with her father. Twelve weeks a year. Three months. With extra weekends where possible.

She'd known it would come to this. Considering the distance between them, Isla would need to spend large blocks of time with Kody rather than custody arrangements where parents alternated every weekend. But the thought of not having her baby with her for weeks … it hurt worse than she could've imagined.

She'd never get to spend the holidays with her daughter again. She'd be the serious parent, overseeing homework and extracurricular activities, while Kody got to do all the fun stuff. She'd miss out on Christmas and Easter and other holidays when they'd usually lounge around in their pyjamas all day, eating junk food and binge-watching old favourites like *Gilmore Girls*.

Tash considered herself practical. She'd always made the best of her life, even when things had got tough. But for the first time in ages this situation had her floundering. What would she do with all that time on her own? No driving Isla around, no movie marathons on the weekends, no lunches to make. She'd been single and independent in Melbourne and loved it. But her world had shrunk considerably since then. Sure, she'd been thinking of finishing her degree but that would only take up so much time.

'I know it seems like a lot when the weeks are consecutive, like the six weeks in the summer holidays, but she'll live with you the rest of the time …' He trailed off when she staggered to the nearest dining chair and collapsed onto it. 'This is fair, Tash.'

'I know,' she murmured, her response barely above a whisper. 'It's just that I can't imagine not seeing my baby for that long. All summer …' Tears filled her eyes and she tried to blink them away, to little effect as they trickled down her cheeks. 'I know this had to be done and you deserve to spend as much time with her as possible, but seeing it in print is very different to thinking about it.'

Tash expected him to apologise for taking control of the situation and doing it on his own, especially after last night. She expected comfort, kind words. But when she dashed away her tears and looked up, he was staring at her with something akin to regret.

'This could've been so different if I'd known about her all these years,' he said, folding his arms.

'We're back to this? After all that's happened?'

'We slept together, Tash, and you think that should wipe away the first thirteen years of my daughter's life—the years I've missed?'

He was deliberately trying to hurt her. That could be the only reason for him reducing everything that had happened—building a relationship with Isla, recovering from his trauma in Wellington, accepting her help, growing closer—to a shag.

A deep-seated ache expanded in her chest, potent and strong, until she could barely breathe. 'You need to leave.'

'This shouldn't change our friendship, Tash, for Isla's sake.'

'Thanks for the reminder but I've always put Isla first.' She stood and stomped to the door, belatedly realising he couldn't walk the distance between their houses without a detrimental effect on his ankle. 'Let's go, I'll drop you off.'

Wisely, Kody kept his mouth shut for the short drive and when he got out of her car and closed the door, she took great pleasure in doing a burnout in the dust.

She hoped he choked on it.

CHAPTER
39

The following Friday night, Kody sat at a darkened table at the back of the roadhouse, casting surreptitious glances around in the hope of seeing Tash. She'd be working tonight; all hands on deck for the blues night according to Ruby. The owner was a lot younger than he'd imagined and she'd been thrilled he'd agreed to perform tonight. She'd been accommodating with his request for anonymity too and had a plan to keep the locals in line. He hoped it would work, because if the media got wind of his whereabouts, his quiet life over the last month or so would be gone, and he wasn't quite ready to give it up yet. He wanted to spend more quality time with Isla and mend fences with Tash, who'd avoided him since he'd handed her the custody agreement, only communicating through brief texts about times she'd drop Isla over.

He didn't know why she'd reacted so badly to the agreement. He'd been more than fair and since they'd slept together he wanted to ensure everything had been spelled out before they pursued ... whatever it was they'd be doing for the rest of the time he was in town.

So much for that.

He couldn't get that night out of his mind. Back when they'd first met she'd been shy about her body, and he'd been more than glad to educate her. What she lacked in experience she made up for in enthusiasm and they'd been great in bed.

But that night at the roadhouse, and later at her place, had left him stunned. Tash had been a confident, wanton woman who had seduced him with her mouth and her hands and he'd been blown away. They'd always had sparks, and whether it was due to maturity or time spent apart or their bodies recognising each other on some visceral level, that night with Tash had been memorable. And he couldn't get it out of his head no matter how hard he tried.

He hoped to talk to her tonight, to have a chat after the gig, maybe get a lift home with her. Though if the last few days were any indication she'd call him a taxi rather than be holed up in the car with him for fifteen minutes.

'Ready to start?' Ruby slid into the chair opposite, her eyes glittering with excitement. 'I can't believe *the* Kody Lansdowne is playing here tonight.' She puffed out a breath that ended in a pout. 'Damned annoying I couldn't publicise it though. It would put this place on the map.'

He laughed. 'You can plaster it on every social media app in the universe once I leave town but for now, secrecy is paramount.'

She nodded, suddenly serious. 'For Isla and Tash, I get it.'

'Thanks.'

She stood and he experienced a flash of fear like he'd been kicked in the chest. Dumb, because he'd already been on stage here. He could do this.

'Where's Tash?'

'Right here,' she said from behind him, and Ruby gave a brief nod.

'I'll give you a few minutes before introducing you,' Ruby said, then slipped away.

'You ready to do this?' Tash took the seat Ruby had vacated. She wore her hair snagged in a high ponytail, a tight navy T-shirt and denim jeans. The place obviously didn't have a dress code, but he preferred this laid-back look. Tash had slicked pink gloss on her lips and mascara darkened her lashes. She looked beautiful and his heart gave an almighty leap that left him breathless.

Concern creased her brow. 'You don't look so good.'

If she only knew his fear of performing had been replaced by a greater fear: losing her. The last time they spoke he'd acted like a jackass, belittling what they'd shared to just sex. He'd panicked because they couldn't have a meaningful relationship, but damned if he didn't want to try.

Clearing his throat, he said, 'I'm fine. Just jitters.'

'Anything I can do?'

'You've done enough.' Before he could reconsider the decision to touch her, he reached across the table and snagged her hand. 'Honestly, Tash, I couldn't have done any of this without you. You gave me a much-needed kick up the bum by pushing me out of my comfort zone to seek help, you've listened when I needed you to and you were here for me when I confronted my fear of performing.' He raised her hand to his mouth and pressed a kiss on the back of it. 'Thank you.'

She blushed and he wished he were bringing colour to her cheeks by other means. Man, he needed to get his mind out of his pants and focus.

'You're welcome,' she said. 'And I'm sorry about freaking out over the custody papers. They're a necessity. I get it. It's just tough for me, when Isla's been my world for so long.'

She'd always spoken her mind and he loved that about her. No game playing like some other women he'd dated. Tash owned up to her feelings and moved on. He could learn a lot from her.

'I understand.'

Sliding her hand out of his, she pointed at the stage. 'I think you're on.'

He glanced up to see Ruby stepping behind the microphone. Wolf-whistles and cheers broke out as she grinned and held up her hands.

Tash stood and moved around the table to lean down, her lips an inch from his ear. 'I'd tell you to break a leg but knowing you, it'd be your good one.'

He laughed and quickly turned his head, snatching a kiss before she knew what was happening. To his surprise, she lingered, pressing her lips to his, sending his libido skyrocketing, before easing away and melding into the crowd.

Ruby glanced at him and he gave a slight nod. That good-luck kiss had buoyed him but it didn't settle his nerves completely. His gut churned with trepidation though his hands were steady as he flexed and unfurled his fingers, limbering them up.

Ruby picked up the mic and moved to the front of the stage. 'Ladies and gentlemen, welcome to The Watering Hole's famous blues night.'

'Shouldn't that be infamous?' some smart-arse called out, accompanied by raucous laughter.

With a grin, Ruby held up her hand to silence them. 'Tonight, we've got a special treat for you and I want you to let me finish before asking questions, okay?' Ruby knew how to command a room because nobody spoke and she continued, 'Our performer tonight is a megastar. He's sold out concerts all around the world and is Australia's most famous rock export.'

A low hum filled the room, with the occasional titter, as Kody slunk further back into the shadows. He knew this was a risk, one he was willing to take because it was time to get his band back together and this small country venue would be the perfect place to do it.

'Tonight is his first gig in a while and he's doing me a personal favour by performing. But he's also in Brockenridge to take a break from the rigours of fame and until now, no paparazzi have caught wind of his whereabouts. And I'd like to keep it that way. So that means no one in this room breathes a word of this to anyone. No posts on social media. No texts to friends. Nothing. If you keep his identity under wraps, he will get his entire band to perform a personal gig for the whole town at the next blues night, free of charge.'

Unable to maintain silence any longer, a guy yelled, 'Are you talking about Kody Lansdowne and Rock Hard Place? My kid mentioned he's in town and I didn't believe her.'

Ruby paused for emphasis before nodding, and all hell broke loose.

Foot stomping and screams and yells filled the air and Kody smiled. This was one of the parts he loved most about the music industry: the fans. The genuine, die-hard fans that queued for hours to buy tickets, who wore memorabilia, who would go to any lengths to prove their loyalty. He was counting on the latter to keep his location a secret for now.

Ruby tapped the mic, trying to get the crowd to shush. 'Remember, folks, if you want Rock Hard Place entertaining you in Brockenridge, enjoy Kody's performance tonight but don't tell anyone.'

'We're not bloody galahs, Rubes, of course we'll keep our traps shut,' someone shouted, with rumblings of agreement.

'Now, it gives me great pleasure to welcome Kody Lansdowne to the stage.' Ruby beckoned him and Kody stood, rolled his shoulders and shook off his nerves. 'Come on up here, you rock star.'

Kody grinned and stepped into the light, and the crowd went wild again. About one hundred and thirty country folk in various shades of denim and flannelette clapping over their heads.

He raised a hand in greeting and stepped onto the stage and it wasn't until he sat on a stool with the guitar on his knee that he realised he hadn't baulked. He hadn't hesitated a second when he had the support of these people and that buoyed him for the future.

He could do this, perform in front of crowds again. Not be terrified that something would go wrong at every concert and people would die. What happened in Wellington had been a freak accident and it had taken him a long time to accept that and get to this point. He wouldn't waste time dwelling any longer. He'd give these people what they'd come to hear. The blues.

A hush fell over the crowd when he played the first chord and from that moment on he never looked back. He did covers by blues legends like B.B. King, Stevie Ray Vaughan, John Lee Hooker and Janis Joplin. He sang from the heart, from a place deep inside that had been locked away since Wellington, a place that Tash had helped crack open to set him free.

His voice soared and his fingers played and by the end of the longest set of his life, he almost keeled off the stool in relief. The thunderous applause rang in his ears as he took a bow and walked off the stage.

Into Tash's arms.

He should've known she'd be there waiting for him, supporting him, holding him up when he was near collapsing.

If he'd changed over the years, she had too. This wasn't the same woman who'd walked away from him thirteen years ago because she didn't trust him to make the right choice. This was a woman who would stand by her man and he hoped to god he could convince her of that for however long they had left together.

She led him through the kitchen and out the back door to a wooden table and benches. 'Wait there,' she said, gently pushing him down onto the bench before trotting back into the kitchen.

She reappeared a few moments later with a carafe of a creamy drink and two glasses.

'Is that what I think it is?'

She smiled, poured him a glass, and slid it across. 'Remember those banana smoothies you used to guzzle after a gig? I thought one might hit the spot now.'

'You're incredible, you know that?'

He didn't have the heart to tell her he'd stopped drinking smoothies when he left Melbourne because it was yet another thing that reminded him of her. Strolling down Acland Street in St Kilda after a gig at the Princeton, desperate for something smooth and icy cold to soothe his throat. Being a nursing student she'd been all about health and had insisted banana smoothies were packed with goodness so he'd humoured her, surprised to find they helped restore his energy after a draining night.

'I'm not the guy who just made that crowd's year. Heck, their whole decade,' she said, pride in her voice. 'You were amazing up there. Your voice ...' she choked up, and he gave her time to pull herself together. 'It's better than I remembered, a much deeper timbre, with the right touch of vibrato.' She kissed her fingertips with dramatic flair. 'Perfection.'

She made it sound like she hadn't heard his music in years. Maybe she hadn't?

'When's the last time you heard me sing?'

She took an inordinately long time to respond. 'At the Princeton thirteen years ago.'

'What?'

She grimaced. 'I couldn't do it to myself, listen to you after you became famous.'

'Why?'

'Because it killed me walking away from you and I didn't need any reminders of what I'd lost.'

She sounded so raw, so pained, that he held out his hand to comfort her. But she didn't take it. Instead, she backed away.

'Tash, I've got feelings for you—'

'Don't, please,' she murmured, clasping her hands together in front of her like a school principal about to deliver an unpleasant speech. 'I've always had feelings for you, and they never went away despite what happened. Then having you back here, telling you the truth about everything, reconnecting …' She shook her head, biting her lip. 'I feel so much for you, Kody, but it doesn't change anything. My life is here, yours is on the road and I won't be a woman who pines, waiting for whatever scraps of affection you dole out if we happen to be in the same town for a day or two.'

The bluntness and logic he'd been admiring earlier now made his gut clench. She was right. There had to be a way, but damned if he could think of it.

'Hey, you two.' Alisha stepped out of the kitchen and headed towards them. Kody didn't know whether to be annoyed at the interruption or grateful. 'Sorry to interrupt but I have something really important I want to ask Kody.'

Tash backed away more. 'I'll leave you to it.'

'No, stay, it's fine,' Alisha said, her eyes glowing in the darkness as she stared at him. 'You were amazing, Kody, and I know this is a lot to ask, but if you're around in two weeks, will you sing at my wedding?'

The smart thing to do would be to refuse. He'd be getting his walking boot off in a fortnight and he'd envisaged heading back to Melbourne for physio while rearranging what's left of the New Zealand tour and perhaps coordinating an Aussie one, giving him time to spend with Isla. But Alisha looked so hopeful, and she was Tash's best friend, so he found himself nodding.

'Sure.'

Alisha let out a loud whoop, did a little jig and clapped her hands. 'I can't believe this. Thanks so much.'

'No worries,' he said, watching Tash for a reaction.

But she remained stony-faced and stiff, like she couldn't wait to get away from him. And as Alisha prattled on about dates and venues and number of guests, he only half-listened, wondering how he and Tash could have such strong feelings yet still walk away from each other.

CHAPTER
40

As Jane approached the bar to order drinks for Louise and Bec, she ran into Tash.

'Hey, that was some blues night,' Jane said. 'How on earth does Ruby know Kody Lansdowne?'

Tash grinned and crooked her finger. 'I'll let you in on a little secret. I'm the one who knows Kody and I used my substantial influence to get him to perform tonight.'

'Good for you. You're friends?'

'Something like that.'

Jane didn't understand Tash's secretive smile. Maybe Tash had a crush on the rock star and wanted to be more than friends? Whatever the reason, it wasn't her place to ask. They'd always been polite to each other over the years but Jane didn't know the waitress that well. 'I'm guessing you won't tell me how you know him if I ask?'

Tash tapped the side of her nose and winked. 'That's on a need-to-know basis, I'm afraid.'

'I figured as much.' They laughed, and Jane hoped Tash would answer her next question, the one she really wanted to ask her.

'Can I ask you something that's not rock-star related?'

'Sure.'

'I know you got out of town for a few years, then came back. What was it like escaping?'

If Jane's odd question fazed Tash, she didn't show it. 'I loved the freedom of not living in a fishbowl, of not having every action scrutinised, of not being judged. But you know something? There's a lot to be said for a small town, because once people get past their hang-ups, they can be pretty damn supportive too.' Tash's gaze drifted over the crowd who'd stuck around for a few drinks after Kody's performance and she smiled. 'It took me a long time to figure that out.'

Jane mumbled an agreement and Tash shot her a glance. 'Are you thinking of leaving?'

'Yeah. Considering I've lived here my entire life, it's time.'

Tash hesitated, as if she wanted to say more, before reaching out and patting her on the arm. 'Do it. Who knows, you may end up like me and realise that time away from this place actually makes you appreciate it more when you return.'

Doubtful, as Jane had no intention of returning to Brockenridge once she escaped. 'Thanks.'

'No worries, and good luck.'

As Jane watched Tash move between tables, chatting and laughing with patrons, completely at ease, she wondered if there would ever come a time she'd feel as comfortable in this place.

Considering she intended to flee and not look back, absolutely no way.

Jane raised her wine glass, waiting for Louise and Bec to do the same. 'To renewing old friendships.'

'To us,' Louise echoed, and Bec added, 'To moving forwards.'

They clinked glasses and sipped at their wines, yet another uncomfortable silence extending between them. It had been easier with Kody Lansdowne performing as the music had prevented any awkward pauses in conversation. Jane had organised this impromptu get-together at the roadhouse as a way of purging more of her past. Confronting her mother had been cathartic but not nearly enough. She'd once been best friends with these girls, not that she'd treated them well. Back then she'd emulated Gladys, expecting everyone to kowtow to her, and that's what Louise and Bec had done. The three of them had never been equals; Jane had resided at the centre of her own universe and expected the other two to bask in her light. She'd been a bitch. But it was never too late to make amends and while she couldn't change the past she could make an easier future.

'I can't believe we got to see Kody Lansdowne perform live tonight,' Louise said. 'Choosing Ruby's place for us to catch up is a nice touch too.'

Jane searched for any sign of sarcasm and found none. Maybe they'd all changed for the better. 'Yeah, his performance was phenomenal, and Ruby's been great, considering how awful I was to her in high school.'

'We all were.' Bec grimaced. 'Why did we do that?'

'Because we were young and stupid and ten foot up ourselves.' Louise's dry response made them laugh. 'And we thought Jane walked on water so we did everything she said.'

'You're right.' Jane shook her head, mortified she'd been so awful back then. 'I was a horrible person and I'm sorry for dragging you two down with me.'

'Hey, we weren't blameless, not by a long shot.' Sadness clouded Louise's eyes. 'Though a small part of me does wonder if karma is real and all that bad shit we did back then is coming back to haunt us.'

'Don't believe in it.' Bec snorted, but her gaze shifted away. 'Though considering you've got a cheating arsehole for a husband, I've got four kids and no money, and Jane's single and stuck in this dead-end town, maybe karma really is a bitch.'

'Hey, I chose to stay here.' Jane lifted her glass.

'Why?' the other girls asked in unison, and the three of them laughed again.

But Jane couldn't give them an honest answer, not when her rationale had been petty and hadn't worked anyway. Making the decision to leave now might be impulsive but it felt right and she couldn't wait.

So she changed the subject. 'Should we get Ruby over here for a drink?'

Louise and Bec hesitated, before nodding.

'Be right back.' Jane stood and scanned the diner. She couldn't see Ruby so she headed towards the bar to ask Aldo, the bartender. However, she'd only made it halfway across the room when an arm snaked around her waist from behind and she jumped.

'Miss me, hot stuff?'

She spun around, dislodging the possessive arm, and glared at the bleary-eyed guy staring at her with a wolfish grin. She couldn't remember his name but she recognised him, some smarmy sales-man she'd flirted with a few years ago when he'd passed through town. He'd have to be forty-something but dyed his hair too dark, had a fake tan and whitened teeth. A city guy, fake and sleazy, the kind of man she'd deliberately targeted in the past because it would piss off her mother. He made her skin crawl.

'I have a boyfriend,' she said, her tone firm. Not that she could class Mason as such, but what he didn't know wouldn't hurt him.

The man leered at her, before shrugging. 'Too bad.'

She breathed a sigh of relief when he lurched away, in search of another clueless woman like she'd once been. But she'd barely taken three steps when another guy waylaid her.

'Hey there, Janey-Jane.' He slung an arm across her shoulder. 'How are you?'

Jane suppressed a shudder. This guy was older and possessive. A sheep farmer from New South Wales, he came through town every few months. She'd liked him because he lavished attention on her. He made her feel special in the same way her father had. Considering his age, no prizes for guessing she had daddy issues and that's what had attracted her to him in the first place.

'I'm fine, thanks, but I have a boyfriend now.'

She shrugged off his arm and he looked her up and down, sceptical. 'Last time I saw you, you were single and loving it.' He leaned in too close and she gritted her teeth against the stench of his woodsy aftershave. 'What happened to fun-loving Jane?'

Annoyed he hadn't got the message, she took a step back. 'Already told you, I'm seeing someone, so back off.'

He must've heard something in her tone because he held up his hands in surrender. 'Don't be so touchy, love. See you round.'

'Not if I can bloody help it,' she muttered to his retreating back, only to turn and see Mason standing behind her. How long had he been there? Had he heard that exchange?

By his thunderous expression, he had. Great.

'You okay?' He touched her arm and she nodded.

'Fine.'

'Who were those guys?'

'Mistakes.'

She expected him to push the issue, and was relieved when he didn't. The last thing she wanted to do was rehash her crappy taste in men before he came along.

'Am I the guy you're seeing?'

She blushed. 'That was an excuse I used to fob them off.'

'But what if you were? Seeing me for real, that is?' He slipped his hand into hers, intertwining their fingers. 'I know I said I'd be leaving town once I got Mum up to speed with the French side of the baking, but I've been doing a lot of thinking and I want to stick around.' He leaned down to whisper in her ear, 'See if we can make this thing between us work. What do you say?'

Jane wanted to say 'hell, yeah' but she couldn't. He wanted to stay; she wanted to leave. Brockenridge held nothing for her anymore. She'd confronted her mother, she'd learned the truth about her father and she needed a clean start. Having those two sleazes approach her sealed it. Unless she got away and created a fresh start in a place where nobody knew her, she'd always be misjudged in this town.

Mason obviously took her silence as consideration, because he continued, 'I've given up my lease on my apartment in Paris. So I'm officially homeless, unless you fancy a roommate?'

Her heart gave a funny twang and she clutched onto his hand like she'd never let go. But she had to. She'd wasted enough of her life doing things for other people: making her dad proud; making her mum mad; making herself miserable. Time to start living her life, even if part of her had already fallen for Mason and walking away from him would be the hardest thing she'd ever had to do.

'I'm leaving,' she said, giving his hand a squeeze and releasing it. 'You're a great guy, Mason, and I like you a lot, but it's my time now. You've done so much. You've travelled and lived abroad and become successful in your career, while I've done nothing. Our timing really does suck, but I have to do this, for me.'

'I understand,' he said, but the gruffness in his tone told her he wasn't happy.

They stared at each other for an interminable moment before she said, 'I'm here with friends and I'm looking for Ruby to join us, so I better get back to them.'

'So that's it?'

She didn't warrant his hint of bitterness. They hadn't been in a relationship. She owed him nothing. But as she nodded and walked away, she couldn't help but wonder if, after all the stuff-ups in her life, she'd just made the biggest mistake yet.

CHAPTER

41

It had been late by the time Tash got home after her shift last night and Isla had been asleep, then up early and on the school bus before Tash had waken. The sitter had said she'd gone to bed early, listening to Rock Hard Place's greatest hits. Of course; her father was all she could talk about these days. Which would make the news Tash was going to deliver when she picked her up from school shortly very welcome.

After Kody had declared his feelings for her last night at the roadhouse and she'd articulated why they couldn't be together, Tash knew she had to get things between them back on a platonic level. So first thing this morning she'd signed the custody papers and dropped them off at the lawyer. Kody had texted her a few times and called twice; she'd ignored him. No point rehashing the hurt. They couldn't be together and she needed some time and space from him, otherwise she'd be tempted to renege on her stance to not date him if he tried to sweet-talk her.

And he would. He'd always been good at that. She'd been powerless to resist Kody at his charming best and, last night, she'd come
close to throwing caution to the wind and agreeing to a relationship, whatever that may entail.

But she couldn't be some rock star's groupie, not at her age. She
had responsibilities and a good example to set. What would Isla
think if Tash fell into Kody's arms whenever he came to town? It
would definitely send her impressionable daughter the wrong message: that it was okay to wait around for a man, to put his needs
first, to be passive rather than proactive in a relationship.

No, she'd never do that to Isla. And she wouldn't do it to herself
either. Which is why she had to set clear boundaries, starting today.

She pulled up outside the school gate as her mobile beeped.
Turning off the engine, she slid the phone from her bag and glanced
at the screen. Kody. Again. She was on the verge of ignoring him
when the first two words of his message caught her eye.

I'm leaving.

She sucked in a breath and read the rest.

Heading back 2 Melbourne 4 band meeting.

I've let Isla know.

Will be back in a week.

A pain so swift and sharp it made her gasp lodged in her chest.
Silly, to have a physical reaction to news she'd been expecting all
along. But after last night surely he could've said goodbye in person, at least to his daughter?

Though it wasn't Isla that Tash was concerned about and she
wished she'd accepted one of his calls today. Now she'd never know
what he'd wanted and once again she'd be stuck in this town, mull-
ing what might have been with the man she loved.

Loved?

Oh no. No, no, no. She shouldn't love him. She couldn't.

But what if she did?

Reeling from the realisation, she couldn't muster an appropriate response to the text so she shoved her mobile back in her bag and focussed on her breathing. She needed to calm the hell down because Isla would be here any minute and her daughter would take one look at her and know something was up.

Yet she couldn't ignore that pesky L word. When did she fall back in love with Kody? They'd hardly spent enough time together for it to happen. And most of that time had been fraught with resentment and anger on his part, guilt and self-recrimination on hers.

That's when an even more startling realisation nudged its way into her conscience.

Had she never fallen out of love with him?

She'd devoted the last thirteen years to raising Isla and hadn't been interested in relationships with other guys, when many single mums had a healthy dating life and made it work despite the demands of motherhood. Kody had been it for her and she never could've anticipated that he'd still be rocking her world all these years later.

The door opened and Isla slid into the car, shoving her bag under the console. 'Hey, Mum.'

Pasting a smile on her face, Tash turned. 'Hey, sweetie, how was school?'

'The usual. PE and drama rocked, the rest sucked.'

This response was nothing out of the ordinary and Tash would usually give a gentle lecture about the importance of all subjects for a good VCE score in order to further her education. But she didn't have the heart for it today.

'Everything okay, Mum?'

'Sure.'

Isla studied her face, her astute gaze way too mature for an almost-thirteen-year-old. 'Are you sad because Dad's leaving?'

'No, I understand he's got work to do in Melbourne,' Tash said, sounding brusque. She softened it with, 'But we've worked out the custody agreement and you'll be spending heaps of time with him.'

Isla's eyes lit up. 'Really? When?'

'All the school holidays and he'll try to squeeze in weekends here and there when he can.'

'Awesome.' She grinned, before surprising Tash by reaching over and hugging her. 'Thanks for sorting all that out, Mum. I know it must be hard on you seeing an old boyfriend, but I'm glad you and Dad can be friends now.'

'Yeah, we're friends,' Tash parroted, sounding idiotic but struggling to keep her composure. Because 'friends' conjured up visions of just that: Tash having to hear about his latest girlfriend, more than likely from Isla, who would think nothing of enthusing over her father's newest glamorous, model-thin babe. She'd hear all about his decadent life and how he lavished Isla with treats, while she'd be stuck in Brockenridge lamenting decisions of the past.

She needed something to focus on, something to take her mind off the fact she'd lost Kody and for too many months of the year she'd be losing Isla too. The obvious choice would be to finish her nursing degree. She'd have the time and throwing herself into study while maintaining her job would guarantee she'd have minimal downtime to dwell and stress.

Oblivious to her whirling thoughts, Isla released her and snapped on her seat belt. When Tash made no move to start the car, Isla waved a hand in front of her face.

'Mum, you're really spaced out.'

'That's because I'm thinking of finishing my nursing degree,' she said in a rush, knowing that confessing to Isla made it real. 'How do you feel about that?'

'I think it's fantastic.' Her daughter's nose crinkled in the same cute way it used to when she was three. 'But all that study. Yuck.'

'I'll let you in on a little secret.' Tash crooked a finger at her. 'I'm actually a nerd at heart who loves studying.'

Isla rolled her eyes. 'I always knew you were an alien from another planet,' she said, and laughed.

Tash joined in, feeling lighter than she had a few moments ago. 'On that note, let's head home and I'll whip you up a batch of my famous outer space oatmeal cookies.'

'Deal.'

Tash managed to make small talk with Isla all the way home, inserting the proper 'uh-huhs' and 'no ways' at appropriate points in the conversation. But her mind was elsewhere, dwelling on a sexy rock star who'd stolen her heart yet again without trying.

CHAPTER

42

Nostalgia swamped Kody as he strolled along Beach Road in the direction of the Princeton. He'd traversed this route countless times as a teen and later in his early twenties, when he played nightly gigs. The Princeton had been the band's first gig and their last in Australia. He'd been a fool for avoiding his home city because of a failed relationship. Then again, considering Tash had been avoiding his calls and texts, maybe he'd done the right thing.

What had she expected him to do, sit around and wait for her to come to her senses? He'd laid his heart on the line, and she'd sliced and diced it and handed it back on a platter. He knew there'd be obstacles to them getting together. Hell, the last thing he wanted was a long-distance relationship but he'd been willing to take a risk because it was her. His Tash.

The kicker was, his yearning to be with her had nothing to do with her being the mother of his child and everything to do with his own selfish needs. Namely, she was the only woman who'd ever really got him. And the years apart hadn't eradicated that. If anything, the older, wiser versions of themselves seemed to meld even better than before.

He understood her reservations. He had the same himself, especially about what would happen to his relationship with Isla if he started something with Tash and it all went pear-shaped. But he hadn't got this far in his life without taking risks and he believed this one was worth it. Why couldn't she feel the same?

As he turned into Fitzroy Street, familiar aromas thrust him back in time. Sautéed onion and garlic from the best pasta restaurant in Melbourne, cumin and garam masala from a spicy Indian café, and lush cinnamon and vanilla from a gelateria. He'd sampled them all with Tash by his side and being back here without her seemed ... wrong.

Shaking off his nostalgia, he pushed through the main door of the Princeton. Yanni would be in the back room near the pool tables and as he wound his way through the bar, empty save for a few bar staff cleaning up after patrons who'd probably stumbled out of here only a few hours earlier, Kody wondered what would have happened if he'd never taken a chance and gone to LA. Would he still be here, performing gigs, wishing for something more? Would he be in a relationship with Tash? Married? Regretful and bitter that he hadn't chased his dream?

That's when he realised she'd given him the ultimate gift.

Freedom.

Because she was right, damn it. If she'd told him about keeping the baby, he wouldn't have abandoned her. Considering his upbringing, when he'd yearned for a stable family and parents that loved him, he never would've left. But he would've stayed for the wrong reasons. Obligation didn't make for a good relationship long term and his regret may have turned him into a shitty dad too.

It was time to let go of his lingering resentment towards Tash and move forwards. Who knows, maybe she sensed that in him and that's why she'd shot him down when he mentioned a relationship?

Only one way to find out.

Once he'd wrapped up business in Melbourne, he intended on heading back to Brockenridge to sort out his future.

As Kody entered the small back room reserved for bands to chill between sets, he spied Yanni scrolling through his phone and emotion tightened his chest. Yanni was the brother he'd never had and he'd stood by him through so much. He hoped he would understand the decision Kody had made.

'Hey, bozo,' he called out, and Yanni's head lifted, a goofy grin spreading across his face.

'Hey, putz.' Yanni stood as he approached and they embraced, slapping each other's backs, before releasing. 'Apart from the limp, you look good. Country air suits you.'

'It does.' He sat and rested his forearms on the table. 'It's weird being back in Melbourne after all this time.'

'Yeah, especially considering it's your home city.' Yanni slugged him on the arm. 'So tell me everything.' He shook his head. 'I can't believe you have a kid. What's she like? How are you getting on? How's Tash?'

'Isla's great. And she's into music, which is fantastic. She asked me to teach her guitar so I've been doing that. She's a quick study.' His throat tightened and he cleared it. 'And she's accepted me like I've always been around, which is pretty damn amazing.'

'I'm happy for you, mate. Do you have any pics?'

'Yeah.' Kody slid his mobile out of his pocket. He hadn't taken a lot of photos of Isla because he hadn't wanted to creep her out, but he'd snapped a few when she'd been practising guitar, and a couple when they were watching some crappy reality show. Different angles, different lighting, but all highlighting how damn lucky he was to have a kid like her. 'Here.'

He held out his phone and Yanni's eyes widened. 'Shit, man, she's the spitting image of Tash, but she has your eyes.'

'Yeah, I know, freaky.'

Kody scrolled through a few more pics, resisting the urge to puff out his chest with pride at how amazing his daughter was. When he pocketed his phone, Yanni pinned him with an astute stare.

'You're not coming back to the band, are you?'

He should've known his best mate would read his mind.

'It's more complicated than that.'

'And does this complication have anything to do with Tash, considering you haven't mentioned her despite me asking?'

Kody huffed out a sigh. 'I'm in love with her.'

'And have you told her that?'

'Sort of.'

Yanni punched him on the arm again. 'Bozo, you already screwed up with her once before.'

'But that wasn't my fault. She lied to me.'

'Yet you walked away when she told you she was going to abort your baby?' Yanni sounded incredulous, and slightly judgemental. 'Come on, man, you had a choice back then even though you're probably telling yourself you didn't.'

Kody held up his hands. 'Hey, I know, okay? And I've come to terms with it. But things are more complicated now.'

'Because of Isla?'

'And you. You and the guys are my family, I don't want to let you down.'

'You're thinking of quitting the band completely?'

'Hell, no. But the changes I want to instigate will affect you all, which is why I wanted to run a few ideas past you first.'

'Okay, shoot.'

'Rock Hard Place is still on top. We're selling out concerts, our downloads and streaming are through the roof. Because of this popularity I reckon we can pick and choose gigs, when we record, that kind of thing. We don't have to do the manic tour thing anymore. And this way we all get to explore what's beyond the band, you know?'

Yanni didn't answer for a few seconds and Kody braced for his idea to be shot down. Then Yanni said, 'I think it's a great idea.'

'Yeah?'

'Hell, yeah.' Yanni thumped his chest. 'I'm sick of being a bachelor. I want a family. Seeing Daz with his kids ... anyway, I'd love to chill out in Brockenridge more often, see what's out there for me beyond the band. That town gets under your skin a little, you know?'

'It has a unique vibe, that's for sure.' The quiet country town had crept under his guard in a way he'd never expected and if he had his way, he'd be spending a lot more time there.

'With a little luck, we might be neighbours?' Yanni's sly wink made Kody roll his eyes.

'Considering Tash doesn't want a bar of me I don't think I'll be moving in with her any time soon.'

'You'll sort it out. Love makes us do crazy things.'

'Speaking of crazy, I kind of promised the owner of the roadhouse where Tash works that the band would perform a gig there.'

'What the—'

'Tash and Ruby, the owner, helped me out.' Kody realised he was fiddling, tracing gouges in the worn wooden table, and interlocked his fingers to stop. 'Those concert deaths messed me up real bad, man. I couldn't even look at a guitar let alone touch it. But I worked through my shit with professional help—' he held up his hand, '—don't say I told you so, because we both know you were right. Anyway, it was hard getting up on stage again but I did it, and I thought doing a low-key gig in front of a hundred might help me face my fears, which it did. But to maintain my privacy, Ruby got everyone to keep their mouths shut with the promise we'd do a gig.'

'Consider it done,' Yanni said with a brisk nod. 'The boys have been worried about you, so I'll invite them all up to my place for a weekend, we'll chill, have a barbie and play this gig.'

'Knew I could count on you, mate.' Kody reached across and slapped him on the back. 'I know the boys will be here soon and we have to break the news about our cut-back schedule to Tony, but do you think you could keep all that stuff about Tash and Isla private?'

Yanni nodded. 'Our illustrious manager is going to have a coronary but he'll have no choice but to accept our decision. As for the rest …' He shrugged. 'News is going to get out about you having a kid. Then the paparazzi will descend. If you don't give them something, they'll make shit up and that'll be worse for all of you.'

'Yeah, I know, I'll discuss a plan with Tony, then I'll get Tash onboard.' The last thing Kody wanted was for her life to be disrupted because of him. That would do him no favours when he had every intention of convincing her how good they were together.

'So back to my original question: how is Tash?'

'As stubborn and gorgeous as ever.'

Yanni chuckled. 'Your grin says it all, putz. She's the one.'

'Yeah, she is, and it fucking terrifies me.'

Yanni hesitated, a flicker of worry in his eyes. 'Just make sure you get everything sorted before the news breaks, because being in this biz can be tough on the families.'

'Daz has managed to shield Bess and the kids well, and they're divorced.'

'Yeah, but it takes work, which is why I'm advising you to put things into place to protect Tash and Isla.'

'Thanks, mate, for everything.'

'No worries.' Yanni stood. 'I'll go rustle up drinks before the boys get here.'

'Thanks,' Kody said, waiting until Yanni left before sliding his phone out of his pocket again.

Still no missed calls or messages. He wanted to badger Tash to listen to him, but he'd already done enough of that and she'd ignored him completely. Besides, the news he had to deliver would be best done face to face.

The sooner he wrapped things up in Melbourne and headed back to Brockenridge, the better.

CHAPTER
43

Having one too many wines with Louise and Bec last night hadn't been a good idea considering Jane's head still throbbed after midday. But she'd needed the numbness that came with alcohol oblivion because if she hadn't drunk after walking away from Mason she would've blurted the whole sorry tale to the girls and that would've been poor form considering they'd only just re-bonded.

She'd enjoyed spending time with them, and regretted not doing it sooner. She couldn't believe she'd wasted a decade of her life wrapped up in a stupid vendetta against her mother trying to prove a point. Then again, Louise and Bec had their fair share of problems, so she didn't blame them for letting the friendship lapse. And considering their very real difficulties, hers would've seemed trite and selfish. Besides, divulging her dilemma about Mason would've made it real and she didn't want to admit to herself let alone others that she may have made a mistake.

When a guy like Mason Woodley was interested in a relationship, you shouldn't dismiss it. But that's exactly what she'd done and she'd been second-guessing herself ever since. Which explained why she'd taken the drastic step of listing her house with the real estate agent first thing this morning and had booked a week in a fancy hotel in Melbourne, giving her enough time to source a rental property in person.

She had to get out of Brockenridge. She had to leave the past behind. Even if it felt like she was abandoning a possible future before it had begun.

To make matters worse, Mason had texted her, asking her to meet him at the patisserie to do a last-minute check on her work before the grand opening in a few days. She could've refused but that would be unprofessional and he'd done nothing to warrant that kind of behaviour. So she'd do this final check, bid him a civilised goodbye, and head back home to start packing. A simple plan that came unstuck when she arrived at the patisserie to find the windows covered in opaque sheets. Weird, considering the windows hadn't been covered while the renovations were being done. Maybe Mason wanted to make the opening extra exciting by doing a big reveal on the day with all his fancy-schmancy baked goodies on display?

She tried the doorknob. Locked. Her mobile beeped with an incoming message.

Come around the back.

Annoyed he was playing games with her, Jane trudged around to the rear entrance. She knocked and the door swung open, revealing Mason in chef's whites. They should've made him look dorky; she'd watched enough reality cooking shows on TV to know this outfit did nothing for the wearer. But of course Mason rocked it, the crispness of the white jacket accentuating his tan and making him look more delectable than the pastries he created.

'Thanks for coming,' he said, his genuine smile making her heart race.

'You made it sound important that I do a final check, so here I am.' She stepped into the small hallway leading to the kitchen on the left and the seating area on the right. Rich aromas tantalised her: sugar, nutmeg, honey, roasted nuts. 'You've been busy,' she said, as her stomach rumbled.

'Hope you're hungry.' He placed a hand in the small of her back, a gesture she secretly loved, as he guided her towards the dining area.

'I didn't come here to eat ... oh—' She gaped at a table set for two in the middle of the room, covered in tiny pastries of every description: eclairs, madeleines, mille-feuilles, petit fours, beignets, pains au chocolat and macarons, arranged artfully on white platters designed to bring out their vivid colours. Saliva pooled in her mouth and she swallowed. If Mason thought the way to a woman's heart was through her stomach, he was damn right.

He propelled her forwards and when they reached the table he pulled out a chair for her, waited until she sat, then pulled up a chair next to her, so close their knees touched. 'I wanted you to see what you'd be missing out on.' His gaze locked on hers, challenging.

She sighed. 'We're not just talking about pastries, are we?'

'Of course not.' Mason gripped her hand and, rather than snatch it away, she savoured one last touch. 'I understand your need to leave Brockenridge, I truly do, but I think we've got something special I'd like to explore. Why don't you take a trip? However long you want, but come back to Brockenridge to live—'

'I can't.'

When his jaw went rigid with tension, she knew she'd have to give him something to get him to back off. 'You saw what happened at the roadhouse with those two sleazes? That's what I'm known for in this town.' She flung the truth at him, tilting her chin in defiance to stare him down.

To his credit he didn't flinch but his eyebrows rose a fraction. 'Yet you've lived here for over a decade since school finished when you could've left at any time?'

'You're not judging me?'

He shook his head. 'Whatever you've done, it's in the past—'

'People have long memories. You know the small-town mentality of a place like this.'

'Then we'll create new memories.' He shuffled a little closer, until their thighs aligned and she could feel the heat radiating off him. 'You wouldn't be afraid of a little gossip otherwise you would've left years ago, so tell me why you're really leaving now?'

'Be careful what you wish for,' she murmured, trying to extract her hand from his but he wouldn't let her. 'My dad died when I was nineteen after a major blowout with my mum. I overheard some of it. She didn't want a child, only had me to get my dad's wealth, that kind of thing. The argument escalated and she ended up saying she wished he was dead. He got in the car and hit a tree ...' She blinked back the tears burning her eyes. 'The lack of skid marks suggested it was deliberate.'

'Shit, Jane, I had no idea, I'm sorry.'

'I blamed Mum. I expected her to grieve like I did. Instead, when I asked her about it, she shut me out. Which was nothing new, considering she'd treated me like a hindrance my entire life, but I thought after Dad died things might be different, she'd feel guilty or something and reach out ...' She shook her head. 'Instead, in her warped way, she resented me more, so I stayed in town and did some dumb-arse things to shame her. None of it worked, of course, and we ended up avoiding each other. She's done some hateful stuff I can't fathom.' She blew out a breath. 'I've confronted her, and she came clean about a lot. She wants us to forgive and forget, but I'm not ready for that yet.'

She looked him in the eye. 'I need to get away, gain a new perspective, discover who I am beyond this town.'

'Then I'm coming with you.' He took her other hand and pulled her to her feet. 'Do you want to know why I didn't renew the lease on my apartment in Paris? Because you're here and I thought this was where you wanted to be. I did it to prove to you how invested I am in us.'

'But why?'

They'd barely dated and hadn't even had sex. Why would a guy like him give up so much to be with a girl like her?

'Because I've fallen for you,' he murmured, before brushing a soft kiss across her lips. 'Every obstinate, stunning inch of you, and I want to explore what this spark between us could turn into.'

In that moment, Jane understood the meaning of having a lightbulb moment. She'd been blessed in the looks and body department, and had wielded her sexuality since she'd hit her teens. Yet here was this amazing, thoughtful, gorgeous guy wanting a relationship with her even though she hadn't used her body to get what she wanted. How much more proof did she need he could be a keeper? Joy filled her chest and she laughed for the sheer hell of it.

'That wasn't the reaction I was expecting.'

'I'm happy,' she said, beaming at him. 'So does this mean once the patisserie is functional you'd be willing to come hang out with me in Melbourne?'

He nodded, his eyes glinting with happiness. 'Wherever you are, I'll be there.'

Jane flung herself at him, plastering her mouth to his, desperate to show him how much his sacrifice meant. He deepened the kiss, groaning into her mouth.

As delicious as those pastries looked, they'd have to wait until later.

CHAPTER

44

As soon as the driver passed the 'Welcome to Brockenridge' sign, Kody texted Isla. As much as he couldn't wait to see his daughter after a week away, he didn't want her around for what he had to discuss with Tash. Relieved when she responded, saying she'd be at netball practice for the next hour before going to Alisha's wedding, he directed the driver to Tash's place.

Another gem of information Isla had provided: Tash was at home doing some research while Isla was getting ready at Ellen's before her friend's father would drop her off at the town square for the wedding. The research bit piqued his curiosity. What was Tash up to? He hoped it had to do with her nursing degree, because she deserved to follow her dream. With him by her side, if she'd have him.

His attempt to convince her the two of them should be together hadn't gone so well last time. They'd both declared feelings for each other but she'd understandably closed him down. She thought he'd leave her because of his career. He had to show her how a relationship could work between them, with a little compromise.

The driver had been respectful of his need for silence on the drive back from Melbourne—feigning sleep had helped—but once they hit Brockenridge and Kody opened his eyes to text Isla, the guy wouldn't stop badgering him for information regarding the band's next tour and how many women he'd slept with.

Reluctant to tell the driver to shut the hell up, he kept his responses to a minimum, grateful when the car pulled up outside Tash's place. After handing over the fare and a tip, he headed up the path towards the house and around the side to the back door.

He liked the informality of the country, how everyone knew everyone else. It soothed the long-buried loneliness that had plagued him for as long as he could remember. Living on the road had been one long adventure but there was a lot to be said for having someone special to share it with.

Knocking on the door, he mentally rehearsed what he'd say. He'd had enough time to do it on the drive but whenever he got to the part about revealing his true feelings he'd stall, even in his head. Dating him would be tough and even though he'd laid out a plan with Tony, the band's manager, to limit the fallout once news of Isla broke, he knew Tash would hate any unwarranted attention. Back in his days playing at the Princeton when he'd been a nobody, he'd seen the way she'd eye the groupies, regulars who attended gigs every Thursday, Friday and Saturday nights. He'd teased her about being jealous once and she'd laughed it off, but he'd noticed her wariness whenever one of the groupies approached him.

How much worse would it be for her now, when women thought nothing of slipping their phone numbers—and worse—into his pocket? When they pulled down tops to have their bras or breasts autographed? When they'd send naked pics? Thankfully the band had PR people to filter the pics out these days but it had been bad at the start, the lengths women would go to in order to get near a rock

star. Then again, he counted on the townsfolk of Brockenridge ral-
lying around Tash once the news broke. Country folk wouldn't put
up with much crap and he counted on the paparazzi soon tiring of
the story and moving on.

When she didn't answer, he knocked again, only to glimpse
movement from behind the sheer curtain. Stifling a grin, he called
out, 'I can see you're in there. Avoidance is futile.'

He heard a muffled, 'Damn it,' and grinned as she opened the door.

'Miss me?' He rested a hand against the doorjamb, deliberately
casual, knowing it would rile her. He shouldn't, not when he
wanted her to hear him out, but he couldn't resist, she looked that
pissed off to see him.

'Don't flatter yourself.' She opened the door wider. 'I guess you'd
better come in considering you sent the driver packing.'

'Where's that country hospitality Brockenridge is supposed to be
famous for?'

'That's only reserved for friends.'

'Ouch.' He pretended to stagger and stepped into the kitchen,
waiting until she closed the door before taking the folded docu-
ment out of his pocket.

She eyed it warily. 'What's that?'

'A plan.'

'For?'

'You and me.'

Her eyes widened and she backed up a few steps. 'Kody, we've
been through this. Anything between us isn't feasible—'

'I'm stepping away from the band.'

Her jaw dropped. 'You can't. That band is your life.'

'No, my life is here. With you and Isla.'

Colour suffused her cheeks and he could almost see the wheels
turning in her head.

'What are you saying?'

'That I want to prove to you I'm in this for the long haul.' He unfolded the paper, smoothed it out and held it up. 'If we're going to do this right, the way the news gets out is important, so a press release will control it.'

She stared at him like he'd sprouted another head. 'You want to announce to the world that you have a daughter? Are you nuts? Media will be all over this place like ants at a picnic.' She shook her head, not even glancing at the paper. 'No way.'

Knowing she'd react like this, he laid the paper on the nearby dining table. 'Give me some credit. I've spent the time in Melbourne reorganising my life so I can be with you and Isla as much as possible, so the least you can do is hear me out.'

She visibly deflated. 'Sorry. You know me, always ready to make rash judgements.'

He bit back a smile, her moroseness incredibly endearing. 'Yeah, I do know you, yet I still want us to be together. Go figure.'

'Stop it,' she muttered, but he glimpsed a smile. 'Okay, I'll listen.'

'I'm not leaving the band, but we're cutting back, big time. No more long tours. We're old enough and successful enough to pick and choose what we do these days, so that means focussing on recording and less live gigs.'

Her lips compressed, her silence telling. She wasn't impressed.

'I want to put down roots for a while, explore a relationship with you, be a dad to Isla, without having her travelling between us. So I'll get a place in Brockenridge, see how it works out.' He held up his hands like he had nothing to hide. 'No pressure, Tash. I just want you to know I'm not jerking you around, that I'm serious about us.'

The tension underlining her mouth softened. 'Those are some major changes for you. Are you sure about it?'

He nodded. 'Absolutely. The boys are onboard too. We've been on the road too long. About time we came home to Australia and concentrated on our local fans.'

She didn't speak for a while and when she did, it was to murmur, 'I'm a fan.'

Hope flickered to life. 'Then that pretty much guarantees I'll be focussing on you.'

She smiled and he wanted to punch the air and let out a happy whoop.

'I need some time so I can think about this, because I always weigh every decision involving Isla carefully.'

She was making him sweat and he bit back a grin. 'How much time?'

Her smile widened. 'As it turns out, no time at all, because I'll be returning to study fairly soon, completing my nursing degree part-time while working, so it'd be handy having you around.'

He laughed at her joke, as an invisible weight lifted off his shoulders. 'So that's the only reason you want to give us a go? For my general dogsbody skills.'

She tapped her bottom lip, pretending to think, before snapping her fingers. 'That, and some other *skills* you have.'

He crossed the kitchen in three quick steps, his ankle not twanging at all, to sweep her into his arms. 'So you want to use me for my body too?'

'Over and over again,' she murmured against the corner of his mouth a moment before she kissed him.

'Lucky I married Harry today otherwise I reckon I'd give you a run for your money with Hot Pants.' Alisha nudged Tash, who hadn't taken her eyes off the stage since Kody had stepped up to perform a great rendition of Billy Idol's 'White Wedding'.

'Huh, did you say something?' Tash cupped her ear and leaned over. 'I think you did, but I didn't hear because I'm too busy perving on my boyfriend.'

Alisha laughed. 'I'm so glad you two are back together. And I'm also glad he got that walking boot off in time to slip into those leather pants.' She fanned her face. 'It's indecent, I tell you, and I'm a married woman now.'

While Tash loved the way those tight pants highlighted Kody's assets, she had every intention of getting more indecent with him later.

'You're blushing,' Alisha said, with a smirk.

'It's the heat.'

'Sure thing.' Alisha gestured at the five hundred-strong crowd milling about the marquee in the town centre. 'I can't believe my small, intimate, closest friends and family only wedding turned into this.'

'Quit your moaning, you love it,' Tash said, rapt to see her boyfriend—she'd never get tired of calling him that—on stage in front of most of the town.

'I guess I'll have bragging rights for life, with Kody Landsdowne performing at my wedding.'

Ruby sidled up to them and bumped Alisha with her hip. 'So you didn't mind me swapping the roadhouse as your wedding venue and organising all this?'

'This town has been my life for so long, it was a great idea,' Alisha said, shooing away a fly in danger of becoming stuck in her veil. 'I even saw my introverted husband busting a few moves with some of those old chooks. You inviting half the town has been worth seeing that.'

'How often are you going to call him your husband after today?'

'All the time.' Alisha held her left arm out, admiring the shiny gold band on her ring finger. 'Can't believe I'm married. Poor Brenda and Cyril had given up hope, I think.'

'So had we, you old spinster,' Ruby said with a chuckle, earning an elbow from Alisha.

'When's Connor going to make an honest woman out of you?'

'We're eloping,' Ruby said. 'Less angst.'

'True,' Alisha said. 'But who's going to forget today? Brockenridge folk are going to be talking about this legendary wedding for decades.'

'You deserve the spotlight, sweetie, after some of the shit you copped growing up.' Tash slipped an arm around her waist and squeezed, raising her champagne glass with the other hand. 'We've all come a long way.'

'I'll drink to that,' Ruby said, beckoning to a waiter and snagging another two champagnes, one for her, the other for Alisha, before raising her glass in a toast. 'To us. And those lucky bastards we love with all our hearts.'

'To us,' Tash and Alisha echoed, clinking glasses, as Jane strolled over, holding hands with Mason, the dishy new baker in town.

'Congrats, Alisha,' Jane said. 'Great wedding.'

'That's what happens when you have my famous boyfriend perform at your nuptials,' Tash deadpanned, and they laughed.

'Ladies, will you excuse me while I go check on the cake?' Mason asked, looking more like a model than a patissier in his tux.

'It's perfect, Mason, thanks,' Alisha said. 'But I did see Harry hovering near it earlier so you better go see he hasn't added an extra macaron or two.'

'I'll come with you,' Jane said, staring at her man with obvious adoration. 'We're leaving for Melbourne tomorrow and I'm not letting this guy out of my sight before then.'

'She's a ball and chain already.' Mason rolled his eyes before planting a kiss on Jane's lips.

Tash chuckled, but before Jane could leave she stepped closer and said softly, 'All the best with your fresh start. He's divine.'

Jane flashed her a grateful glance before falling into step with Mason and heading for the buffet marquee, as Tash spied Kody signing autographs and waving her over.

'On that note, ladies, my sexy man is calling me.' She downed the rest of her champagne and leaned over to give Alisha a quick hug. 'I'm so happy for you. And this is the best day ever.'

Alisha's eyes shimmered and she blinked rapidly. 'Your best day ever will come when you and Hottie McHottie tie the knot with Isla as your bridesmaid.'

The thought made Tash want to bawl too. 'Considering we've only been back together for a few hours that's not going to happen any time soon, but I appreciate the sentiment.'

'Go be with your man,' Ruby said, giving her a gentle shove. 'I think Connor and Harry have finished being total groupies and are heading this way.'

Tash smiled at her friends and headed towards the stage, where Kody had ducked into a makeshift room where he'd warmed up. When she reached the canvas door his hand snuck out, grabbed hers and tugged her inside.

'Hey, watch the dress,' she said, laughing as he picked her up and twirled her in his arms.

'Why? I'm going to tear it off you later anyway.'

She smacked his chest playfully. 'Cut the bad-boy act. I know you're a softie on the inside.'

'Only for you,' he murmured, nibbling on her earlobe. 'You know that last song was for you, right?'

'"White Wedding"?'

When he didn't speak, Tash eased away to find the man she loved staring at her with hope.

'What do you think about you and me having one of those some day?' He grasped her hand and pressed it to his chest, directly over his heart. 'We've got a lot of lost time to make up for.'

Tears of joy burned the back of her eyes as she leaned into the love of her life and whispered, 'If that's a proposal, my answer is hell yes,' a moment before she kissed him.

CHAPTER
45

Two weeks later

'Where are we going?' Tash asked, as Kody closed the back door and snagged her hand. 'We have to be at the roadhouse in twenty minutes.'

'It's a surprise.' Kody lifted her hand to his lips and pressed a kiss to the back of it. 'Besides, do you really think anyone's going to begrudge the band going on a few minutes late?'

'Good point.'

True to his word, Kody had ensured Rock Hard Place would be performing at Ruby's blues night and the event had been a sell out. Considering the crowd expected, Ruby had hired a sound technician to set up giant speakers and a screen in the car park so folks who missed out on a ticket could watch outside.

'Let's get this show on the road.'

Walking hand in hand, they headed for the driveway. As they neared the car, Tash spied Isla sitting on the bonnet, her legs swinging as she tapped at her phone.

'I can't believe she's ours,' Kody murmured, his grip on her hand tightening. 'She's an amazing kid.'

'She has the best of both of us,' Tash said, her heart full to bursting when Isla glanced up, caught sight of them, slipped off the bonnet and ran towards them with joy on her face.

'Dad's got a surprise for us,' Isla blurted, hopping excitedly from one foot to the other like a kid half her age. 'And he won't give me any clues.'

He laughed. 'Why don't my two favourite girls in the world get in the car and you'll soon find out what it is?'

Isla rode shotgun, giving Tash the opportunity to study the loves of her life, their profiles so similar her heart ached. She remained silent as Isla chattered, her enthusiasm making Kody laugh.

They headed out of town a short way before Kody turned onto a dirt road not far from the dried-up creek where the high school kids hung out to get up to mischief. As far as she knew there was nothing on this road but as it started to gradually climb she noticed a killer view. When they reached the top of a steep incline, Kody pulled over and switched off the engine.

'Here we are,' he said, getting out of the car and flinging his arms wide. 'Home sweet home.'

Tash chuckled as confusion crinkled Isla's forehead.

'It's a scrubby old hill, Dad.'

'Where our house is going to be built.' Kody beckoned them in close. 'A home where we can be a family.'

Isla's face lit up. 'You're the best, Dad.'

'I second that,' Tash said, slipping into the family embrace, staving off tears that threatened to fall at any second.

'I love you both so much,' Isla said. 'I'm going to explore a little, okay?'

'Sure, kiddo,' Kody said, releasing her, leaving Tash to snuggle into his arms.

She tilted her face up to his. 'You're amazing, you know that, right?'

'Right back at you.'

He kissed her and Isla yelled out, 'Gross. You better not be doing that all the time when you're married and we're living in our new house.'

Tash smiled as they separated. She knew she was the luckiest woman in the world to be granted this second chance. 'I love you.' As Kody rested his forehead against hers, she murmured, 'But why did you bring us here now? You could've waited until after the gig.'

'Because I'm shitting bricks at performing with the band for the first time in months and I needed the distraction.'

Tash laughed. 'You'll be fine. You're *the* Kody Lansdowne, and folks in this town already love you.'

'Yeah, but this is different …' The amusement in his eyes faded. 'It's the first time we'll be on stage together since Wellington, and I'm bloody petrified.'

'I know.' She cupped his face between her hands. 'I also know you've got this.'

When she pressed her lips to his, she hoped she conveyed her belief in him, because though she'd never admit it, a small part of her was freaking petrified too.

'Stop that,' Isla yelled, breaking the tension. They smiled as their daughter added, 'You two really are gross but I love you anyway.'

Time stood still as Tash watched the love of her life perform.

She clapped and stomped and whistled along with people she'd classed as friends her entire life as Rock Hard Place played one classic hit after another, raising the roof on The Watering Hole.

There'd been a hiccup when Kody initially took to the stage, a hesitation as he strummed his first chord and the words hadn't come. She'd willed him to look at her and, somehow, their eyes had met across the packed room. Corny as it seemed, everything had been okay. He'd visibly relaxed as he moved a fraction closer to the microphone.

When he'd sung the first note, Tash had cried with relief, silent tears trickling down her cheeks. The haunting melody filled the air, raising the hairs on her arms.

He was singing her song. The one he'd written especially for her all those years ago, the one that never failed to make her heart swell.

As he crooned about fate and heartbreak and star-crossed lovers, their eyes met again, and she knew this time they would be together forever.

'Isn't he amazing?' Isla leaned in to her and Tash slid an arm around her daughter's waist, hugging her tight.

'He sure is, sweetheart.'

'I'm so happy we're going to be a real family,' Isla said, the joy in her daughter's eyes mirroring hers.

'That makes two of us …' She trailed off as the deep timbre of Kody's voice reached the last verse. The man of her dreams singing about a forever kind of love.

The kind of love they shared.

ACKNOWLEDGEMENTS

While I'm a city girl, small country towns hold a special place in my heart. Their warmth makes me want to recreate the same vibe in the rural romances I write and I hope I've done that again in returning to Brockenridge, my fictional town based on Echuca, a real town on the Murray River that I love.

It takes a team to bring a book to fruition and I'd like to thank the following people.

Rachael Donovan, my publisher at Harlequin Australia, for loving my books. Being published by Mira and having you champion my rural romances is fantastic.

Julia Knapman and Kylie Mason, your editorial guidance helps polish my manuscript into the final product. I appreciate it.

Sarana Behan, the publicity hours you put into *Long Way Home* helped propel sales and I'm so grateful. Fingers crossed *Second Chance Lane* flies off shelves too.

Shirley Tran Thai and Christine Armstrong of the HarperCollins Design Studio, who created my amazing covers. Shirley, the gorgeous colours of *Second Chance Lane* pop and Christine, your beautiful design contributed to *Long Way Home*'s success. Very grateful to you both, as the cover is what draws a reader's eye first and I'm so lucky mine are stunning thanks to you.

Annabel Adair, for your comprehensive proof edits.

The entire team at Harlequin Australia and HarperCollins Australia, with special shout-outs to Sue Brockhoff, Adam Van Rooijen and Johanna Baker, for placing my rural romances into readers' hands.

Jacqui Furlong, the Field Sales Manager at HarperCollins. Huge thanks for getting my books into stores and organising a fantastic launch.

Erica, the manager at Robinsons Bookshop in The Glen, for championing my books and throwing a fabulous book launch.

My agent, Kim Lionetti, for being my support in this ever-changing business.

Rachael Johns, for featuring *Long Way Home* as a book of the month on her online book club, spreading the love for my venture into rural romance.

For the bookshops, librarians, reviewers and bloggers who help spread the word about my books.

For my family and friends who took the time to let me know how much they enjoyed *Long Way Home*, and are looking forward to this one.

Martin, for your ongoing support.

My boys, who shared in my excitement at the launch of *Long Way Home* and took loads of shelfies for me as we spotted it in various bookshops. You know there'll be plenty more shelfies to come, right? Love you.

My loyal readers, I'm eternally grateful you buy my books. Our lives are so hectic these days and knowing you take the time to read my stories means a lot. I hope you enjoy revisiting Brockenridge and have as much fun delving into the lives of the characters initially created in *Long Way Home* as I did bringing them to life on the page.

Happy reading!

Nic x

Turn over for a sneak peek.

Summer of Serenity

by

NICOLA MARSH

Available October 2021

mira

CHAPTER

1

One thing Jy hated more than seeing pictures of his ex-wife and her slick husband in the society columns of Melbourne newspapers was being summoned by the Education Department. He loathed bureaucracy.

But he loved shaping young minds, so he'd suck it up and front the big wigs. For the third time in two months—some kind of record for the principal of an elite private school, apparently.

'Mr Bosch will see you now, Mr Atherton.' The PA pointed to a heavy wooden door to his right. Like he needed the instruction. He'd been privy to the condescension and censure behind it already. What could they say this time? He'd already been warned and he'd chosen to flout the rules. More fool him.

Mustering a tight smile of thanks for the PA, he opened the door.

To face a firing squad.

Nothing quite as dramatic, but this time, Gus Bosch, chief education officer for the state of Victoria, had a backup team: three fellow cronies in their sixties wearing matching grim expressions.

'Take a seat, Mr Atherton, and we'll get started.' Gus didn't bother introducing his mates. Jy hoped that meant he wouldn't be staying long.

Closing the door, Jy resisted the urge to slip a finger between his collar and his neck. He'd been wearing a suit and tie daily since he'd graduated uni and started teaching fourteen years ago; didn't mean he had to like it.

The four men stared at him as he crossed the room and sat opposite them—spine ramrod straight, shoulders back, hands clasped in his lap: perfect minion posture.

'Thanks for coming in today,' Gus said. Like Jy had been given a choice. 'We'll make this brief.'

Good. The briefer the better so Jy could get back to what he did best: running Korrungal Grammar, the small private school he'd worked at for the last five years and been in charge of for the last twelve months.

'Rest assured, we've heard all your concerns regarding the new curriculum and taken them into consideration. And it's because of your passion for education in this state that we're sending you to Acacia Haven.'

Gus's monotone grated on Jy's nerves as much as the CEO's outlandish proclamation. 'What do you mean you're sending me? I'm a principal. I can't be shipped off anywhere.'

A groove dented Gus's brow and his lips thinned. 'You're not being shipped. We need someone with your experience and expertise to ascertain whether the school is viable.'

Jy struggled to hide his growing horror. They were sending him to some godforsaken place he'd never heard of to shut down a school? This was a major slap on the wrist. An archaic punishment for having the balls to stand up to these dinosaurs with their antiquated ideas of what constituted a good education.

When he remained stubbornly silent, trying to get his rising temper under control, Gus continued. 'We've already teed up your deputy to take over your role for the month you'll be in Acacia Haven.'

Jy would deal with the traitor Olga, his vice principal, later. She could've given him a heads up at least.

'We want you there for the first four weeks of the new term to ascertain why their VCE results are the lowest in the state and if there's any chance to rectify. If not …' Gus shrugged, as if closing down a school meant nothing. 'We expect a full report and will take your recommendations into account.'

That'd be a first, considering they'd shot him down when he'd voiced his opinions on their proposed changes—while Science, Technology, English and Mathematics were still valued, they wanted to invest more money into humanity teachers than STEM—in a very public forum of senior teachers and principals from all around Victoria. He'd stuffed up. He should've kept his big mouth shut.

'Do you have any questions?'

He had a feeling they wouldn't want to answer anything he had to ask. Like 'Why are you treating me like a naughty child being sent to detention?' Or 'Why would I want to spend the last month of summer in some hick town I've never heard of?' Or 'Where the hell is Acacia Haven and is it as hokey as it sounds?'

Instead, he cleared his throat and said, 'When is the report due?'

Gus raised his eyebrows, apparently surprised by his acquiescence. 'After you return … the first week of March, is fine.'

Nothing was remotely fine about this ludicrous situation and Jy didn't appreciate being treated like a recalcitrant insubordinate. But he was coming up for long service leave in April after being in the education system for almost fifteen years and the last thing he wanted to do was give these guys an excuse to screw him over somehow.

'We'll email you the details and if you have any questions after that, feel free to contact me.' Gus stood and extended his hand. 'Good luck.'

Jy hid a grimace. He had a feeling he was going to need it.

CHAPTER

2

Jy saw three things as he hit the outskirts of purgatory. Two girls, barely school age, making daisy chains on the side of the road. A rogue roo up on hind legs staring balefully, like he wanted to leap out in front of the car and add to Jy's woes. And an ocean so blue his eyes hurt.

He didn't mind the sea; he remembered beachside holidays as a kid fondly. In fact, those weeks spent in Sorrento or Rosebud or Ocean Grove with his folks were the only times he saw his parents truly relax. For the rest of the year, Sylvie and Angus Atherton coexisted in polite indifference, staying married for the sake of appearances and little else. So he'd cherished those snatched weeks by the ocean when he'd sit next to his dad on a pier, rods in their hands, raspberry icy poles in the Esky. They never caught a fish, not once; it didn't matter, because he liked hanging out with his father, the sun on their backs and the breeze on their faces. Not catching anything had an added bonus of getting fish and chips for dinner and he couldn't taste salt and vinegar without remembering those days.

When his mum spied the paper packet in his hands as he trudged sand all over the floor, her eyes would light up in a way they never did at home in their small weatherboard in Chadstone. She liked a treat as much as he did and for an all-too-short hour he'd share a meal with his folks on the porch, the distant sound of the waves crashing on the back beach a pleasant distraction, and pretend like everything was okay.

But he wasn't at a seaside jaunt now. For the last four weeks of summer, he had to atone for his sins in godforsaken Acacia Haven. That's what it felt like, being sent to this tiny town three hours from Melbourne—and three hours from the best barista in bay-side Brighton—like he was being punished.

Not that he'd given Gus and his brigade any indication how truly pissed off he'd been. He'd bide his time, give them their precious bloody report, and look forward to utilising his long service leave by taking the last term off. He had plans for those four months and no way in hell he'd let some bureaucrats derail him.

As he crested a small hill leading towards town, the ocean vista widened into a cerulean crescent, and for a moment he released his residual bitterness and took in the view. To his right, a sheltered bay with towering cliffs. To his left, a calm stretch of ocean with a rock poking out smack dab in the middle, like a giant nose. And in between, a main street lined with shops leading all the way to the beach at the bottom of the hill.

He slowed below the recommended speed limit and cruised up the street. Along with the requisite pub, small supermarket, post office and bank that most small Victorian towns featured, this place had an abundance of eclectic shops and cafés with equally distinctive names: Vegan Vault, The Cool Candle, The Love Lotus, The Okra and The Knick Knack Shop. Rainbow-coloured banners fluttered in the brisk sea breeze, beckoning the few people strolling the street into the shops. Sandwich boards were propped along the footpath, advertising sesame cucumber salads, chilli cauliflower steaks, grilled shiitake and asparagus tacos and quinoa burgers.

Jy's stomach rumbled, reminding him he'd grabbed a muesli bar with his takeaway coffee before he hit the road, but none of what he'd just seen sounded appetising. A chicken parma at the pub was more his scene but first, he had to swing past the school.

He was not looking forward to this. Gus had reassured Jy the Education Department hadn't told the school the reason behind his arrival but it wouldn't take Einstein to figure it out, especially when he was stuck here for four weeks. They'd know he was making a note of their every move with the sole intention to close them down.

There was no other option.

He'd read the reports Gus had emailed and they weren't pretty. Acacia Haven College had eighty-nine students of various ages and grades, most of whom barely passed the national standard exams set every two years. As for their VCE results, the few kids who actually sat the exams failed more often than not. In comparison, kids in nearby Inverloch outranked them by sixty percent. Not good. As Gus had said, they had the lowest results in the state and nothing Jy did could change that.

This wasn't a fact-finding mission for some bogus report Gus wanted. He'd been sent here to shut this school down.

And that made him the bad guy before he even set foot in the place.

The droning voice from his satellite navigation told him to turn left at the end of the Main Street, drive another kilometre, then take a slight left and his destination would be dead ahead. He followed the instructions but when he pulled up outside what looked like a massive wooden shearing shed, he glanced at the screen again. It still displayed the bullseye, indicating his destination was dead ahead.

This was a school?

Shaking his head, he parked under a towering eucalyptus and got out of the car. His back twinged from the long drive and he linked his hands, stretching overhead, before taking a step and stopping. Should he put his suit jacket on? As Gus had reminded him many times, he'd be a representative of the Education Department while in town and he had to act like it. The warning had pissed him off. What did the old guy think, that Jy would do a nudie run along the beach's foreshore?

This was the first day of a new academic year in a small country town. Strutting into a school where he wouldn't be welcome, wearing a suit and tie, probably wouldn't endear him to the teachers, so he left his jacket in the car and undid an extra button on his shirt. He'd been tempted to wear jeans as a silent finger towards Gus, but he'd settled for a suit. He had to present a professional front because the last thing he needed were the local teachers snitching on him to the board.

Opening his big mouth had landed him in this predicament in the first place. He'd seen a lot of changes in curriculum during his time as a teacher but the latest proposed updates had sent him into a tailspin. He'd always been old school in his approach to learning but open to possibilities. Yet the current recommendations, to focus on pouring money into expanding humanities and cut funding so all schools wouldn't have counsellors to deal with escalating mental health issues, ensured he couldn't keep quiet. He'd approached the department with his concerns, twice. Being a respected principal at an elite private school meant he usually had clout.

Not this time. Instead, he'd been sent to Acacia Haven to effectively close their school down and that's something he wouldn't be able to shake. His stellar reputation would be tarnished and those bozos at the department knew it.

Gritting his teeth, Jy strode towards the long wooden building. On closer inspection, it was an L shape, probably delineating between primary and secondary students. He bounded up the rickety steps and pushed open one half of a double door.

To find the place empty.

He entered and the familiar smell of a classroom calmed him. Crisp paper, ink, the pungent tang of a few teens who refused deodorant and the faintest waft of old banana leftover from recess. While bordering on the unpleasant, the scents grounded him as he wound his way between the tables and chairs to the front of the room, where an open laptop sat on a desk in front of a massive whiteboard.

But not a teacher in sight. He was supposed to meet with Hugo and Jill St Clair. Hugo taught secondary, Jill primary, and according to the Education Department, he had to hold them both accountable, though Hugo was on the chopping block considering the shoddy VCE results.

When he reached the desk, a movement outside caught his eye and his jaw dropped as he peered out the window. A woman of about seventy, wearing a flowing black kaftan with her hair in grey dreadlocks, was juggling in front of a group of laughing and clapping students. A man around the same vintage held sway with another group trying to light fires with sticks. And a third woman, young, blonde, sat in a large circle of kids, with rows of tiny bottles lined up in front of her and a few beakers.

With a shake of his head, Jy headed outside. If this was how Hugo and Jill taught he'd have his work cut out for him. As he approached the groups he saw they were much smaller than the reported eighty-nine students who studied here. In fact, there was about half that number and he made a mental note to look into the truancy rates. Not actually attending classes would have a massive impact on final grades in year twelve.

To the kids' credit they didn't glance his way, their attention riveted to their respective teachers. Though the young woman with the tiny bottles noticed him and stood, unfolding herself with a lithe grace that had him admiring her without realising it. She was tall, at least five ten, with blonde tousled hair half-way down her back and big blue eyes that pinned him with cool distrust.

He smiled and raised his hand in a wave. She frowned in return.

Yeah, they were expecting him.

She said something to the kids, who were scribbling notes in exercise books, before approaching him with long, easy strides, her colourful skirt swishing, her simple black tank top skimming her curves. He liked how she moved, with confidence and an ease that had him wishing he felt that comfortable in his own skin.

When she reached him, her lips thinned in disapproval and she arched a brow. 'Can I help you?'

'Jy Atherton,' he said, holding out his hand.

She stared at it like he'd offered her crap on a plate.

'I'm here to—'

'We know why you're here,' she muttered, folding her arms, leaving him no option but to lower his hand. 'You want to close down the school.'

'I'm here to ascertain the viability of education in this region—'

'Can you hear yourself?' She snorted; a rude, disparaging sound. 'You sound like a pompous ass.'

Rather than being insulted, the damnedest thing happened. Jy felt like laughing. At six three, he usually towered over people and he liked having this woman go toe to toe with him, standing up for what she believed in. Pity it had to be a decrepit school with poor results that had to be shut down.

'I'm not your enemy. I'm here to get a feel for the place and write a report, that's it.'

'Bull.' She squared her shoulders, her glare so fierce he had to bite back another smile. 'Some slick city suit doesn't come all the way out here and hang around for a month if it's just to "write a report".' She made inverted comma signs with her fingers. 'At least have the decency to tell the truth.'

'Maybe I would if the person I was conversing with had the decency to introduce herself.'

He scored a direct hit as flicker of remorse made the indigo flecks in her eyes glow.

'Summer O'Reilly.' She eyeballed him, defiance stiffening her shoulders. 'Giving you a heads up. You're not going to be popular around here.'

He shrugged. 'Then lucky I'm not here to win any popularity contests.'

Her eyes narrowed but not before he'd seen fury deepening the blue to midnight. 'You have no idea what you're up against here. We're a tight-knit community doing our best for our kids and the last thing we need is some clueless know-it-all bustling in and throwing his weight around.'

She almost choked on the last word and a flicker of pity made him want to reach out to her. Instead, he held up his hands in surrender. 'I'm not the bad guy you've built me up to be. And for the record, I don't want to be here any more than you want me here, but I had no choice.'

'What did you do to get exiled here?'

He couldn't have put it better himself but no way in hell he'd be giving away that much information to a woman he barely knew, a woman who was technically the enemy.

'The Education Department has set me a task. I intend on completing it to the best of my ability.' Damn it, he did sound like the pompous ass she'd accused him of being, so he tempered his response with, 'Things will go a lot smoother if you cooperate and we all get along.'

'Cooperate? With you?' She took a step back and swept him from head to foot with an imperious glance and damned if a jab of unexpected lust didn't shoot through him. 'I'd rather eat meat.'

A burst of laughter escaped. He couldn't help it. 'Let me guess. You frequent the Vegan Vault.'

'My eating habits are none of your business,' she said, but he glimpsed a slight twitching at the corners of her mouth. 'Now, if you don't mind, why don't you come back later when the kids are at lunch and I'll introduce you to Jill and Hugo.'

He had no intention of going anywhere but the kids were starting to cast curious glances their way and he didn't want to disrupt their learning. By those reports he'd read, they needed all the help they could get.

'You weren't mentioned as a teacher in any preliminary reading I did regarding the region?'

He saw he'd inadvertently touched a sore spot as she drew herself up to her impressive height and folded her arms again. 'Come back later and we'll discuss my role, among other things.'

'Like?'

'How you better shelve any preconceived ideas you have of Acacia Haven and this school, because no-one in this town is going to let some upstart bureaucrat like you barrel in here and tear down a vital part of this community.'

With one last scathing glare, Summer turned on her heel and stomped away, her long paisley skirt swishing around her ankles. Only then did he notice the brash, mouthy teacher was barefoot. Combined with the juggling, the fire starting and the essential oil bottles, it merely reinforced what he already knew.

He didn't fit in here and the next four weeks would be hell.

talk about it

Let's talk about books.

Join the conversation:

facebook.com/romanceanz

@romanceanz

romance.com.au

If you love reading and want to know about our
authors and titles, then let's talk about it.